EXPATRIATES

EXPATRIATES

A Novel of the
Coming Global
Collapse

James Wesley, Rawles

Dutton

DUTTON
Published by the Penguin Group
Penguin Group (USA) LLC
375 Hudson Street
New York, New York 10014

USA | Canada | UK | Ireland | Australia | New Zealand | India | South Africa | China
penguin.com
A Penguin Random House Company

REGISTERED TRADEMARK—MARCA REGISTRADA

LIBRARY OF CONGRESS CATALOGING-IN-PUBLICATION DATA
Rawles, James Wesley.
Expatriates : a novel of the coming global collapse / James Wesley, Rawles.
p. cm.
ISBN 978-0-525-95390-6 (hardcover)
1. Political fiction.   I. Title.
PS3568.A8437E97 2013
813'.54—dc23
2013015366

Printed in the United States of America
10 9 8 7 6 5 4 3 2 1

Set in Arno Pro
Designed by Chris Welch

PUBLISHER'S NOTE

DISCLAIMERS

The making and/or possession of some of the devices and mixtures described in this novel are possibly illegal in some jurisdictions. Even the mere possession of the uncombined components might be construed as criminal intent. Consult your state and local laws! If you make any of these devices and/or formulations, you accept sole responsibility for their possession and use. You are also responsible for your own stupidity and/or carelessness. This information is intended for educational purposes only, to add realism to a work of fiction. The purpose of this novel is to entertain and to educate. The author and Dutton shall have neither liability nor responsibility to any citizen, person, or entity with respect to any loss or damage caused, or alleged to be caused, directly or indirectly by the information contained in this novel.

This novel is dedicated to my wife, "Avalanche Lily,"
for her inspiration, encouragement, and diligent editing.
She has filled the enormous gap in my life after Linda
("The Memsahib") passed away.

The LORD also will be a refuge for the oppressed, a refuge in times of trouble. And they that know thy name will put their trust in thee: for thou, LORD, hast not forsaken them that seek thee.

—PSALMS 9:9–10 (KJV)

DRAMATIS PERSONAE

Jacob "Jake" Altmiller—Hardware store owner/manager in Tavares, Florida.

Janelle Altmiller—Real estate agent. Wife of Jacob Altmiller. Daughter of Alan and Claire McGregor. Sister of Rhiannon Jeffords.

Lance Alan Altmiller—Son of Jacob and Janelle Altmiller. Eleven years old at the onset of the Crunch.

Captain Soekirnan Assegaf—Captain ("Kapten") of the Indonesian Navy patrol boat *Sadarin*.

Sam Burnu—Aborigine ex-convict groundskeeper, Marrakai Heights, Northern Territory, Australia.

Caleb Burroughs—Australian Army WO1 warrant officer.

Randall "Rabbit" Burroughs—Oil and gas seismic crew member. Brother of Caleb Burroughs.

Bruce Drake—Oil and gas seismic crew member.

Thomas Drake—Retired farm foreman. Paternal uncle of Bruce Drake.

Alvis Edwards—Salt and hide broker, Wyndham, Western Australia.

Vivian Edwards—Wife of Alvis Edwards.

Edward Hadley—Private pilot, Alice Springs, Australia.

Paula Hadley—Private pilot, Alice Springs, Australia. Wife of Edward Hadley.

Peter Jeffords—Christian missionary from New Hampshire, living in Quinapondan, Samar Island, Philippines.

Rhiannon Jeffords—Christian missionary, originally from Bella Coola, British Columbia. Wife of Peter Jeffords. Daughter of Alan and Claire McGregor. Sister of Janelle Altmiller.

Sarah Jeffords—Daughter of Peter and Rhiannon Jeffords. Seven years old at the onset of the Crunch.

Lyle Jenkins—Mayor of Mount Dora, Florida.

Samantha Kyle—Disabled RAAF veteran and home automation systems specialist, Palmerston City, Northern Territory, Australia.

Byer Levin—Mayor of Tavares, Florida.

Tomas Marichal—Former Marine, self-employed gunsmith. A builder of custom AR-15 and AR-10 rifles and carbines in Tavares, Florida.

Tom Martinson—Mayor of Tangerine, Florida.

Alan McGregor—Semiretired cattle rancher, Bella Coola, British Columbia. Father of Ray McGregor, Janelle Altmiller, and Rhiannon Jeffords.

Claire McGregor—Wife of Alan McGregor. Mother of Ray McGregor, Janelle Altmiller, and Rhiannon Jeffords.

Ray McGregor—Afghanistan War veteran and military historian. Originally from Bella Coola, British Columbia. Living in Newberry, Michigan. Son of Alan and Claire McGregor. Brother of Janelle Altmiller and Rhiannon Jeffords.

Joseph Caylao Navarro—Jeepney barker, living in Quinapondan, Samar Island, Philippines. Sixteen years old at the onset of the Crunch.

Paul Timbancaya Navarro—Coastal fisherman in Quinapondan, Samar Island, Philippines. Owner and captain of FV *Tiburon* and part-time instructor of the Filipino Martial Arts. Grandfather ("Tatang") of Joseph Navarro. Called Tatang by both his relatives and friends.

Chuck Nolan—American petroleum geologist originally from Texas, living in Casuarina, Northern Territory, Australia.

Ava Palmer—A GIS technician and Australian National University college student raised in Casuarina, Northern Territory, Australia.

Major General Rex Raymond—Special Operations Commander Australia (SOCAUST), near Bungendore, New South Wales, Australia.

Colonel John "Jack" Reynolds—Commander, 7th Combat Service Support Battalion (CSSB), in Enoggera, Queensland, Australia.

Rudolfo Saguisag—Retired Philippine Navy NCO. Nicknamed Dolpo.

Lisa Schoonover—Clerk and accountant at Altmiller's Hardware in Tavares, Florida.

Ralph Simmonds—Immigration officer with the Department of Immigration and Citizenship, Darwin, Northern Territory, Australia.

José Valentin—Former U.S. Army radio repairman. A photovoltaic power sales and service technician with Altmiller's Hardware in Tavares, Florida.

Quentin Whittle—Former bush logger and commercial hunter, Rapid Creek, Northern Territory, Australia.

Adhi Wulandari—*Perantara insinyur* ("intermediate engineer"), Semarang, Central Java, Indonesia.

AUTHOR'S INTRODUCTORY NOTE

Unlike most novel sequels, *Expatriates* is contemporaneous with the events described in my previously published novels *Patriots*, *Survivors*, and *Founders*. Thus, you need not read them first (or subsequently), but you'll likely find them entertaining. Another novel is planned for the series. Check out my blog, www.SurvivalBlog.com, for updates.

1

A GLIMPSE

"Don't look like a Snicker's bar if you don't want to get eaten."

—Clint Smith, founder of the Thunder Ranch shooting school

Tavares, Florida—
June, Four Years Before the Crunch

They came into the store so quickly that Janelle Altmiller didn't have time to react. There were three of them, all men in their early twenties wearing hoodie sweatshirts. As they ran up to the counter, two of them pulled out handguns. Janelle was petrified. In a flash, she realized that she was unarmed, and that her husband, Jacob—who *was* armed—was out of sight in the back of the store, running the panel saw. He was cutting up a piece of plywood for a customer. The noise of the saw would drown out her voice, even if she were to shout for help.

The shortest of the three men tossed a pillowcase to Janelle and ordered, "Fill it! Dump the cash tray and the cash *under* the tray in, too." She quickly opened the cash register and complied. As she handed the sack back to the man, one of the others, with an acne-scarred complexion, hissed, "You pick up the phone in less than five minutes and I'll come back here next week and empty this gun into you."

The three men fled just as Janelle heard the sound of the vertically mounted Skilsaw winding down. She ran toward her husband in a panicked dash. "We've just been robbed," she shouted over the noise. Jake hesitated only for a moment before unholstering his SIG pistol. He started walking toward the front of the store, cautiously. Behind him, Janelle said, "Three young black guys, all wearing hoodies. Two of them have guns." Jake glanced at the open cash register and the register's empty cash tray sitting at an odd angle.

They heard tires screeching outside the store. Jake picked up his pace and jogged to the hardware store's front entrance. As he ran out the door, he caught just a glimpse of an older Ford Taurus racing down the street. He stopped and lowered his pistol. Then he noticed that his hands were shaking.

"Call 911! Black Ford Taurus sedan. Tell 'em they're headed south on State Road 19!" he shouted to Janelle. Then muttering to himself, he added, "And they'll be lost in the traffic and down in Orlando before the cops even get out of the donut shop."

Their store had been burglarized the year before, so they'd added bars to the windows and beefed up the back door. But they hadn't expected an armed robbery during the day. To Janelle, robberies had seemed like something that happened only to jewelry shops, liquor stores, and gas stations—and then mainly in Jacksonville or Orlando.

The robbery made the Altmillers seriously reconsider security for their small hardware store. The store had been established by Jake's grandfather, who had bought the 2.5-acre lot for just twelve hundred dollars during World War II. Situated south of the Dora Canal, it had been in continuous operation since 1946. It was also the last family-owned, independent hardware store in Lake County. All of the others had long since been affiliated with chains like Ace or True Value, or run out of business by the big-box giants like Home Depot and Lowe's. And while they'd suffered their share of shoplifting, this was the first time they'd ever been robbed at gunpoint.

A few days after the robbery, the Altmillers added four miniature security cameras that recorded directly to their PC's hard drive. One of these cameras was deliberately set up at a low angle to avoid the classic "view of the top of the perp's baseball cap." Another camera was aimed at the front entrance, and contrasting strips of colored tape were added at one-foot intervals running up both sides of the door frame. When seen in surveillance footage, these markings would allow them to approximate the height of a suspect after a robbery.

Most importantly, Janelle and Jake began to carry their pistols daily. They both took the three-day fighting pistol immersion course taught by Florida Firearms Training in Okeechobee. This was Janelle's first formal firearms instruction. For Jake, who had taken two previous classes by other instructors, the comprehensive course made him realize how much he still had to learn. They both made a point of doing monthly practice shooting sessions at the local range on Sunday afternoons when the store was closed.

Janelle stood just five feet two inches tall—eight inches shorter than her husband. Her rounded hips and short trunk made most hip holsters uncomfortable for her. Drawing her pistol from a hip holster was ungainly because of the short distance between the top of the holster and her armpit. She tried several types of right-handed holsters before settling on a modified Kydex cross-draw holster made by Multi Holsters. She concealed it with the blue Altmiller's Hardware logo canvas vests that they wore to identify store employees. By wearing the vest unbuttoned, she could draw the pistol quickly if needed. On the few occasions when a customer caught a glimpse of the holstered pistol, it usually triggered compliments rather than ridicule. Florida, after all, had one million concealed carry pistol permits—the most of any state. There was a reason it was nicknamed the Gunshine State.

2

DOUBTS

"Ever since the religion of Islam appeared in the world, the espousers of it . . . have been as wolves and tigers to all other nations, rending and tearing all that fell into their merciless paws, and grinding them with their iron teeth; that numberless cities are raised from the foundation, and only their name remaining; that many countries, which were once as the garden of God, are now a desolate wilderness; and that so many once numerous and powerful nations are vanished from the earth! Such was, and is at this day, the rage, the fury, the revenge, of these destroyers of human kind."

—John Wesley (1703–1791)

Semarang, Indonesia—
May, Two Years Before the Crunch

Adhi Wulandari was an ambitious *perantara insinyur*, an intermediate engineer, with a midsize electronics company in Jakarta. He had just survived a big layoff. This had been the first time the company had let go more than just assemblers. Two friends from his department—one from New Zealand and one from Singapore—were the company's only foreign-born employees. Without warning, they had been told to pack up the personal contents of their cubicles and were escorted out the door. It soon became apparent that all of the others singled out in the layoff were non-Muslims, leaving the company with a one hundred percent Muslim staff. The circumstances of the lay-off troubled Wulandari.

The next day, word came of a lucrative new video camera assembly contract. *Why would the company need to lay off anyone when they've just received a new contract?* Wulandari wondered. Everyone else seemed happy to still have their jobs, so they didn't ask many questions.

While reviewing the drawing specifications for the new assembly contract, Wulandari noticed that the drawings were incomplete. The diagrams showed only one half of a clamshell housing marked CAMERA CASE, a battery, and a digital timer. The large round center section of the housing was a blank spot in the drawings, marked simply as CAMERA POSITION (TBD). The empty space also seemed unusually large for a digital camera, given their recent miniaturization. Even stranger, there were no molded projections in the plastic to hold a camera in place.

All of the parts for the assembly project came in from several other subcontractors: 252 unmarked gray plastic cases from an injection molding company in Tasikmalaya, boxes of aluminum screws from a fastener supply company in Banjarsari, 252 five-year-life 48-volt lithium manganese dioxide batteries sourced from China, bundles of green LEDs from a parts vendor in Jakarta Tangerang, and 252 generic programmable digital timers made by Omron.

The battery specification also struck Wulandari as unusual. Rechargeable lithium-ion batteries would have been a better choice for a camera system. *Why would they specify a 48-volt disposable battery, and why did they need one with such a high voltage and amp-hour rating?* He surmised that they wanted to emplace "set and forget" espionage cameras for several years, but the specifications still seemed incongruous.

When the 252 timers arrived, he grew even more suspicious. They were packed in cardboard boxes labeled OMRON AUTOMATION—a major electronics company in Jakarta Selatan—but the timers themselves were completely unmarked. Every other electronics subassembly he'd ever worked with had carried at least a maker's name and part number. The lack of any markings further piqued his curiosity.

The camera boxes had only a pair of 48-volt DC power input wires, a mini-USB controller port, two pairs of 20-centimeter-long 48-volt output wires, and another 40-centimeter pair of thinner leads in a contrasting color, with smaller connectors that were attached to the low-current, low-voltage green status light LEDs. These were left dangling for later assembly, which was not common practice.

Wulandari asked his supervisor why they were doing only part of the assembly, but the senior engineer offered no explanation. "I don't know. We are just the subcontractor." And when Wulandari asked about the customer, his boss said, "They tell me it is a secret project for the BIN. I think it must be some kind of spy camera." The Indonesian Badan Intelijen Negara—the Indonesian equivalent of the CIA—was notoriously secretive. Another employee, however, was told that it was a project for the National Institute of Aeronautics and Space or Lembaga Penerbangan dan Antariksa Nasional (LAPAN). Wulandari didn't know who to believe.

Wulandari also raised concerns about the flimsy aluminum screws that were specified for mounting the camera's timer and battery, as they would be easily deformed when the cameras were eventually serviced. Once again, his concerns were brushed aside. "I have no idea why aluminum. That is just what they ordered."

After all of the parts had arrived, the assembly of the cameras was completed in just one week and resulted in a very profitable contract for the company. The 252 camera housings—with batteries and timers installed and LEDs attached—were then packaged and sent by truck to another small company farther south in Banten Province, ostensibly for installation of the cameras.

The camera case contract was soon forgotten by most of the company's employees. But Wulandari's doubts about it persisted until almost three years later, when the camera cases made news headlines, erasing all doubt about their true purpose.

3

LIFE IN OZ

"A society that does not defend itself is doomed. A system that remains passive in the face of attack deserves to go under. Those unwilling to defend freedom will become unfree. To stand idly by is to commit suicide."

—The late Brian Crozier, *Strategy of Survival*

Fifteen Miles Northeast of Bulman, Northern Territory, Australia—November, One Year Before the Crunch

It was late in the afternoon, and the three men were tired. They had already lowered ten of the high-explosive seismic charges down the previously drilled shot holes, and this would be the eleventh of the day. Sweat was dripping off the end of Chuck Nolan's nose. Randall "Rabbit" Burroughs, one of Chuck's "jug hustler" assistants, lifted the thirty-four-pound yellow plastic tube of Geoprime dBX explosives to the mouth of the hole. The thousands of feet of cables and geophones, or jugs, laid out by the team over the rough, dry terrain would capture the reflected acoustic energy released from these explosive charges and provide an image of the underlying geologic strata.

Looking up from the reel of thin two-strand electrical wire that was resting in the payout stand, his other assistant, Bruce Drake, said, "Hey, mate, you forgot the suspension cord."

"What?" Burroughs asked.

Just then, the tube slipped from Randall's sweaty fingers. The five-inch-diameter plastic canister briefly lodged at a slight angle in the top of the bore, but then straightened itself and continued its fall before Burroughs could grasp it again. The wire payout wheel spun rapidly with a loud whirring sound.

Chuck yelled, "Run!" at the top of his lungs.

Run they did, in three different directions. They were still sprinting and just ten yards from the bore when the explosives tube hit the bottom of the hole. The sharp jolt of bottoming in the bore set off the blasting caps. Instantly, the main charge detonated. An enormous cloud of red dust loomed up from the bore and from the soil near it. The ground lurched beneath their feet as dirt and rocks came raining down around them. Chuck felt at least two clods or small rocks hit his yellow plastic bump cap, and one glanced off his shoulder. Another hit the side of Chuck's Jeep.

After running a few more yards, Chuck stopped and looked back. As the cloud of red dust started to dissipate, he could see that his assistants were still in one piece and running. Even though his ears were ringing, Chuck started laughing uproariously, greatly relieved that they had escaped the blast unscathed.

Drake stopped and yelled at Burroughs. "You mongrel! You're a few sandwiches short of a picnic!"

After catching his breath, Drake added, "You better keep running, Rabbit!"

Still laughing, Chuck muttered to himself, "Just another day of oil fossicking in the Merry Old Land of Oz."

Despite their proximity to the blast, there was no damage to the trucks, other than a shattered passenger-side rearview mirror on Chuck's Jeep. Rabbit Burroughs had been complaining of a headache all day, and had twice mentioned that he thought he was coming down with the flu. That was his explanation for failing to attach the nylon parachute cord that was normally used to slowly lower the seismic testing charges. They laughed off the incident on their drive back to

Darwin, although Rabbit Burroughs spent the next three days sick in bed with the flu.

Two weeks later, the replacement side-mirror assembly Chuck had ordered arrived. He bolted it on without the assistance of the dealership, but when he'd finished, he was confronted with a strange sight: His perennially filthy Jeep had one *clean* mirror housing. It was enough to compel Chuck to take his truck to the car wash for a long-overdue cleaning.

The self-service car wash on Vanderlin Drive was run by a genial man in his thirties. By his looks, Chuck assumed the man was half Aborigine. Instead of being coin-operated like the car wash in his small hometown in Texas, this one used credit cards for payment. Washing the accumulated red dirt from the truck took three full cycles.

Chuck wore his cowboy hat as protection from the glaring sun. As he worked, he hummed the tune to the song "I'm So Ronery" from a political parody movie featuring puppets, which he had seen many years before. Just as he was finishing up the last cycle, he heard a woman's voice from behind him. "What's T-T?" she asked.

He turned to see a tall young woman with curly, sandy-brown hair, wearing short pants and a simple blouse. Her index finger was pointing to the large red decal on his truck's back window, with overlapping capital *T*s.

Momentarily flummoxed at the unexpected sight of the woman, Chuck answered haltingly, "That's, uh, Texas Tech, ma'am."

Mimicking his Texan accent, she asked, "Are you new in these parts?"

Chuck laughed. "No, I've been here about eight months. I'm in the oil business."

Dropping the accent, the young woman said, "A genuine Texas oilman. You're practically a walking cliché with the left-hand drive steering wheel, the Wranglers, and the Stetson hat. You're quite the poser."

She cocked her head and added, "But I would have thought we'd meet here long before this. I'm usually here two or three Saturdays a month, especially in the summer."

"That's because I only give my truck a bath about once a year."

She laughed, the warm sound causing Chuck to smile.

Chuck shoved the dribbling sprayer rod into the holder mounted on the masonry-block wall. He turned to face the young woman, saying, "My name's Chuck Nolan. Pleased to meet you."

"I'm Ava . . . Ava Palmer."

Chuck tipped the brim of his hat and nodded to her in response, and Ava burst out laughing. "I've met some posers, but you take the prize," she exclaimed.

"I'm just being me, ma'am." He cleared his throat and asked, "Assuming that you're single, can I buy you lunch?"

"You Texans do start off at a gallop, don't you?" Ava replied.

"When I meet a lovely single lady, I don't waste any time."

She paused for a moment and then said, "Lunch . . . Why not? I was just about done using the chamois on my car. Give me a sec, and then follow me over to Fasta Pasta—the takeaway. Do you know it?"

"The one in the shopping mall on Trower Road?"

"Right!"

Chuck grinned. "I'll be right behind you."

It was just a short drive to the takeaway restaurant. Ava was driving a Toyota RAV4 that was several years old but well cared for. They ordered pasta salads and took their plates to some outdoor tables in the shade of a casuarina tree—the tree species for which the town was named. Chuck had also bought them each a can of Passiona—a passion fruit soft drink—to have with their meals. He missed the larger soda fountain drinks that he was accustomed to in the States. Australia, he had learned, was "the land of no free refills."

After some pleasantries about the weather and a discussion on the relative merits of clean vehicles versus truly utilitarian vehicles, Ava asked, "So, Chuck, Texas Oilman, what's your story?"

"I'm an oil fossicker. I shoot reflection seismic surveys for oil and gas exploration. You know what they say: 'Little boys who play with rocks either end up in jail or become geologists.'"

Ava cocked her head and commented, "I thought there were plenty of Aussies available to do that work. No offense, but why would they hire someone from the back side of the planet for that?"

"Well, I have bachelor of science and masters degrees in geology with a specialty in geophysics. I liked Red Raiders football so much I just had to stick around those extra two years and earn that second degree. I'm glad that I did since the market is really hot now for folks with a specialty in geophysics."

Ava looked taken aback by his credentials. "I see. So how did you get your start, after Texas Tech?"

"After I finished my masters, I went to work for Vecta Oil and Gas, in the States. I started out in the office, but I eventually found my niche in leading a seismic acquisition team for oil and gas exploration. I liked working outdoors and traveling much more than I did any five-day-a-week job at the corporate office. In my first three years, I worked with the company's seismic crews in Texas, Colorado, Montana, and North Dakota. Eventually, my manager asked me to move to North Dakota full-time, where the company was making a major investment in a geologic play known as the Bakken oil shale—sorry, am I boring you with all this?" asked Chuck.

"Not at all," Ava assured him.

"Okay, we were shooting a large 3-D seismic survey with follow-up plans for an aggressive drilling program. The Bakken shale play is really booming. But I very quickly got tired of the winters in North Dakota. They're really brutal. I knew that I wanted something different, or at least someplace more *habitable and warm*. So I started searching for other oil and gas opportunities . . . especially jobs outside the United States."

"So why Australia?" asked Ava.

"Well, one evening I was doing some web wandering, and I stumbled upon Australian Oil and Gas Corporation headquartered in Darwin. One of my lab instructors in college was an Aussie and told great stories about the country. More or less on a lark, I updated my resume and e-mailed it. I was pleasantly surprised when I got a quick response. Eleven days later, I was on a Qantas jet bound for Sydney, reading the old novel *In The Wet*, by Nevil Shute. I took a Virgin flight up to Darwin, and by the time I got there I was already onto my second Shute novel, *The Far Country*. Those books were a pretty good crash course on Australian culture."

"More than a bit dated," Ava interjected. "But yes, his books did capture the culture, back in the 1950s. People in this part of Australia have changed a lot less than they have down in the big cities."

"I was surprised that the company gave me a job offer right on the spot, at the end of my second interview," Chuck continued. "Turns out they were looking for a person that had a strong background in both seismic acquisition and seismic prospecting, and I fit the bill. They said that they'd expedite my work visa, pay all of my moving expenses, yada-yada-yada. So here I am. I like the climate here. It is a lot more conducive to my hobbies—especially shooting, hiking, and mountain bike riding—than living in the Dakotas ever was."

Ava nodded in agreement and forked up more of her pasta.

After a pause to take a sip of soda, Nolan asked, "And you, Ava?"

"I'm just a year out of high school, and saving up the money to attend the ANU, starting in the upcoming first term this January. I'll be studying computer science. Right now I'm just a GIS technician, plotting and confirming map coordinates, using ArcMap. It's all very boring, repetitive work, but I want to expand on my current rudimentary programming skills to learn how to actually *write* programs, not just use them like a worker bee for the rest of my life."

"That's great. And so you're single, not engaged or ..."

Ava laughed. "Back to the full gallop, are we?"

Chuck grinned sheepishly.

"Before we delve off into potential, or shall we say *hypothetical*, matrimonial topics, Mr. Chuck Nolan, I have a big fat question for you."

"Shoot."

"Are you a Christian?"

"Well, yeah. I went to church when I was a kid. I went to Sunday school and all the usual—"

Ava cocked her head and interrupted, "Yes, but do you know Jesus the Christ as your personal savior?"

"I've never thought in those terms," Chuck admitted. "I mean, I've never studied the Bible as an adult, you see. I really wouldn't know where to start."

Ava pushed the remains of her plate aside and said, "Do you have a Bible, a King James?"

Chuck nodded.

"Since you understand shooting, then you will understand 'missing the mark.' This is man's biggest problem. I suggest you start by reading the Gospel of John—he depicts Jesus' work to solve man's biggest problem very plainly. See if that speaks to you. And if it does, then ask Jesus into your heart."

Ava stood up from the table and gave a little wave.

"Wait! I need your phone number," Chuck protested.

Ava pulled out a pen and wrote on the back of their lunch receipt. "Here's my mobile number. I *would* like you to ring me up, Chuck. But before you do, I'd really like you to be able to tell me, with sincerity, where you stand with God."

4

SISTERS

"You can kid the world, but not your sister."

—Charlotte Gray

Tavares, Florida—
September, One Year Before the Crunch

J anelle Altmiller was depressed. She had spent the last hour on the Internet, checking on comparable houses for one of her real estate clients. What she found confirmed the continuing deterioration of the real estate market in central Florida. Despite all the talk of "recovery" in the market, prices were still down everywhere she looked. Even more depressing were the huge number of foreclosed properties, and the average time on the market for homes that sold—thirteen months to sell a house in Lake County.

If Janelle and Jake had been forced to rely solely on her property sales commissions, they would have already been bankrupt. Thankfully, Jake had the income from the hardware store that he'd inherited from his late parents. The store was small, and its location at the south end of Tavares was not optimal, but visits from their regular local customers were still fairly steady.

Jake Altmiller's willingness to go the extra mile for his customers was almost legendary. He would special-order parts from anywhere in the country for just about anything. He even had the knack for sweet-talking manufacturers into providing uncatalogued parts for machinery that were not normally available individually and sold only as assemblies or subassemblies. Jake had also developed extensive contacts with dealers in secondhand equipment and parts, which saved his customers a lot of money.

The other thing that kept the hardware store going was their small assortment of firearms ammunition and gun accessories. While most other hardware stores had dropped firearms from their lines many years ago, Jake had kept this part of the business running. He did so more out of his personal interest in guns and his stubborn nature than with much profit in mind. For his regular customers, Jake would special-order guns at just twenty-five dollars over cost using his Federal Firearms License (FFL). He also served as an FFL transfer dealer for any of his customers who bought guns online through websites like GunBroker.com. His willingness to do so attracted all of the serious gun hobbyists in and around Tavares. The walk-in business and the pace of special orders had gotten frantic after the Newtown massacre in 2012. With calls for bans on manufacture and importation, many American gun owners who previously had little interest suddenly wanted a semiauto rifle and a big pile of spare 30-round magazines.

The biggest customer for Altmiller's gun department was Tomas Marichal, a former Marine who was semiemployed building custom AR-15 and AR-10 rifles and carbines. Marichal was practically a fixture at Altmiller's gun counter. Although he ordered a lot of AR-15 and AR-10 lower receivers through Jake's FFL, Tomas spent most of his time shooting the breeze about guns and telling war stories about his five deployments—three to Iraq and two to Afghanistan. There were times when Marichal waxed on a bit too long, and Jake regretted ever purchasing the pair of tall padded stools in front of the gun counter.

To bolster his business at the store even more, Jake also sold photovoltaic panels and inverters. Although he discovered that some of his "off grid" customers were illicit marijuana growers, which he took steps to "weed out," the photovoltaic part of the business soon developed its own loyal clientele. Over the past year, Jake had installed twelve photovoltaic panels on the roof of their house and another twenty-four panels on top of the store, more as a demonstration of the capabilities of a PV system than out of any desire to save money on his utility bill or to "go green."

He chose an OutBack brand inverter that was slightly larger than they needed, in part because he planned to eventually add more photovoltaic panels for the house, and because he wanted to have an inverter with 220-volt AC capability so they could run their well pump. The panels were mounted on racks facing southward at a thirty-degree angle, to roughly match the twenty-eight-degree latitude of Tavares.

Jake Altmiller's right-hand man at the store was José Valentin. José, a thirty-one-year-old former U.S. Army radio repairman, handled most of the photovoltaic power sales and service issues. He was a third-generation American whose grandparents had been born in Cuba but had emigrated to the United States shortly after Fidel Castro took power. Jose stood only five feet eight inches and had the wiry build of a bantamweight boxer. Since Tomas Marichal was also a Cuban American with prior military service, Valentin often joined in the Bravo Sierra sessions at the gun counter. Because Valentin had served in the Army, and Marichal's prior service was with the USMC, there was plenty of good-natured interservice rivalry and ribbing between them.

Quinapondan, Samar Island, the Philippines— One Year Before the Crunch

Peter and Rhiannon Jeffords helped run an orphanage in Quinapondan on the southeast coast of Samar Island. Shortly after they arrived from the United States, they had added a breakfast program and afterschool ministry for local children. These children all lived with their parents but were so desperately poor that many started the day without breakfast. So in addition to feeding the orphanage residents, they began feeding more than 150 local schoolchildren.

At thirty-two years old and 135 pounds, Rhiannon's petite five-feet-three-inch stature had grown plump, though her light brown hair looked the same as it did when she first met Peter. She dressed modestly and never wore any jewelry other than her wedding band. She always felt mismatched when standing next to her husband, who was two years older, six feet three inches, and lean, and had handsome, chiseled features. Aside from a receding hairline—for which he compensated by often letting his dirty-blond hair grow bushy—Peter Jeffords could have had a career in modeling. Peter tended to wear jeans and Ban-Lon short-sleeve shirts in subdued colors. He always carried a CRKT brand B.U.L.L. pocketknife but refused to wear a wristwatch or carry a cell phone.

The Jeffords' house was a simple nipa hut, locally called a *bahay kubo*, with only 280 square feet of floor space. It sat on tall, almost stiltlike piers and had a steep-pitched roof that was thatched with a long grass called cogon. The gables were left open for ventilation. The hut was built almost entirely of nipa palm wood, *kawayan* bamboo, and rattan. (The latter was called *yantok* by the locals.) There were eight steps up to the high porch. The area beneath the house—the *silong*—had a table for kitchen chores, but Rhiannon disliked working there because of the pig manure that was underfoot.

Recently, they had learned of a new lighting technique that was being used in many homes in the Manila area to save electricity costs during the day and they decided to use it in their home, too. They took clear, empty one-liter soda bottles and filled them with water and two cap measures of bleach; then they cut holes in their roof in strategic locations. The bottles were then installed so that they were half inside and half outside of the hut. During the day, each bottle provided the equivalent lighting of a 50-watt lightbulb.

The family's most valuable possession was a dark blue Mitsubishi L300 minivan. It had come to them providentially—a gift from a wealthy friend in New Hampshire who had heard that the Jeffords were in need of transportation on the island. It was one those "God Things"—a wire transfer for twelve thousand dollars arrived just a day after Peter and Rhiannon had prayed together for the first time about their need for a vehicle. Peter often said that the Mitsubishi L300 was too fancy a vehicle for a humble pastor. The modern boxy-looking vehicle seemed incongruous parked beside their modest nipa hut parsonage. The Mitsubishi was just one year old and had only fourteen thousand miles on the odometer when they bought it two years before the Crunch, when their daughter, Sarah, was only five years old.

In the months leading up to the Crunch, and in the first week of the hyperinflation, Rhiannon spent many hours on the phone and on Skype with her older sister, Janelle, who lived in Florida. The sisters had grown up together on a remote cattle ranch outside of Bella Coola, British Columbia. Though they now lived a world apart, they still felt a very close bond. With the unlimited calling provided by Janelle's voice over IP phone, they were able to talk for about an hour each weekday. It became a daily ritual for Janelle to call at eight A.M.—which was eight P.M. for Rhiannon. They would both do their household cleaning, laundry, and dishwashing while they shared news and stories.

Rhiannon also received care packages from Florida and British Columbia via balikbayan boxes. These two-cubic-foot boxes would take between thirty and sixty days to arrive. Many of these packages containing clothes and other essentials were sent by her brother, Ray McGregor, who lived in Michigan.

Ray was definitely the oddball of the McGregor family. He was a Canadian Army Afghanistan war veteran who had gone on to study military history at Western University in London, Ontario. In his senior year, however, he had dropped out to work on a book about World War II veterans in Michigan.

Often living in a fifth-wheel "toy hauler" camping trailer towed behind his pickup truck, Ray had first lived in Ypsilanti, Michigan, and later relocated near Newberry, in Michigan's Upper Peninsula. Most recently, he kept his trailer parked on a sprawling farm that belonged to the Harrison family. Four generations of the Harrisons had lived on the farm. Ray had met the Harrisons when he began a series of taped interviews with Bob Harrison, who was a B-24 bomber pilot in World War II.

With the exception of a few of his articles that were published in *Military History* magazine, Ray was a failure as a writer. He had never found a literary agent who was willing to work with him, and his four uncompleted manuscripts had never been published. He made most of his meager living cutting firewood.

The last e-mail Rhiannon received from Ray before Internet service was disrupted read:

Dear Rhi:

Things are getting bad here, even in the Upper Peninsula of Michigan. I parlayed the last of my cash into food and fuel. The inflation is so crazy that to wait just one day would mean I'd only get half as many groceries for my money.

I talked with Mom and Dad via Skype. I'm not sure how it is in the P.I., but here in the U.S. the phone lines are getting flaky AND are jammed with calls. Dad said they are doing okay, but they sound befuddled by the economic situation. Dad asked me for advice on finding a stock that would be safe to invest in. Ha! I suggested putting all of their remaining cash in food, fuel, salt blocks, bailing twine, and ammo.

My old friend Phil Adams told me that I need to "Get Out of Dodge" ASAP. The plan is for Phil to meet me at the ranch. I'm not sure if I can get enough fuel to get out west, though. I think I can trade some ammo for fuel.... I also have a few silver dimes and quarters, but those are effectively now my life savings. They are worth a fortune, at least in terms of the Funny Money U.S. Dollar.

I'll be praying for both you and Janelle and your families.
May God Watch Over You,

—*Ray*

5

PLATEAU

"I was born and raised in that religious atmosphere which for three hundred years has never varied in its extreme devotion to peace. Yet I know that peace comes in the modern world only to those nations which are adequately prepared to defend themselves. The European Allies are now paying in blood and disaster for their failure to heed plain warnings. With adequate preparedness they might have escaped attack."

—Herbert Hoover, radio address, May 27, 1940

Tavares, Florida—
October, the First Year

One of the Altmillers' full-time employees, Lisa Schoonover, worked as their ordering clerk and accountant. Because the store was independent, they didn't have the advantage of the automated ordering systems that were common at chain hardware stores. This made Lisa indispensable to the smooth operation of the store. It came as a shock when Lisa announced her resignation just after the stock market crash. She explained that she and her family were "bugging out" to live with relatives in Oneida, Tennessee. The town was on the Cumberland Plateau, an area that Lisa had predicted would be safe, if times ever got desperately bad.

In recognition of her five years of faithful work, Lisa was given a store credit in lieu of her final paycheck for her choice of merchandise at twenty percent below cost. She carefully selected a shopping cart full of batteries, ammunition, nails, screws, garden hoses, gardening seed, and rolls of kerosene lantern wicking.

Altmiller's Hardware was on a commercial street, but their house, at the back end of the same deep lot, faced onto the residential street of Magnolia Avenue. The house was bigger than they needed since they had only one child. The 2,500-square-foot one-story house had a very gently sloping roof, which was typical for Central Florida. It had been built in 1973 by Jake's father on the site of the original 750-square-foot house, which his late mother had called the Swelter Shack.

When Janelle married Jake and they moved in, she learned to love the house's breezy open-floor plan. Jake remodeled the house in 1998, and with his handyman's flair continued to work on the interior, changing most of the major appliances and adding two zone air conditioners. Their home's water supply came from a grandfathered shallow well that also supplied the store.

Soon after they were married, piles of lumber had begun encroaching farther and farther into Janelle's garden in the backyard. After repeated requests to remedy the situation, she reached the breaking point—every husband knows when this has happened. She spent an hour moving lumber by herself and then insisted that Jake move the rest of it and construct a white picket fence to divide her yard from the store's lumber storage area. This solution kept peace in the family, interrupted only occasionally, when the fence was smashed in forklift mishaps.

One afternoon, just as she was finishing up the comps for her client, Janelle's son, Lance, came running into the room. He was eleven years old but had the intellect of a seven-year-old. The experts told her he would probably not advance any further, intellectually. In addition to his learning disability, Lance had difficulty conversing with both children and adults and rarely made eye contact. He spent many hours with a pencil or small felt-tip marking pen, endlessly repeating the same simple drawings and doodles.

Jake and Janelle loved their son very much and gave him lots of attention. They chose to homeschool him rather than send him to public

school, an arrangement that gave him the best chance for full development while sparing him the agony of being teased and bullied by other
students. Though he never said it, Jake was disappointed that Lance
would never grow up to inherit the family business.

The media called the economic crisis the Crunch. It was a credit collapse
and economic depression that made the Great Depression of the 1930s
seem small by comparison. The global credit market had come unglued.
All around the world, markets were in free fall. Credit had completely
dried up. Cities, counties, states, and even national governments were in
default. Consumer prices soared. Interest rates skyrocketed. Firearms,
ammunition, and precious metals prices soared simply because they could
not be printed. While Helicopter Ben was busy convincing the world that
the Treasury goose could continue to lay golden eggs, bonds collapsed.
Derivatives contracts cratered, leaving counterparties for trillions of dollars in contracts twisting in the wind. Corporations of all sizes announced
huge layoffs. The crisis started in the United States, but it quickly spread to
other countries and paralyzed the global economy.

As the world plunged into chaos, Janelle and Rhiannon found com-
fort in comparing their experiences of the economic crisis from their
different vantage points in Florida and the Philippines.

One thing they had in common was the abundance of tropical fruit
just outside their doors. Janelle's backyard in Tavares had six large orange trees, two tangelos, and a forty-year-old avocado tree that had
grown to overshadow nearly half of the yard. Meanwhile, in the vicinity
of her nipa hut on Samar, Rhiannon could locally pick an abundance of
durian fruit—a local favorite despite its strong odor—as well as lychee,
pineapple, banana, santol, malunggay leaves, and guavas (*bayabas*).

Once the mass inflation started, Jake, Janelle, and José had a meeting. Jake realized that unless something changed quickly, their store

shelves would be stripped clean, and they would be left holding nothing but worthless dollars. José suggested a "cash only" policy and regularly ratcheting up prices, but Janelle wanted to go a step further and post a "silver only" sales policy. The discussion was fairly brief. Janelle pointed out that their entire inventory would be irreplaceable until normal industry and transportation were reestablished. As Janelle put it, "We should think of what we currently have on the shelf as our *legacy* inventory. If we replace it with anything that we pick up in barter, it will mainly be used, secondhand stuff, and it should be priced accordingly. It would be foolish to sell what we have now cheap."

The others agreed.

After a two-day period while they were "Closed for Inventory," they reopened with a carefully hand-painted sign on a four-by-eight-foot sheet of plywood displayed inside the front door, hanging from the ceiling on chains. It read:

Altmiller's Hardware Payment Policy:

ONLY Silver or Barter Accepted for Payment.

NO Paper Currency, Credit Cards, or Checks!

NO EXCEPTIONS!

Until further notice, we now accept ONLY pre-1965 U.S. silver dimes, quarters, half-dollars or silver dollars, at 10 times face value, or 99.9% silver trade dollars and bars.

No pennies or clad coins accepted.

To calculate your prices in silver:

Take the shelf tag prices and divide by 10. That is your price in 90% silver (pre-1965) coins. So a $3 tagged lightbulb will cost 3 silver dimes (30 cents).

99.9% silver trade dollars and bars are also accepted at the following ratio:

0.0715 troy ounces per silver dime or 0.715 troy ounces per dollar of face value (10 dimes or four quarters). Hence, a 1-Troy-ounce trade round or bar equals $1.40 face value in pre-1965 coinage. (Loaner calculators are available on request.)

Nickel Small Change Policy:

As needed, we will make "small change" in real nickels (pre-composition-switch vintage nickels), at the ratio of 50 nickels per silver dime (500 nickels per silver dollar). We MAY at our discretion take nickels in payment for small purchases, but only if nickels are in full 50-coin rolls.

Note: Some choice hard goods such as guns, ammunition, high-cap magazines, clean steel hardware, batteries, and sealed liquor bottles MAY be considered for barter, on a case-by-case basis. See Jacob Altmiller for details.

Sorry for Any Inconvenience
J. Altmiller, Owner and Manager

The only items that had their prices recalculated and retagged before the Altmillers reopened the store were irreplaceable guns, ammunition, gun accessories, empty gas cans, cans of two-cycle mix and four-cycle TRUFUEL, and charged propane cylinders. Those prices were all tripled or quadrupled.

During one of their regular calls, Rhiannon and Janelle were discussing the Crunch and how things were obviously getting much worse in America's big cities. The riots and looting were spreading. After recounting a long list of cities where riots had occurred, Janelle moaned, "I'm really worried, Rhi."

She took an audible breath, and continued, "On Fox News they're saying that in a lot of cities, the police and firemen aren't showing up for work because they're too worried about their own families to leave their homes. There's also reporting that some of the telephone and power utility workers are staying home, too. Nobody knows how much longer the power will stay on."

Not wanting to upset her sister even more, Rhiannon adopted a reassuring tone. "Well, just know that we'll be praying for y'all and—"

Their connection unexpectedly went dead. They both made dozens of attempts to reach each other in the days and weeks that followed. At first Janelle got "All circuits are busy now" automated messages. But a week later, there wasn't even a dial tone. It was then that Janelle feared it might be years before she'd be able to speak to her sister again.

6

FORTIFICATION

"Until recent times, every child had a rifle of his own as soon as he was old enough to understand his father's instructions. With it he hunted game and birds, killed snakes and protected himself against the dangers of rural life. When he was grown, he passed knowledge of the rifle down to his own son.... The tradition of arms is an American tradition born of generations of self-reliance, self-sufficiency and independence...."

—T. Grady Gallant, *On Valor's Side*

Tavares, Florida—
October, the First Year

While the store was closed, José Valentin went to work installing a buzzer-activated latch on the front door, similar to those that had long been used at jewelry stores and some pawnshops in Orlando and Miami. He did all this work as Jake stood guard behind him with the L. C. Smith double-barrel shotgun he'd inherited from his grandfather.

As José was testing the completed door latch, he said, "You know, boss, you really need a couple of better long guns. That blunderbuss and your .30-30 just won't cut it when Schumer hits the fan."

Jake nodded. "I suppose you're right. What do you recommend?"

"Instead of that side-by-side, you should get something like a Saiga shotgun with a detachable magazine. And instead of your .30-30 cowboy gun, you should have an AR-10 or maybe an FAL if you can find one. Marichal can hook you up, but they won't come cheap these days."

"Prices are all relative, José. If you put it in terms of, say . . . the value of the lives of my wife and son—"

Valentin interrupted. "Ehhhh-xactly."

After his discussion with José, Jake made a series of trades with Marichal. In all, Jake traded 110 ounces of silver in 10-ounce and 50-ounce bars—his entire hoard that he'd accumulated since 2001—plus a promissory note for another hundred ounces of silver. In exchange he received two of Marichal's most valuable and irreplaceable guns: a Russian-made Saiga-12 shotgun with six spare plastic 10-round magazines and a LAR-8 variant of the AR-10 with nine 20-round steel FN FAL magazines. The Rock River Arms LAR-8 was designed to accept either FN FAL or L1A1 magazines.

A new sign outside the door announced: LIMIT: TWO CUSTOMERS IN STORE AT A TIME. THANKS FOR YOUR PATIENCE. The Altmillers also erected an inexpensive fabric gazebo awning in front of the store, where customers could queue in the shade before entering the store to do business.

As one of the few functioning businesses left in town, setting up the gazebo had the unintended consequence of creating a place of barter for customers as they waited. This eventually spilled out into the paved parking lot in front of the store, turning it into a six-day-a week bazaar. By the time customers reached the head of the line, they had traded for the silver coins they would need to make purchases inside.

One important change before Altmiller's Hardware reopened was that Jake hired Tomas Marichal as a full-time security guard. He was paid three dollars per day in pre-1965 coinage, or his choice of store merchandise at cost, in barter. He was also provided display counter space to sell his own extra guns, which he priced at what first seemed to be exorbitantly high prices. For example, a run-of-the-mill DPMS

brand M4gery with iron sights and five spare magazines was priced at
$350 in silver coin. Even with his high asking prices, though, Marichal
gradually sold most of his AR-15, AR-10, and SIG556 rifles.

Tomas Marichal was an imposing figure at six feet two inches and a
muscular 230 pounds. In his new role, he became a fixture at the store.
In essence, Tomas was on duty twenty-four hours a day. He slept on a
folding bed in the back of the store, and he was encouraged to be armed
at all times. He took this seriously, opting to carry both an M4gery carbine and a Glock Model 23 pistol everywhere he went, with three spare
magazines for each in belt pouches.

Jake and Janelle habitually carried guns as well. They both had SIG
P250 pistols in Blade-Tech hip holsters—his chambered in .45 ACP,
and hers in .40 S&W. Jake also kept his loaded Saiga-12 shotgun behind
the store's front counter at all times and the RRA LAR-8 by his bedside.

To avoid setting any patterns that could be exploited, Tomas was encouraged to take his breaks for meals and errands at sporadic, unpre-
dictable times. He often took advantage of Janelle's home-cooked
meals, which the Altmillers provided to encourage Tomas to stay in the
store as much as possible. His meals were usually brought to him by
Lance, who idolized Marichal. The boy called him "our store's soldier."

Both the two-customer limit and the silver coin pricing were unpopular at first, but these practices were soon emulated by many other local
businesses after word came that several stores in Orlando and Leesburg
had either been looted or had their entire inventory sell out in a matter
of days.

Since the Altmiller's Hardware building had been built in the late
1940s, it had pre-air-conditioning architecture, with spacious screened
windows. Even better, it had a raised pagoda center section roofline
that provided exceptionally good natural light and ventilation. While
ventilation wasn't a big issue at the onset of the Crunch in October, by
the following July, many other businesses had to shut down or relocate.
Their almost windowless architecture turned them into humid saunas
in the post-grid power era. Worst of all were the tilt-up slab buildings

that had become popular in the 1980s and beyond. These relied heavily on fluorescent lighting and air-conditioning since they had few, if any windows. With rolling blackouts and the eventual failure of the power grid, these buildings became little more than unbearably hot, humid, dark caves. Jake was thankful for both his store's architecture and its PV panels. As part of the Old Florida—both culturally and architecturally—Jake and his family were far better prepared for the Crunch than most.

7

SOLDADOS

"Shortly before World War I, the German Kaiser was the guest of the Swiss government to observe military maneuvers. The Kaiser asked a Swiss militiaman: 'You are 500,000 and you shoot well, but if we attack with 1,000,000 men what will you do?' The soldier replied: 'We will shoot twice and go home.'"

—Historian Stephen P. Halbrook, as quoted by
Bill Buppert in *ZeroGov: Limited Government,
Unicorns and Other Mythological Creatures*

Tavares, Florida—
November, the First Year

Rumors began to circulate about Cuban raiders in the Florida Keys and on both the east and west coasts of the Florida peninsula. The concern was that they would start to loot inland regions. There was even talk of a full-scale Cuban invasion. When Janelle brought up these concerns in the store one day, Valentin immediately dismissed the rumors. "The Cuban army couldn't fight their way out of a paper bag."

Valentin, however, later admitted to Jake, "Papa Fidel may be dead, but they're still a bunch of commies down there. I have no doubt that they'll come and loot in Florida, if they have the chance."

Surrounded by three large lakes, Tavares effectively sat on a peninsula. The economy of the region was dominated by theme parks. There was not just the Walt Disney World resort, which included four theme parks, two water parks, and huge resort facilities, but also the two Universal Studios parks, SeaWorld, and many minor spin-off tourist traps in greater Orlando. They all had brought throngs of visitors year-round. The local saying was, "Directly or indirectly, everyone works for the Mouse." Or more derisively, "for the Rat." Even before the Crunch started in earnest, Disney World tourism dropped to nil, and everyone felt the pinch.

In Tavares, the locals were nervous, but they felt comfortably isolated by the lakes, which eliminated several potential avenues of approach. The town conscripted a levy of armed men to man the roadblocks. Each man between ages eighteen and sixty was expected to do an eight-hour guard duty shift five days of each month. There were very few exceptions made—only those with chronic health conditions were excused, but even these men were expected to pay the daily wages in silver for substitutes to stand duty during their assigned shifts.

Eventually, the roadblock levy rules were liberalized, allowing more substitutions. A few men served as substitutes for three or even four others, which provided a way to make a decent living just by standing guard duty. These men soon went by the nickname Suntanned Soldados, given the many long hours they spent manning the roadblocks. A few men tried to claim noncombatant status because of their religious objection to being armed, but they were told to report for duty anyway and serve as unarmed "runners" or as medics.

The men at the roadblocks were in constant radio contact with the police department. It was initially the police, bolstered by more than a dozen recent combat veterans, who formed the Quick Reaction Teams (QRTs). They would be called up anytime a sizable force of looters was spotted. The attrition rate at the roadblocks was low, but on the QRTs it was surprisingly high. They lost an average of one man a week—either killed or wounded so badly that they couldn't return to duty. By the end of the first year, there had been a complete turnover; only two of the pre-Crunch police officers were still with the force.

The Lake County Sheriff Department's heaviest weapon was a

Barrett semiauto .50 BMG rifle. Lake County had a National Guard armory in Eustis. The 2nd Battalion, 124th Infantry Regiment at the Eustis Armory had several .50 caliber M2 Browning heavy machine guns, and its anti-tank unit had TOW missile systems that could be mounted on up-armored Humvees. These weapons, however, were essentially worthless because no ammunition was kept on site. All of it was stored in bunkers at an Ammunition Supply Point (ASP) eighty miles away at the Camp Blanding Joint Training Center near the town of Starke. The Eustis National Guard Armory also had sections of 81 mm and 60 mm mortars, but it was the same story: mortar tubes, but no mortar bombs. Only their M16s, M4s, and M240 light machine guns were put to use, but only with very limited ammunition that was scrounged up locally. The 5.56 and 7.62 NATO ammo that they needed for these was in very short supply and traded as if it were gold.

Up until the 1970s, Tavares had been a somewhat distinct community with its own identity. But Tavares and all of the area along U.S. 441 from Orlando to Ocala and along U.S. 27 from Clermont to Ocala became known as Greater Suburbia. Most of the region became a continuous commercial retail strip. It was as if Central Florida transitioned from a collection of *towns* into an amorphous *shopping experience*. The sense of community was lost, and only the extremes of the Crunch brought part of that back in a defensive instinct. Tavares as "town" concept was restored only as a protective community to delineate "us" from "them," with the "them" meaning the riffraff in Orlando. Once this concept crystallized, the roadblocks went up.

Tavares became a law-and-order stronghold for several reasons. Not only did the lake-dominated geography limit avenues of approach, but Tavares was the county seat and had a rather imposing Justice Center (with county jail and courthouse). The Lake County Sheriff's Department headquarters were also in town.

When the Crunch set in, the local citizens were already quite well armed and most of them believed strongly in the right to keep and bear arms. As a base of operations, the police, National Guard, and local citizens groups were able to maintain law and order and create a relatively stable and free community where a barter economy developed.

The local economy was enhanced by the chain of lakes and other area lakes because water transportation—mostly rowboat and small sailboat—connected the cities of Tavares, Mount Dora, Eustis, Leesburg, and the communities of Howey-in-the-Hills, Astatula, and those near the Ocklawaha River.

It was the scarcity in the region that dictated the roadblocks. There was no longer any significant agriculture nearby, so the citizens had to scramble to become self-sufficient. Most of the large citrus groves had been killed by the freezes in the 1980s and replaced by residential developments. The small groves that remained and the backyard trees became threatened by disease—greening and canker—which killed some trees.

Most of the "muck" farms—wetland converted to vegetable farms—near Zellwood and Apopka reverted to swamp because of environmental regulations. After the Crunch, however, this process was quickly reversed.

By the early 2000s, there was very little commercial cattle production in the area—just a few hobby farms and ranchettes. Immediately after the Crunch, all of the heifer calves were saved for breeding stock, but it was an agonizingly slow process to build up production. Anyone with a dairy cow was considered rich. Heifer calves were pampered and closely guarded. Their asking prices were enormous—as much as two ounces of gold. The local lakes and rivers provided fish, turtles, and alligators, but within two years they were fished out. By that time, however, gardening had begun to flourish, as had raising chickens, rabbits, ducks, and pigs.

The population of Florida was dominated by retirees. Largely because of untreated chronic health conditions and starvation, the state's population dropped thirty-five percent in the first twenty-four months following the Crunch. The Great Die-Off had begun.

8

FOSSICKERS

"The people are immensely likable—cheerful, extrovert, quick-witted, and unfailingly obliging. Their cities are safe and clean and nearly always built on water. They have a society that is prosperous, well ordered, and instinctively egalitarian. The food is excellent. The beer is cold. The sun nearly always shines. There is coffee on every corner.... Life doesn't get much better than this."

—Bill Bryson, *In a Sunburned Country*

Casuarina, Northern Australia— November, One Year Before the Crunch

Chuck's first Christmas in Australia gave him some culture shock. Since Christmas came at midsummer, the holiday mainly revolved around swimming pool parties and barbeques. Instead of citrus and fruitcakes, the fruit most often served with holiday meals was mangoes. There was some turkey served at Christmas, but prawns and crayfish predominated. There was a lot to like about Australia, but it took some adjustment.

Although he missed his home, Chuck took infrequent vacation trips to see his family in Texas. Part of his reluctance to travel was his frustration with the U.S. government's TSA agents, who made his life miserable. Because he worked regularly with explosives, all of his clothing, belts, wristwatch band, and even the exterior of his luggage were perennially contaminated by trace amounts of dBX and PETN—the explosive filling used in detonating cord. The legions of blue-gloved "Scope and Grope" TSA drones were endlessly swabbing pieces of passenger luggage and running the swabs through their spectroscopic scanners. It all got worse in 2012 when the TSA fielded their Picosecond Programmable Laser scanners. These scanners were particularly sensitive. And, instead of scanning just a few random swabs, they were able to scan the clothing of *everyone* who walked by.

Many times Chuck missed his scheduled flight because he was shunted off to TSA back rooms for "interview" interrogations and secondary searches. He would often be left to sit by himself for what seemed like ages. He would mumble to himself, "Two by two, hands of blue," and watch the minutes tick by on his wristwatch. The process was always agonizing.

Invariably, the TSA agents would seem hesitant, consult among themselves, and then push his case up the chain of command. A senior TSA agent would then personally interview Chuck, who would *again* have to explain the nature of his work. He'd then be released as "free to go," but without any apology.

Chuck lived in a one-bedroom leased cottage in Casuarina. He had originally looked in the nicer adjoining suburb of Tiwi, but he couldn't find a cottage in his price range. He didn't need much space because he had brought just a few possessions with him from the United States. These were mostly boxes of books, clothes, and a couple of guitars. Even though it was a long drive from most of his job sites, he chose the town because it had good shopping and a seven-screen cinema. He was not much interested in shopping personally, but he knew that shopping malls and movie theaters attracted young women. The shopping malls, he reasoned, were his best chance of meeting a potential spouse, since it drew shoppers from as far away as 125 miles. Of course, once he met Ava, his proximity to the malls no longer seemed very important.

The evening after their first meeting, Chuck lay anxiously in bed, thinking about what Ava had said to him. Finally, realizing that he would get no sleep, he turned on his bedside light. Normally when he had trouble sleeping, he would get out his twelve-string guitar and play familiar tunes or improvisations until he felt sleepy. But tonight what she had said was hounding him. He dug through one of the boxes of books that he'd had shipped from his parents' home in Texas but had never unpacked, and found his dusty Bible.

"Matthew, Mark, Luke, and John," he recited, as he turned to the book of John. He began to read. At first he tried to remember exactly what Ava had said, as if it was a note jotted down in one of his college lectures. "Personal Savior" was what she had said. But then he just got into reading. Chuck recognized John 3:16. *Yes, I believe in Jesus*, he thought. *I'm smart enough to see that none of us would be here if it wasn't for God making us.* But moving on to the next verse, he saw that there was more. It said that whoever did not believe would be condemned. He pondered the word *condemned. That has to be something more than just being mistaken—condemned to Hell?* he wondered. He came to chapter six and was perplexed by Jesus' bizarre sermon about his body being bread. That story had confused him in Sunday school, and it was not any clearer now. But as he read the rest of the book, it began to come into focus. Jesus *was* the good shepherd. He really was born on Earth to die for sinners.

Over the next few days, Chuck kept reading. He raced through the book of Acts, amazed by Paul's conversion. He reached Romans, and everything fell into place. He would later learn to love Paul's epistles for their depth and brilliant insight. Paul spelled out in concrete terms what Chuck had been trying to understand. He was a sinner. This sin was much more than the porn that he'd watched until he got his life straightened out during his freshman year of college. He realized that his indifference was a dishonor to his Creator. He prayed quite simply, "God, Lord, I've been going the wrong way, ignoring everything you've done. I've only been interested in my plans, and not cared at all that you made me. I've been your enemy! Thank you for showing me that. Thank you for dying for me. That's insane! But I need it. I need you to forgive me and save me."

One evening, a month after he had become a saved Christian, Chuck called Ava's cell phone number. He told her earnestly, "I do know where I stand with God now, Ava. I had always reckoned that if God took care of His business, and I took care of mine, we'd be all right. But I get it now. John's gospel is about God coming to us and saving us. The fact is, I thought I had it together, but I was flat wrong. I kept reading and got to Paul. I realized I was dead—absolutely dead in my sins! God showed me that I needed Him. Christ died for my sins so that I could live with Him. I can't ignore that! He's given me real life."

He could hear Ava weeping. She said, "Thank you, Lord, for this answer to prayer."

Casuarina, Northern Australia— December, the Year Before the Crunch

Chuck's Jeep had nearly 187,000 miles on the odometer. The vehicle's left-hand steering arrangement was a constant source of amusement. With amazing regularity, someone from the oil company would attempt to jump in as a passenger, on the driver's side. This would be met with comments like "What, are you chauffeuring today, sir?" Even better was when Burroughs brought his brindled Great Dane with them on their fossicking trips. Chuck would sit behind the wheel in the left front seat, the dog would sit in the right front seat, and Burroughs and Drake would sit in the back. They loved seeing the expressions on the faces of the motorists in approaching cars, because to them it looked as if the dog was driving.

When they had begun working for Nolan, both men were in their early thirties, divorced, and recovering alcoholics. Chuck did his best to keep them away from beer. His main weapon was his ice chest, which he constantly kept full of their favorite soft drinks. For Drake, it was Bundaberg Ginger Beer, and for Burroughs it was Solo brand lemon soda.

For himself, Chuck usually carried ice-cold water in a pair of Coleman wide-mouthed backpacking water bottles that were so well worn and battered that their markings had been completely rubbed off. He found that avoiding sugary sodas was best for maintaining his desired body weight. But on particularly hot days, he liked to have a Schweppes Passiona. He tried to keep a couple of those—or the Kirks brand Pasito equivalent—in the bottom of the ice chest, but he often found they had been filched by his men.

Chuck Nolan's employer, AOGC, had begun focusing on true rank-wildcat exploration in recent years and had started an aggressive seismic exploration program to find areas for future drilling. (A "rank" wildcat venture was exploration of a long distance from existing well-heads.) Chuck did most of his prospecting work in the Bonaparte Basin and Daly Basin, south of Darwin, or in the McArthur Basin, east of Darwin. Occasionally, he would work as far south as the Birrindudu Basin, but it was a long drive into hot and dry country, and he dreaded every trip there.

Chuck particularly liked the exploration style of AOGC in that they relied upon conventional 2-D seismic data, which required far less manpower and "men on the ground" than the large, manpower-intensive 3-D surveys he previously led back in the United States.

While some of the other seismic prospecting crews transported enormously heavy 58,000-pound peak force seismic vibrators, he preferred to work with his explosives team. Depending on the terrain, this work was less time consuming and required only a small crew and, as Nolan claimed, gave a stronger and higher-resolution image of the underlying formations. He often said: "My idea of the perfect day of fossicking is to get in and get out fast, make things go boom, and leave big dust clouds. I like to start early and get home early."

Typically, he would go on preliminary surveys by himself or with just one assistant to survey the terrain and to lay out future seismic surveys, recording GPS coordinates along the way. Another crew would methodically drill the shot holes, in patterns of up to thirty-six bores.

That same crew would also lay out the thousands of feet of cable and geophone jugs, to receive the reflected energy from each shot.

After the crew had finished, Chuck's team would return to the completed shot holes, set up their recording instruments, and carefully lower the large Geoprime dBX explosive charges into the holes. The company had started out using gelignite, but in more recent years, partly because of environmental regulations, they had switched to Geoprime dBX, a high explosive that was specially tailored for seismic acquisition. The explosive was made by Dyno Nobel. The Geoprime dBX variant they used was packaged in thirty-four-inch-long bright yellow plastic cases that were five inches in diameter. The cases were threaded at the end, so multiple charge cases could be combined by simply screwing them together, to provide a detonation of the desired force.

Just before the detonation they would "roll tape" while igniting the charges—although in the modern context, this meant high-resolution digital recording rather than the magnetic tape equipment of years ago. Later, this recorded digital data would be painstakingly processed by AOGC's "boffins" into 2-D seismic sections or data volume of the earth's underlying structure, which would then be analyzed by the company to assess the economic potential of hydrocarbons in the area. In addition to oil and natural gas, the company also searched for coal and coal bed methane gas. As Nolan frequently told folks, the process was similar to a medical ultrasound, which creates an image of the internal human body. In fact, ultrasound technology was based upon oil field seismic technology.

Chuck was often called in to help with the interpretation of the data. The boffins tended to work hacker hours, wandering into the office as late as two P.M. and staying as late as midnight. To Chuck, who liked to start work at six A.M. and be home by three thirty P.M. on his office days, the disparity in hours was frustrating.

Every major oil company had a specialized seismic group in their exploration departments, and each company carefully guarded their secrets for advanced imaging and interpretation technology. One of AOGC's reasons for hiring Chuck was to capitalize on his 2-D interpretation skills. Much like a radiologist interpreting an ultrasound or CT-scan image, Chuck had a particularly keen eye for assessing the hydrocarbon potential from a set of seismic images. Seismic interpretation was as much an art as it was a science.

Aside from Chuck, most of AOGC's oilfield and survey crews came from bogan backgrounds, although given their high salaries, they were often called CUBs—cashed-up bogans. Chuck found their culture rather interesting. Many bogans, he noticed, had Southern Cross tattoos. The tattoo's familiar pattern of stars from the Australian flag, however, had become synonymous with racism against the aboriginal population and their deep dislike of immigrants, an attitude Chuck openly disagreed with.

Despite their diverse backgrounds and differing opinions, Chuck got along quite well with the men on his crew. There was plenty of joking and some good-natured teasing, as well as discussions about current events, sports, celebrities, and different brands of cars. Whenever they mocked Chuck for being an American and driving a Jeep, he would crack jokes about popular Holden cars, which were either built in Australia or imported from other countries and sold under the Holden name. He was fond of saying "Holden isn't a family name, but an acronym that stands for Heap of Lead Doing Essentially Nothing." During a conversation with a drilling crew foreman, Chuck couldn't help but ask, "Why do Holdens have heated rear windows?" The foreman, always game for Chuck's jokes, shot him a questioning look. Chuck paused a beat before answering, "So their owners can keep their hands warm when they're pushing them."

9

BARGAIN HUNTING

> "It is a commonplace that the history of civilisation is largely the history of weapons.... A complex weapon makes the strong stronger, while a simple weapon—so long as there is no answer to it—gives claws to the weak."
>
> —George Orwell, "You and the Atomic Bomb"

Casuarina, Northern Territory, Australia—February, the First Year

Chuck began spending most of his weekends with Ava. They had long conversations about a wide range of topics, but mostly about theology and the Christian life. Just as their relationship was blossoming, however, Ava moved away to begin college at the ANU. They carried on via e-mail and phone calls, but Chuck missed her company. To compensate, Chuck did more reading, attended Bible studies, played his guitars, and went hiking. He would have also liked to do some target shooting and hunting, but the bureaucratic challenges of importing any of his guns from Texas were daunting.

When Chuck Nolan casually mentioned to his fossicking crew that he was interested in buying a rifle, Bruce Drake said, "Well, you've got to meet my uncle Thomas. He's our family's biggest gun guy. He has a lot of guns, and he's quite the roo hunter. He was a farm foreman, but he's retired now."

Despite Chuck's immediate interest in meeting Bruce's uncle, he didn't see Thomas Drake until a month later. In the interim, he learned, Uncle Thomas had done some thorough background checking on Nolan.

They met face-to-face for the first time at the Casuarina Gun Club rifle range, where Thomas was a member. It was a small club—the sort where each member had a key to the padlock on the gate.

The club had been established just a few years before, as an alternative to the Darwin Clay Target Club, which catered to trap and skeet shooters. There, some of the rifle shooters had felt the deep divide between the shotgun shooters and the rifle shooters. They felt like the rifle shooters were treated as second-class citizens. Even in the Northern Territory, which had a reputation for its casual and nonbureaucratic government, getting the permits and inspections required to establish the new range had taken a frustrating three years.

It was a hot afternoon, and Chuck and Thomas were the only shooters there. For a new club, the facilities were Spartan: Some earthen butts that had been bulldozed at various distances. A dozen shooting benches with posts made of ironbark eucalyptus and their tops and seats cut from plywood. Concrete had not yet been poured, but the forms for the concrete walkways were already under construction. A temporary shade structure covered only four of the benches.

Initially, they spent some time chitchatting as Thomas stapled a pair of targets on the frames at the 200-meter butts and set up his spotting scope. Thomas had brought three rifles with him that day: a Mauser sporter that had been rechambered to .243 Winchester with a heavy bull barrel, a BSA Model 15 .22 rimfire target rifle on a Martini single-shot action, and a Scout-sporterized .303 No. 4 Mk 1 Short Magazine Lee-Enfield (SMLE) bolt action. It was the latter rifle that Drake had hinted he might be willing to sell.

Their first half hour of shooting was quite deliberate, as Drake shot the Mauser .243 in three-shot groups from a sandbag rest, comparing the accuracy of four different hand-load batches that he'd made, which had slightly different powder charges. Chuck was impressed to see that

Thomas had a detailed shooting log book wherein he made notes on the temperature, humidity, and estimated wind speed. After he'd found the most accurate load, he gave Chuck the chance to shoot the rifle. Shooting from the rest, his three-shot group measured less than two inches—larger than Drake's best group, but still quite respectable.

Next, they shot the .303 caliber SMLE. Drake mentioned that he had inherited it from a relative in New South Wales where registration wasn't required until after the Port Arthur tragedy. This rifle had been tucked away in the back of a closet and overlooked until after the registration deadline. When Thomas had inherited it, he didn't have the heart to turn it in. Before they started shooting, Chuck mentioned, "I've been doing some research, and I've read that there is a particular sequence for loading the ammo into SMLE stripper clips so that the rifle won't jam."

Drake nodded. "Ah, so you have been doing your studies, have you? I've heard that you're a man with close attention to detail. You're right about that. Since these cartridges are rimmed, you have to be careful that they go into the chargers just like this."

With Chuck watching carefully, Thomas dexterously loaded a stripper clip. He did it in a way so that, as the cartridges were sequentially pushed out of the magazine by the bolt, the cartridge rims wouldn't get tangled up.

Chuck liked the rifle. It had a butter-smooth action and it had been partially sporterized with a good-quality forward "scout" style scope mount and a Schmidt & Bender long eye relief scope that was worth almost as much as the rifle itself. The rifle's 10-round magazine, which could be rapidly reloaded with 5-round stripper clips (or "chargers" in the British Commonwealth shooting lexicon) was a nice plus. He would have preferred a more modern SMLE chambered in 7.62 NATO, but those were quite scarce.

Chuck noticed that the ammo they were using was the later vintage noncorrosively primed ammunition made in Greece in the 1970s, with an HXP head stamp. He would have given anything for some more-recently manufactured American-made Federal brand .303 British soft-tip hunting ammunition. Having once used that ammunition, he had been able to put two-round groups from a cold barrel into the same hole on paper at one hundred yards, from a well-cleaned, cut and re-crowned barrel. He had even read that in the early 1980s, the American Olin-Winchester plant had produced modern military ball (FMJ) .303 British under contract for the U.S. government, to be sent to the Afghans fighting the Soviets at that time.

The rifle was a No. 4 Mk 1 model and was stamped ROF(F)—which indicated that it had been manufactured by the Royal Ordnance Fac-tory at Fazakerly, England. As was typical of sporters, the forward por-tion of the handguard wood had been removed, and the remaining handguard tapered and rounded at the tip. Seeing this made Chuck cringe, as he hated to see original military rifles altered. However, he was glad to see that the sporterizing had at least been done neatly and that the scope mount and scope had been expertly installed.

Chuck shot five rounds through the SMLE rifle. With the high mag-nification spotting scope, he could see that all five shots had hit in a five-inch radius. This was good accuracy for two hundred yards—at least for a SMLE.

"That's a fair grouping for that rifle when using surplus ammo. I think it suits you. Would you like to buy it?" Thomas asked.

Chuck smiled and said, "Yes, I like the idea of owning an American-designed rifle."

"What? Lee-Enfields are *British*."

Chuck shook his head and said politely, "Actually, the SMLE was a design *refined* in England by the Enfield arsenal, but the original de-signer was James Paris Lee, who was born in Scotland and raised in Canada, but he moved to the States in the 1850s. He was a naturalized American citizen, and that's where he became a gun designer."

"Oh."

Chuck asked hesitantly, "Is it registered?"

Thomas snorted derisively and said, "Nah. Do you realize there are more unregistered guns than there are registered ones in this country? After the Port Arthur muck-up, us Aussies got wise and either started building hiding places in our walls or sharpened our spades."

Chuck raised an eyebrow, and asked with a wry grin, "Some midnight gardening, eh?"

Drake laughed. "Too right."

Chuck tested the rifle's magazine release, popping the magazine in and out twice, and said, "You know, a Texan without a rifle is like an Englishman without an umbrella."

Drake chuckled and gave him one last scrutinizing stare. "Okay, Chuck. Here's what's what: For five hundred dollars Australian, I'll give you that rifle with the scope and sling that are on it now, and I'll include eighty rounds of that Greek .303 ball."

Chuck thrust his hand forward for a handshake, and half shouted, "We have a deal."

Later that day, after thoroughly cleaning the rifle, Chuck did a Bing web search to find a ballistic "drop table" for .303 ball cartridges, calculated from two hundred to twelve hundred yards. After all, the .303 British cartridge was considered underpowered by modern standards (starting its drop even before two hundred yards), although the bullet's relatively large grain weight still made the round accurate as well as a heavy hitter within six hundred yards. He printed a copy, trimmed it with scissors, and neatly taped it to the left side of the rifle stock, just forward of the magazine. While some gun collectors found this practice unsightly, Chuck was strongly in favor of practicality over style. He wanted to have a quick reference to the rifle's ballistic characteristics handy at all times.

The same evening he began searching for dead space in his cottage. He needed a hiding place for the SMLE and its ammo and accessories. Tapping on the thin veneer paneling on the partition between his bedroom and the combination living room/kitchen, he discovered a hollow sound. Rather than the FIBEROCK plasterboard that had been used on the inside of the exterior walls, he found that this partition had been shoddily constructed. The paneling had simply been nailed to bare studs using small brads. He found one panel above the built-in dresser that would be the right size to hold the SMLE and accessories. This panel was three feet wide by four feet tall. On the reverse side of the wall in the living room, there was an electrical outlet, but since it was in the corner of his intended cache section, he didn't anticipate that it would be a problem.

The next morning, Chuck drove to the shopping mall in Casuarina and bought a package of 20 mm diameter Velcro tabs at a department store. These tabs had glue-backed adhesive. Then he drove to the All Tools store on Winnellie Street in Darwin and picked up a few hand tools.

Back at the cottage, he sized up the job. He noticed that if he pulled the paneling down from the top, it would probably scrape the ceiling and leave a mark. So he worked from the bottom. He found that the brads the builder had used were quite thin, and had just a very slight flare at their head ends. This meant he was able to gingerly pull the paneling off, with the brads staying in the studs, and their head pulling through the paneling. Once he had the first ten inches loose, the rest of the panel came off easily. With the paneling removed, he used his hammer to nail the protruding brads down flush.

Chuck found that his intended cache space was bisected by a piece of AC electrical wire that angled down to the outlet box. The wire would get in the way of storing the rifle, so he made a trip to an electrical supply store where they sold wire by the roll or by the meter. It was twice as expensive when it was purchased by the lineal meter, but he only needed to buy 1.5 meters. He also bought an assortment box of wire nuts, a combination wire cutter/stripper tool, and a roll of electrical tape.

After again returning to the cottage, he found the circuit breaker for the living room outlet and de-energized it. Once he had the junction box open to extend the wire, he realized he had the opportunity to hardwire in a GoldenRod dehumidifier. So he substituted larger wire nuts and stubbed off a short length of wire, and he capped its conductors with wire nuts.

He oiled the SMLE heavily and stowed it in the wall cache along with the bandoleers of ammunition, even including his cleaning supplies. He didn't want to leave anything out in plain view that might arouse suspicion. The Enfield rifle fit nicely in the shallow space, but only when its bolt handle was removed.

The Velcro tabs worked wonderfully. The cache was virtually undetectable, yet he could access it in just a few seconds. The finishing touch was adding a row of cup hook screws inside beneath the top stud to provide a place to hang his cotton bandoleers of ammunition.

He ordered a twelve-inch-long 220/230 VAC GoldenRod dehumidifier on the Internet. It arrived a few days later and took just a few minutes to wire in. The dehumidifier drew only 50 watts, so the expense of operating it was negligible. Chuck slept better knowing the rifle and ammunition would be protected from corrosion. Rust was a constant enemy in Australia's Top End.

Chuck took the rifle out only for occasional outback target shooting and roo hunting. He eventually bought another 280 rounds of .303 ammo but was able to find just one spare magazine. He was careful to always carry the rifle in a guitar case, in case any of his neighbors were nosy.

A few weeks after he bought the Enfield rifle, Chuck Nolan met Caleb Burroughs through Randall Burroughs, his younger brother. Caleb was a warrant officer in the Australian Army with a specialty in logistics. He found his job frustrating because although he handled logistics *related* to the Australian Army deployments in Afghanistan, he never had the opportunity to go to Afghanistan himself. He resigned himself to "pushing paper" for the Army but often grumbled that as a logistics planning officer, it was unlikely he'd ever have a chance to go to "The Sharp End." He kept himself in top-notch physical condition, always hoping that he would be deployed to Afghanistan, but he never was.

Randall introduced Chuck to his brother when Caleb was home on semiannual leave, and the two immediately hit it off. In Chuck's estimation, Caleb was a much different man from his brother. While Rabbit was crude and impulsive, Caleb was refined and reserved. And unlike Rabbit, Caleb was well educated, and well read. Rabbit's tastes ran toward men's magazines like *Maxim*, while Caleb read *Guns & Game* magazine and *Journal of Military History*. He also subscribed to *Quadrant*, a conservative literary magazine. Born in the same year and just three days apart, Caleb and Chuck also shared tastes in movies and novels—particularly old Westerns—and both were shooting enthusiasts and admirers of the Australian novelist Nevil Shute.

As a serving army officer, Caleb was rarely at home in Darwin, but he and Chuck continued their friendship via e-mail and Skype. For months on end, they had wide-ranging debates on everything from politics to the peculiarities of the ballistics of various .303 British cartridge loadings. One of their longest-lasting e-mail debates concerned the multiple voting scheme proposed by Nevil Shute in his novel *In the Wet*. Caleb liked Shute's "seven vote" scheme, while Chuck proposed having only one vote per citizen, but making land ownership, an IQ test, and/or military service prerequisites to voting rights. As an Australian Republican Movement (ARM) member, Caleb suggested that anyone with a title of nobility who received a welfare payment should be excluded, which started another round of debate. Caleb and Chuck became good friends, politely sparring over these issues.

10

DOWNLOADS

"Pro captu lectoris habent sua fata libelli." (Loosely translated: "According to the capabilities of their readers, books have their destinies.")

—Terentianus Maurus, *De Litteris, Syllabis, et Metris*

Casuarina, Northern Territory, Australia—March, the First Year

Chuck Nolan and Caleb Burroughs were both news junkies and watched world events closely. When it became apparent that another global credit crisis like 2008 was approaching, they began sending each other permalink URLs for articles from news websites like DrudgeReport.com and WorldNetDaily.com. Links from these sites led them to "hard money" investing websites like TheDailyReckoning.com, ZeroHedge.com, SovereignMan.com, and GaryNorth.com. Investment websites then provided entrée to a plethora of Austrian economics, libertarian, and survivalist sites.

Four months into this shared web wandering, Caleb declared in one of his e-mails, "I've taken the Red Pill, bro. I can now see that the mainstream media has been feeding us horse by-products. We need to get *ready*. There's a storm coming."

Chuck sent a reply. "I concur. It looks like it's going to hit the fan in less than two years, and possibly much sooner. We need to get smart on bartering, gardening, self-sufficiency, commo, advanced first aid, the whole works. Suggestions?"

> "I vote that we start out with resources out there that are free for
> the picking. I can download hundreds of military manuals as
> PDFs. There are also thousands of free books on the Internet.
> We should download those and put them on redundant memory
> sticks. The cost of storage media like thumb drives has gotten
> ridiculously low. I just saw an ad for a sixteen *giga*byte stick for
> just twenty-two AUD. That's about the same price as a sixteen
> megabyte stick was just a few years ago! Just one stick could fit many
> *hundreds* of books and manuals, especially if they are compressed."

Chuck responded, "Okay, you start with military manuals, while I gather civilian books. We make two copies of each, plus copies on our laptops, and then mail the redundant copy sticks to each other."

Forty-eight hours later, Caleb wrote back, "Great idea. I started out with more than forty Aussie army manuals. I also have access to an Australian Defence Force mirror website of the American military database site called Army Knowledge Online (AKO). It is a treasure trove of information.

> "Here are the manuals I was able to download just this evening:
>
> Survival and Evasion, FM 21-76-1
>
> USMC Survival Manual, MCRP 3-02F
>
> Camouflage, FM 5-20
>
> Camouflage of Vehicles, FM 5-20B
>
> Field Hygiene and Sanitation, FM 21-10
>
> Improvised Explosive Devices or IEDs, TM 31-210
>
> Infantry Rifle Platoon-Squad, FM 7-8
>
> Ranger Handbook, SH 21-76
>
> Survivability, FM 5-103

NBC Protection, FM 3-4

NBC Decontamination, FM 3-5

Special Forces Unconventional Warfare, TC 18-01

M16 and M16A1 Rifles Operator's Manual, TM 9-1005-249-10

Sniper Training, FM 23-10 å

USMC Sniping, MCWP 3-15.3

Counter Guerilla Operations

Jungle Operations

Long Range Surveillance Unit Operations

Military Mountaineering, FM 3-97.61

Special Forces Use of Pack Animals, FM 3-05.213 (FM 31-27)

Claymore Mine, FM 23-23

Obstacles, Mines, Demolitions, FM 90-10

Ordnance and Explosives Response

Ranger Unit Operations, FM 7-85

USMC Scouting and Patrolling, MCWP 3-11

Military First Aid Manual, FM 4-25-11

US Army Tactical Combat Casualty Care (TCCC) Correspondence Course

NATO Emergency War Surgery

Combat Lifesaver Home Study Course

Special Operations Forces Medical Handbook (2001)—Note: there is a newer edition, but it isn't in the online free libraries and it is *beaucoup* expensive.

Have you had the chance to search for civvie books?"

Later that evening, Chuck sent an answer: "You betcha. I already downloaded the LDS Preparedness Manual from the Mormon Church and went to the Hesperian Foundation website and downloaded 'Where There Is No Doctor' by

David Werner and 'Where There Is No Dentist' by Murray Dickson. I also found mention of sites where I can download the following, gratis, and will do so over the course of the next few evenings:

Survival and Austere Medicine: An Introduction

Ship Captain's Medical Guide

Medical Drugs and Equipment for the Team Physician

Journal of Special Operations Medicine

"I also read a recommendation that I get physical copies of these books:

Wilderness Medicine, 5th Edition, by Paul S. Auerbach

2012 Nurse's Drug Handbook

Ditch Medicine: Advanced Field Procedures for Emergencies by Hugh Coffee

Medicine for the Outdoors by Paul Auerbach

The Merck Manual of Diagnosis and Therapy

Primary Surgery: Volume 1: Non-Trauma by Maurice King

Primary Surgery: Volume 2: Trauma by Maurice King

The Sanford Guide to Antimicrobial Therapy 2012 Edited by David Gilbert

Tactical Medicine Essentials by E. John Wipfler

Wilderness Medicine, Beyond First Aid, 5th Edition by William W. Forgey

Wilderness 911 by Eric Weiss

Wounds and Lacerations: Emergency Care and Closure by Alexander T. Trott, MD

The Doom and Bloom Survival Medicine Handbook by Joe Alton, MD and Amy Alton

"Buying all those could blow my budget, especially if I have to order them from book companies in the States. I'll have to be selective about what I buy. That last one by Joe Alton of 'Dr. Bones and Nurse Amy' fame is a real prepper medical book written by a real deal prepper MD. From fish hooks to frostbite, surgery to stockpiling medications—it's all in there. I will let you know what else I find. OBTW, over the next few evenings, I plan to dig into the following:

"Project Gutenberg: 33,000 free public domain e-books! But be advised that some books there are way out of date, so they *do not* follow modern fire safety, lab/chemical safety, and machinery safety standards.

The Australian Small Farm Permaculture and Sustainable Living website has lots of free e-books.

E-Books Directory

Steve's Pages: Another gold mine! *Thousands* of free firearms manuals and military manuals. At a minimum, we should be sure to download the exploded diagrams and the user manuals for each of our guns.

"I think AKO has only current manuals, so you might check GlobalSecurity.com. They have lots of free military manuals (text only).

"And a civilian site called PR68.com has lots of links for U.S. military FMs and TMs—especially radio manuals.

"Oh, and Wikipedia has some links to PDFs of U.S. military manuals. For advice on stocking up, I downloaded a copy of 'The Alpha Strategy' by John Pugsley. And for some good Christian doctrine and Bible study, the Institute for Christian Economics site, established by Dr. Gary North, has lots of free books. I'll be getting a lot of those.

"I'm also considering buying the forty-two-year compendium of *The Mother Earth News* on CD-ROM. Ditto for the compendium of *Backwoods Home* magazine. Both are American 'back to the land' magazines with a wealth of info on self-sufficiency.

"I just had another idea. How about all of those instructional videos
(outdoor survival, gardening, shooting schools, etc.) on YouTube? I
found a website called YouTube Downloader that has free software, so
we can SAVE those videos onto our hard drives or to memory sticks.
Way cool."

The following week, Chuck e-mailed Caleb: "Just when I thought we
had assembled a fairly complete library, I found out that there are a couple of
websites that offer ALL of Wikipedia on DVD. There are a couple of options. The
skinny version is text only, but the fat one has all the photos and illustrations.
This might be a good idea for something to add to our library."

Caleb replied: "<Snarkasm On> Yes, but consider: When they do the Wikipedia download, they had to take a *snapshot* of the site contents. At any given
time, especially Saturday evenings when college students have been drinking,
some of those pages are being vandalized. So just consider that the Idi Amin
Wikipedia bio page we get on DVD might say, 'General Idi A. Meany, Notorious
Egg Sucker, President of Bananaland . . .' <Snarkasm Off>"

11

THE MISSING UMBRELLA

"All politicians will allow, and most philosophers, that reasons of state may, in particular emergencies, dispense with the rules of justice, and invalidate any treaty or alliance, where the strict observance of it would be prejudicial, in a considerable degree, to either of the contracting parties. But nothing less than the most extreme necessity, it is confessed, can justify individuals in a breach of promise, or an invasion of the properties of others."

—David Hume, *An Enquiry Concerning the Principles of Morals*, 1777

Surabaya, Indonesia—August, the Second Year

Soekirnan Assegaf was excited to get his first command, even if it was one of the smallest ships in the Indonesian Navy. His most recent assignment had been as a weapons officer aboard the large patrol boat KRI *Tenggiri*. (The ship had formerly been called the *Ardent* when it was in service with the Royal Australian Navy.) Much of that time had been spent cruising the Strait of Malacca. It had only been three months since Assegaf had been advanced in rank from *Letnan Satu* (first lieutenant) to *Kapten* (captain). Unlike most of his contemporaries, who were receiving logistics and staff officer assignments, he was getting his own ship.

The bad news for Assegaf was that his new home port would be at Manado on Sulawesi island. This port was considered the gateway to the Celebes Sea. It was 675 miles from Surabaya and more than 1,000 miles from his family's home in Jakarta. He would have only one or two leaves each year, and undoubtedly his transport to Jakarta would be on slow and noisy C-235 or C-295 combination cargo and passenger logistics flights, with several island-hopping stops along the way.

Assegaf's new assignment was to command KRI *Sadarin*. Depending on the perspective of who saw it, *Sadarin* could be described as either a large boat or a small ship. It was fifty-one feet long and displaced twenty-three tons when fully fueled. It was in the Hawker de Havilland *Carpenteria* class, powered by a pair of MTU diesels. These engines produced 1,360 horsepower and gave *Sadarin* a top speed of twenty-nine knots. The boat had been built in 1977, but since then it had been re-engined twice—most recently in 2010.

With its standard fuel tanks, *Sadarin* had a range of 950 miles at eighteen knots. A typical patrol was five days, but the frequent picket duty patrols were an agonizing fourteen days. Living for such a long stretch of time in cramped quarters and subsisting on plain, uninteresting rations often led to short tempers. Stowing extra fuel in 45-liter bladders strapped down in spare berths, extra water in crates on deck and extra provisions in every available space made the small ship seem even smaller.

The crew of *Sadarin* was normally ten, but for picket duty the crew had just eight men, and three of them weren't even sailors. They were *otaks* ("brains") that had been detailed from Tentara Nasional Indonesia Angkatan Udara—the Indonesian Air Force. These three men had no other duty than to stare at air-surface radar screens around the clock.

Assegaf loved the power and agility of his boat. He became famous for shouting in English the command, "Ludicrous Speed," a quote from one of his favorite American comedy films. Seldom content with cruising *Sadarin* at the nominal fuel-conserving sixteen knots, he often came back into port dangerously low on fuel. Behind his back, Assegaf's men called him either Speed Racer or Kapten Ludicrous.

In 2002, Indonesia had been forced to cede the islands of Ligitan and Sipadan (near eastern Borneo) to Malaysia by order of the International

Court of Justice. This made the entire Indonesian military machine obsessed with defending their territory and exclusive waters. In particular,
the Indonesian Navy had closely watched the oil-producing Ambalat region of the Celebes Sea since 2002. The frequent patrols of *Sadarin* were
just one small part of that increased vigilance.

Even before he was given command of *Sadarin*, Soekirnan Assegaf
had earned a reputation for being impulsive and stern in handing out
reprimands to subordinates. But he was also fairly sensitive to the
needs of his men while on long patrols. Unlike most other skippers of
patrol boats, he encouraged his men to fish once they were well away
from the port of Manado. The fresh fish supplemented their usual diet
of yams, breadfruit, rice, sago, kangkung (water spinach), dried fish,
krupuk crackers, canned chicken, and canned mutton.

Assegaf also allowed movies and music to be played on board, often
piping songs from MP3 players directly into the ship's speakerphone
system. Both when he was a naval cadet and later in his career, he spent
an inordinate portion of his pay on movies for his collection. Many of
these were pirated copies that he bought on the back streets of Surabaya for only twenty thousand rupiah apiece or about two dollars each.
Some of the more recently released films were muddy duplicates that
had actually been surreptitiously videotaped inside Jakarta movie theaters, so occasionally they'd see the silhouette of a head popping up at
the bottom of the screen, or the conversation of obnoxious movie patrons would be mixed in with the movie's dialogue. On board *Sadarin*,
almost every night at sea was movie night, and there was seldom a repeat. The exception was usually Maria Ozawa movies.

Assegaf's penchant for American movies did not go unnoticed by his
superiors. Without his knowledge, he was placed on a watch list by Indonesian Naval Intelligence. His personnel file was flagged by one of
the more devout Muslims on the counterintelligence staff at his base
headquarters. Even though Assegaf was loyal to the Jakarta government, some of his personal habits were flagged as "suspicious." Members of his crew were questioned at intervals about his behavior, his

religious practices, his preferences in entertainment, any foreign contacts, and whether or not he had made any comments about the Jakarta government, or about Indonesia's role in the expansion campaign in the Philippines.

There was an unspoken division and preference within the Indonesian military that viewed "seculars" with suspicion, and gave promotion and assignment preference to devout Muslims. In the last few years before the global Crunch began, rapid promotion blatantly went to those who were outwardly devout carpet bowers. Indonesia's secular constitution was sharply eroded, most noticeably starting in 2003 when *Sharia* law was recognized in Aceh province. This process started to spread in the early 2010s, and by the time of the Crunch, it went into high gear. The increasingly muzzled Indonesian press at first called this Acehinization but later more discreetly called it "moderation of morals" or "return to devout values."

Acehinization flew in the face of the nation's tradition of Pancasila state ideology, which had asserted that Indonesia would recognize multiple religions but be *secularly* governed. Most recently, under legislation spearheaded by the Islamic Defenders Front (FPI) and the Justice Welfare Party (PKS), kissing in public had been banned, as well as "lascivious clothing." To some clerics, the new dress code was interpreted as head-to-toe coverage for women, even in Indonesia's sweltering climate. All of these steps were heralded as "defense against Western decadence."

The PKS, which was directly patterned after the Muslim Brotherhood, began to assert more and more control over all the branches of the Indonesian military. Non-Muslims were increasingly marginalized and sometimes targeted for malicious rumors, "morals investigations," and negative efficiency reports.

Indonesia's population of 225 million included 197 million Muslims. Kapten Assegaf was one of the many who were "Muslim in name only." In the eyes of the new Acehinated Navy, his stance was not career enhancing. In the new Indonesia, the radical imams had slowly

been putting a theocracy in place for more than a decade. Most of Assegaf's contemporaries saw it as inevitable. Some of the more radicalized
ones who were PKS members actually embraced the change. The dis-
senting "decadent" minority started derisively calling the fundamentalists the Jerks of Java.

In the early 2000s, the Laskar Jihad, led by Ja'far Umar Thalib was in
the media spotlight. These jihadis were directly influenced by modern
Saudi Wahhabism. After a couple of years, Laskar Jihad appeared to die
out. In actuality, it went underground, burrowing into many government ministries in Indonesia and Malaysia. The jihadis eventually
gained control of every branch of government, including the armed
forces. The culmination came with the seating of the new president,
just before the Crunch. His green lapel pin told the world that the radical Islamists controlled every apparatus of the government, from top to
bottom. The *Reformasi* (Reformation) era had ended and the *Sarip*
era—the era of the theocrats—had begun. They had completed their
silent coup with little more than whispers of dissent in the heavily state-
controlled press.

The Crunch was the final blow for the Indonesian moderates. The
radical fundamentalists that dominated under the new president
pointed to the economic collapse as an "aha" moment and proof that
"Western decadence" and non-Islamic banking practices had been
what precipitated the collapse. This cemented their power and marked
a radical shift in their foreign policy. From then on, open jihad became
their byword.

Indonesia and Malaysia had experienced a simmering conflict since
the end of hostilities in 1966. But as time went on, the tensions lessened, and they became regular trading partners. As the Crunch set in,
this bilateral trade grew increasingly more important, as global trade
collapsed.

Several things worked synergistically to unite Indonesia and Malaysia: The new presidents of both countries were distant cousins and both
were strident Wahhabists. Just before the Crunch, Indonesia had assisted

Malaysia both in earthquake relief and in setting up desalinization plants during a drought. Then came the "fairy-tale romance" between the son of the Indonesian president and the daughter of the Malaysian president, which culminated in a marriage that was played up intensely by the mass media in both countries, much like British royal weddings. Ironically, the conservative clerics, who had ordered the removal of the mushy soap operas from Indonesian television, left a vacuum that was partly filled by media coverage of the romance and marriage.

As Caleb Burroughs heard all this on the BBC broadcasts, he thought about how his mates over in Afghanistan would go on high alert when the word *wedding* was listed in the intel officer's portion of the commander's brief. *Wedding* was almost always a code word for a jihadi attack. It seemed a cruel irony to have it actually touted as such in the media. *Life imitates art*, he thought to himself.

Shortly after the much-publicized wedding, a variation on the Austrian *anchsluss* occurred in Malaysia wherein it quickly became a puppet state of Indonesia. The state-controlled mass media in both countries tried to put a positive spin on the takeover, calling it the *perkawinan* (marriage) of the two countries.

The kingdom of Brunei also made special concessions that effectively put Indonesian theocrats in control of the country. Remarkably, these changes in Malaysia and Brunei all took place without a shot being fired. These *anchslusse* were the ideal outcome for Indonesia because they needed *all* of their available military power for their planned invasion of the Philippines, Papua New Guinea, and Australia. They could not have spared the manpower that otherwise would have been needed to occupy Malaysia and Brunei.

The Royal Malaysian Navy (RMN) soon transferred most of their large ships to the Indonesian Navy at nominal cost. These included their recently launched guided missile destroyer (KD *Sabah*), two frigates, two corvettes, three nearly new landing craft, sixteen *Ligan* class new generation fast attack craft, two 37-meter Fast Troop Vessels (FTV), as well as the majority of their replenishment ships and military transport ships.

Meanwhile, the sultan of Brunei "gifted" Indonesia his navy's four 41-meter *Ijhtihad* class fast patrol boats and all three of his 80-meter *Darausalam* class multipurpose patrol vessels, complete with missiles and helicopters. All of these Bruneian ships were only a few years old and had been built to be state of the art. With all this talk of jihad, the Sultan felt obliged to donate the ships. To do anything less might have triggered a fundamentalist uprising in Brunei.

Ironically, the Indonesian government, which under previous leadership had spoken out so forcefully against the Jamaah Islamiyah militants and the Bali bombing, would less than two decades later be espousing many of the same fundamentalist Islamic goals, and building their own time bombs.

A few years before the Crunch, Australian Prime Minister Julia Gillard had urged schoolchildren to prepare for the "Asian Century" by learning Asian languages. Little did she know that Bahasa Indonesia would become the most important language to learn because Indonesia culture would soon be forcefully injected into Australian life.

It was no great surprise when China invaded Taiwan. They'd been itching to do so for decades. But Indonesia's next moves had not been fully anticipated by Australia's strategic analysts. What the analysts overlooked was the full significance of the loss of American military power in the Pacific region. Without the American presence, many nations in East Asia felt emboldened.

Australia signed the Nuclear Non-Proliferation Treaty in 1970 and ratified it in 1973. But even before then, they were dependent on America's military might to assure peace in the Pacific region. Now the Americans were gone. All around the eastern periphery of Asia, alliances were shifting. The posturing and saber-rattling began. Borders were stretched. Old territorial disputes reemerged. Ethnic minorities were sent packing. Darkness was falling on the Pacific.

12

NIPA

"I learned how much of what we think to be necessary is superfluous; I learned how few things are essential, and how essential those things really are."

—Bernard Fergusson, *Beyond the Chindwin: An Account of Number Five Column of the Wingate Expedition into Burma 1943*

Quinapondan, Samar Island, the Philippines—October, the Second Year

Rhiannon heard a knock at the door of their hut. When she answered, three elders from the local church stood before her. They asked to talk to both her and her husband, declaring that they were quite concerned about the safety of the Jeffords in the unfolding invasion. As they explained it, they thought it was important for the Jeffords to flee to Manila or even leave the country entirely, both for their own safety and for the safety of the villagers. One elder admitted, "We are willing to hide you, but we are pretty sure the Indos will start torturing and killing us until we give you up."

The Jeffords knew they had to leave the Philippines. All through the following year they prayed for the means to make that happen. All of the scheduled Philippine Airlines and Cebu Pacific flights out of Calbayog City were sold out for months in advance. And even if they made it to Manila, there were no longer any scheduled flights to the United States.

As missionaries, they had few possessions with them on the island. Anything bulky had been left in storage with relatives and friends in New Hampshire and in Florida. Other than their car and some hammocks, almost everything else they owned could fit in eight suitcases. They pared this down to five suitcases for their planned voyage. Their hammocks, extra clothes, kitchen utensils, linens, and extra luggage were given to friends at the mission school.

Meanwhile, the news kept getting worse. Moro Islamic Liberation Front (ILF) guerillas were making increasingly brazen and atrocious attacks. Catholic church buildings—the most outward symbol of Christianity in the island nation—were burned wherever the ILF went, and anyone wearing religious apparel, or carrying rosaries and crucifixes, became the targets of disfigurements or even murder, usually via machete.

A recent rumor circulated that the government would only defend Luzon Island and let all of the islands to the south fall to the ILF. Samar Island and neighboring Masbate Island were directly in the path of the Islamic guerillas. The Indonesians and their surrogates were systematically taking control of all of the southern and central Philippine islands. There were reports that ILF soldiers were hunting down Christian missionaries and torturing them before beheading them.

Just as the Jeffords had begun to feel panicked about their situation, Joseph Navarro, a teenage Jeepney barker showed up at the school. Joseph's job as a barker was to call out the routes and drum up customers. But his job also gave him free rides almost anywhere, and the opportunity to make some money on the side. He often sold used cell phones, cell phone SIM cards, and prepaid telephone calling cards. He regularly made deliveries to the mission school, which was on one of his routes. Joseph only casually knew the Jeffords, but he approached Peter and asked, "Kuya, I hear you want to get to Luzon. My grandfather, Paul Navarro, says he will take us in his outrigger boat—a carag boat called the *Tiburon*—if you can help buy the diesel fuel. It's a big fishing boat."

"Is it big enough to carry us and all of our luggage?" Peter asked.

"Oh, yeah. *Ang Malaking barko*—a big boat. I've been helping him run her since I was twelve."

"He'd really be agreeable?"

"I think so," Joseph replied. "We are really tight. I'm his *Tuazon*, you know, his youngest grandson."

"It sounds like you are his favorite grandson, too."

Joseph, who was modest, nodded and looked embarrassed when he heard that.

The Jeffords met Paul Timbancaya Navarro a few hours later. They learned that everyone called him Tatang (grandfather), even people who were not related. He had a strong reputation in the community, both as a fisherman and as an instructor of the Filipino Martial Arts (FMAs). Now in his early seventies, he had reduced both occupations to just part-time endeavors.

Paul Navarro was sitting on his porch reading an *Abante* tabloid when Joseph and the Jeffords arrived. He gazed up from his paper and said quietly, "I heard you need to get to Luzon."

"That's right," Peter answered.

The old man set aside the newspaper and said, "This very familiar to me, from a long time ago. It is just like the Huk uprising, right after the World War Two. I was a little boy then. Our family originally lived on Luzon, but my dad decided to flee to Samar, in 1948. This was during the Huk Rebellion. Rumor had it that they were going to try to recruit my father by force, or that there was a price on his head. So he got wise and fled. He thought he would be safer if he moved our family completely off of Luzon. He chose to come here to Samar, where he already had a few relatives."

Peter nodded. "That was a smart thing to do."

"Yes, when there is trouble like that, with hundreds of soldiers coming your way, you don't try and stand your ground. That will just get you killed. What you do is pull up anchor and get the heck out of there. That is what my dad did, and it saved all our lives, in my family. This is wisdom."

From his history reading, Peter Jeffords knew that the Huk Rebellion had been a communist-led uprising of peasants, primarily on Luzon. The name of the movement was a Tagalog acronym for *Hukbo ng Bayan Laban sa Hapon*, which was often shortened to *Hukbalahap*, or simply just *Huk*. The acronym stood for "People's Anti-Japanese Army," which was how the communist rebels got their start. The Huks were eventually defeated by the army during the presidency of Ramon Magsaysay.

"Even after it was safe to return to Luzon, my father decided to stay on Samar. That worked out okay, too," Tatang said.

After a long pause, Tatang Navarro said, "I will take you."

Again and again, the Jeffords expressed their thanks. They wore huge smiles and felt tremendous relief in the knowledge that they would be escaping the ILF. They knew that Mr. Navarro's generous offer had just saved them from almost certain death.

They went to see Tatang Navarro's boat late that afternoon. Peter and Rhiannon liked the look of the boat. It was thirty-eight feet long with a five-foot wide hull, and a thirty-inch draught. For stability, it had traditional double-pole outriggers called *carags*. The boat had a graceful upswept triangular transom, but its well-proportioned bowstem was incongruously tipped with an old car tire that had been painted white for use as a mooring buffer. Overall, the boat had attractive lines, but it was obviously built more for utility than for style. What *Tiburon* lacked in chromed fittings, it made up for in solidity and native charm.

A pair of large white horizontal canvas awnings covered *Tiburon* in the rear and amidships. The awnings were elevated in shallow inverted Vs, suspended from short masts. They had reinforcing rods down the center and numerous guy lines to keep them taut. Unless the winds were unfavorable, the awnings could be left unfurled day and night.

Tacked up above the chart box were newspaper clippings—most of them about Filipino boxer Manny Pacquiao, a national hero and distant cousin of Navarro's late wife—and a few faded printouts of digital pictures showing some of their particularly large catches of fish that had filled the hold.

Tiburon's engine was a Mitsubishi straight block four-cylinder, a naturally aspirated diesel with a 2,659 cc displacement. This reliable engine produced 80 horsepower. It was equipped with an auxiliary belt-drive alternator, which was used to charge a pair of 6-volt deep cycle marine batteries. The batteries were needed to operate an electric Power Block winch for hauling in the fishing nets. This was a smaller version of the big winches used on commercial purse seiners. The engine's exhaust pipe, one of the few stainless steel fittings on the entire boat, emerged just below the center of the transom rail.

Their original plan was to motor *Tiburon* northward to Batangas in southern Luzon only 170 nautical miles—about a fourteen-hour trip at twelve knots. The next morning, however, word came that the ILF and Indonesians also planned to invade Luzon in their jihad campaign. Peter and Tatang began a series of meetings on the old man's porch to discuss alternative destinations.

Unfortunately, most of the Pacific islands were not self-sufficient. If the Crunch lasted for another year, Peter anticipated that many Pacific islanders would be starving to death. Peter summed it up. "Continental land masses have resources that just aren't available on island nations."

They weighed the merits and drawbacks of different destinations. They even considered going as far as the United States, but the vast expanses of the central Pacific Ocean were more than they could handle. To motor their way 5,300 miles to Hawaii and then another 2,500 miles to San Diego seemed far too uncertain, and well beyond the capabilities of their coastal fishing boat. Rhiannon had also been hearing reports of a total collapse of law and order throughout the United States, with the worst of the chaos on the East and West coasts. Most of their news came from Radio Australia, which was still in operation.

Most of the other international shortwave broadcasters had gone off the air. In the end, northern Australia seemed like their safest bet.

Tatang had always burned a mix of petroleum–based "dino diesel" and various plant-derived oils in *Tiburon*'s engine. He was proud to exclaim, "This engine, she's an omnivore. She can burn coconut oil, palm oil, peanut oil, corn oil, you name it!"

To surreptitiously get to Australia through Indonesian-controlled waters, Peter realized that FV *Tiburon* was actually better suited than the larger and ostensibly more seaworthy steel boats docked in Samar's harbors. Because Paul Navarro's boat was constructed of wood, it was radar transparent. The only significant radar reflector was the engine block, and most of that was below the waterline and therefore less visible to radar. Even the ship's wheel was made of wood. As was typical of locally made boats, oversize wood mooring bitts were used instead of the stainless steel ones used on nearly every boat from First World countries. And since *Tiburon* was built in the late 1990s, its two diesel fuel tanks—forty and forty-five gallons—were made of HDPE plastic rather than steel.

Pointing out these features, Peter added, "Just look at how the outriggers are lashed on with heavy fishing line rather than bolted on with big stainless steel fixtures like they'd be if this were an American-made boat. Even the chainwale is plywood, not steel. What you have here is a stealth boat, Tatang."

Tatang's expression changed to a huge gap-toothed grin. "Radar can no see her?"

"That's right," Peter replied. "I'd much rather be in your radar-invisible boat going eight or ten knots than I would in a big fancy steel yacht going twenty-five knots. Those ships would have big radar signatures and be obvious targets. But *Tiburon* will likely just slip through unnoticed if we can keep out of sight, visually."

After a pause, Peter continued, "My dad was an engineer who worked on the periphery of the stealth aircraft programs for the U.S. Air Force. His little company only made special heating pads that were used to cure the composite materials used in the wing and fuselage sections. But I had some long conversations with him about radar and radar wave reflectivity. It all comes down to this: Composites, fiberglass, and wood are good because they don't reflect radar waves, but metal is bad because it reflects radar like a mirror. Even though this boat is thirty-eight feet long and has four feet of hull above the waterline, it has a radar cross section—or RCS—that is probably smaller than that of an eight-foot-long aluminum skiff with just one foot of hull exposed above the waterline."

Tatang nodded to indicate he understood and Peter continued, "This boat won't give a sharp radar return like a modern boat. It will probably look fuzzy, like an indistinct blob. In daytime, when we are drifting or have a sea anchor out, we won't look like much more than a piece of driftwood. At night, when we are under power, the motion against the radar screen background will make it obvious that we are a boat, but of course on radar we won't look like anything more than a local fishing boat. The chance of someone dispatching a patrol boat or a cutter to investigate, I think, will be quite low."

Peter walked around the boat, closely examining it, then came back to Tatang, who was sitting in the helm chair. Peter said, "The anchor and the motor winch will be an issue for radar. The anchor is on a rope, rather than a chain, which is good, but it is stowed on the foredeck. That's almost like mounting what they call a radar corner reflector for all the world to see."

Tatang gave a toss of his hand and said, "No biggie, Pastor Jeffords. I can trade that, easy, for a poor man's anchor. Those are made out of concrete. They cast those flat, what-do-you-call discs, so they don't roll off a boat. The only metal is a little loop of rebar."

Jeffords nodded. "*Perfecto.*" Then another thought crossed his mind. "And what about the Power Block winch? There is a lot of metal there. Can we dismount it and stow it below?"

"Sure, but if I'm selling my nets, I might as well sell the winch, too."

13

CHARTS

"Technology is a blessing for those who understand it and can develop and maintain it. It can be a snare for those who can only depend on getting it 'off the shelf.' If it malfunctions they are lost. Tools, supplies, and technological equipment should play a part in anyone's survival plans, but they should not play a part that overreaches the person's ability to deal with it."

—Karl Hess, *A Common Sense Strategy for Survivalists,* p. 37, 1981

Quinapondan, Samar Island, the Philippines—October, the Second Year

The next day they started looking at Navarro's nautical charts. Tatang summarized their options. "There are two ways we can go: either down through the Moluccas or down through the Celebes Sea, which is more roundabout."

Jeffords, always the punster, couldn't resist quipping, "As I once informed a young Catholic priest, celibacy ain't all it's cracked up to be."

Joseph laughed, but the subtlety of the play on words escaped his grandfather.

Tracing his finger on the chart, Jeffords said, "Well, Darwin in northern Australia is our nearest safe landfall. So through the Molucca Sea, then the Banda Sea, and then Timor Sea would be the most direct route."

Looking to Tatang, he asked, "But I suppose the more important question is, given all the variables and imponderables, which route will give us the *least* chance of running into any ILF or Indo warships?"

Tatang looked slightly puzzled—perhaps by Peter's use of the word "imponderables"—so Joseph translated this question into Tagalog.

"The only bad danger is the Makassar Strait up against Malaysia. There could be ships of the Indonesian Navy there," Tatang replied.

Peter nodded. "Okay, we'll make sure to avoid that. So we take the Molucca route?"

Tatang nodded, but Peter asked, pointing at the chart, "What about this string of islands between the Molucca Sea and the Banda Sea? Look, it's Pulau This, Pulau That, Pulau The Other Thing without much water in between them."

Joseph and Tatang consulted rapidly in Tagalog.

Joseph then translated. "Grandpa says there's not many people in the Spice Islands—no cities, just villages, so it is not too risky, especially if we time it so we slip between those islands at night."

Jeffords nodded. "Okay, then that's the route we'll take, and we'll put our trust in God to see us safely through."

Tiburon's engine, Tatang said, was less than two years old and had been run for only about five hundred hours. By Filipino fishing fleet standards, it was considered brand-new.

Tallying the various containers and adding it to the capacity of the boat's two existing tanks, they came up with a grand total of 503 gallons. At 7.29 pounds per gallon, the fuel would weigh 3,667 pounds. At three quarts per hour at three-quarter throttle, that gave them 377 hours of engine run time—or thirty-one and a half days—assuming twelve hours per day with the engine running. With good weather, catching favorable winds and currents, and with Gods' providence, they might make it the 2,800 nautical miles to Australia in twenty-eight days. If the winds were not favorable, it might take as long as thirty-eight days. According to their calculations, they would run out of fuel in thirty-one and a half days unless they found a place to refuel en route.

Their greatest challenge would be that after leaving Samar they would be entirely in hostile Islamic waters until they approached Australia. There would be no friendly ports where they could purchase fuel. East Timor was already under Indonesian control, and they expected to find warships blockading Papua New Guinea.

Jeffords pondered for a few minutes and reran the calculations. Then he asked Tatang, "How much lube oil does the engine use?"

"It's a brand-new engine, so it burns *at most* maybe one quart a week. I use the what-ya-call forty weight."

Jeffords said, "Okay, we should set aside a gallon and a half for lubrication, even though we'll probably need less than half of that."

Once the fuel discussion had been sorted out, they focused on *Tiburon*'s white-and-light-blue paint scheme, which was clearly not good for camouflage. Tatang consulted one of his neighbors, Rudolfo Saguisag, who went by the nickname Dolpo. Dolpo had served for many years as an NCO in the Hukbóng Dagat ng Pilipinas—the Philippine Navy, often just called the PN. He had retired from the navy four years before the Crunch. His last duty station had been with Naval Forces Central (NAVFORCEN), serving on rigid hull inflatable boats.

Dolpo's experience was mainly in small boats and onboard frigates. After hearing about their camouflage concern, he advised Tatang to use the U.S. Navy's defunct Measure 21 camouflage paint scheme. He pulled a naval camouflage reference book from his bookshelf, and after a couple of minutes of searching through the pages, he turned to the page that showed Measure 21. "Here," he said. "Have the paint store match these colors. That is the best camo coloring for being out on the blue water. It is a little too dark for inshore, but *perpekto* in deep water." He then jotted down a note that read: "Navy Blue 5-N on all the vertical surfaces and Deck Blue 20-B on all the horizontal surfaces and canvas."

Two days later, Peter learned that Tatang had traded his nets and floats for 150 rounds of .22 Long Rifle ammo, which had practically become a currency unto itself since the Crunch. The electric motor winch was traded for 20 rounds of .30-06.

The engine, he explained, burned about three quarts of diesel or coconut oil ("mantika") per hour. The nearby Caltex station had long since sold out of all types and grades of fuel, but with some begging and pleading, a number of neighbors were willing to sell a total of eighty-five gallons of diesel.

In addition to the dino diesel, the Jeffords were able to buy coconut oil. Most of this was "Light Centrifuged Coconut Oil" in five-gallon plastic buckets labeled with maker names like NARDIAS, MPC, and CIIF Oil Mills.

They also managed to buy ten and a half gallons of corn-based cooking oil (made by the Bagiuo, Sun Valley, and Sunar companies), eight gallons of palm oil, six gallons of soybean oil, eleven bottles and cans of olive oil, and even a few bottles each of sunflower, peanut, and camellia oil. Realizing that this still wouldn't be enough, they asked around and found twenty gallons of used deep-fryer oil available from a fried fish stand owner in Calbayog, as well as fifteen gallons of 10W40 motor oil, much of it in one-quart plastic bottles. It cost them more than 800 Philippine Pesos (PHP), but Tatang assured them that the various types of oil could mix with the diesel fuel, though no more than fifteen percent by volume. "We put in just a little bit of this fryer oil each time we refill the main tank," he explained.

Before it was taken aboard, the used deep-fryer oil was carefully strained through three thicknesses of T-shirts, a slow process that removed all of the blackened particulate matter.

As he started the filtering process, Joseph asked his grandfather, "Do you want it to be stored in this can, or in this big plastic bottle?"

The old man answered in Tagalog, *"Pakilagay naman sa bote ang mantika"* ("Please put the oil in the bottle"). He added in English, "Mr. Jeffords says he want as many plastic containers as possible since metal ones are radar reflectors. We are stealthy boys."

Jeffords recognized the Tagalog phrase. In the two years leading up to his first missionary trip, he had seriously studied the language. Ironically, his assignment turned out to be in the central Philippines, where Visayan and Waray were spoken much more frequently. Peter's knowledge of Tagalog came in handy only around people like Navarro, who was originally from Luzon.

They indeed tried to buy and repackage as much of the oil as possible in plastic bottles. The few steel containers were stowed below the waterline. They agreed to use up all of the fuel in these metal containers first so they could discard the containers immediately after they had been emptied into the main tank, by sinking them. Given the wide variety of oil that they planned to burn and its dubious purity, they took the precaution of buying four spare fuel filters.

With both the U.S. dollar and the Philippine peso in free fall, nearly all of the various fuel and oil purchases were barter transactions. They started by bartering the gasoline they could siphon from the Jeffords' car and what they had in cans. They were able to negotiate two gallons of diesel in trade for each gallon of gas, since gas was already more scarce, and because it was common knowledge that coconut oil could be substituted in diesel engine cars, trucks, or boats.

Tatang's standard practice was to start the engine with "dino diesel" before switching to draw from the tank of coconut oil. Then, just before shutting down, he would switch back to the petroleum-based diesel tank.

The most disappointing transactions occurred when Tatang traded his truck for 110 gallons of coconut oil, and the Jeffords exchanged their Mitsubishi L300 Versa Van minivan for 130 gallons of coconut oil and 40 gallons of palm oil. The car was only three years old, but in the new post-Crunch economy, cars with gasoline engines were not highly valued. If the Mitsubishi had been a diesel, they might have been able to trade it for enough coconut oil for their entire trip. The rest of the fuel was bought with Philippine pesos of rapidly diminishing value and by bartering Rhiannon's laptop and some silver pesos that Joseph had inherited from his maternal grandmother.

Their arsenal for the voyage consisted of Tatang's well-worn but serviceable M1 Garand semiautomatic .30-06 rifle, Joseph's takedown .22 rimfire Ruger 10/22 rifle, and Tatang's 26.5 mm Geco flare pistol. The latter was designed just for signaling, but Tatang had a 12 gauge flare insert sleeve for the gun. Inside of this insert, he could use a second insert—a chamber adapter for .38 Special revolver cartridges. This made the flare gun into a crude single-shot pistol. Lacking both a rifled barrel and sights, the pistol could not be fired accurately beyond a few yards, but it was better than nothing.

Peter's main concern was their most potent weapon, the M1 Garand. "Is it zeroed?" he asked Tatang.

"Oh, yeah, on a paper target it shoots right where you are aiming it at one hundred steps."

Peter had once fired an uncle's M1, but he didn't know how to field-strip it or clean it. Tatang showed him how, though he had some difficulty in relating the rifle parts nomenclature in English.

Most of Tatang's ammunition was black-tipped armor-piercing (AP) ammunition. It was all stored in 8-round en bloc clips. Tatang had only eleven loaded clips left—seven of AP, and four of plain "ball" full metal jacket ammunition. With such a small supply, they realized they would have to make each shot count.

With just one solid battle rifle in hand, Peter did not feel comfortably well armed for the voyage. When he mentioned this to Rhiannon, she retorted, "What did you want? A 20-millimeter deck gun? We have what we have, and we'll be vigilant. The rest is up to God."

14

IN FULL FLIGHT

"We have an unknown distance yet to run, an unknown river to explore. What falls there are, we know not; what rocks beset the channel, we know not; what walls ride over the river, we know not. Ah, well! we may conjecture many things."

—John Wesley Powell

The ANU Campus, Canberra, Australia—October, the First Year

The campus was near chaos. Many students felt stranded by the economic turmoil. News outlets were exaggerating the scope of the crisis by focusing on the severe insulin shortage and deaths from ketoacidodis and diabetic comas. Australia had *no* domestic insulin manufacturing capability. Up until the late 1970s, Australia had been a major producer of animal-sourced insulin, but in recent years they had become entirely dependent on foreign supply.

Several hysterical students in Ava's dormitory were sobbing. The ATMs were shut down. Many students lacked any transportation to get home. The major department stores like Coles and Woolworths were having huge runs on merchandise, and reports of looting were becoming more frequent. Imported goods were the most sought after since it had become obvious that foreign trade was shutting down. One young man in Ava's dormitory was buying up as much cocoa powder and coffee as he could find.

Witnessing the spreading panic, Ava and her roommate discussed their options. "I'm getting out of here," Ava declared. "God only knows how bad things are going to get in the big cities. I'm not going to wait to see."

Her roommate agreed. "We should get back to our homes straight away."

"At least you've got it easy," Ava replied. "You'll be safe at home in just over an hour. I've got thirty-two hundred kilometers of road to travel."

Knowing that every minute counted, Ava packed just the essentials, leaving behind all of her impractical clothes, her high-heeled shoes, and her large collection of Japanese manga and magazines. She selected only five books from her bookshelves: two Bibles, a concordance, and a 1950s vintage cookbook that had belonged to her grandmother. She offered anything that was left to her roommate, who was also starting to pack.

Ava's plan was to drive to Altona first since the Geelong refinery was there, and she expected it to still have petrol available. She reckoned that if they didn't have fuel in a refinery town, there wouldn't be fuel anywhere.

When Ava stopped by the hardware store on the way out of town, she found that proper petrol cans were completely sold out, but she did find a twenty-inch-long blue plastic funnel with which she could fill the tank from odd containers, and four fairly sturdy ten-liter steel cans that had originally held olive oil. Ava also scrounged eighty plastic one-liter bottles with screw caps. She filled forty of them with water since she never traveled through the outback without plenty of water. Next, she talked a filling station manager into letting her fill the other forty plastic bottles with petrol. He kindly said, "I'll turn a blind eye if the containers you use aren't legit."

The odd assortment of containers was a fire brigade safety officer's nightmare. Ava positioned the weakest containers—like the repurposed soda bottles—at the far rear of the roof rack. She decided to empty those into the tank first.

After a brief phone call to Chuck, Ava departed the ANU at two A.M. Before she hung up, she did her best to reassure Chuck she'd make it. "My RAV4 burns about eleven liters per one hundred kilometers. So it'll take three hundred forty-one liters to get me home. If I can just find a couple of places with fuel available, I should be good."

"Okay, just be very careful," Chuck responded. "Find safe places to sleep. I'll be praying for you. And don't worry about calling your parents. I'll let them know that you are on the way."

After all that anxiety, her drive turned out to be anticlimactic. It was just two very long days of driving. Gasoline was scarce, but she did find a few stations open, though they were only willing to take cash. And the price per liter had nearly doubled.

Rather than renting a motel room, she simply drove off onto an unmarked rutted red dirt road to sleep once she reached the point of exhaustion, making sure her vehicle would be out of sight from the highway. After reorganizing her load, she was able to fully recline her seat, though it was still far from comfortable. Ava slept fitfully for six hours, awakening before dawn. After taking just a minute to step out to relieve her bladder and to gulp down some water, she started her vehicle and pressed on.

She arrived in Casuarina at nine P.M. the next evening, utterly exhausted. After embracing her parents, she declared, "I'll tell you the full tale in the morning. Right now, I need some sleep."

The following morning, the news on the television was filled with headlines of continuing riots in all of Australia's major cities. The entire Australian Army and Army Reserve had been mobilized or alerted to respond. The Reserve was fully mobilized, while the Standby Reserves (which consisted of older veterans who were not required to actively drill) were placed on "call up" status. News broadcasters reported heavily on the further deterioration of the economies of the United States and Japan. It was also announced that the prime minister would be giving a major televised address at six that evening.

Ava's parents rescheduled their dinner so that they'd be able to watch the speech. They clustered around the television in anticipation. The PM had recently been appointed, with many promises of a conservative shift in policies.

The smiling PM exuded an air of confidence as she walked up to the podium. She began:

"Good evening. The global financial crisis is still worsening, and its shock waves are being felt here in Australia. In consultation with the cabinet, and with industry and banking leaders, we've had to make some difficult decisions. For the time being, to allow the Australian economy to survive, for free commerce to carry on, and for the Australian people to press on with their normal lives in peace and prosperity, we came to the conclusion that Australia needs economic independence and self-sufficiency.

"We've therefore formulated a bold plan, which I'll be outlining tonight. This plan will require the cooperation of the Australian people. We've always had a digger can-do spirit, a fair dinkum attitude, and our own way of doing things. The ongoing riots and the insulin supply crisis are not the key problem at present. Quite the contrary, they are merely *symptoms* of the massive dislocation that has taken place, and that dislocation was caused by immoderate government spending and the massive debt—both public and private. Artificially low interest rates created the illusion of prosperity and huge artificial bubbles in shares and in house prices. Clearly, the bubbles have burst. Attempting to reinflate them would be a huge blunder. The only way to restore law and order and stable supply chains is to get the economic trolley back on its tracks. For our economy to recover and to thrive, it will require some hard work and imagination.

"I've directed the Reserve Bank of Australia to cease production of all banknotes for a period of four years. Unlike many other nations which are suffering the ravages of mass inflation, our people need the assurance that we will have a *fixed* money supply. And with the advent of polymer notes, it is realistic to think they will hold up in circulation for four years. At the end of that four-year period, new banknotes will be produced, but strictly for the purpose of one-for-one replacement. We will have *zero* banknote inflation. **Zero.**

"The Commonwealth of Australia has the agricultural strength, the mining strength, and the industrial strength required to be fully independent. Adapting to changing circumstances will at times be painful, but we simply must prepare ourselves to go it alone. Loss of jobs and industry began with Gough Whitlam and the Lima Declaration. The exigencies of an independent economy will reverse that trend. We need a free market and a level playing field.

"Settlement of all outstanding foreign trade contracts will be left up to the best judgment of the parties involved. If our own government is a contracted party, then we reserve the right to settle in Australian dollars, in gold, or in foreign currencies as we see fit. Our trading partners, particularly in APEC, will need assurance that they can continue to trade with Australia with confidence.

"The assured flow of some trade goods such as pharmaceuticals will require government intervention in the short term, but in general our approach will be to let free market economics prevail. In free markets, prices reach equilibrium with astonishing speed. Let's just let the free market work, shall we?

"Next, I have ordered the immediate repatriation of all of Australia's national gold reserves from the Bank of England. Our current reserves are just over eighty metric tons. A small portion of our gold will be immediately repatriated by air transport, but the rest will be coming by ship. Rest assured, it is *all* coming back to Australia as soon as possible.

"We will establish a fixed rate of exchange of ten thousand Australian dollars per ounce of gold, and one thousand Australian dollars per ounce of silver. This might sound arbitrary, but it is in fact far less arbitrary, far less capricious, and far less fictitious than what we've witnessed with currencies and finance in recent years. We were living in a financial fantasyland, and we need to definitively set that behind us.

"The Aussie dollar will become fully convertible to gold and silver in a program that will be phased in over a period of three years. Under our bimetallic plan, we will adopt a fixed ratio of ten ounces of silver per ounce of gold. This ten-to-one ratio will encourage the production of silver, which will be needed for the purpose of minting new silver coinage next year.

"A variety of new gold and silver coins ranging from one-twentieth ounce to one ounce will be minted starting next year. These new coins will include a hardening alloy to make the coins hold up to the rigors of circulation.

"Within eighteen months, every bank in the Commonwealth will be equipped to exchange gold and silver with their customers. Once in place, gold and silver can be exchanged for either polymer currency or silver or gold coins upon the demand of the customer. The minting costs for the new coins—the *seigniorage*—will be paid by the government. These bank metals windows will be able to accept everything from gold nuggets and gold jewelry, to soft gold koalas and silver kookaburras, to pre-decimal silver coins and exchange them directly for the new hard gold and silver coins once they are available. A new large cupronickel penny will also be produced to make small transactions more practical.

"The present-day coinage will become obsolete in twenty-four months. But banks will be required to exchange the old coins indefinitely for either polymer notes or like value of the new coins. The defunct coins will be recycled, providing useful commodities for industry.

"Australia has traditionally been thought of as a gold producer, but we also have reserves of seventy thousand tons of silver. We are now the world's fourth-largest silver producer. The new currency regime will encourage an expansion of gold and silver production, with much greater profitability for miners. And with the stability provided by a fully convertible bimetallic currency, *everyone* wins.

"All but one of our foreign exchange markets have been temporarily suspended. The exception is New Zealand. We are in consultation with the New Zealand government, encouraging them to adopt a similar bimetallic standard. As for our many other trading partners, exchange rates and mechanisms will be reestablished one by one, only after thorough investigation and consultation. Most rates will be free-floating, but a few rates will be fixed for a period of two years. We will take steps to ensure that all key commodities continue to be imported to keep the wheels of industry turning.

"We have a few immediate goals: First, we must concentrate on law and order. We have taken steps to assure that. Crime and wanton destruction of property will not be tolerated.

"Next is national self-sufficiency. Publicly owned ground in agriculturally suitable regions will be sold off to encourage small-scale agriculture. Even some public lawn areas will be made available for community vegetable gardens for a period of six years. I most strongly encourage private landowners to also convert their lawns and flower gardens into vege gardens. Australia can and *will* be food self-sufficient.

"Oil and natural gas exploration will be encouraged, as will further development of the Coober Pedy shale oil deposits. Many environmental regulations will be temporarily suspended to assure food and energy independence. Development of renewable energy resources including wind, solar, geothermal, and hydroelectric will be encouraged through tax breaks and a few modest

subsidies, particularly to encourage the development of the domestic capacity to produce photovoltaic power panels. Australia
can and *will* be energy self-sufficient.

"We can do this, Australia. Yes, there will be some shortages.
Yes, there will be some redundancies. Yes, there will be some
challenges. We merely have to set our minds to this and make it
happen. I am confident that with God's providence, we can and
we will. May God bless Australia."

Ava's father sighed. "Well, her economic plan sounds top-notch, but
all of that gardening she mentioned will be a backbreaker. I suppose it's
time for me to sharpen my spade."

15

UNFETTERED

"God, who foresaw your tribulation, has specially armed you to go through it, not without pain but without stain."

—C. S. Lewis

Quinapondan, Samar Island, the Philippines—Late October, the Second Year

Because they were able to haul *Tiburon* out onto a beach at high tide, painting it went quickly. The entire boat, the carags, the awning canvas, and nearly all of the fittings were painted in the two blue camouflage colors.

Not content with the glossiness of the completed paint on some of the exposed exterior of the boat, Peter used six full spray cans of Boysen brand matte lacquer paint, which made it look essentially flat, even in full sunlight. Although he knew it was necessary, Tatang was sad to see his boat lose its once bright appearance.

During the painting and packing phase, either Peter or Tatang would sleep in *Tiburon* each night to guard it, with the flare pistol close at hand. The paint fumes were horrendous, but they couldn't risk having the boat or any of its contents stolen.

Peter and Tatang scrounged nautical charts from all over the island. They mainly needed charts of the Molucca Sea, Banda Sea, and the Timor Sea. They even managed to find a coastal waters chart for Australia's Northern Territory and Western Australia.

With the help of twenty villagers, they were able to get *Tiburon* back into the water during high tide. Only then did they begin to load fuel, food, water, and baggage. Half of the water was in plastic containers that were lashed down on the center deck and foredeck, bundled in old fishing nets. Used returnable glass soda pop bottles predominated. Some of the water was carried in blue five-gallon jugs. A few of the bottles, jugs, and plastic buckets seemed questionable to Rhiannon, like the used bleach bottles which imparted some chlorine taste to the stored water. Nonetheless, they stowed just over 400 liters—enough water for one liter per person per day, for eighty days.

The Navarros' food stores were mostly sacks of smoked fish and plastic buckets of rice, *pancit* (rice noodles), and beans. They also carried smaller quantities of mami (ramen) noodles, Ma Ling canned pork, casava, *pan de sal*, Kraft Eden cheese, Magnolia drink mix, and instant Calamansi iced tea. Their soap came in the form of big solid Surf brand bars.

They packed three jars of peanut butter, but only because Tatang had it on hand. He liked making a Filipino peanut butter stew called *kare kare*. He never used it for making sandwiches. Rhiannon wished they had a dozen jars of the peanut butter. Not only was it a very compact form of protein, but it was also a natural cure for loose bowels.

The Jeffords brought two cardboard boxes of food packed in jars, retort pouches, and cans from their nipa hut. These were mostly canned fruits and vegetables, SPAM, fish crackers, RAM brand tomato sauce in retort pouches, Swift corned beef in retort pouches, Century brand tuna, and peanut butter. After the refugees began to pour in from Mindanao, they couldn't find any more canned goods at *any* price. The few people who had any were hoarding them for their own evacuation contingency plans. The Jeffords pledged that all of these canned foods would be used sparingly.

The stories that the Mindanao refugees told were frightening. The ILF soldiers repeatedly forced professions of faith in Allah. Those who refused, or who seemed insincere, were immediately shot or beheaded,

often with a *bolo* machete or a longer *kampilan* machete. Some of the
most bloodthirsty Indonesian killers were actually in the Kopassus—
the Indonesian Special Forces.

One of the refugees, a Catholic priest, recounted to Peter what he
had heard from a colonel in the Intelligence Service of the Armed
Forces of the Philippines (ISAFP.) The ISAFP colonel told him that
three ILF officers captured in separate engagements broke under pressure of intense interrogations and gave nearly identical details on the
ILF's plans. First, they would take the rest of the central islands. Then
they would take Luzon, bolstered by the Indo-Malaysian Army and
Navy. This would put the entire Philippine archipelago under their
control. Once their grasp of the Philippines was consolidated, they
planned to invade Australia within two years.

Peter was incredulous, but the priest was insistent. "They want it *all*."
The priest described how they had brutalized the residents of Cebu,
Bohol, Negros, Panay, and Leyte islands. There, he said, they were absolutely merciless, killing nearly all of the adult non-Islamic men and
systematically raping the women. "They are moving faster than they
did on Mindanao. Back during the long guerilla war there, they moved
slowly and made political gestures in exchange for 'autonomous regions' because the world was watching. Now they are moving like der-
vishes, with amazing speed and utter ruthlessness. The world is *no
longer* watching, and it is a real bloodbath."

The priest also described how the Indonesians had transitioned to
overtly arming the ILF guerilas, providing them with vehicles, landing craft, night vision gear, and communications equipment. The islands of Mindaro, Masbate, and Samar were generally considered next
on their list of targets. For that reason, the priest planned to continue
on northward as soon as he could.

When rumors of invasion began, local mayors and clans were seen
arming themselves with homemade shotguns. Danao guns came out
from hiding. Despite the official statistics, the Filipinos were fairly well
armed.

Hundreds of other refugees came from Mindanao, and the other central islands began coming to Samar, mainly in small boats. They heard of one clever young man from Dinagat Island who made a solo crossing just after the ILF landed there and all the available boats had already left. Wearing a water skiing life vest, he lashed himself to a *Little Mermaid* novelty children's swimming kickboard and propelled himself with a pair of snorkeling swim fins. All that he carried with him was a plastic bag full of candy bars, a pocketknife, a pair of sunglasses, and a tube of SPF 45 Water Babies sunscreen. Trailing behind him on separate pieces of twine were seven soda pop bottles. These 1.5-liter bottles were each half full of fresh drinking water when he started out. His harrowing crossing to Samar took thirty-eight hours.

Hearing these traumatic stories made the Jeffords pick up the pace of their provisioning. A week before they departed, Rhiannon made sure they all started taking daily multivitamin tablets. Her father, a veteran deer and elk hunter, had often told her that good nutrition was crucial for maintaining peak night vision.

Typhoon season in Southeast Asia could be expected from May to November, though the peak months were September and October. Tatang mentioned that FV *Tiburon* had survived Typhoon Bopha in 2012 only because he wisely hauled the boat out two days before the storm made landfall. Many other boat owners on Samar who didn't do likewise witnessed their boat hulls being shattered and sunk by the pounding surf.

Earlier in the month, they had heard that the invasion of Samar could come as soon as November. Moving quickly, they rushed to finish provisioning *Tiburon* so they could put out to sea before the island was blockaded. The Navarros and Jeffords set October 25th as their departure date. It put them at risk of foul weather at the tail end of the typhoon season, but they agreed that waiting any later would put them at far greater risk of running into ILF or Indo picket ships.

Once loaded, the combination of fuel, food, water and baggage, and passengers put *Tiburon* down perilously low in the water. Jeffords estimated that in all, the boat was carrying about 2,700 kilograms, which was dangerously near its maximum safe cargo capacity in calm seas. But Tatang said he was expecting good weather for at least the first week. He promised that as long as the weather held and they consistently kept the bilge pumped, they would be fine. After the first week, the boat would be considerably lighter and would sit much higher in the water. "I know this boat. I know what she can take. *Magkabati*. It will be all right."

Rudolfo Saguisag came to visit them just as they were finishing stowing their supplies. The old man came limping up to the pier, leaning heavily on his cane. "I'm here for my final inspection tour," he said.

Tatang laughed and said, "Welcome aboard!"

Dolpo eased himself down to *Tiburon*'s aft deck. He looked admiringly at the fresh blue paint. "These are good colors for the open ocean. And not too *lustroso*. How you say—glossy? Flat is good. You don't want no reflections."

Echoing Tatang's earlier observation, Dolpo said, "Your boat is sitting pretty deep in the water, but she'll lighten as you expend your fuel and provisions."

Dolpo looked at the boat again before adding, "You should get a sextant if you take any other trips later. I'm not sure how long those GPS satellite things are still going to be working. I hope that when you punch up your house, the lat/long numbers are still the same as your place mark. Once they start to drift, it means that the GPS can no longer be trusted."

They showed him their two GPS receivers. He agreed that it was wise to have two, including one that was wired into the boat's 12-volt power, and one that ran on small AA batteries. Dolpo nodded. "Redundancy is always good."

Next, they showed him their binoculars. There was a compact pair that Rhiannon had used for many years as an amateur bird watcher, and a much larger pair that belonged to Paul Navarro. Dolpo picked them up and said, "Let me teach you an old trick, what I learned in my brown water days."

He turned to Joseph, and asked, "You got some electrical tape, *galán*?"

Joseph answered with a quick nod.

Dolpo gestured toward the open hatch. "Joey, you go below and get me a roll of tape, an old cardboard box, and some scissors or a real sharp knife."

The boy did as he was asked. He emerged less than a minute later with a large roll of black Duck tape and a Stanley box cutter knife in a one-foot-square box that had originally held a rice steamer.

The old man said, "*Mabuti, mabuti.*" Working quickly and deftly, Dolpo cut six-inch-wide strips of cardboard. In less than two minutes, he had attached cardboard tubes that were a tight friction fit on the outer barrels of the binoculars. Rhiannon looked puzzled, but Peter grinned as he realized what Dolpo had done.

"When you are standing watch, you don't want the sun to reflect off the lenses and give away that you are there," Dolpo explained. "These hoods will keep any reflections from happening. You make sure you use these anytime there is daylight, okay *na*?"

16

CROSS SECTION

"Men are qualified for civil liberty in exact proportion to their disposition to put moral chains upon their own appetites.... Society cannot exist unless a controlling power upon will and appetite be placed somewhere; and the less of it there is within, the more there must be without. It is ordained in the eternal constitution of things, that men of intemperate minds cannot be free. Their passions forge their fetters."

—Edmund Burke, 1791

Quinapondan, Samar Island, the Philippines—Late October, the Second Year

The Jeffords and Navarros motored out the inland waterway under the Quinapondan Bridge on the evening high tide. Their goal was to travel southeast all night long to get them well beyond line of sight of Mindanao, and any coastal boats and their short-range radars. Once they were at least fifty miles offshore of Mindanao, they would turn due south.

Sleeping in *Tiburon* was very uncomfortable. With so many five-gallon buckets of coconut and palm oil strapped down inside both sides of the hull, it left only a twenty-inch-wide crawl space in the middle. Here, Tatang had laid long scraps of Zamboply brand plywood atop the keelson. These were topped with scraps of old handwoven *banig* mats. The plywood often wobbled and shifted, despite having copra husks wedged beneath them. The addition of four thin foam mattresses made sleeping just marginally more bearable.

To make matters worse, the combined smells of the diesel exhaust, diesel fuel vapor, various cooking oils, dried fish, *bagoong* (shrimp paste), ginger, *patis* (fish sauce), body odors, and lingering paint fumes were potent, especially when the wind dropped.

After the initial exhilaration of getting clear of Samar and into open water, the realization sank in that they faced a long trip in cramped, uncomfortable quarters. *Tiburon*'s V-hull cross section was decent, but at times it acted more like a flat-bottom skiff than a modern chined boat design, doing little to dampen the effect of waves. Instead of lapping up the sides, they slapped noisily, depending on the boat's presentation to the wind and waves, adding to the vibration and drone of the engine. In all, the effect varied between just tolerable and downright miserable.

Even before they got under way, one of their biggest concerns was the safety of seven-year-old Sarah. To protect her from falling overboard and drowning, they purchased a child's life vest. They supplemented it by attaching a nine-foot-long nylon rope that was kept constantly clipped to either Peter or Rhiannon's belt with a carabiner. Thankfully, Sarah had a placid demeanor and was content to play with toys and dolls at her mother's feet for many hours each day.

From their first night at sea, they ran *Tiburon* with her navigational lights turned off. Tatang wisely taped down the switches for these lights to prevent them from being turned on out of force of habit. Other than lights in the cabin—which were used exclusively with the companionway storm hatch closed—their only light came from the dim glowing dial of the compass and the small screens on the GPS receivers and the depth finder when any of those were switched on. Realizing how far light could be seen on a dark night, they kept these screens covered by rags to subdue their glow, uncovering them just when needed.

They developed a routine that if anyone on deck wanted to go below after dark, they would give three rapid knocks on the companionway hatch. Then the hatch would be opened from within, *after* the cabin lights were switched off.

Like many coastal fishing boats, *Tiburon* had no head other than a tall, wide-bottomed urinal bucket for the cabin, and a pair of ropes fastened to the deck forward of the transom to hold on to, so that whoever had their buttocks projecting off the stern wouldn't fall overboard. As the only adult female aboard, Rhiannon found these ablution accommodations presented a privacy challenge. The transom was in full view of whoever was manning the wheel. Tatang and Joseph were gentlemanly, however, and would sing out, "I'm looking straight at the bow, Mrs. J., no worries!"

One evening shortly after the change of watch at the wheel, Peter and Rhiannon heard Tatang and Joseph in an animated conversation in rapidfire Tagalog. All Peter caught with certainty was Tatang twice saying the words *dalawang uri ng isda*, which he knew meant "two kinds of fish."

After Tatang had gone below, Peter asked Joseph, "What was all that about?"

"Tatang says that being out here dodging the ILF's navy is just like this: There are only two kinds of fish in the ocean: fish you can eat, and fish that want to eat *you*. We just need to choose our course carefully—far away from the islands so we don't run into the ILF fish, the kind with guns."

"That sounds like sage advice to me."

As they motored each night, they usually trolled for fish, which added great variety to their diet and was their main source of protein. Once in a while they would hook a fish that was too heavy for their tackle and would break their lines. Tatang was worried that if this happened too many times, they would run out of fish hooks.

To avoid detection, their Standard Operating Procedure (SOP) was to run the engine and make their forward progress at night. At daybreak, unless there was another boat or an island in sight, they would usually set their sea anchor—a fourteen-foot-long cone of cloth. The only exception was when the current was favorable to their intended course. Then they allowed *Tiburon* to drift, but they kept a close eye on the GPS. If the direction of the current changed, they would set the sea anchor. During daylight hours they did their best to sleep, leaving just one of them on watch to scan the horizon with binoculars. They traded off on this duty at two-hour intervals.

At dusk they would eat their "dinner-breakfast," start the engine, and press on. They were close to the equator, so the periods of daylight and darkness never varied by more than twenty minutes, seasonally. They essentially had twelve hours of travel in darkness, and twelve hours in stealth mode in daylight.

To maintain light discipline, all of their checks on the charts were done below with the storm door slid shut. They plotted a tiny dot with an ink pen once per hour while they were making forward progress.

By SOP, whenever they saw or heard an aircraft, they would throttle back to one knot to stop creating any visible wake. They kept this SOP even at night. They would then wait twenty minutes after the plane could no longer be seen or heard to advance to three-quarter throttle.

Washing with salt water made everyone feel uncomfortable and they never felt quite clean. The sunshine caused chapped, cracked lips that petroleum jelly never fully healed. Sunburned ears, noses, and necks were another irritation. The smells of seawater, fish, coconut oil, and the cooking spices became pervasive. Together, they were just *the smell* that was the constant reminder that they weren't still at home in their nipa hut. The boat's constant motion was at first unnerving to Peter, but it later became almost calming, like a cradle being rocked. Jeffords concluded that he would never want a career working at sea, but he could bear up to it for a couple of months.

Their daily routine gradually turned into a blur. He prayed several times a day. Often they were prayers that he wouldn't get short-tempered in the cramped confines of the boat. The few excitements came when fish were caught, or when the sight or sound of a plane prompted them to stop their engines and anxiously wait to see if they had been detected.

Ahead of them, the vast expense of the South Pacific seemed endless. There were so many things that could go wrong and bring their voyage to an abrupt end. *Tiburon* was a small boat in a big ocean.

17

FOX HUNT

"If you know the enemy and know yourself, you need not fear the result of a hundred battles. If you know yourself but not the enemy, for every victory gained you will also suffer a defeat. If you know neither the enemy nor yourself, you will succumb in every battle."

—Sun Tzu, *The Art of War*

Tavares, Florida—
January, the Second Year

Looter activity dramatically increased in Central Florida as the cities ran out of food. Bands of looters that numbered from five to sixty—some on foot and some in vehicles—fanned out from the larger cities like Orlando. Their attacks began with soft targets, mostly isolated hobby farms owned by retirees. Their modus operandi was to stealthily approach a house late at night while the occupants were sleeping. Then they'd smash windows and charge in rapidly, in the modern home-invasion mode. The property owners who survived the initial assault were often bound and interrogated. The truly unlucky were raped and killed. The looters would stay for the night, systematically stripping the farm of food, fuel, guns, ammunition, liquor, batteries, and precious metals. Livestock was often crudely butchered in barn stalls, with the looters cutting meat into fifty- to seventy-pound chunks with the hide still on. They left behind only the heads, forelegs, and gut piles.

The looter gangs quickly grew in size and sophistication. They began sending small scouting parties ahead to spot targets. These scouting teams used SSB CB radios to relay back the GPS coordinates of soft targets. At first, their idea of great communications security (COMSEC) was simply reading the GPS coordinates over the air in reverse sequence. Later, they adopted simple transposition ciphers for their messages, but these proved to be quite easily decrypted.

The Lake County sheriff consulted the president of the local ARRL-affiliated ham radio club and was told: "All it takes is at least two hams equipped with loop or small yogi antennas, compasses, maps, and enough time to get lines of bearing, or LOBs, on a ground wave signal before it goes off the air. Those LOBs are plotted on a map. The intersection of two LOBs is called a cut, and it takes three or more LOBs to establish an accurate fix with a halfway-decent circular error probability. From there, you just move in to narrow it down to an individual house or vehicle."

He continued, "We have a lot of club members who are adept at DFing in the field. They've all been in our 'Fox and Hound' group. They track each other down just for fun."

Members of the club gladly volunteered. Their vehicles preceded small convoys of QRT vehicles. Pinpointing the houses or vehicles that were the source of the transmissions was relatively quick in lightly populated ranch lands but more tedious and time-consuming in suburban neighborhoods.

The looter spies were mainly found hidden in abandoned houses. They simply moved vehicular CB radios indoors and connected them to one of a half dozen charged car batteries that they had brought along. Their amateurish attempts at COMSEC turned out to be their downfall. By reading aloud lengthy coded messages (from simple and easily decrypted transposition ciphers) in five-letter groups, they were on the air for as long as twenty-five minutes per broadcast. This gave the ham radio operators plenty of time to track down their locations.

———

Tomas Marichal generally enjoyed being the guard for the hardware store, but the long hours were wearing him down. Eventually, both José and Jake began taking two-hour guard shifts once a day on a rotating schedule.

Tomas was concerned that even though he alternated between standing in different corners of the store, someday he'd be caught in an inattentive moment and shot by an armed robber. He voiced his concern to Jake. "What we need is some sort of armored guard booth *inside* the store. We need something like the bulletproof kiosks that they have for cops and security guards, like at the big shopping malls."

After discussing this possibility, Jake, Tomas, and José all sketched some ideas for an armored guard booth, but their designs all lacked sufficient visibility. Then José suggested buying the teller windows from the now defunct Bank of America branch on West Burleigh Boulevard.

Jake learned that control of the bank building had reverted to the owner who had leased it to the bank. The building was sitting vacant. Jake made arrangements to meet the owner. They walked through the frame of the bank's smashed glass front door, with chunks of shatterproof glass crunching beneath their shoes. Birds had already started to nest inside the building. The interior was a shambles. Mortgage brochures, bank forms, and worthless Federal Reserve Notes littered the floor. But the four Plexiglas teller windows—each with a round metal voicimeter mounted at chest level and a rotating cash tray at counter level—were still intact. Jake was pleased to see that each Plexiglas window sat in a stout steel frame.

As Jake was taking measurements, the owner offered an explanation for the state of the bank. "B. of A. closed the branch after the inflation hit. They really did their customers dirt. When depositors came for their money, they didn't have enough cash on hand, so they gave everyone cashier's checks for their full balances and closed their accounts. People asked, 'Where am I supposed to cash this?' and the manager just said, 'That's your problem.' Even worse were the people who had safety deposit boxes. They only gave them one week to empty their boxes. When I repossessed the building, I found the main vault door was open, there was a huge pile of empty deposit boxes, and more than twenty boxes had been drilled open. Drilled by whom, I can only speculate."

Jake shook his head in disgust, and said, "I never liked B. of A. I've heard some horror stories about how they handled their ag loans with the orange growers." Jake finished jotting down the dimensions in his notepad. Then he looked up and said, "My offer is one hundred seventy-five dollars face value in silver coin."

"For each?" the building owner replied.

"No, one hundred seventy-five dollars face for *all four* of them. And we'll handle all of the removal, transport, and cleanup."

"But these are bulletproof . . . and they probably cost a fortune."

"No, they're bullet *resistant*, and they're just like hundreds of others that I can find in abandoned banks all over Florida."

The owner was clearly disappointed by the offer, but after a moment's hesitation he extended his hand to shake on the deal. Jake and a crew of four men came to dismantle and haul off the teller windows the next day.

The new guard booth was constructed near the middle of the store to give it a commanding view. It was pentagonal and used the teller windows on four sides and the door from a Winchester Silverado gun vault on the fifth side. Beneath the four teller windows, the first thirty inches up from the floor were plate steel, constructed of two quarter-inch thicknesses of Grade 50 hot-rolled A572 steel. Above these were bolted the teller windows with their rotary cash trays still attached. The booth's roof was just one quarter-inch thickness of steel, but it was firmly welded in place. Two thicknesses of the steel went over the triangular spaces between the window frames. The voicimeters were converted into gun ports that were latched shut from the inside.

Gasoline to run the arc welder was in short supply, so Tomas decided to use his oxyacetylene torch. Welding gases had become a valuable commodity, so he charged as much for the oxygen and acetylene as he did the steel when he put in his time and materials bid for the job. After the cutting and welding was done, Tomas smoothed the rough edges with an angle grinder. Then Janelle did the painting, starting with gray Rustoleum primer, and then adding two coats of white lacquer paint. The ten-gauge steel vault door was left in its original granite gray color with a Winchester factory logo near the bottom.

The vault door was only fifty-four inches tall, so the guard had to stoop whenever passing through it. It had originally been designed to open only from the outside, but by removing the inside panel and installing a secondary wheel, it could be quickly opened from the inside. In the event that the exterior lock dial was scrambled, the combination lock mechanism's back cover was left loose so the lock's three notched plates could be realigned with a pin punch. A large wooden block was cut so someone inside could prevent the vault's locking bars from opening, in case any miscreants ever gained access to the vault door's combination.

A tall swivel chair with a bucket seat allowed anyone manning the booth to be able to quickly turn to any of the four windows. It immediately became apparent, however, that the booth would need better ventilation. Two large rectangular vents were cut in the top, using a cutting torch. Expanded metal mesh was welded over the top of each vent, and sliding metal plates with handles were installed to block the vents in an emergency.

The final touch for the booth's security was suggested by Tomas: a set of high-pressure SCUBA air tanks that could be cracked open in the event that armed robbers tried to use tear gas or some other irritant to flush out the guard. Tomas surmised that closing the top air vents and then opening an air tank valve slightly would create a positive overpressure so no irritants could get into the booth.

The air tanks came from a SCUBA shop on Highway 441 in Mount Dora. Though there was probably still some work for commercial divers on the coast, in inland Florida, SCUBA diving had mostly been recreational. So dive gear was available for a pittance after the Crunch. The shop owners were happy to sell Jake two steel "120" dive tanks, which were both fully charged with 107 cubic feet of air at three thousand pounds per square inch.

The armored guard booth was quickly dubbed the Pentagon, and it spawned plenty of nicknames. Whoever was manning the booth was called the Chairman of the Joint Chiefs or just the Chairman. Any reading materials inside the Pentagon were called the Pentagon Papers.

Despite all the jokes, the Pentagon was taken very seriously. The shotgun, AR-10, and piles of loaded magazines in the continuously manned Pentagon made it abundantly clear that the Altmiller's store would be a tough nut for any robbers to crack. The booth was greatly admired by the store's patrons. One elderly lady commented, "I wish I had a house built like that."

18

QUISLINGS

"A government by representatives, elected by the people at
short periods, was our object; and our maxim at that day
was, 'Where annual election ends, tyranny begins.'"

—Thomas Jefferson, in a letter to Samuel Adams, February 26, 1800

Tavares, Central Florida—
August, the Second Year

In the second year of the Crunch, word came that a provisional government (ProvGov) had been formed at Fort Knox, Kentucky. It was
led by Maynard Hutchings, a man who had no government experience other than being a member of the local County Board of Supervisors. Now Hutchings fancied himself the dictator of the United States.
The ProvGov grew very quickly because it had both the U.S. Army
units and gold depository at Fort Knox to back it up and lend it some
respectability. The rise to power of Maynard Hutchings was more
about being in the right place at the right time than it was about states-
manship, oratory, or his political acumen.

The ProvGov filled the power vacuum left when the East Coast suffered a massive loss of life, partly due to an influenza pandemic that struck
the eastern seaboard particularly hard from New York to South Carolina
during the first winter of the Crunch. Without antibiotics available, the
disease ran wild, especially in the cities. The new government rapidly
spread outward, "pacifying" territory in all directions. Any towns that

resisted were quickly crushed. The mere sight of dozens of tanks or APCs was enough to make most townspeople cower in fear. What it couldn't accomplish through intimidation, the ProvGov accomplished with bribes.

The ProvGov soon began issuing a new currency. Hutchings' administration cronies spent the new bills lavishly. Covertly, some criminal gangs were hired as security contractors and used as enforcers of the administration's nationalization schemes. Some of these gangs were given military vehicles and weapons and promised booty derived from eliminating rival gangs that were not as cooperative. Hit squads were formed to stifle dissent through any means including abductions, arson, and murder. Nobody was ever able to prove a link between the ProvGov and these squads, but an inordinately large number of conservative, pro-sovereignty members of congress from the old government disappeared or were reportedly killed by bandits.

Within the first three months of launching the new government, Hutchings was in contact via satellite with the UN's new headquarters in Brussels to request peacekeeping assistance. The old UN building in New York had burned, and the entire New York metropolitan region was nine-tenths depopulated and controlled by hostile gangs. At first, Hutchings had naïvely assumed that the UN's assistance would be altruistic, with no strings attached. It was only after the first UN troops started to arrive in large numbers that it became clear that UN officers would control the operation. Eventually, Hutchings became little more than a figurehead. The UN administrators held the real power in the country. They had their own chain of command that bypassed the Hutchings administration and they had direct control over the military.

In Tavares, news of the ProvGov's rise to power came first via rumors. But then two copies of a widely circulated DVD reached Tavares in December. It was a video of ProvGov President Hutchings making a State of the Union speech. By the time Jake and Janelle got a copy, José reported, "Yeah, I already seen it on the DVD player built into my neighbor's minivan. That Hutchings is a big fat blowhard. I don't trust him or the ProvGov any farther than I can spit. The whole thing is borderline *fascist*, if you ask me."

The DVD that Jake Altmiller watched came to him from Mayor Levin. It had a mirror side so badly scratched that he wondered if it would even work. With ample photovoltaic power at their house, they were able to watch it on the television in their living room. Tomas and several neighbors joined them. The video looked professionally produced and started with an image of an American flag fluttering in the breeze, with an accompanying audio track of a brass band playing "Hail to the Chief." The video then cut to an auditorium in which a podium adorned with the familiar presidential seal had been placed.

The applause made it sound as if a large crowd was present. A man in a dark suit that must have come from a Big Man's suit shop stepped up to the microphone. Reading from notes, he began:

"My fellow Americans: The United States is slowly recovering from the greatest tragedy in its history. I have recently been provided a detailed report on the extent of the catastrophe from the administration's chief scientist. Some of the report's findings are as follows: In the past three years, an estimated one hundred and sixty million of our citizens have died. Most who died succumbed to starvation, exposure, and disease. Of the deaths by disease, more than sixty-five million were caused by the influenza pandemic that swept the eastern seaboard. Without antibiotics available, the disease simply ran rampant until there were no more hosts left to attack in the heavily populated regions.

"At least twenty-eight million are estimated to have been killed in lawless violence. In addition, more than five million have died of complications of preexisting medical problems such as diabetes, heart disease, hemophilia, AIDS, and kidney disease. Hundreds of thousands more have died of complications of tonsillitis, appendicitis, and other ailments that were heretofore not life-threatening. The distribution of population losses ranged from in excess of ninety-six percent of the population in some northeastern metropolitan areas to less than five percent in a few areas in the High Plains, Rocky Mountains, the intermountain areas of the West, and the Inland Northwest. Order has been restored in only a few states, but we are making rapid progress.

"As you are no doubt aware, the economy is still in complete disarray. The formerly existing transportation and communications systems have been completely disrupted. In the coming months, our biggest priority will be on revitalizing the petroleum and refining industries of Oklahoma, Texas, and Louisiana. Next, we will strive to get electric power back on line in as many areas as possible. With bulk fuel, natural gas, and electrical power available, it is hoped that agriculture and the many industries critical to our nation's economic health will be reestablished.

"Here at Fort Knox, we have taken the lead in rebuilding a new United States. Already, with the help of security forces from other United Nations countries, we have pacified the states of Kentucky, Tennessee, Mississippi, and Alabama. But there is much more to be done. America must be put back on its feet again economically. Never again can we allow the economy to get so out of control. Strict economic policies will ensure that there will never be a repeat of the Crash. Wages and prices will, by necessity, be controlled by the central government. Many industries will have to be government-owned or government-controlled, at least in the foreseeable future. Reasonable limits on the press will stop the spread of unfounded rumors. Until order is completely restored, the federal and state constitutions have been temporarily suspended, and nationwide martial law is in effect. The single legitimate seat of power is here at Fort Knox. It is only with central planning that things can be put back in order rapidly and efficiently.

"Kentucky, Tennessee, Mississippi, and Alabama are already under the control of nine United Nations subregional administrators.

I will soon be dispatching UN regional and subregional administrators to the other areas that have independently reestablished order. These include Maine, New Hampshire, and Vermont, the southern portion of Georgia, most of Texas, part of Louisiana, most of Colorado, southwestern Oregon, all of Idaho, all of Utah, eastern Washington, all of Wyoming, and most of North and South Dakota.

"The UN Regional Administrators will oversee the many tasks required to accomplish a complete national recovery. For example, they will be setting up regional police forces, which will be under their direct control. They will oversee the issuance of the National ID Card. They will appoint judges that they deem properly qualified. Each Regional Administrator will bring with him on staff a regional tax collector and a regional treasurer who will handle issuance of the new national currency. Rest assured that the new currency is fully backed by the gold reserves of the national depository.

"I hope that you, my fellow citizens, will do everything in your ability to assist your new Regional Administrators, the subregional Administrators, their staffs, and those that they appoint under them. Only with your cooperation will America be able to quickly restore itself to its former greatness."

There was thunderous applause, and Hutchings raised both his hands to wave to the crowd.

Just as Janelle switched off the television with the remote control, José yelled, "What a load of horse *caca*! He reminds me of that kid Cartman from the cartoon show *South Park*. When he gets deputized, he starts shouting, 'I am a cop and you will respect my author-i-tahh!'"

They all laughed.

"Any guesses as to what he meant by 'strict economic policies'? Are you thinking what I'm thinking?" Jake asked.

"Yeah. It all sounds like *big government* central planning," Janelle answered.

———

Three weeks after the Altmillers had watched the DVD, news came that the Provisional Government's army had begun "pacifying" North Florida. According to ham radio operators, the ProvGov's troops often treated reluctant towns and cities still held by elected governments with the same brutal tactics they used on looter bastions.

It was a while before any of the Provisional Government's actions were felt in Tavares. One of the first instances came when the ProvGov distributed a poster that outlined the UN-mandated gun laws. It read:

B-A-N-N-E-D

Effective Upon Posting in a prominent place in each county and in effect until further notice, the following items are hereby banned from private possession by the recently enacted Amplified United Nations Small Arms and Light Weapons (SALW) Normalization Accord:

1. All fully automatic or short-barreled rifles and shotguns (regardless of prior registration under the National Firearms Act of 1934).

2. Any rifle over thirty (.30) caliber, any shotgun or weapon of any description over twelve (12) gauge in diameter.

3. All semiautomatic rifles and shotguns, all rifles and shotguns capable of accepting a detachable magazine.

4. Any detachable magazine, regardless of capacity.

5. Any weapon with a fixed magazine that has a capacity of more than four (4) cartridges (or shells).

6. All grenades and grenade launchers, all explosives, detonating cord, and blasting caps (regardless of prior registration under the Gun Control Act of 1968 or state or local blasting permits).

7. All explosives precursor chemicals.

8. All firearms regardless of type that are chambered for military cartridges (including but not limited to 7.62 mm NATO, 5.56 mm NATO, .45 ACP, and 9 mm parabellum).

9. All silencers (regardless of prior registration under the National Firearms Act of 1934).

10. All night vision equipment including but not limited to infrared, light amplification, or thermal, all telescopic sights, and all laser aiming devices.

11. All handguns—regardless of type or caliber.

12. Other distinctly military equipment including but not limited to armored vehicles, bayonets, gas masks, helmets, and bulletproof vests.

13. Encryption software or devices.

14. All radio transmitters (other than baby monitors, cordless phones, short-range wireless devices, or cell phones).

15. Full metal jacket, tracer, incendiary, and armor-piercing ammunition.

16. All ammunition in military calibers.

17. Irritant or lethal (toxin) chemical agents including but not limited to CS and CN tear gas and OC "pepper spray."

18. All military-type pyrotechnics and flare launchers.

Exceptions only for properly trained and sworn police and the military forces of the UN and The Sole and Legitimate Provisional Government of the United States of America and Possessions.

Any firearm or other item not meeting the new criteria and all other contraband listed herein must be turned in within the ten (10) day amnesty period after the UN Regional Administrator or subadministrator, or their delegates, arrive on site. Alternatively, if federal or UN troops arrive within any state to pacify it, a thirty (30) day amnesty period will begin the day the first forces cross the state boundary. All other post-1898 production firearms of any description, air rifles, archery equipment, and edged weapons over six inches long must be registered during the same period.

Anyone found with an unregistered weapon, or any weapon, accessory, or ammunition that has been declared contraband, after the amnesty period ends will be summarily executed.

As ordered under my hand, Maynard Hutchings, President (pro tem) of The Sole and Legitimate Provisional Government of the United States of America and Possessions.

That poster got the residents of Lake County, Florida, in an uproar. Almost immediately, there was talk of organizing resistance. As the ProvGov army moved deeper into North Florida, horror stories began to circulate. The army was absolutely brutal in asserting its authority. In one town, they massacred more than one hundred people as a reprisal for the shooting deaths of two ProvGov soldiers. The victims were buried in a mass grave.

Eight counties in North Florida were soon officially declared "pacified," but in actuality, resistance fighters remained active. In the counties farther south, hundreds of small guerilla cells were forming, training, and caching supplies for what looked like would be a protracted war of resistance. The patriot media discouraged the guerillas from forming any bands larger than nine members, for fear of infiltration and annihilation by the ProvGov or their quislings. They reasoned that a profusion of small independent cells with no central leadership could never be defeated. This was "leaderless resistance" in its purest form.

Tavares, Florida—Late December, the Second Year

Janelle Altmiller was at home with her son, Lance. While she was in the master bathroom folding laundry, she heard Lance shouting in the kitchen. "Hey, stop! My dad says strangers can't be in the house!"

When an unfamiliar gruff voice told her son to shut up, Janelle's blood ran cold.

She drew the XD pistol from her holster, then dashed into the bedroom and reached across the bed to flip the silent alarm switch that was mounted under the bottom center of the bed's headboard. It was one of four switches that had been installed in the house after the Crunch. She rolled back up just in time to see a stranger standing in the doorway, holding a revolver in one hand and a bundle of large plastic cable ties in the other. She brought the pistol up, got a "flash" sight picture, and fired three times, hitting the man twice in the chest and once in the jaw. He staggered backward, and she shot him once more, hitting him at the top of his right eye socket. He landed on his back in the hallway, dropping the revolver as he fell. She heard someone screaming. It took her a moment to realize that *she* was the one screaming. Janelle didn't know what to do next. After just a moment to consider, she maneuvered back to the bathroom, looking for cover. She knelt down beside the door frame and lined up her sights on the open bedroom door. Her ears were ringing.

She heard another man's voice asking, "Javi?"

A few seconds later, she heard the man shout, "No way! No freakin' way!"

It was quiet for nearly a full minute. Obviously, the surviving intruder did not want to step forward and make himself a target. Janelle wondered if he had fled. Or perhaps he had gone outside to approach the master bathroom window from behind her. A wave of anxiety and panic went through her. She was afraid to take her eyes off the doorway to look over her shoulder.

Still in the house, the man shouted, "Listen: I've got your kid here. Throw out your gun and . . ."

To Lance, it sounded like the world had exploded. In a deafening roar, Jake and Tomas fired almost simultaneously through the living room's sliding glass door, striking the home invader with a hail of #4 buckshot from the Saiga shotgun and .223 bullets from the M4gery.

The man never got a shot off in response.

Lance thought there were only two men who had invaded their home, but Jake, Janelle, and Tomas methodically cleared all of the rooms in the house and then both the front yard and the backyard, just to be certain.

When they stepped back inside, they found Lance lifting the head of the dead man in the living room, holding his hair. "These guys are really, really dead."

"Not like on TV, is it?" Tomas asked.

Lance stood up and said, "No. It's louder. And it's *messier*."

They found that the two men had broken in by simply slashing one of the window screens and stepping into the living room. After that, the

Altmillers never left the sliding windows open unless they were directly guarded by an adult with a long gun.

Janelle had many sleepless nights after that incident. Eventually, she came to the realization that her home was defended far better than most, and that she had to trust in those defenses. But she never felt quite the same about the security of their home. And every time she locked their bedroom door, the events of that day would flash into her mind.

19

WATER

"You know what's wrong with karate, Jerry? It's based on the ridiculous assumption that the other guy will fight fair."

—James Garner, as television private detective Jim Rockford, *The Rockford Files* episode "Backlash of the Hunter," 1974; screenplay by Stephen J. Cannell and Roy Huggins

On Board *Tiburon*, Sulawesi Sea— October, the Second Year

After just six days at sea, the boat's reverse osmosis water maker broke. It was a crucial piece of equipment, providing them fresh drinking water. Just a small tear in its membrane made it useless.

After the water maker broke, they prayed for rain so they would be able to harvest rainwater from the awning canvases. They also started scanning the charts, looking for small, uninhabited islands where they'd be able to go ashore to gather coconuts. Tatang said that coconut water had saved many a sailor from dehydration.

They found a suitable island eighteen days after the water maker broke. It was scarcely a quarter mile long, it looked uninhabited, and most importantly, there were no other islands within line of sight. They spent several hours circumnavigating the island reef. There was a large gap on the west side that looked deep enough to accommodate *Tiburon*, even at low tide. This would be important in case they had to make a quick getaway.

They pulled into shore at just before nine A.M. and did a quick, armed reconnaissance. The island was indeed uninhabited, and the few rusty cans they found strewn on the ground looked as if they'd been there at least five years. They soon set to work. Joseph did most of the climbing. He would shimmy up a palm tree and call, "Look out below!" Their foraged green coconuts quickly grew into a large pile.

At the end of the first day on the island, they pushed *Tiburon* back offshore, and dropped anchor a quarter mile out to sea. This, they reasoned, was a safer place to spend the night. If nothing else, they didn't want any rats on the island stowing away.

They took advantage of being anchored and fished for squid that night, using a flashlight. The squid, attracted to the light, could simply be scooped up with a hand net. They caught two buckets full. They had to keep the bucket lids snapped on to keep the slippery squid from escaping. Black ink squid adobo was one of Tatang's specialties.

At the end of the second day, they had gathered all the green coconuts they could possibly carry. For the sake of expediency they decided to load them onto *Tiburon* unhusked. The coconuts filled up all of the available space and their weight put *Tiburon* just as deep in the water as she had been when they first left Samar. This made everyone nervous. They pushed off just before sunset as the tide was coming back in to lift the boat from the beach.

They husked the coconuts as they traveled southward. First they would cut off both ends of the green coconuts with Tatang's *itak* machete, and then they would husk them on a large chisel that Tatang attached upright to the transom with a pair of eight-inch C-clamps. It took three days just to work the pile down to the point where three of the passengers had places to sleep. And it took a full week to husk three quarters of the coconuts. They discarded the husks off the stern as they worked. Gradually, *Tiburon* lightened, bringing the waterline back to a comfortable level. Originally, Peter Jeffords had wanted to husk all of the coconuts, but Tatang insisted that the remainder of the coconut hoard would keep better if the husks were left on.

The coconut water became their water substitute. They even used it for cooking the rice, along with a bit of seawater, for savor. It gave the rice a delicious flavor that was both sweet and salty. It tasted a bit like *suman*, a traditional Filipino rice sweet cake that was made with coconut milk, usually wrapped in banana leaves.

After a week of eating fresh coconut meat and drinking mostly coconut water, however, Rhiannon and Joseph both developed diarrhea. By eating three large spoonfuls of peanut butter per day, they regained regularity.

Instead of sinking the empty coconut oil and palm oil containers, as they had in the past, they began to save them, refilling the bottles with any sources of fresh water they might find.

Their diet consisted of rice and fresh fish for at least two meals per day. If they had a poor day of trolling, which rarely happened, then they resorted to using some of their supply of dried fish. Jeffords marveled at the amazing variety of fish and sharks they caught. He only recognized a few of them by name, but he was usually happy to eat the daily catch. They did most of their cooking in a greasy fry pan on a propane stove that was cleverly gimbal-mounted, attached to the bulkhead just forward of the pilothouse. They could cook on that in all but the roughest seas.

To conserve their small supply of propane, they cooked their rice each day using a large rectangular pot with flange hooks that pressed against the engine's exhaust manifold. The engine's constant heat kept the water in the pot at just below a boil, making it a simple task to cook rice. Tatang had seen this on other fishing boats, so he had a tinker custom-make the pot for him soon after *Tiburon* was built.

While they ate some of the rice seasoned with only salt or seawater, for the sake of variety some batches contained adobo, ginger, *bagoong*, *patis*, or teriyaki sauce. The array of fish species and the various rice seasonings broke up the monotony of their diet. The seasonings, they discovered, were part of what made the discomfort of the cramped quarters of *Tiburon* bearable. Once every three or four days, Joseph would prepare an extra batch of rice at dawn and stir-fry it with different seasonings, tossing in a few bits of fish, a can of peas, and a can of water chestnuts. This special meal always lifted everyone's spirits.

They tried to keep a good sense of humor, often joking, singing songs and hymns, and telling stories. They also looked forward to sunset each night. Not only were the tropical sunsets beautiful, but the darkness meant greater protection from observation.

The three men and little Sarah did well adjusting to being at sea and to the change in diet. But Rhiannon suffered regularly from seasickness, and the change in diet caused her to alternate between diarrhea and constipation. She began to lose weight rapidly, though, thankfully, her extra weight gave her some reserves from which she could draw.

Sarah adjusted remarkably well to the sea voyage. Always curious about all the workings of Tatang's boat, she was constantly asking questions about everything from its engine to the weather to what fish she ate. She spent many early evening hours at the edge of the coaming near the wheel—the boat had few proper grab rails—asking endless questions. Tatang smiled and answered as many questions as he could with the enduring patience that grandpas are famous for having with children. Sarah was still at the "sponge" age of brain development, so she began to pick up some Tagalog phrases. Rhiannon and Peter had both spent months in language classes, but did not pick it up nearly so quickly.

The weather varied, but was generally fair. Most afternoons would cloud up, as was the norm for the tropics, but there wasn't much rain. Each rain shower was cause for celebration. The canvas awnings were carefully held in a V shape to capture as much of the rainwater as possible, in every available container. Then, once the containers had all been filled, everyone on board took turns washing their hair and showering half-clothed in the runoff from the canvas.

There was an hour or two of quiet time in the early evening of most days after their "breakfast" but before it got dark enough to safely start the engine and get under way. Tatang took advantage of this time to teach everyone the Filipino Martial Art called Pekiti-Tirsia Kali. This art emphasized fighting with sticks, knives, or any object that could be pressed into service from baseball bats to hand tools.

There was just enough room on the aft deck for Tatang and one student at a time to spar. The others sat farther forward to watch and learn.

They did most of their knife-fighting practice using a pair of ten-inch-long tubes of tightly rolled scrap cardboard. These proved to be effective training tools. The bruises they left were reminders that this training was in deadly earnest. Even little Sarah got some training, particularly about pressure points and bone joint anatomy.

The engine stopped running unexpectedly, twice. Both times, it turned out to be a clogged fuel filter. Until these repairs were completed, everyone was quite anxious. Unlike many other small boats in the region, they had no way to revert to sailing, and being in hostile waters, they couldn't radio for help. And because of the outriggers, *Tiburon* could not easily be adapted to rowing. Without a functional engine, the boat would be nothing more than a piece of driftwood at the mercy of the currents, winds, and tides.

The only other problem with the boat on the journey was that the propeller drive shaft seals began to loosen, emitting a trickle of water whenever the drive shaft was spinning. This was more of an annoyance than cause for alarm, however, since the automatic bilge pump easily kept up with the leak.

When they first discovered the leak, Tatang told Peter and Rhiannon: "You know, back in the nineties I had a friend on Samar who had a twenty-five-footer. He had a drive shaft seal totally blow out because the bearing seized and the shaft started to spin, all wobbly. They were looking forward so they didn't notice the flooding, at first. They tried stuffing rags around the shaft, but by then, the boat she was half flooded, and they only had a puny bilge pump. She sunk only five miles off of Samar. They barely made it back to the island. Good thing they were strong swimmers."

In the days that followed, Rhiannon seemed obsessed with the seals. She would get up from her sleeping mat several times each night to inspect them, using a flashlight. After a few nights of this, she became convinced that the leak was not worsening further and started to get more sleep. But for the rest of their voyage she still inspected the seals more frequently than was probably needed.

20

E&E

"When it all comes down, the last man standing is going to be standing there in shorts and sneakers [armed] with a '98 Mauser, and all the ninja-looking guys belly up at his feet— with all their cool gear."

—Louis Awerbuck

On Board *Tiburon*, the Banda Sea— Late October, the Second Year

The seas were calm and the night was almost pitch-dark. It was overcast, the quarter moon had not yet risen, and the Jeffords could barely distinguish the horizon. They motored on, regularly checking the compass and the GPS.

Tatang sat dozing in the side chair while Peter held the wheel. As he gazed ahead, Peter saw the flare of a cigarette lighter about four hundred or five hundred yards ahead—someone lighting a cigarette in the deck of a boat of some sort. Jeffords hesitated for a moment, and then cut the throttle to bring *Tiburon* to slow maneuvering speed. He swung the wheel sharply. The motion roused Tatang. Peter ducked his head toward the old man's ear and whispered, "Quiet." He could hear excited voices in the distance.

A pair of big diesel engines rumbled to life. Just as Peter completed their turn about and the *Tiburon*'s stern was pointed toward the strange boat, a searchlight snapped on and began scanning. Peter slammed the throttle forward and he said, "Take the wheel!"

Peter stepped away from the helm and snatched up Navarro's M1 rifle. Tatang took the wheel and shoved hard on the throttle, but he found that it was already wide open. The searchlight found them, blindingly bright. Peter's eyes had been accustomed to the darkness and this change overwhelmed his senses. There were more shouts from the other boat. It was now five hundred yards away and had started to turn toward them. Peter judged that it was a fifty-footer, and it had the profile of some sort of pilot-house patrol boat, with pedestal-mounted machine guns, fore and aft. Before it completed its turn, he could make out the boat's hull number: 855. Tatang muttered, "We're in a tight spot, aren't we, Mister J?"

Across the dark sea, Kapten Assegaf switched on *Sadarin*'s hailer, emitting a high warble. Then he keyed his microphone and issued a warning to stop, in Indonesian. He repeated the command in Dutch, and then English: "*Hou vast!* You are ordered to stop, or we will be shooting." The young, impetuous captain was grinning. He knew the outrigger boat was no match for his boat, with its pair of MTU diesels. Despite a few patches to its hull that gave her more drag than in her early days, *Sadarin* was still a very fast patrol boat.

The patrol boat was quickly gaining on *Tiburon*. Peter crouched behind the stern rail, put the rifle to his right shoulder and clicked its safety bar forward with the front of his trigger finger. He said aloud, "Help me get out of this, Lord." Then he took aim at the searchlight. The glare was intense.

He fired three times in rapid succession. The third shot hit the searchlight, extinguishing it. Tatang then immediately jerked the wheel, turning *Tiburon* sharply to starboard. The .50 caliber M2 Browning on the forward deck of the patrol boat sputtered to life, firing blindly in reply, in a deep staccato.

To Peter's dismay, moments later a second searchlight snapped on and began to scan. Tatang muttered something which Jeffords recognized as a Tagalog reference to excrement.

Peter fired two shots at the searchlight. The second one hit the mark, again casting them into darkness. Immediately after, Tatang wisely swung the wheel again, this time hard to port. The .50 caliber fired again blindly. The muzzle flashes were all they could see. The first few rounds passed over their heads. Every fifth round was a tracer. The arc of the tracers increased farther and farther to starboard. Tatang changed course once more, quartering away from *Sadarin*. Between bursts from the machine gun, they could hear excited shouts from the Indonesian crewmen. Two Indo sailors with Pindad SS2 5.56 mm assault rifles joined in, blindly firing in long, fully automatic bursts. But like the big Browning, all of their bursts were fired high and wide—nearly all toward their previous heading.

After a minute, they were about a thousand yards away from the patrol boat. Peter realized that his rifle was more than half empty, so he fumbled for a minute to unload it and reload it with a full 8-round clip from his pocket. The Garand, he knew, had the limitation of an "all or nothing" ejecting cartridge clip—there was no way to top off the rifle without changing the clip completely. He wanted to be ready with a full 8-round clip in case he had to fire again.

Captain Assegaf used his bullhorn again, this time ordering his own crew, "*Diam, diam!*" The shooting stopped. Realizing what was happening, Peter whispered urgently, "Stop, stop! *Preno!*"

Tatang chopped the throttle and then turned off the engine completely. Moments later, the Indonesian captain shut his engines down, too. It was eerily quiet and still quite dark. Below deck, two of the Indonesian Air Force radar technicians were wailing and crying, convinced that they were about to die for failing to do their jobs.

Hoping to hear the engine of *Tiburon*, the Indonesians were listening intently. It was so quiet that Jeffords could hear the sound of squeaking footsteps on the deck of the patrol boat. There was an anxious, questioning voice from below deck and then another shout of *"Diam!"* from Captain Assegaf, this time without the benefit of the bullhorn.

Peter crept toward the helm chair. The storm door slowly slid open. Rhiannon's head popped out. Peter reached across the door and clamped his hand across her mouth. He leaned forward and whispered into her ear: "An Indo patrol boat. I shot out their lights, so now it's cat and mouse. Keep Sarah and Joseph super quiet."

Rhiannon gave an exaggerated nod and quietly descended back into the cabin, sliding shut the storm door as gently as possible.

The unnerving quiet continued for two minutes. *Sadarin*'s signals officer approached Captain Assegaf to report that there was no radar contact. Worse yet, the ship's sonar could be used only as a depth finder. It was not designed to locate other vessels. Assegaf began cursing loudly. He ordered hand flashlights and a flare gun be brought up from below, but there was some difficulty in finding the waterproof box that held the flare gun and flares. Instead of its usual location, it was inadvertently hidden under a pile of life vests. This led to even more consternation and shouting.

By the time they started scanning with the hand flashlights, the two boats had drifted apart and were separated by 1,250 yards. Because the Indonesians' flashlights lacked sufficient range, the sailors had no luck spotting *Tiburon*. Captain Assegaf let loose a long string of profanity and slapped his signals officer on the side of his head. Frustrated, he impetuously fired up the boat's diesels. He hesitated for a moment, and then took a guess at *Tiburon*'s last heading, but he guessed wrong. He turned *Sadarin* thirty degrees to starboard as he advanced his throttles to three-quarters, pushing the boat up to twenty knots.

Peter inched up to Tatang and asked in a half whisper, "Now that they're started their engines, won't that mask the sound if we start ours?"

The old man thought for a moment and then answered, "Yeah, but they could stop any time and listen again, and then they'd hear where we are. We'd really be in the *kamalasan*. Right now, they don't know if we are pirates, smugglers, or refugees. And even refugees are probably all 'shoot on sight.' We are safer just drifting for now, Mr. J. It is still six hours to the daylight, and the clouds will stop most of the moonlight. The moonrise won't be for about two hours. Just pray hard that they get far enough away that they can't hear our engine."

Jeffords did pray, fervently.

The Indonesian patrol boat was more than a mile away when they began launching parachute flares. But at that distance, they didn't throw enough light to reveal *Tiburon*'s position.

Even worse than the misplaced flare gun kit was the fact that up until fifteen days before, *Sadarin* had been equipped with a pair of Fulinon Gen 3 light amplification night vision goggles (NVGs). But the Indonesian Navy had requisitioned the NVGs from every ship less than 25 meters in length for an unspecified "priority tasking." Assegaf assumed this meant the Philippines campaign. He was furious. If he had the NVGs or at least if he had the flare gun close at hand, then the intruder would not have been able to slip away.

Rhiannon and Joseph came up on deck. "Sarah is asleep," Rhiannon reported in a whisper.

Peter had the binoculars out, trying to gauge the distance between *Tiburon* and *Sadarin*. He started to chuckle and said, "I told you that you have a stealthy boat, Tatang."

Tatang put on a huge grin that Peter could see even in the very dim light. "Yes, she's a stealthy old shark, and she just put those Indo bastards on a what-ya-call wild geese chase."

The two men shared a laugh.

After another half hour, when the Indonesian flares could barely be seen six miles away, Tatang restarted *Tiburon*'s engine. He turned the bow to the southeast, quartering away from the Indonesian boat. Speaking at a normal level for the first time since the incident began, Tatang said, "Now, we gotta put a lot a miles between them and us before the daylight. They'll try to get a patrol plane up to look for us, sure as anything." He pushed the throttle forward all the way to its stop and added, "Go, baby, go."

Joseph said, "Do you know how lucky we are?"

Rhiannon shook her head and said, "Poor choice of words, Joey. The word isn't lucky, it is *blessed.*"

As dawn broke, after a fruitless night of searching, Assegaf had a long talk with his first mate, an old NCO who had seventeen years of service with the navy. They discussed how they would write their report of the incident with the "unidentified fishing boat." They agreed that it would be counterproductive to complain about the lack of NVGs and that the misplaced flare gun kit should be blamed on a junior-grade sailor and a reprimand issued before they returned to port.

Assegaf's next conversation was with the senior radar technician to determine why the radar couldn't detect the fishing boat. After a brief lecture on radar fundamentals, the NCO explained that the ship's radar had a feature called "near field clutter rejection." Thus, the radar *did not display* any target less than two kilometers away if it was moving at less than twenty kilometers per hour and if it had a radar cross section smaller than that of a small boat or passenger car.

Kapten Assegaf fumed about the fishing boat getting away. More than just the disappointment, it was writing the After Action Report that troubled him. Given the recent political shifts within the TNI-AL, his report would have to be *very* carefully worded.

21

RABBLE IN ARMS

"Believe in your cause. The stronger your belief, the stronger your motivation and perseverance will be. You must know it in your heart that it is a worthwhile cause and that you are fighting the good fight. Whether it is the need to contribute or the belief in a greater good, for your buddy, for the team or for your country, find a reason that keeps your fire burning. You will need this fire when the times get tough. It will help you through when you are physically exhausted and mentally broken and you can only see far enough to take the next step."

—MSG Paul R. Howe, U.S. Army Retired, from *Leadership and Training for the Fight: A Few Thoughts on Leadership and Training from a Former Special Operations Soldier*

Tavares, Florida—
January, the Third Year

Living in Tavares had at one time seemed isolated and relatively rural to the Altmillers. But after the Crunch, they felt uncomfortably close to Orlando. The more than two million people in the greater Orlando area were constantly on their minds. There were troubling reports of widespread looting in downtown Orlando, and then successively larger raids pushing out in waves to Winter Park and Alamonte Springs, and Oviedo. When word came of a 2,000-looter raid on Apopka, the town elders and police chiefs of Mount Dora,

Tangerine, and Tavares held a joint meeting. It was agreed that they would send experienced military scouts to Apopka and beyond. They also alerted some traders with contacts near Orlando that there were rewards of up to ten ounces of silver for anyone with firm word of any planned looter gang movements. They would also set up and continuously man outposts on Highway 441. They made provisional plans to raise a large force of armed men to block and repel the expected raid.

Highway 441, also known as the Orange Blossom Trail, was a divided four-lane highway. It was the obvious avenue of approach, if looters from Orlando were going to come in force as they had in recent raids. On the Apopka raid, the looters had been preceded by a bulldozer that had been crudely upgraded with armored steel plates and periscopes. This bulldozer had easily smashed two intervening roadblocks, sending Apopka's defenders into a disorganized retreat. The looters spent two days in Apopka, looting, raping, and burning. They left very little of value.

Combining the intelligence derived from recently captured looters and information provided by the Mount Dora scouts, it became clear that the looter gang had plans to hit Tangerine and Mount Dora in about two weeks. A group of Afghanistan veterans and good ol' boys from Astor selected an ambush site on Highway 441 near Zellwood between Winfred Avenue and Ponkan Road. This stretch of the highway had a railroad track on a raised ballast bed on the west side of the road and some recently cleared fields to the east. The open ground was still dotted with stumps. The trees had been cut for firewood and there were plans to plant corn there once the stumps were removed.

They set up an obvious line of defense, blocking both directions of the highway with abandoned truck trailers that came from a now defunct CITGO fuel station and truck scale, immediately to the north, at the corner of Winfred Avenue. The owner of the station—a man from Georgia who had bought the company just before the Crunch—donated them willingly, once he learned that his property would be just *inside* of the defensive perimeter. The trailers were strongly attached to each other with three-quarter-inch steel cables and formed a "Lazy W" shaped chain that extended from the railroad tracks of the northwest side to the fuel station on the southeast side.

Based on updated intelligence, a large ambush was formulated by the mayors of Mount Dora and Tavares. Realizing that they'd need more men, the mayors asked for additional volunteers from Zellwood and the many smaller communities east and west of Tangerine, like Lane Park, Bay Ridge, and Plymouth Terrace. The message they spread was: "Adults in good walking shape are asked to bring their guns to Tangerine. Be there no later than four P.M. on Tuesday. Wear camouflage. Bring lots of water and enough food for overnight. Rifles preferred, but shotguns okay if you have buckshot or slugs. Bring at least eighty rounds per man. Bring a heavy coat for overnight outdoors."

The ambush was in a classic L shape, with the roadblock forming the short leg of the L. The longer leg of the L was along the reverse side of the railroad track, which provided both concealment and cover for the ambushers. Some of the men with the heaviest weapons—mostly .308 and .30-06 rifles—were positioned behind the trailer roadblock, because it was anticipated that they would have the opportunity to fire enfilade down the length of the ambush kill zone.

By prior agreement, the ambushers gathered in Zellwood on the afternoon of January 21st. Jake Altmiller and Tomas Marichal arrived at three thirty after a seven-mile walk. Janelle and José were guarding the house and the store, which was temporarily closed. The men had been trickling in all afternoon from as far as twenty-five miles away. Most arrived on foot, but a surprising number came on bicycles.

Jake sized up the men and the handful of women. Nearly all of them wore camouflage, as requested, but this came in a dizzying assortment of military and civilian patterns. Jake, who had no military experience, wore a ripstop nylon Battle Dress Uniform (BDU) in the Woodland pattern. He had bought these a decade before at a St. Vincent DePaul thrift store. They'd cost him just twenty dollars for both the pants and the shirt. Janelle had removed the Air Force insignia with a seam ripper shortly after he brought them home. In the following years he had worn them for some duck hunting, but more frequently for painting, so they had copious spatters of dark brown deck stain, and forest green paint from his house trim. His jacket was an old faded olive drab Army M65, also from a thrift store. Jake also wore a MultiCam boonie hat—a more recent acquisition. The BDUs fit him well. Jake's weight was around 185 before the Crunch but had recently dropped to 175 pounds. He attributed this to being deprived of ice cream, which he used to have for dessert almost every evening.

Tomas, as a USMC vet, looked more regulation and strack with an entirely matching set of MARPAT digital "digiflage" camo utilities, and a matching boonie hat and field jacket. People like Tomas were so obviously prior service (belt buckle centered, bootlaces tucked in, and so forth) that there was no doubt whatsoever. Others, who wore odd assortments of camos and who had dangling bootlaces, clearly had no military experience. A few others were hard to pin down, at least at first glance. There was clearly a duck hunting crowd: They all wore civilian camouflage pattern clothes from head to toe. Not surprisingly, a lot of them carried shotguns rather than rifles.

It was fairly easy to distinguish between the Army veterans of various vintage, as their clothing and gear often told the tale of when they had served. Some of the oldest Army vets wore green fatigues or tiger stripe camouflage. These were Vietnam veterans—or at least Vietnam era wannabes.

Then there was the Woodland pattern, which could be spotted widely throughout the crowd. The specific pattern dated the men wearing it as having served from the late 1970s to the turn of the century. The print was so ubiquitous that the men wearing it nearly outnumbered all the other camo patterns combined.

Next were the Army Combat Uniform (ACU) wearers. This was a grayish digital camouflage pattern that had been worn in Iraq, Afghanistan, and Bosnia, coming home in the duffel bags of veterans who served up until 2012. The ACU pattern was generally disliked because it made the wearers look like gray blobs at a distance, and it was not an effective camo pattern in most environments.

Last were the MultiCam OCP wearers, who had served in Afghanistan and elsewhere in more recent years. Similarly, the Marine Corps
and Air Force veterans wore uniforms that were telltale signs of their
years of service.

Added to the mix was a strange assortment of camouflage that ranged
from Swiss Alpenflage and British DPM to Rhodesian splinter pattern.
Tomas had to name many of these patterns for Jake, who assumed that
most of them had simply been bought as military surplus. But he had no
idea whether the men who wore them were the genuine article—
veterans of those nations—or just guys who liked to play paintball on
weekends. He suspected that the latter was more often the case.

The briefing was to be held at just after six P.M. As men continued to
arrive in large numbers before the appointed hour, everyone was asked
to top off their canteens and Camelbaks from a pair of tan Florida
National Guard water tank trailers parked nearby. The disorganized
crowd that formed at the four brass toggle spigots on each of the Water
Buffalo trailers was Jake's first indication of the wide range of experience in the assembled crowd. Clearly, some of these men had never
even been in a Boy Scout troop. Seeing so much water get spilled on the
ground and so many men milling around was frustrating. Tomas
moaned. "What a goat rope. Whatever happened to the old 'form two
lines of two'?" The chaotic process took almost an hour. "Whoever organized this didn't think it through, and didn't think about security,"
Tomas observed. "Just one crude explosive could disable a large percentage of the force. Pitiful."

After the water trailers fiasco was over, Tom Martinson, the portly
mayor of Tangerine, gave a speech. With some help, he climbed up in
the back of a pickup truck bed. He pulled out a notepad and shouted,
"Your attention, please."

It took a while to get everyone quieted down. Reading from his notepad, he said, "I want to thank everyone for coming. As you know, some
grievous wolves are on their way here. We all heard what they did to
Apopka and we have to stop them from doing the same here. If we don't

stop them, and stop them *hard*, then they'll just keep doing this in all directions throughout Central Florida."

There were shouts of agreement from the crowd.

Martinson continued, "We now have solid intelligence that a large looter force has been assembling down on the Western Beltway next to Lake Marshall, northwest of Apopka. They plan on advancing toward Tangerine before daylight tomorrow. We've prepared an excellent ambush site near Zellwood and the looters are expected to pass by there as early as 0900. Now I'm not going to sugarcoat this: There is an *army* of them. But if we take them by surprise, the numbers won't matter. It'll be a turkey shoot."

Then Martinson reached down with his hand to help up a Baptist church pastor into the pickup. The pastor said a brief prayer for safety. The word *Amen* was deeply echoed in the crowd.

Jake felt reassured, knowing he was surrounded by men of faith.

The pastor said, "God's Word in Psalms 37, verses 5 through 15, reassures us with this:

'Commit thy way unto the Lord; trust also in him; and he shall
    bring it to pass.
'And he shall bring forth thy righteousness as the light, and thy
    judgment as the noonday.
'Rest in the Lord, and wait patiently for him: fret not thyself because
    of him who prospereth in his way, because of the man who
    bringeth wicked devices to pass.
'Cease from anger, and forsake wrath: fret not thyself in any wise to
    do evil.
'For evildoers shall be cut off: but those that wait upon the Lord,
    they shall inherit the earth.
'For yet a little while, and the wicked shall not be: yea, thou shalt
    diligently consider his place, and it shall not be.
'But the meek shall inherit the earth; and shall delight themselves in
    the abundance of peace.

'The wicked plotteth against the just, and gnasheth upon him with
    his teeth.

'The Lord shall laugh at him: for he seeth that his day is coming.

'The wicked have drawn out the sword, and have bent their bow, to
    cast down the poor and needy, and to slay such as be of upright
    conversation.

'Their sword shall enter into their own heart, and their bows shall be
    broken.'

"May God bless and protect all y'all."

Then the mayor stepped forward again and shouted, "We don't want
any negligent discharges, so leave your chambers empty for now." There
was a loud clatter of guns being unloaded, with their muzzles pointed
skyward. One shotgun went off in this process, which evoked scornful
laughter and lots of derisive comments like "Nice!" and "Thanks for letting the whole county know!"

Martinson shouted, "*That's* what I was warning you about. We can't
afford to have that happen down at the ambush. Leave your chambers
empty until just before the order to fire. It just takes a moment. The element of surprise is crucial. I need you to now *quietly* route-march to the
roadblock on Highway 441 with *no* use of flashlights. It is about four
miles from here to the site near Zellwood." He gestured to his right.
"Take one of the sack lunches here only *if* you didn't pack enough chow
for both dinner tonight and breakfast tomorrow. You will receive further orders at the roadblock. God bless and protect you. Move out!"

There were four hundred paper sacks lined up five rows deep on the
sidewalk. Jake observed that about three hundred fifty of these sack
dinners were taken. He later learned that each sack contained a large
hunk of soft bread, a four-ounce Ziploc bag of peanuts, and an orange.
Tomas was disgusted that so many men had come so ill-prepared.
"What a bunch of pogues," he muttered. The perfunctory briefing also
angered Tomas. He had expected a full-blown mission prep in standard
"Op Order" format.

22

THE WAIT

"There's no such thing as life without bloodshed. I think the notion that the species can be improved in some way, that everyone could live in harmony, is a really dangerous idea."

—Cormac McCarthy, in Richard B. Woodward's "Cormac McCarthy's Venomous Fiction," *New York Times Magazine,* 1992

South of Tangerine, Florida—
January, the Third Year

The ambushers walked to Zellwood by the light of a nearly full moon. Once there, most of them were directed down the grassy strip just west of the railroad tracks. They were asked to "stand on line with one hand raised, and rest it on the shoulder of the man next to you." In the darkness and given their inexperience, it took forty minutes to get straightened out. This aggravated Tomas, who had become accustomed to being around well-trained Marines. Finally, after their interval was established, the order was passed: "Get down, facing the tracks."

It was not until everyone was in position and three successive head counts were passed up the line that the planners knew their exact strength. There were 1,082 ambushers. On the long side of the L, the men were organized into groups of roughly one hundred, based on the interval of the telephone poles on the far side of the highway. They were told that a captain was assigned to command all of the men between each pair of poles.

Two reserve forces of two hundred men each were positioned in the woods at both tips of the L. Rather than providing blocking forces to prevent being outflanked as they had intended, in the end they provided massed firepower to cut down any of the looters who attempted to escape the ambush zone.

Given the wide variety of experience, lack of familiarity working together, and the sheer size of the ambush teams, the planners wisely decided to keep things simple. A static ambush was feasible, but any attempt at maneuvering these untrained men might result in confusion, panic, or even worse, a friendly-fire accident. Without a standard uniform, it would be difficult to distinguish friend from foe once units started to maneuver. A simple static ambush would be the safest plan.

Jake and Tomas rested prone in the "caterpillar" facing the railroad tracks. There were lots of whispered questions—mostly asking what was going on. After a few minutes, a man wearing a MultiCam uniform walked down the line to Jake and Tomas's section and introduced himself. Once every twenty feet, he repeated, "I'm your captain. I had a deployment in Iraq and three in Afghanistan, so trust me. We are going to kick some tail and take names tomorrow. Just get comfortable and keep very quiet. Further orders will follow."

Jake and Tomas were among the best-armed men in the ambush. Jake had his LAR-8 while Tomas has his DPMS AR-10 rifle. They each had nine 20-round magazines of ammunition.

The two men were just an arm's width apart with their rucksacks positioned at their feet. In the moonlight he could see that there was a large monopole tower supporting a billboard sign off to their left, on the far side of the tracks. Highway 441 could not be seen, because of the raised railroad bed ahead of them.

The railroad bed had been elevated just a few months before the Crunch, as part of a regional railroad company upgrade designed to give the tracks better flood protection. This construction program was partly federally funded. It converted tracks that had heretofore been at just above street level and put them up on a five-foot-tall earthen berm that was topped by a thick layer of two-inch minus chert rock. The berm and ballast still looked freshly constructed.

They lay there quietly, with each man absorbed in his own thoughts. Jake fiddled with a chunk of chert rock that at some point had rolled down from the berm ahead of him. He started thinking about chiggers. Those biting insects were particularly fond of his flesh. He was glad it was January, and not June. Then his mind wandered to the song "Orange Blossom Special," and he tried to recall the lyrics. The tune and the lyrics occupied his mind for several minutes, but his thoughts eventually returned to the upcoming ambush. He dreaded the prospect of deliberately taking lives.

Just after midnight, Jake asked Tomas in a whisper, "Does it bother you that some of these looters coming here in the morning from Orlando are going to be *Cubanos*?"

Tomas answered, "Naw. Look at who we got here alongside us: Every skin tone and accent of speech you can imagine. Whites, blacks, Cubans, and even some Seminole Indians. Same for the bad guys. But this *isn't* about skin color. It's about respect for life and property. We respect the right to safeguard life and property and they don't. Plain and simple. We want to live in peace and help each other out, but all they think about is taking, taking, taking. Orlando didn't get the nickname Whorlando for nothing. There are some really low-class thieving people there. And yeah, they do come in all colors."

A young black man armed with a .30-30 Winchester lever gun on the other side of Tomas had overheard Tomas. He said, "Some of them may be black like me, but they're no-account *trash*."

A few minutes later the man on Jake's left struck up a whispered conversation. He was wearing a camouflage jacket and a matching cap with a prominent Realtree company logo on the front. He appeared to be in his fifties. The man held a stainless steel Ruger Mini-14 Ranch Rifle that had been wrapped with camouflage tape to reduce its glare. He also carried a M1911 Colt, .45 ACP—also stainless—in a Kydex hip holster. He whispered, "If we let these bastards get through, they're going to *decimate* Mount Dora and Tavares. They'll rape, they'll kill, they'll burn houses, and they'll loot everything. They'll even eat our dogs."

"Yeah, I've heard how they operate," Jake replied. "They're like the Mongol Horde, only better armed. Worst-case scenario is they come and then they *stay* and lord it over us for a few months. I guess you heard what happened when the looters from Miami moved up the coast from Boca Raton to Vero Beach. Like a swarm of locusts, and they *stayed*. I heard that they took some women as slaves and kept them chained up—with padlocked chains around their necks. They're absolutely barbaric."

The man in the Realtree camo nodded. "All four of my grandparents and a bunch of my great-aunts and great-uncles died in the Holocaust. And my mother almost died of starvation before her camp was liberated by the British Army. She was in a camp called Neuengamme-Geilenberg, on the Elbe River. That's near Hamburg. She was still just a little kid when they broke open the camp gates in May of 1945. I grew up hearing her say, 'Never again.' She gave me my first gun, a Remington .22 pump, for Christmas when I was eleven years old. Then she bought me an M1 carbine for my sixteenth birthday. My friends all thought that was pretty cool, that my mom liked guns."

After a pause, he continued. "She'd often show me the tattoo on her left forearm. It was H-1938. By coincidence 1938 was the year she was born. She'd show me that tattoo and she'd say, 'Never give up your guns. And never let them *take* you. Never!'"

Tomas chimed in. "Damned straight, *never* surrender. And never let *anyone* put you behind barbed wire. It's better to die on your feet, fighting, than to die on your knees, begging for mercy."

The night was spent in nervous anticipation. Only ten percent of the ambushers slept. These were mostly the men who'd had the longest walks. Just a few of them snored, and for this they got poked in the ribs and cussed out. Throughout the night a few orders and reports were passed down the line in whispers, at odd intervals. Most of them made sense.

"No talking above a whisper."

"No lights or smoking."

"Quiet."

"Looters are expected at ten A.M."

"Resist the urge to peek over the berm."

"You're a bunch of schoolgirls. Whispers only!"

The January night was chilly by Florida standards. A few of the men complained but were quickly chided. "Shut up. Deal with it. In another few hours you'll be complaining that you're too hot. So just shut up." Jake had a heavy jacket and a pile cap. Tomas curled up in his poncho liner. He took pity on the young black man next to him, who had only a light jacket. He loaned him a Navy watch cap and a spare quilted field jacket liner that he normally kept bundled in his rucksack to use as a pillow when sleeping in the field.

The looter army was led by escaped convicts. They left the north end of Orlando before dawn, as expected. It was little more than a large, disorganized mob. They had no forward or flank scouting elements. They assumed that their superior numbers would overwhelm any defenders. They also had a false sense of security provided by the armored bulldozer, which they had used successfully twice before.

As they advanced, many of the looters sang chants, most of which were nonsensical. One of the largest groups was singing, "We gonna get some, get some, today." The rest were variations of the same idea, the longest-running chant going, "Take some, take some, take some more. Get some, get some, get some more."

The looters advanced in staggered clumps of twenty to fifty people rather than in proper fighting array. Their numbers were overwhelming. In all there were over four thousand armed male looters, plus a few hundred unarmed women and teenage boys. The latter had come along hoping to find loot or perhaps "pick up" weapons in the wake of a successful raid.

The looters were armed with a motley assortment of weapons that ranged from lever-action Winchesters and Marlins to pump-action shotguns of various brands and vintages, to a few AKs, ARs, FALs, HKs, and M1 carbines. Only a few of them carried spare magazines in proper ALICE or MOLLE pouches. They mostly wore civilian clothes in a wide range of colors, and baseball caps, visors, and straw sun hats. Nearly all of them carried rucksacks and backpacks that hung loosely— indicative that they planned to fill them with booty. Many of them pushed or pulled a variety of carts—again, mostly empty or holding empty gas cans—for their expected loot.

On average, the ambushers were armed better than the looters, with a higher ratio of battle rifles. There were a few exotic guns including several Steyr AUGs, a belt-fed Shrike .223, an HK G36 clone, and a SIG PE-57. Most of the ambushers carried at least a hundred spare cartridges or shotgun shells, which was twice the average carried by the looters. Despite the disadvantage of smaller numbers, they were better organized, and better disciplined. And most of them would also have the advantage of firing from behind the cover of two steel railroad tracks. History has always shown that although outnumbered, the advantage goes to the defender who is thinking of nothing else but holding the line so that the oncoming horde might not assail his family or homestead. They waited in the darkness. A few slept. Many of them prayed. All of them worried.

23

MAD MINUTE

"... Then the Gods of the Market tumbled, and their smooth-tongued wizards withdrew / And the hearts of the meanest were humbled and began to believe it was true / That All is not Gold that Glitters, and Two and Two make Four / And the Gods of the Copybook Headings limped up to explain it once more.

"As it will be in the future, it was at the birth of Man / There are only four things certain since Social Progress began. / That the Dog returns to his Vomit and the Sow returns to her Mire, / And the burnt Fool's bandaged finger goes wabbling back to the Fire;

"And that after this is accomplished, and the brave new world begins / When all men are paid for existing and no man must pay for his sins, / As surely as Water will wet us, as surely as Fire will burn, / The Gods of the Copybook Headings with terror and slaughter return!"

—Rudyard Kipling, "The Gods of the Copybook Headings," 1919

Highway 441, Near Zellwood, Florida— January, the Third Year

The morning of January 22nd dawned with clear skies. It would be a sunny day. As the sky in the east lightened, a stack of photocopied one-page flyers was passed down the line, with the whispered words, "Share these—just one copy for every five men, pass them down."

The sheet read:

Instructions to Our Roadblock Ambushers

If we fail today, we'll be dead or slaves tomorrow.

Obey the orders of your Captains of Hundreds.

Noise, light, odor, and smoke discipline are essential.

If you need to poop, then dig a cat hole. (Odors can go a long distance.)

No smoking or talking above a low whisper.

Leave your rifle and shotgun chambers empty and safeties on.

If the ambush is sprung too early, we'll be out-flanked. Wait until they are right in the middle of the kill zone.

Keep on your bellies—you'll live longer.

DO NOT advance from behind cover at the trailers or up to the RR tracks until ordered.

Keep your heads down! This cannot be overemphasized.

DO NOT fire until you hear rapid firing at the front end of the ambush.

Take only well-aimed shots.

Concentrate on that front sight post: everything else should be somewhat blurry.

Keep shooting until all of the looters are dead. Once they drop, take very deliberate shots at any looters that are still moving. (And any that might be faking death.)

DO NOT advance into the ambush kill zone until ordered by the captains.

Stay down. This is NOT a traditional military ambush, so we will not immediately charge into the kill zone. Allow plenty of time to let the wounded looters bleed out before advancing.

Pray hard. Psalms 91. May God bless this endeavor.

(By mutual agreement, after concerted prayer)

—Mayor Lyle Jenkins—Mount Dora

—Mayor Byer Levin—Tavares

—Mayor Tom Martinson—Tangerine

As full daylight came, a few men nibbled on food from their pockets. Jake could now see the billboard sign better. It had been painted black, and both sides said RENT THIS SIGN, along with a phone number—yet another victim of the economic decline that had preceded the Crunch. Jake and Tomas shared a granola bar. As they did so, Tomas said, "I wish I had a helmet. That would double my life expectancy."

After a beat, Tomas continued. "I've been thinking about something. You know how you were teasing me about carrying too much gear? Well, one thing I've got in my ALICE pack is a couple of sandbags. When I was in the Marines, our battalion commander always insisted that each of us carry four sandbags. At first we hated that, since we were always humping around a ton of stuff, like we each also had to carry two mortar rounds. But those sandbags later turned out to be useful for a lot of things other than ballistic protection. For instance, we used them for packing speedballs."

"What's a speedball?" Jake asked.

Tomas explained. "That's something that both the Army and Marines use, depending on the tactical situation or terrain, when part of a unit is under fire, and the rest of the guys are masked by terrain. When the guys up front, who are pinned down and doing most of the shooting, call back for a speedball, you take a sandbag and put in a couple of bandoleers of 5.56, a belt box of 7.62, and a few water bottles, and carry it forward."

Jake looked incredulous. "You think we're going to get pinned down?"

"No, no, no. I'm just explaining why amongst all my other gear I have three sandbags in the bottom of my rucksack. I say we fill them with soil here, and then we can lay them on the railroad track to give us a few more vertical inches of frontal protection. Hey, we've got the time, and it might give us a slight advantage."

The man with the Mini-14 next to them chimed in. "I'll take that third bag, if you don't mind."

"Sure, no prob."

The three men spent the next fifteen minutes quietly scraping sandy soil into the olive drab nylon bags using Marichal's canteen cup as an impromptu shovel. Once the bags were filled, they used some black plastic cable zip ties from Jake's pack to close each of them.

More orders were passed down the line in a sporadic succession as the morning progressed:

"Don't panic if we get flanked. Mass your firepower."

"Looters are expected at ten thirty A.M."

"Share your water."

"Quiet."

"Looters are expected at eleven A.M."

"Pray for success."

"Quit grumbling and be patient."

"Keep your heads down or you'll ruin this ambush."

"Quiet."

"Looters are expected at ten thirty A.M."

"Keep your safeties on."

"Keep quiet."

"Looters have been sighted less than three quarters of a mile south."

"Keep your heads down."

It was now above seventy-five degrees and Jake was getting a headache. He continued to look in the direction of the highway. At 10:40, Jake heard the looter's armored bulldozer as it chugged toward the roadblock. The clanking of its steel tracks was almost as loud as its engine. Tomas started looking anxious. He took off his MARPAT field jacket and stuffed it into the top of his ALICE pack.

Soon they could all hear the chants of the advancing looters in the distance. The bulldozer passed by, and the vanguard of the looter army approached. The amount of noise that came from the looters was surprising. As they got closer, Jake could hear shuffling feet, conversation, laughter, clanking metal, wobbling shopping cart wheels, and intermittent chanting.

Tomas half rolled over to Jake and whispered just inches from his ear, "Yep, there are *lots* of them, but this is amateur hour."

Jake was also feeling warm, so he peeled off his field jacket, keeping his arms low. He quietly crept down to his rucksack and stowed the jacket. Then he pulled on the pack, trying to stay as close to the ground as possible. He handed Tomas his own pack, and he put it on. Once they were prone again, Tomas whispered, "Showtime, any moment."

He had just finished speaking when the deep reports of a Barrett semiauto .50 from the Lake County Sheriff's Department initiated the ambush. Just five shots from the Barrett aimed at the armored bulldoz-er's engine brought it to a screeching halt, in a cloud of black smoke, just twenty-five feet short of the roadblock trailers.

There was a crackle of gunfire, as the looters probed the tree line to the west of the roadblock where they thought the Barrett .50 shooter might be hidden. Then a whispered order came. "Low crawl to the tracks. Stay prone. Keep as quiet as possible." Jake crept forward up the berm, dragging his sandbag alongside him, in a leapfrogging motion. As he topped the railroad bed, he was startled by the sight of the huge number of looters, who were still ambling forward, nonchalantly. There were *thousands* of them. Then came an audible collective gasp from the looters, as the heads of the hundreds of ambushers came into view along the railroad tracks.

The second phase of the ambush began with an overwhelming roar of gunfire. This was the proverbial Mad Minute that Jake had often heard José and Tomas talking about. With the ambushers almost shoul-der to shoulder, the brass and fired shotshells came down like hail-stones. The firing started as a continuous roar. The looters immediately began to run, mostly to the rear and toward the field of tree stumps on the far side of the highway. Just a few of them had the discipline to drop to the ground in the grassy median between two stretches of the high-way pavement and return fire. But these men were all quickly targeted and shot.

Despite their numerical superiority, the looters were overwhelmed by the ambush. Most of them were in absolute panic. They ran, only to be cut down by the withering rifle and shotgun fire. Many of the looters were trampled by the weight of the sheer number of their fellows trying to flee.

Only a few looters ran *toward* their ambushers. Tomas later com-mented to Janelle, "Those were probably the handful that had military training and had been taught to *charge* an ambush. But they couldn't get through our wall of lead. Talk about a target-rich environment."

In a later conversation with Jake and José, Tomas also mentioned that the ambush had been "at least a full order of magnitude larger than anything I've ever seen in my *life*. It was devastating. And to see it all pulled off so well by a bunch of civilians was even more amazing."

The tempo of the firing gradually died down. The casualties among the ambushers were light. Only fifteen men were wounded and seven killed. Most of these were head, neck, arm, or shoulder wounds. Four of the head wounds were instantly fatal. Three men accidentally injured themselves with ricocheted bullet jacket fragments. By resting their scoped rifles' forends on the railroad track, they unwittingly put their rifle bores in alignment with the second track. Because the scopes were mounted parallel but two to three inches *higher* than the axis of their rifle bores, it *appeared* that they had clear shots, but some of their low-angle shots actually hit the track just an arm's length forward of their muzzles.

Jake and Tomas were virtually unscathed. Jake, however, did have a hot piece of .223 brass go down the collar of his shirt. It left a painful nearly horizontal red burn at the base of his neck in the perfect shape of the brass that would become a distinctive scar.

The ambush was a lopsided success. Dead looters were scattered across the highway lanes, the median, and in the adjoining fields in huge numbers. As the ambushers' rate of fire dropped to just sporadic shots, Jake could hear screams and moans from wounded looters.

The man next to Jake had a 3-9-power variable scope mounted on his Mini-14. He turned the ring of the scope to 9-power and then began deliberately scanning the bodies of the looters. He rested the forend of his Ruger on the sandbag that Tomas had given him for a steady aim. Whenever he saw a chest rising and falling, or any other sign of life, he would take a head shot. He continued this for fifteen minutes. After most men had finished shooting and busied themselves with reloading, the man in the Realtree cap shot another fifty rounds, changing maga-zines twice. During the second magazine swap, he muttered, "There are still a lot of them playing possum." The occasional rifle fire sounded up and down the line as others were taking similar coup de grâce shots.

About twenty minutes after the most intense firing of the ambush, an order was passed down the line: "Reload before the order to advance." Very few men needed this reminder. But there was still the clatter of many rifle actions as nervous men double-checked that their guns were fully loaded. Jake still had five loaded magazines, and Tomas had four. They deliberately shifted their empty magazines to the rearmost pouches on their web gear to avoid confusion.

A few yards down the line, a man shouted, "I'm down to two rounds. Any y'all got a spare M14 magazine for my M1A?" A loaded magazine was quickly passed down the line to him, with the proviso, "You owe me, big-time. Make every shot count."

Jake heard two similar requests made in rapid succession—one for .30-30 ammunition and one for .243 Winchester ammunition. Both requests were filled. Then a man just fifteen feet down from Jake and Tomas shouted, "I need some .25-06." After a pause, he said with greater urgency, "Does anyone have any .25-06, please? I've got *zero* rounds!"

Someone heckled. "You gotta be kidding. This ain't the wide-open prairie. You should have bought a .308."

A whistle was blown and the captains relayed the order down the line. "Forward!"

Nearly everyone stood up, many of them unsteady after so many hours in a prone position. A few stayed behind to tend the wounded. The ambushers pressed forward in an uneven skirmish line. There were sporadic shots as men shot at looters suspected of playing dead.

The bodies of many of the looters were in tangled clumps. Most of them were in the grassy median between the two paved lanes of the highway or in the field beyond. The smell of the blood and the smell of the feces were overpowering—as many of the looters had been shot through the intestines or had involuntarily soiled themselves. There was blood everywhere—far more than Jake Altmiller had expected. In places where the bodies were closest together, the ground was *flooded* with blood, collecting in bright red, half-inch-deep puddles that were already starting to turn black around their edges. A few of the ambushers vomited at the horrific sight.

As they walked forward, Tomas commented, "*Christo.* I seen a lot on my deployments, but never anything quite like this."

What surprised Jake the most was seeing all the stray shoes. Nearly everywhere he looked, there were shoes and sandals that the looters had lost in the panic of the ambush, especially in the tightly packed groups where they had trampled each other.

Less than a hundred of the looters had escaped into the woods at the southeast end of the ambush zone. The ambushers first checked all of the bodies for signs of life. There were many coup de grâce shots, mostly using pistols and revolvers since rifle ammunition was considered precious. Two unarmed black teenagers were found playing possum near the southeast of the ambush. The leaders of the ambush let them live so they could deliver a message. "You *run* back to Tampa and tell them what happened here, and warn them what happens to any looters who head up this-a-way."

Thousands of weapons and more than a hundred thousand rounds of ammunition were collected. A few of the guns had been rendered inoperable by bullet hits, but most of them were still serviceable, albeit sticky with blood. Others had been ruined—like shotguns with their barrels pierced by rifle bullets—but they could still be salvaged for valuable parts. Since the looters had outnumbered the ambushers so heavily, most of the men each went home with between one and four captured guns. Tomas picked up a parkerized Ithaca Model 37 Military and Police shotgun with an 8-round magazine. Aside from one notch in the bottom of the buttstock where a bullet had grazed it, the shotgun was in good working order. Jake got a Springfield Armory XD 40 pistol and three extra magazines. He also found a Kel-Tec SU-16 rifle beneath one of the bodies.

Seeing the Kel-Tec, Tomas declared, "Not the best, but at least those take standard AR or M16 magazines. That'll be good for barter." Tomas showed Jake how to unload the rifle and fold its stock. Once it was folded, the gun fit easily in Jake's rucksack with room to spare.

Stripping the guns, magazines, ammunition, and holsters from the looters turned into a chaotic grabfest. Tomas commented that it was like some giant piñata had burst and rained down guns and magazines. The nicest gun they saw recovered was a Tavor TAR-21—a bullpup configuration .223 rifle designed in Israel. The gun's new owner was ecstatic. The rapid-pace gun snatching was followed by countless impromptu barter transactions. One ambusher took the initiative to shout, "I got two AKs and a Glock .40 here. I'll trade all three of them for a FAL or an M1A." Everywhere around them, trades were being made. It looked incongruous to see this trading going on, as everyone was walking amidst so many lifeless bodies. As Jake later recounted the scene to Janelle, "It was like some strange flashback of the aftermath of a medieval battle, with the peasants stripping the swords and bows and armor from the bodies of the defeated army. It was just surreal."

Several uniformed police officers from Mount Dora and Tavares filled shopping carts with the less desirable guns that had been passed over. There were mostly single- and double-barreled shotguns and .22 rifles. Jake wondered whether the policemen had been ordered to do this, or whether they were just taking advantage of the situation for their own gain. In either case, no looters would have these weapons now.

Jake noticed that the man who had just been asking for .25-06 ammunition had found himself a CETME .308 rifle. The rifle looked a lot like an HK91, but it had a wooden stock and forend. Jake nodded to the man, and said, "That'll do. Scrounge as much .308 ball ammo as you can."

Tomas added his own advice. "You may have heard that CETME will also take G3 or HK91 magazines, but you might have to file on the mags a bit, depending on the receiver's tolerances." Jake always marveled at the depth and breadth of firearms knowledge that Tomas possessed.

After most of the ambushers had started walking homeward, a pair of D6 bulldozers were started and walked around the north end of the roadblock. With many successive passes, they cut a four-foot-deep trench for a length of 350 yards for a mass grave. A few of the most widely scattered bodies were dragged in by hand, but most of them were simply pushed into the grave with the bulldozer blades. Before the grave was refilled with earth, a Catholic minister gave a funeral oration.

Jake and Tomas didn't talk much as they walked home. Their elation at the success of the ambush was tempered by its bloody aftermath. Jake summed it up when he resignedly said, "It had to be done." He didn't sleep well for a month.

24

MADAGASCAR

"A very few—very few—isolated locations around the world, where it was possible to impose a rigid quarantine and where authorities did so ruthlessly, escaped the disease entirely. American Samoa was one such place. There not a single person died of influenza.

"Across a few miles of ocean lay western Samoa, seized from Germany by New Zealand at the start of the war. On September 30, 1918, its population was 38,302, before the steamer *Talune* brought the disease to the island. A few months later, the population was 29,802. Twenty-two percent of the population died."

—John M. Barry, *The Great Influenza*

Tavares, Florida—
January, the Third Year

Two days after the big ambush on Highway 441, Mayor Jenkins of Mount Dora and Mayor Levin of Tavares had a private meeting at Levin's home a few hundred yards east of the Ruby Street Grille. This was the fourth time they had a face-to-face meeting since the Crunch began. To get to the meeting, Mayor Jenkins motored west in his 14-foot Glasstream, a twenty-year-old boat that before the Crunch he had used mostly for fishing. After the Crunch, he found it was one the safest ways to travel without a bodyguard, so he often used it to get to meetings and to go barter for local produce.

Not only were the two mayors old friends, but they looked like book-ends. They were graying and pudgy, and both wore khaki pants. They were each native-born in their respective towns, and they had attended the University of Central Florida at the same time. Levin had earned a bachelor of science in criminal justice, while Jenkins had majored in business administration. Oddly, their bond didn't stem from being in the same fraternity or living in the same dormitory. It was because they were both country boys, and both commuted to the university. Unlike the rich city kids in the dorms, who were constantly partying, Levin and Jenkins were relatively sober and studious. And since they drove to their parents' homes each night, they always felt like *observers* of the campus life, rather than fully immersed participants. As commuter students, they developed their friendship in quiet conversation at the university library.

Their careers were different, but their success had been roughly parallel. Levin rose through the ranks of the Tavares Police Department to become chief of police. He was a savvy investor who had put all of his liquid assets in silver in 1999. Silver had bottomed two years later, but in subsequent years it had seen tremendous gains. Meanwhile, Jenkins had launched several businesses—which he sold in quick succession. When he was in his thirties he got the itch for politics, starting with the Mount Dora City Council and the County Board of Supervisors. Both men had married in their mid-twenties and then had small families. They both had homes on Lakeshore Drive, although Jenkins had a much larger one.

They first talked briefly about two familiar topics: finding sources of fuel that might be bartered, and developing markets to keep local citrus fruits and corn from going to waste. Then Mayor Jenkins adopted a more serious tone. "Some of the men who were in the two big reserves at the far ends of the ambush have complained that they were short-changed when the distribution of the weapons from the looters took place. Most of those reserve forces were composed of men—and a few ladies—from Bay Ridge and Plymouth Terrace. I've been hearing, in no uncertain terms, from the mayors in both towns. They're complaining they got *shorted*."

"Distribution? It was more like a free-for-all. It looked like that Free Cheese Day riot they had in Miami. We were both at the ambush and saw what happened. I think I was closer to the trailer roadblock than you were. Down at my end, during the 'distribution,' there were some harsh words, and even some shoving going on."

"Well, they still feel like they got shorted. So I think we ought to give them those shopping carts full of guns that our officers collected."

Mayor Levin nodded. "Fair enough. Let's throw 'em a bone. We'll give them each about a hundred guns. In fact, let's also offer Plymouth Terrace that armored bulldozer. It's not much use to either of us—since it is more offensive than defensive. It should be fairly easy for them to find another engine to put in it."

After nodding sharply and letting out a sigh, Byer Levin continued, "I have something much more important that we need to discuss, Lyle."

"What?"

"I had a long talk with my son this morning. As you know, he's a ham radio operator and my main source of information on the Big Picture, throughout the southeast and beyond. He's up past midnight most nights, scanning through the ham bands and international broadcast bands. He says there's report of a stomach flu, a *very bad* flu, that is working its way down the coast from the Northeast. It's now in the Carolinas. It's hard to tell exactly, but if all the chatter on the amateur nets is true, it is killing hundreds of thousands of people, and it may kill *millions* before it is done. And from the reports, it's not the flu itself that is the real killer, but rather the diarrhea that comes with it."

Lyle Jenkins looked stunned. "I think it's time to call 'Madagascar.'"

Byer cocked his head in question.

Lyle went on. "When I was younger, I used to play a computer game called *Pandemic II*. In that game, the president of Madagascar is always quick to isolate the country to prevent the encroachment of any pandemic. It kind of became a standing joke among gamers, and the term *Madagascar* even started being used by epidemiologists. 'Going Madagascar' is essentially slamming the doors shut—a total quarantine—in the hopes of avoiding the spread of an infectious disease. Since we have the lakes as natural barriers, we may have a chance."

"Then that's what we'll do."

Within a few days, the *soldados* manning the roadblocks around Mount Dora and Tavares had been given new instructions to turn back *everyone*, until further notice.

A new roadblock was set up on the bridge over the Dead River to the north, and they built up a heavy defensive line south of Mount Dora. Another new roadblock was established on the Lake Harris Bridge, on Highway 19. This isolated them from the town of Howey-in-the-Hills.

The mayors issued identical proclamations, calling for special precautions to be taken at shared wells, curtailing public gatherings, and urging frequent hand washing. The proclamations also asked all residents to salute each other rather than shake hands. This was reminiscent of the flu pandemic during World War I, when saluting also became the custom.

Though they were unpopular at first—since they stifled local commerce—the full quarantine roadblocks and other measures worked. While most cities and towns in Florida lost up to thirty percent of their populations in the two waves of flu that followed, Tavares and Mount Dora completely avoided the pandemic.

The pandemic die-off brought an end to large-scale looter forays out of Orlando. Afterward, the looters raids were never in groups larger than forty people. There were still substantial losses by the roadblock teams and QRTs in Tavares, but they could be sustained.

25

INTO THE DEEP

"Kriget är icke en ström eller en sjö utan ett hav med allt ont."
(Loosely translated: "War is not a river, or a lake, but an
ocean of all that is evil.")

—Gustavus Adolphus

On Board *Tiburon*, Celebes Sea—
November, the Second Year

On their third night of motoring through the Celebes Sea, Tatang's boat came close to several small low-lying islands. When they shut down the engine at dawn, the GPS showed that they were eight miles from the nearest island on their starboard side and eleven miles to another on their port side. As dawn broke, none of these islands could be seen over the horizon. But as the boat gradually drifted during the day, the palm tree cover of the nearest island came into view. By the late afternoon, they were feeling exposed.

As Joseph was preparing their evening meal, Rhiannon was alarmed to hear a boat motor in the distance. At first they couldn't determine the direction. Rhiannon broke out the binoculars and began scanning the horizon. Tatang pulled his M1 Garand rifle from its case and slipped a spare 8-round clip onto its sling, the bullet tips clinging like interwoven fingers. This gave him a quick reload close at hand.

The boat was approaching quickly from the west. The glare of the sunset masked their approach until they were less than five hundred yards away. Joseph started *Tiburon*'s engine. He instinctively brought the throttle forward and turned away from the approaching boat, presenting their stern to the intruders. Once it was obvious that the boat was headed directly toward them, Joseph pushed the throttle wide open.

The unknown boat was a black Woosung-Zebec 13-foot rigid inflatable, with a large outboard engine. Judging by the rapid speed at which they approached, it was obvious that they could outrun *Tiburon*. It was styled much like the classic Zodiac brand, but produced in South Korea. There were three ILF or Indo soldiers aboard and two of them were armed with Pindad SS2-V1 folding stock rifles.

Still holding the binoculars, Rhiannon declared, "They're wearing camos and they have long guns. They look like .223s." After a pause, she added, "I can spot for you, Tatang." She had grown up hunting deer and elk in British Columbia, so Peter didn't protest. He knew Rhiannon was better qualified for the job.

One of the men in the bow of the inflatable began firing even though they were out of effective range.

Tatang muttered, "No question now." He clicked the Garand's safety forward and took a wrap of the sling around his forearm. He shouted to Joseph, "Keep on a straight course!"

Joseph hunched down over the wheel. His Ruger 10/22 rifle lay across his lap with a 25-round magazine inserted. It would be better than nothing if they needed backup.

Tatang judged their distance at 450 yards away and closing. Both of the men in the bow of the inflatable were now firing in a rapid cadence, semiauto. *Tiburon* was still outside the range of their Pindad .223 rifles but well inside the effective range of a M1 Garand.

On board *Tiburon*, they began to hear bullets zipping over their heads. Kneeling at the stern rail, Tatang took careful aim and began to fire. With each shot, Rhiannon, kneeling beside him, observed with the sun-shaded binoculars and shouted a brief report: "Can't tell . . . Low . . . Can't tell . . . Two feet low . . . You got one—he's down!"

The Indonesian beside the man who had just been shot rolled to his side to change magazines. Tatang fired three more times. His second and third shots hit the exposed soldier. One of those bullets passed through his body and grazed the knee of the soldier at the rear, who was steering the boat. As Tatang fired his eighth shot, he heard the distinctive *ping* of the Garand ejecting its empty clip. He immediately reloaded the rifle with the spare clip hanging from the sling, nearly catching his thumb in the rifle's action in his haste. As he did so, the inflatable, now just three hundred yards astern, veered sharply to the left.

Joseph chopped the throttle, dipping *Tiburon*'s bow. Peter shouted, "They're running!"

The inflatable was now presented broadside to their stern. Both of the men in the bow were down, gushing blood. The pilot in the back of the boat was crouched down, doing his best to escape. Navarro resumed firing at a slightly faster tempo. Rhiannon, still spotting, reported, "Just behind him—lead a little."

Tatang fired again, and Rhiannon called the shot: "Just ahead of him."

The third and fourth shots both hit the soldier. "Hit in the chest. Hit in the head. He's down," said Rhiannon.

With the soldier's hand now off the outboard's spring-loaded throttle, it automatically "dead-manned" to a low idle, and the inflatable ceased throwing any wake.

"Come about, Joey, and bring us alongside, reeeaal slow," Tatang shouted to Joseph. The boy did as he was told.

As they got within one hundred yards, Tatang shouted to Joseph, "If you don't mind, I'm going to finish this up with your .22—the big rifle's ammo is too precious for this." Tatang handed his Garand to Peter and then reached over his shoulder to take the Ruger 10/22 that Joseph held forward.

When they were sixty yards from the inflatable, the elder Navarro resumed firing, with the much quieter .22 rimfire. The old man shot each of the Indonesian soldiers twice more, in the head. He said resign-edly, "We gotta be sure they're really dead." His last shot was fired when they were less than fifty feet away from the Woosung inflatable. After his final shot, he clicked the rifle's crossbolt safety and handed it back to Joseph.

Peter approached Rhiannon and laid a hand on her shoulder. "It had to be done." She nodded in reply, with tears welling up in her eyes.

They could see that there was just one rifle left in the Woosung. Any others had obviously been dropped overboard. The three Indo soldiers were in grotesque death postures. One of the men's jaws had flapped open unnaturally wide on one side, broken by a rifle bullet. The inflat-able boat was a blood-drenched mess.

Rhiannon turned to face her husband. Wiping away a tear, she said, "That's the first time I've ever spotted for someone with bullets coming back from the *other* direction. A bit too exciting." She gave a faint smile.

Peter said, "Yeah, the proverbial two-way shooting range."

Joseph throttled *Tiburon*'s engine back to a minimum and they crept up to the inflatable. Rhiannon said, "I'm going to go keep Sarah occu-pied down below."

Peter nodded. "Good idea."

Rhiannon handed the binoculars to Peter, who began scanning, mostly toward the island.

Tatang used a gaff hook to snag one of the lines that ran down the top of each of the inflation cells. Peter draped himself across the stern rail and held on to the gaff, which allowed Tatang to jump into the in-flatable. The old man did so with a catlike grace that surprised Jeffords.

Joseph said, "I've never seen so much blood, coming from people. Looks like the floor of the *carneceria* on a slaughter day."

Working quickly, Tatang picked up the only remaining SS2 rifle and rotated its safety lever leftward to what he presumed to be the safe posi-tion. He pointed the muzzle skyward and gave the trigger a pull. It didn't move. "She's safe."

Tatang handed the rifle up to Joseph, butt first. He quickly stripped off the web gear harnesses from the three bodies. The harnesses each had four magazine pouches.

There was no question of taking the boat with them. Not only was it now obviously leaking from multiple .30-06 bullet hits, but there was blood everywhere.

Tatang grabbed a rubberized haversack and one empty rifle magazine from the floor of the boat. That left just the bodies and the outboard engine, which was still gurgling. Tatang took another look around the inflatable and then disconnected its four-gallon gas tank. He handed it up to Joseph, saying, "Gas can't work in our engine, but it still could come in handy, maybe to trade." Last, he flicked open his *balisong* folding knife and slashed down the length of both inflation cells—from stem to stern. He spun the knife with a flourish, returning it to a closed position, and tucked it back into his front pocket.

As he stepped back up into *Tiburon*, holding on to the gaff, his feet were already under five inches of water. Starved for fuel, the outboard engine sputtered to a stop. Less than a minute later, the boat slipped beneath the water. The bodies went down with it, although they seemed to linger near the surface while the boat disappeared rapidly out of sight. The weight of the big outboard engine had dragged the deflated boat down, stern first. A few large bubbles escaped from the cells as it sank.

Tatang and Peter paused for a moment to watch the boat's descent in horrified fascination as a few more bubbles rose to the surface of the red-stained water.

Joseph restarted *Tiburon*'s engine. The sun was below the horizon, and the sky was already starting to darken. Navarro gave his nephew directions. "Steer southeast, with the full throttle."

Washing the blood, intestinal contents, and brain matter off of the rifle, web gear, gas tank, and Tatang's shoes required bucket after bucket of seawater. After the fifth bucket, Peter brought a stiff bristle brush up from below deck. It took them another twenty minutes and many more buckets of seawater to get everything cleaned up.

That evening, Tatang took the wheel. Working below, Peter patiently cleaned and oiled the SS2 rifle. He recognized its design. It used the same gas system as the famous FN FAL, but it was scaled down for the smaller 5.56 mm NATO cartridge—the same cartridge used in M16 rifles. Unlike a FAL, the rifle's charging handle was on the right-hand side. Peter would have preferred it to be on the left, like a FAL, since manipulating the bolt on this rifle required either reaching over the top of the receiver with his left hand or removing his firing hand from the pistol grip.

Joseph's cleaning rod for his .22 caliber Ruger rifle worked passably well in cleaning the bore of the new rifle. Rhiannon, Joseph, and Sarah watched with rapt interest as Peter worked. They asked occasional questions about the rifle and its shooting characteristics. The mechanics of the SS2 were easy to figure out, except for its folding stock, which required some practice to push down to rotate shut. Opening the stock was quick and easy, but Peter found folding the stock to be more cumbersome. Rhiannon thought the rifle's spring-loaded action dust cover was especially clever. The rifle's safety selector was of particular interest. It had three positions—the third one was for full-automatic fire. This was the first time Peter had ever handled a fully automatic weapon and the "cool" factor took a long time to wear off. Overall, he was pleased with the rifle.

Because they'd been drenched by seawater, cleaning all of the magazines took longer than cleaning the rifle itself. With the help of Rhiannon and Joseph, each magazine was emptied of its cartridges and then each cartridge individually dried with rags. Each round was carefully rubbed down with coconut oil and then redried with a fresh rag. This time-consuming process took an hour and used up nearly all of Tatang's bundle of rags.

Almost as an afterthought, Peter realized that the magazines could also be disassembled and cleaned. It took him a while to figure out how to slide off the floorplates from the magazines. He used a rag wrapped around a foot-long nipa shaft to dry and then oil the inside of each magazine body, rubbing down their springs, again with coconut oil.

Peter and Joseph reloaded three of the magazines with thirty cartridges each and bagged up the rest of the ammo and the spare magazines. They would need to reinspect them for the next several days,
given the highly corrosive nature of salt water. Jeffords also decided to
let the magazine pouches dry for several days before reinserting any
magazines. In all, there were fourteen magazines for the rifle, and 362
live cartridges.

As Peter finished his work, Joseph looked admiringly at the rifle.
"Mr. Jeffords, God has been good to us. He has delivered us *twice* from
the Indos. And now we have another good rifle with plenty of ammo."

Peter nodded. "And that's the way the Lord provides for his Cove-
nant People. We are undeserving, unworthy, and little better than unre-
pentant sinners. Yet he cares for us, and protects us. We are truly
blessed, and we can only credit all this to Christ Jesus. He died for us."

Joseph grinned broadly. "Amen and amen."

26

SHIPSHAPE

"When all is said and done, Civilizations do not fall because of the barbarians at the gates. Nor does a great city fall from the death wish of bored and morally bankrupt stewards presumably sworn to its defense. Civilizations fall only because each citizen of the city comes to accept that nothing can be done to rally and rebuild broken walls; that ground lost may never be recovered."

—Bill Whittle, "The Undefended City"

On Board *Tiburon*, Celebes Sea—November, the Second Year

On four more occasions, they spotted the lights of small boats in the distance. After determining their courses, they would steer away and bring the engine to full throttle. This brought *Tiburon* up to twelve knots, which was a respectable speed. It wouldn't outrun many boats, but it could outrun some.

They assumed that Palau was already in the hands of the Indonesians, so they avoided making landfall there. Far on the westward horizon, they could see smoke rising from fires in East Timor. Apparently the Indonesians were mopping up the last of the resistance there.

Rhiannon was suffering less often from seasickness, but the frequent bouts of diarrhea had taken their toll. She started their voyage weighing 135 pounds, but she was down to around 120 pounds—they had no way to be sure. Peter had never seen her look so slim, even when they had first met.

Not wanting to attract a lot of attention from customs and immigration officials—since neither Joseph nor his grandfather had passports—they set their course toward Wyndham, a small town 275 kilometers southwest of Darwin.

As Peter was piloting, Tatang Navarro sat next to the wheel. "I don't want us to get deported. You know, we can wait and come in at night to drop you off, and then I can take *Tiburon* back out into deep water and scuttle her if we have to," Tatang suggested.

Jeffords shook his head, and said reassuringly, "I really doubt that will be necessary. Just pray that we'll be well received by the immigration authorities."

Their fuel was running low. The good news was that, after burning most of *Tiburon*'s fuel and after having consumed nearly all their drinking water, the boat was now five thousand pounds lighter than when they left Samar and sitting much higher in the water. They were now making ten knots at three-quarter throttle instead of the seven to eight knots that they had averaged for the first half of the voyage. It had been thirty-two days since they left Quinapondan.

Tatang left Peter at the wheel while he went to repack his gear. He first snatched his laundry off the clothesline and then went below. There, he disassembled his M1 Garand rifle and wrapped the three components in his spare blue jeans, tucking them in his large duffel bag along with the flare gun and all of the remaining .30-06 ammunition and the flares. He had Joseph stow his Ruger .22, ammo, and magazines in a similar way.

As Tatang took the wheel again, he said to Peter, "Joey and I just hid the guns in our luggage. I sure hope we don't have to go through any customs *tae ng bull*."

Jeffords shook his head. "Probably not. That's one reason we picked such a small port."

Rhiannon cleared the rest of the clothes from the line and started to

spruce up the boat. The realization that they would soon be under public gaze spurred her to do some long-neglected cleaning—even scrub-
bing the spot on the foredeck where Joseph usually cleaned the fish.

As they entered the bay, Rhiannon poured the very last of the palm
oil and the last quart of corn oil into the main fuel tank. It looked less
than a quarter full. She said resignedly, "After this, that's all she wrote."
They also had less than one gallon of water and enough food to last perhaps two more days—just a few dried fish and a couple of cups of dried
rice that was starting to go green. The propane for their cookstove had
run out two days before.

Commenting on their scant fuel and food, Peter said, "Is that cutting
it close, or what? Thank you, Lord!" Looking at the chart and comparing it to the GPS readings, Joseph said, "We should be at the port of
Wyndham in less than two hours, Lord willing."

Tatang throttled back to five knots and they picked their way into
the inland waters. The waterway was broad and sheltered, but unfamiliar. They consulted the chart, GPS, and depth finder frequently as they
worked their way toward the Cambridge Gulf, and then south along to
Wyndham. Much of the shoreline was flanked with mud flats and salt
ponds. The portions of the shore with vegetation were dotted with
oddly shaped boab trees.

"How's the fuel, exactly?" Tatang asked.

Rhiannon uncapped the tank and lowered the bamboo dipstick with
practiced precision. Pulling it up, it showed less than an inch of coconut
oil clinging to the end. She said, "Not a lot—maybe three or four
gallons—but we don't have far to go now. If for some reason we have to
divert to Darwin, there is no way we could make it there without refueling. It's all or nothing now."

Peter Jeffords attributed the timing of the food, fuel, and water supplies to Divine Providence. During the last few hours of their journey,
he and Rhiannon hummed and sang the church chorus *Jehovah Jireh*
several times. Tatang and Joseph weren't familiar with it, so they taught
them the words:

"Jehovah Jireh, my provider,
His grace is sufficient for me
For me, for me.
Jehovah Jireh, my provider,
His grace is sufficient for me.

"The Lord shall provide all my needs
According to His riches in Glory,
The Lord shall provide Himself a lamb for sacrifice,
Jehovah Jireh takes care of me
Of me, of me."

Peter generally liked older Baptist hymns, preferring them to most modern praise choruses. He found the latter largely vain and repetitious. As he often put it, "Most praise choruses have a shortage of good doctrine and a surplus of personal pronouns." But "Jehovah Jireh" was one chorus that he *did* like, and he couldn't get it out of his mind in the last few hours of their voyage.

Finally, the sleepy port of Wyndham came into view. The town had less than seven hundred residents and most of them lived inland in the new development of Wyndham East—also known as Wyndham Three Mile—rather than in Old Wyndham. As they pulled up to the town's looping commercial pier, it was just after three P.M. local time. The elevated pier had a paved roadway with several cranes dotted along it and a fuel terminal tower at the south end. There was an empty barge tied up at the center of the pier. Just two yachts were tied up, both at the north end. Nine others—small coastal yachts—were anchored offshore, strung out to the south. Jeffords assumed that their owners were using free anchorage. A row of pallets with shining zinc ingots stood near the center of the pier, being readied for shipment.

The sight of their large distinctive outrigger boat caused a bit of a stir. Tatang expertly maneuvered *Tiburon* to nose her into the pier, just beyond the prow of one of the yachts. Because of the projecting carags, the boat was limited to docking at either the fore or aft.

As Joseph tossed up a mooring line, an aboriginal man on the pier shouted to them, "Where have you lot come from?"

"Samar Island, in the Philippines," Peter replied. "There's a world of Muslim jihad hurt going on up there."

"Yeah, so we've heard. You must be a Yank."

Peter answered. "Yes, I'm from New Hampshire. My wife is originally from Western Canada. We're missionaries."

Another man from the crowd asked, "Is it true the Indonesians are invading the Philippines?"

"I haven't seen that firsthand, but they are definitely using the ILF guerillas as their surrogates. One thing is for certain: The ILF guerillas are killing every Christian they can find in the Philippines."

The crowd was growing on the north end of the pier, gawking at *Tiburon* and listening attentively. About half of them were aboriginal dockworkers and fuel terminal workers.

Peter announced to the crowd, "I'm here to warn you, folks. In less than a year, or perhaps less than that, you can expect to see the Indonesian Navy in these waters, planning an invasion." This sparked a loud murmur in the crowd.

Peter and Rhiannon felt nervous to have the crowd gazing at them, but their anxiety was overshadowed by immense relief to be in port and among English-speaking people. At last they were safe.

27

WYNDHAMITES

"Never forget, even for an instant, that the one and only reason anybody has for taking your gun away is to make you weaker than he is, so he can do something to you that you wouldn't let him do if you were equipped to prevent it. This goes for burglars, muggers, and rapists, and even more so for policemen, bureaucrats, and politicians."

—Aaron Zelman and L. Neil Smith, *Hope*, 2001

Wyndham, Western Australia— Late November, the Second Year

Peter and Joseph snugged up the mooring lines at the pier while Tatang shut down the engine. They began unloading the suitcases from *Tiburon*, carrying them up a ribbed aluminum gangway ramp, which had rollers at the end to adjust for the tide. A woman from the crowd stepped up to Rhiannon and said, "My name is Vivian and you're all welcome to stay at our house in Wyndham East while you get things sorted out."

"God bless you, ma'am," Rhiannon replied.

They were told that the pier was primarily used for exports of live cattle, cattle hides, lead, and zinc. The barge nearby was laden with zinc ingots nominally bound for South Korea, but the shipment was delayed by the international financial turmoil. The pier operator offered them three nights of free anchorage at the pier or indefinite free anchorage amid the larger group of yachts farther out, where a skiff would be required to reach them. Tatang opted for the latter.

After they had unloaded the baggage and their two GPS receivers, they borrowed a skiff from the harbormaster and anchored *Tiburon* using a permanent buoy at the fore end and a concrete anchor at the aft.

With the engine still hot, Tatang gingerly removed the Mitsubishi engine's fuel pump and wrapped it in rags and then a pair of bread bags. The pump went into his duffel bag. He told Jeffords, "Nobody is starting her motor without this."

Vivian soon had them and their bags loaded in her Toyota Estima minivan. Rhiannon was impressed with how quickly and with such wordless economy of motion the woman attached the baggage to the car's roof rack with bungee cords. She looked like she had a lot of experience doing it. Her full name, she said, was Vivian Edwards. Her husband, Alvis Edwards, was a broker in both salt and exotic hardwoods.

In just a few minutes, they were at Vivian's home in Wyndham East. It was a large house and one of the few in town that had a swimming pool. The great room was lined with taxidermied trophy heads from three continents—mostly from Africa. A childless couple, the Edwards' passion was big game hunting. Vivian told them that they had taken many hunting trips to Africa, Canada, the United States, and even Argentina. The floor was mostly covered with tanned hides of everything from bears to zebras. The backs of the couches were draped with gazelle hides. Joseph spent a long time examining the trophy mounts. Neither he nor the Jeffords had ever seen a private trophy mount collection of such magnitude before and they were fascinated. Tatang observed that it was like walking into a museum. To Rhiannon, it was reminiscent of the living room of the house near Bella Coola where she had grown up, though her old house had a much smaller number of deer, elk, and caribou mounts.

Vivian phoned her husband to summon him home early from work.

Alvis arrived a half hour later, eagerly looking forward to meeting his new house guests and hearing about their voyage.

For dinner, Alvis barbequed some large kudu steaks. The steaks had been in their freezer since before the Crunch from their most recent safari in Botswana, sent by air freight to Australia packed in dry ice at considerable expense. After several years of big game hunting abroad, Alvis learned a way—through a friendly local veterinarian—to get around Australia's labyrinthine quarantine laws. Hides and horns were not particularly difficult, but importing frozen meat required including some key phrases in the paperwork and one additional form.

Over the steaks, Alvis commented, "I get a laugh when I hear tourists say they 'went on safari' but all they took were pictures. A camera safari is not a *real* safari."

They were all served water with dinner. Sarah asked for milk, but since the Edwards didn't keep any in their refrigerator, she received a small glass of cream. "We do drink a *little* wine from time to time, but we are careful," Vivian explained. "You know what the Good Book says. 'Wine is a mocker.' It often takes us three or even four dinners for the two of us to use up one bottle."

Both Alvis and Vivian had their speech peppered with foreign words and turns of phrase that they'd picked up on their many overseas hunting trips. For example, they used the Afrikaans word *braai* instead of "barbeque," the Shona word *chirairo* for "dinner," and the Swahili words *karibu* for "welcome" and *samahani* to say "excuse me."

Most of the afternoon and evening was spent with Peter Jeffords providing a detailed account of their journey. The Edwards listened with rapt attention. Their many questions kept Peter so occupied that he was last to finish eating his meal.

After dinner, Sarah was invited to open up the old steamer trunk that served as a toy box. The Edwards kept the box on hand to entertain their nieces and nephews when they came to visit. The toys kept Sarah busy and quiet while Peter and Rhiannon carried on with their tales of adventure. They moved to the living room, where Vivian served coffee and lamingtons—a chocolate-covered cube of sponge cake rolled in dried coconut.

When Peter got to the part of their tale where they had their first shooting encounter with the Indonesians, Alvis couldn't help but interject.

"What were you shooting with?" he asked.

"Tatang's rifle, an M1 Garand. It's an American service rifle that shoots the big .30-06 cartridge," Peter replied.

"Oh, you don't have to explain what an M1 is to me. I used to own one of them, made by International Harvester, it was. But I had to turn it in back in 1996, along with all of my other semiautomatics and pumps after the Port Arthur shootings. That was one of the most heartbreaking days of my life. I turned in five guns for the smelter. That ban is still a very sore point with me. I've switched to all bolt actions, double guns, and few single shots."

Alvis cleared his throat and continued, "I was already cheesed off by the ban, and now that I hear that the Indos may be coming to invade us, I'm even angrier. All of our citizenry's really *effective* guns have been melted down and turned into jaff irons. Those do-gooder socialist Labor dimwits in Canberra have set us up to take a shellacking."

After a pause, Alvis looked at Tatang. "Do you still have that rifle with you, or did you drop it into the drink before you came into port?"

Tatang laughed and pointed to their pile of luggage in the front hall. "No, sir. That rifle, she is disassembled there in my duffel bag. Am I gonna get arrested for that?" he asked with a wry smile.

Alvis shook his head. "Those were banned for many years, but that ban was just repealed. However, I don't know precisely what the legalities are for someone who isn't a citizen. You'd best keep very quiet about it." Then he leaned forward and in an exaggerated conspiratorial whisper said, "Our lips are sealed."

"What about getting entry visas?" Rhiannon asked. "Tatang and Joseph don't have passports. Can you make any recommendations?"

"No worries at all," Alvis answered. "My brother-in-law is with the post office—they handle passports around here and he knows all the Border Protection Service people. Rest assured that I'll have him dummy up your Department of Foreign Affairs or BPS paperwork and also put in a good word for you with the Department of Immigration and Citizenship. After what you've been through, you certainly don't deserve any bureaucratic aggro. You've got a strong case for claiming religious persecution."

"Yes, I suppose that those thousands of summary decapitations *might* qualify as a form of persecution," Rhiannon said drily.

When Peter mentioned that Tatang had been teaching them Pekiti-Tirsia Kali, Alvis interrupted Peter. "Can you show me a bit of that, here and now?"

"Well, we barely have our land legs, but I'm willing. How about you, Paul Timbancaya?"

Tatang half shouted, "Sure!"

They quickly moved a coffee table out from between the couches, and the two men demonstrated strikes and parries. Then, using two rolled-up *SAFARI* magazines, they demonstrated knife fighting and disarming techniques. The last one ended with Tatang twisting Peter's arm and driving him down to the floor with an elbow strike. Peter lay on a sable hide gasping, while Tatang simulated slitting his throat with three slashes of the coiled magazine. Everyone cheered and clapped.

Alvis stood up and exclaimed, "That was a corker! Could we pay you to teach us lessons as well?"

Tatang frowned and then gave a hesitant nod. "I suppose so."

Their conversation went on until ten P.M. An hour earlier, Sarah had already curled up on the couch with a stuffed wallaby from the toy trunk—a *real* taxidermied wallaby—and fallen asleep.

28

THE UTE

"If a thing is old, it is a sign that it was fit to live. Old families, old customs, old styles survive because they are fit to survive. The guarantee of continuity is quality. Submerge the good in a flood of the new, and good will come back to join the good which the new brings with it. Old-fashioned hospitality, old-fashioned politeness, old-fashioned honor in business had qualities of survival. These will come back."

—Eddie Rickenbacker

Wyndham, Western Australia— Late November, the Second Year

Their stay at the Edwards home was comfortable. The two guest bedrooms and a cot in the den easily accommodated them. The next morning, Rhiannon was amazed to see colorful Gouldian finches flitting around in the shrubbery of the yard, followed by a pair of wild Sulphur Crested Cockatoos landing in the tree outside her window. As a birder, these sightings were thrilling for Rhiannon.

"Do you know how much a cockatoo like that sells for in the States?" she asked Vivian.

Mrs. Edwards shook her head. "Thousands, I suppose. They're considered pests here. A big flock of them can do a farm a lot of damage, ricky tick."

When Rhiannon came back into the house, she found Peter and Tatang in a deep discussion. "Tatang has decided to sell his boat," Peter announced.

After Alvis drove to work, Vivian drove Peter, Tatang, and Joseph back to the Wyndham docks. They carried several empty boxes with them and a large For Sale sign that had the phone number for the Edwards's home on it.

They borrowed a skiff, and the three men paddled out to *Tiburon*. Meanwhile, Vivian waited in the minivan and practiced with one of her *Let's Learn Afrikaans* audio CDs.

Not knowing if it would be days, weeks, or months before the boat might sell, they took down the canvas awnings and stowed them below. Then they methodically removed the remaining tools, books, food, spices, memorabilia, and other personal effects from the boat and tidied it up. They left the solar trickle charging the batteries and the automatic bilge pump switched on. With the tiny leak at the propeller shaft seal, Tatang estimated that the bilge pump would cycle only once every nine or ten days.

The cardboard For Sale sign was taped up on the rear awning mast. They left the cabin looking shipshape before closing the storm hatch and locking it. As they paddled away, the elder Navarro said, "Goodbye, *Tiburon*. You've been a good boat and you got us here safe." He looked skyward, and added, "Thank you, Lord." Joseph gave his grandfather a hug, and they both smiled. They were sad to give up the boat, but they knew they badly needed some Australian currency. And because Navarro was unfamiliar with fishing in Australia and lacked the money to buy fuel or new fishing nets, it was unrealistic to think they could go back to fishing to earn their living.

After they were back at the house, Vivian helped Tatang write a bill of sale with the line for the purchaser's name left blank. The boat had no formal registration papers.

On faith, Paul Navarro gave Vivian the signed bill of sale, the cabin storm-hatch key, and the fuel pump.

In an exception to normal policy, the Department of Immigration and Citizenship representative flew from Darwin to Wyndham, rather than having the Jeffords and Navarros report to the local Immigration office. The manager of the local Wyndham office was miffed and started to complain, but he was told that the Australian Security Intelligence Organisation (ASIO) had taken an interest in the case. The department wanted a more senior man to handle the investigation.

The Immigration officer's flight from Darwin was in a Pilatus bush plane that was owned and operated by his second cousin. He tried to give his cousin plenty of business since he always provided reliable, punctual service at the going rate. Plus, the Pilatus was an excellent plane that was capable of takeoffs and landings on very short airfields. He felt quite safe as a passenger in it, especially with his cousin at the controls.

The Protection Assessment interview was conducted over a barramundi luncheon at the house. The Immigration officer, Ralph Simmonds, was a portly and jovial man in his fifties. As expected, the interview turned into a repeat of the Jeffords' story of their escape from Samara, but conspicuously absent of any mention of their possession or use of firearms.

"That is an exceptional story, and you are an exceptional case, indeed," said Simmonds. "You surely deserve a fair go. In my estimation, all five of you are entitled to Class XA visas. It's our special humanitarian Onshore Protection visa and it's what we've been giving the Timorese who have arrived by boat. I have no doubt we'll see some more refugees from the Philippines in the months to come, but being the first to arrive on the north coast this year by sea, you are getting *capo d'astro* treatment. I do want you to do me a favor, however. I'd like you to write a detailed report of what you heard from that Catholic priest and what you've seen with your own eyes for me to forward to some officials in the Australian Security Intelligence Organisation at Canberra. Don't be surprised if ASIO sends some of their boys up here to debrief you as well. What you've said about the possible invasion of Australia is troubling, *troubling* to say the least."

After a pause, he said, "I'll be providing a statement to Customs.

Your baggage and boat have already been inspected." He then added with a wink, "I inspected them myself."

Simmonds turned to Tatang and Joseph. "You will both shortly be issued a Travel Document in Lieu of Passport, as well as visa labels. I'll make sure that they are fully renewable. Welcome to Australia."

Once Simmonds had left, Alvis asked, "So, you are planning to go to Darwin?"

Peter nodded. "Yes, we'll probably just thumb rides. We travel by faith."

Alvis shook his head. "Hitchhiking in Australia is frowned upon. It isn't nearly as easy as in the P.I. or in the United States, particularly for a large group. With five of you and all your bags, you might have trouble finding even a truckie that would have enough room to give you a ride. And there are no scheduled buses—only charters and those are costly."

Vivian gave Alvis a glance with a cocked head. He nodded in response. "I have a little ute in my garage that I could give you. It would be yours to keep."

Peter looked surprised. "A yoot?"

"A utility truck. We call them utes."

"That is extremely generous of you, sir," said Peter.

Alvis laughed. "Don't thank me until you've seen the ghastly thing. It is about ready to rust out, I'm afraid. That Datsun is already wearing its second ute bed. Utilities don't last long in my line of work. The air at the salt yards is a real killer."

When Alvis opened the garage door, Peter could see what he meant. The truck was indeed quite rusty, with crescent-shaped rings of rust around the wheel wells. The rust was so bad that there were even holes in the worst parts of the rust patches. The hood was also deteriorating badly.

Edwards started the pickup and backed it out into the driveway. There was a hole on the muffler, so it was noisy. "I'm afraid that she'll whistle and rattle if you get it up over seventy klicks," he shouted.

The front half of the truck was painted white, but the back half was yellow. When asked about this, Alvis explained, "In the salt business, the ute beds always rust out first. So it's not unusual for us to buy a replacement ute bed from a wreckers."

That evening they went to see a movie at the Wyndham Picture Garden, an outdoor movie theater run by volunteers. They used the outing as a shakedown run for the Datsun. Most of the moviegoers brought folding camping chairs, but some preferred to sit in their cars. Two groups of teenagers brought couches in the back of their utes and parked with the sides of their trucks facing the screen. It was illegal to ride in the back of an open pickup in Australia, but it was explained to them that many rules were enforced "quite casually" in the more remote regions of Western Australia and the Northern Territory.

As they were packing for their journey to Darwin, Alvis handed Peter the title papers for the Datsun. Then he went back to the house and carried out two green metal ammunition cans. "This is some .30-06 ammunition for you. I don't own an oh-six rifle any longer, so this ammo is of no use to us. Most of it is loaded in Garand clips. I've got to warn you, though, it is mostly old U.S. military stuff, so you can assume that it has corrosive primers. With that priming, you'll have to clean your rifle very tidily after shooting it."

Handing Tatang the cans, Alvis quipped, "Who knows, someday you may need this ammo if the Indos or the Chinese come to visit."

Alvis had to leave for work before they had finished packing the Datsun. He shook hands and said his good-byes. He left them with his standing joke. "Well, back to the salt mines."

Since they had no Australian currency, Vivian gave them five hundred AUD in cash so they'd have enough money for fuel. Peter offered to return it, but Vivian insisted it was a gift. Their American and Philippine currency was worthless, but Australian dollars still held most of their value and were generally accepted. Before they left, Vivian gave Rhiannon a hug. "Call me if you need any help at all. May God bless you, no matter where you alight."

They followed the route that Vivian programmed into Tatangs's GPS. The roads were narrow and substandard until they reached Kununurra. The 560-mile drive from Wyndham to Darwin went well except for a leaking top radiator hose. As they neared the town of Katherine, steam coming from under the hood signaled that something was amiss. They stopped and found that the top radiator hose had split. They refilled the white plastic radiator filler tank with most of their remaining drinking water. It was just four miles to Katherine, so they drove to a Mobil Oil station to get help.

Even before a petrol station attendant came around front to help, Joseph declared, "I think the hose is long enough that we can just shorten it. I saw this same thing happen once with my friend Honesto's Jeepney."

After buying fuel and allowing the engine to cool down, they rolled the Datsun to the side of the station. They were indeed able to shorten the hose using Tatang's *balisong* knife. With a screwdriver from the *Tiburon* toolkit, they were able to detach and reattach the hose clamp. As they worked, the station attendant quizzed them, asking about their escape from the Philippines. He was fascinated. Sarah ran and skipped around the pickup, gleefully singing "This Little Light of Mine." By the time they had refilled the radiator and checked for leaks, it was nearly dark. The attendant kindly gave them a dozen used plastic soda bottles so they would have extra water for the radiator on hand for the remainder of their trip.

It was still 155 miles to Darwin, so they decided to spend the night in Katherine. The service station attendant told them that the least expensive hotel was just east of town on the Stuart Highway. The rooms, he said, were around one hundred AUD per night. After their fuel expenses en route, they knew they couldn't afford the lodging and asked the station attendant if there were any other options. "No worries. My uncle is the bishop of the Anglican church here in Katherine. He'll find rooms for you for the night," he said blithely.

They went to sleep that night saying prayers of thanks for God's travel mercies.

29

LODGINGS

"Throughout history, poverty is the normal condition of man. Advances which permit this norm to be exceeded—here and there, now and then—are the work of an extremely small minority, frequently despised, often condemned, and almost always opposed by all right-thinking people. Whenever this tiny minority is kept from creating, or (as sometimes happens) is driven out of a society, the people then slip back into abject poverty. This is known as 'bad luck.'"

—Robert A. Heinlein, *Time Enough for Love*

Katherine, Northern Territory, Australia— Late November, the Second Year

They had breakfast just after first light the next morning. Their host was a retired baker who never got out of the habit of getting up early. After a "brekky" of lamb chops, eggs, and biscuits, they were on the road at eight thirty A.M.

After driving to Darwin, Peter asked directions to the Presbyterian Reformed church, which was doctrinally the closest to his "sending" church in New Hampshire. They were told that the church met on Sundays at the music auditorium of Kormilda College on Berrimah Road. After further inquiries, he was given the phone number of the pastor. Using a borrowed smartphone, Peter called the pastor, and after a brief introduction and explanation of how they got to Australia, the pastor gave them directions to his home.

They spent the full evening with the pastor and his family. The pastor and his wife were originally from New Zealand. He was a very likable man who immediately welcomed the Jeffords and Navarros as if they were long-lost cousins. Before retiring for the night, Rhiannon used the pastor's smartphone to send a text message to Vivian Edwards to let them know the address and phone number where they were staying.

Within a few days, the pastor had found places for them to rent and lined up work for the men. Tatang Navarro was offered a twenty-hour-per-week job as a FMA instructor at the Powerpit Gym in Alawa. Joseph got a thirty-two-hour-per-week job at the same gym—with his time divided between duties as towel boy in the evenings at the front desk, and doing janitorial work after hours. Eventually, he transitioned away from the janitorial duties into a position as a part-time FMA instructor. They lived in a small apartment in Alawa that was within walking distance of the gym. Since they had hardly any Australian currency, Tatang was given a modest cash advance on his first paycheck.

The Navarros' apartment had a kitchen that looked like it was modeled in the late 1960s. Its curved kitchen counter provided lots of dead space behind the cabinets where Tatang was able to construct a hidden compartment to conceal his M1 Garand, Joseph's Ruger .22, the flare gun, and all of the ammunition. The owner of a flower shop gave Paul some bags of silica gel, a desiccant that protected the guns from rust. By putting the silica bags in the oven overnight on low heat, moisture could be driven out to reactivate the silica.

Ten days after they had settled into their apartment, Tatang found a parcel on his doorstep when he came home from work. It was marked NORTHERN TERRITORY COURIERS & MAIL SERVICES. Inside was a box that had been mailed to Darwin from Wyndham.

He opened the inner box and found a cell phone, two cell phone chargers (one AC and one DC), an envelope full of cash, and an envelope containing a letter. The letter read:

Dear Tatang Navarro, Joseph, and the Jeffords Family,

We've been praying that all is well with you in Darwin.

All is well here. Alvis talked with everyone that he knew about finding a buyer for your boat. He did find a neighbor who has always been keen on fishing but who had never owned a boat of his own. Alvis cajoled him into buying yours. He really talked up its seaworthiness and the reliability of its engine.

The gent asked to take it for a test run first. They got the fuel pump back on it straight away, and the engine started immediately. But then it died after idling for just a few minutes. They discovered that it was <u>out</u> of fuel. That shows you how narrowly you sliced things when you arrived at Wyndham! Long story short, they refilled the fuel tank with diesel (which costs a lot these days), reprimed it, and then the engine ran marvelously. He gave $6,200 AUD for the boat, which was a higher figure than we had discussed. So I trust that you will find that satisfactory. In addition to the cash, I have enclosed the gift of a mobile, with 750 prepaid minutes, so you and the Jeffords have no excuse but to keep in touch with us. (You will see it has our number programmed.)

By the by, they've already been out fishing twice on the boat (the second time with us) in deep water with heavy tackle. On their first foray they caught nothing but sharks. (Apropos, I suppose, given the boat's name.) But on the second trip we hit a spot of ~~luck~~ <u>Providence</u> and landed several large fish, including a giant trevally and three tuna. The largest of the tuna weighed more than 300 pounds! It was all quite the thrill.

Let us know if there is anything else we can do to help. We specialize in overcoming difficulties, and we never forget our friends.

We wish you a Purple Patch!
May God Bless You,

                                             Vivian and Alvis

———

The old man read the letter over and over, and so did Joseph. They were pleased to hear that the boat was being put to such good use. The stack of cash seemed like a huge windfall. They were quite grateful and amazed at the Edwards' generosity. Joseph promised to share the letter with the Jeffords family the next day.

Peter Jeffords got a job sorting and hauling farm produce. He worked for one of the church elders who lived in Jingili. The Jeffords rented a small house that was just off Rothdale Road. The job was six days a week and involved long hours, usually starting at five A.M. each day. Though the job didn't pay well, it was steady work, something that had become a rarity in Australia. It also meant that Peter would have the use of his delivery truck, which was critical since the Datsun was not very reliable. He had Sundays off, which was important to him since he didn't want to miss church and Sunday evening meetings. He also had a quitting time in the late afternoon, which allowed him to lead two evening Bible studies and to attend another. Peter had a "lumper" assistant who proved to be invaluable; since he was born and raised in Darwin, he knew all of the local roads.

The Jeffords liked their new house on Rothdale Road. Originally built in the 1960s, the walls were all gypsum board. Peter felt the need to hide his Pindad rifle, but he didn't want to cut holes in the wall of a rental house. So he bought a large 1960s console combination AM/FM stereo and stereo record player at a thrift store. There was little demand for these big antiquated stereos, so it cost only thirty AUD. It had a nice teakwood cabinet. Its design had sweeping legs that set the internal stereo cabinet nine inches off the floor, but the trim in the front, back, and sides extended down another four inches. Peter took advantage of this extra space to build a three-inch-deep gun caching compartment beneath with a plywood lid. Accessing the compartment required flipping the stereo console on its back and unscrewing the plywood, but he didn't anticipate the need to do so very frequently. Since the cabinet was almost six feet long, he had plenty of room for the rifle, magazines, ammunition, and web gear. He greased the rifle heavily before storing it.

They bought three four-kilogram bags of Catsan Crystals—a brand of cat litter that used silica gel as its main ingredient. It was similar to the Fresh Step Crystals cat litter that he'd seen used in gun cabinets back in the States. Rhiannon poured the cat litter into two pillowcases and positioned them at both ends of the hidden compartment before they screwed it shut. Their rifle was thus safely out of sight and safe from the depredations of Darwin's notoriously high humidity.

Both Peter and Rhiannon found that the story of their voyage to Australia was a great way to strike up conversations with strangers, and to then share the Gospel. They didn't hesitate to call their escape from Samar *providential*. Peter included their story in sermons that he delivered as a guest speaker at nine local churches of various denominations.

The Jeffords kept up their friendship with the Navarros through Peter's Bible study meetings, which Tatang, Joseph, and later Joseph's girlfriend attended regularly. The Navarros were dinner guests roughly once a month at the Jeffords's apartment. Tatang often volunteered to be the cook for these meals. He would bring his spices to cook at the Jeffords, because his apartment was so tiny. The Jeffords were also invited to attend exhibition FMA matches at the gym. These were intended to drum up business for the gym. The Jeffords came to most of these, both to see the matches and for the opportunity to eat some of the Navarro's *lumpia* spring rolls—which Joseph and his grandfather made in quantity to serve at each exhibition. Their *Lumpiyang sariwa* made with diced chicken and heart of palm became legendary at the gym.

After his conversion, Chuck Nolan had become active with the Casuarina Baptist Church. The church, nicknamed Casi Baps, had a friendly atmosphere. In addition to the main Sunday services, the church elders hosted several Bible studies. It was at one these meetings that Chuck got into a lengthy discussion about Romans chapter 13, which Chuck had found confusing, especially in the modern-day political context. The elder who was leading the meeting said: "You know, I have an acquaintance in the Presbyterian Reformed Church who just started an eight-week home study series specifically on Romans 13 and those thorny issues, on Tuesday evenings. I think you'll like it. He's an American. His name is Peter Jeffords."

After an introduction by telephone, Chuck was invited to join the Romans 13 study. At his first meeting—which was the second in the series—Chuck was loaned a book coincidentally by another American named Chuck. Pastor Chuck Baldwin. The book was titled *Romans 13: The True Meaning of Submission.* Chuck Nolan dove into the book and soon learned that Romans 13 was about submission to *good* government, and how the verses had been twisted by twentieth-century theologians to somehow justify a loss of personal freedom in America and in other ostensibly Christian nations.

Because of their similar doctrinal views and partly because they were both Americans, Chuck Nolan and Peter Jeffords became great friends. It was through Peter Jeffords that Chuck met Tatang Navarro, which led Chuck to study Pekiti-Tirsia Kali. When Chuck learned that Pekiti-Tirsia Kali started students with edged and blunt weapons, and only *later* taught empty-handed fighting techniques, he was sold. "Finally, I've found a martial art with some common sense!" he declared.

He greatly enjoyed learning the martial art and eventually convinced Ava Palmer to study Pekiti-Tirsia Kali as well. The two practiced sparring with each other whenever they could. In turn, Ava became a close friend of Rhiannon because of their shared love of bird watching. It was Ava who taught Rhiannon the names of many local birds.

The Jeffords and Navarros quickly adapted to life in Australia, but there were difficulties since the economy was still shaky. Widespread shortages occurred because the country had become dependent on imports of processed foods that were sourced from New Zealand, the

U.S., Canada, Malaysia, China, and Argentina. Some specialty foods came from Greece, Thailand, Peru, South Africa, France, and Belgium. Many textiles and electronics had come from China. With these imports sharply curtailed, a huge market in secondhand goods sprang up.

There was a huge run on cigarettes when realization spread that they were all either imported or made in Australia with imported tobacco. Domestic tobacco production had ramped down to nearly nothing in the 1990s. The nation went through what one editorial at *The Australian* called "a national nicotine fit" for nearly two years, while domestic tobacco growing—both commercial and backyard—ramped up and new distribution channels were established. For a short time, tobacco seeds traded at nearly the same price per ounce as gold.

At the same time that people with nicotine addictions were going through withdrawals, so were the millions of Australians who were dependent on antidepressant SSRIs and other mood-altering drugs, most of which were imported. Their withdrawal was particularly painful and led to hundreds of suicides and a few well-publicized mass murders and murder-suicides. In one of these, a man hacked his family to death with a machete before he jumped off the Bolte Bridge in Melbourne.

The department stores became almost empty shells, while street markets thrived. Vehicle spare parts, computers, and computer peripherals were in chronic short supply. The stigma in buying used goods completely disappeared. Some of the most sought-after items were expendable items such as batteries, ammunition, blank DVDs, and blank CD-RWs.

Chuck and Rhiannon adapted well to the rapidly changing circumstances. Their many years of missionary service had accustomed them to living on very little money, improvising, and living self-sufficiently. This made them well suited to a hardscrabble life in a disrupted economy. Meanwhile, their daughter, Sarah, was almost oblivious to their poverty. She remained content in a life without luxuries. As a missionary kid, she had always worn hand-me-down clothes, so her expectations were modest. She soon made neighborhood friends with girls her own age. Running around with her friends, she learned where she could pick wild fruit. She also delved into the local school library, which had free book lending. Sarah was homeschooled, but the school's sympathetic librarian always greeted Sarah warmly when she arrived for her daily three P.M. visits.

30

THE KING HIT

"The backbone of surprise is fusing speed with secrecy."

– Carl von Clausewitz

Australia—February, the Third Year

As the Jeffords and Navarros settled into their new lives in Australia, larger events were in motion that would soon change things for all Australians.

Seven years before the Crunch, an Indonesian plan had called for 750 sleeper agents to infiltrate Australia. The Indonesian State Intelligence Agency—the Badan Intelijen Negara (BIN)—began training a cadre of sleeper agents bound for Australia and Papua New Guinea. Most of these agents came into the country as legal immigrants. A few of the higher-level operatives came in under diplomatic cover and then switched identities. The embassy later faked exits from the country for their original identities, listing them on passenger manifests for flights on Indonesian aircraft.

The sleeper agents were mostly bachelors in their late twenties and early thirties, but included a few married couples. Each agent was given detailed targets and instructed to find work and move as close to their respective targets as possible. Their coded instructions, communication equipment, explosives, detonators, incendiary igniters, timers, and chemical weapons were smuggled into Australia via diplomatic pouch. The term *pouch* is an antiquated term. In modern times it meant entire shipping containers on board cargo aircraft that carried diplomatic seals and were therefore exempt from any inspections by Australian authorities. Similar abuses of diplomatic mail privileges had become widespread in the late twentieth and early twenty-first centuries.

To get this materiel into the hands of the sleeper agents, the Indonesians used their embassy and six consulates that were scattered across the country. Over the course of five years, more than six thousand kilograms of materiel and packets of currency were surreptitiously distributed to the sleepers.

The sleeper agents slipped into the population of eighty thousand Indonesian immigrants already living in the country. A few Timorese tried to warn Australian police, intelligence, and tax compliance agencies of their suspicions of the newcomers. They reported that many of the recent immigrants appeared to have wealth that didn't match their incomes. However, their warnings were largely ignored. There were eventually three raids on immigrant apartments, but the searches revealed no evidence and official apologies were made.

The original plan had been to train and infiltrate 750 sleepers. However, before he signed off on the plan, the Indonesian Armed Forces chief of staff—a devout Muslim—intervened. He ordered an increase in the number of sleepers to 786 and renamed Project 750 to the 786 Heroes Plan. The 786 figure was based on the Islamic mystical significance of the number 786. Eventually, 763 of their trained agents did successfully infiltrate the country.

The training of the Heroes agents was done in five separate groups on five different islands. This maintained a compartmentalized organization. The agents, and even their trainers, did not know the size of the overall program or of the existence of the other groups. Thus, those trained to destroy aircraft with thermite charges had no knowledge of other groups that were being trained to destroy communications equipment. For all they knew, the plan was only to disrupt their particular segment of the Australian infrastructure. By keeping them ignorant of the larger plans, the agents could not reveal the enormity of the overall operation in the event that they were arrested and interrogated.

Coded message activation orders were sent out redundantly via e-mail as Internet greeting cards, and shortwave radio messages on Voice of Indonesia (VOI) at 9.525 MHz. Most of the messages were birth announcements for a baby girl named Ayesha. The coded messages all indicated that February 5th would be Heroes Night.

Many of the sleepers got jobs with Tidy Services Group, a contracting company that had dozens of military contracts in Australia and New Zealand. This was a large company that did building maintenance, janitorial services, laundry and linen, mess hall catering, painting, trash hauling, and even some site security. The legions of Tidymen, who often wore optic yellow uniform shirts, had become ubiquitous on Australian military bases since the 1990s.

In the end, only 712 of the agents carried out their orders. The remainder had become so accustomed to their comfortable new lives in Australia that they ignored their activation orders. They would later claim they never received any orders.

The news of the attacks came to Rhiannon after Peter had already left for work. As she was scrambling some eggs for breakfast, Rhiannon turned on the radio and heard the alarming developments. She immediately picked up her phone and hit the preset button for Peter's mobile phone. When he answered, all she said to him was, "Turn on the radio in your truck, right now!"

Even the initial news reports made it clear that the attacks on RAAF aircraft were a devastating blow. The full tally didn't come until several days later: Sixty-eight of the RAAF's seventy F/A-18Bs, twenty-three of their twenty-four F/A-18Fs, and sixteen of their fleet of eighteen AP-3C Orion maritime patrol aircraft (two had already grounded indefinitely in the United Arab Emirates) were destroyed. The thermite attacks also wiped out all fourteen of the RAAF C-130s in the country (six others were grounded in Afghanistan, for lack of spare parts) and all six of their C-17s. Even though Boeing had decades of commercial operations in Australia, there was not any chance to get parts for the F-18s or the C-17s after the Crunch—the aircraft were indefinitely redlined. One of the most expensive hits was the destruction of all fourteen of the RAAF's newly operational F-35A multirole fighters, which had cost $125 million each.

Meanwhile, on Army bases, ninety-two of the Australian Army's 105 helicopters were destroyed. Two of their CH-47s were also stranded in Afghanistan. The only operational aircraft spared were planes that were either in flight or at remote landing fields during the three-hour window in which the saboteurs emplaced the thermite bombs.

The successful attacks at the airfields were later attributed to the infiltration of on-base concession workers, tipper truck drivers, fuel truck drivers, and contract office janitors. All of the saboteurs were later identified as being Indonesian-born, and all had been New Australians for just a few years.

The simultaneous detonations on the Royal Australian Navy ships were even more devastating. These bombs destroyed forty-one of the navy's fory-two commissioned warships. Forty-one ships were afloat, and one was in dry dock when the time bombs exploded. Unlike the attacks on parked RAAF aircraft, the ship time bombs caused tremendous loss of life. The only ship to escape the bombings was HMAS *Melville*, a 71-meter hydrographic survey vessel, but only because its monitor boxes had been inadvertently delivered to the frigate HMAS *Melbourne*. All six of the charges that had been intended for the *Melville* were still stacked up and forgotten in a paint locker on the *Melbourne* when they exploded.

Launched in 1998 and originally painted white, the *Melville* was pressed into part-time duty in border protection operations starting in 2001. She was then repainted gray. *Melville* was equipped with two .50 caliber machine guns—her only armament.

The fact that the *Melville* had been spared from the bombing attack provided some important evidence about the ship bombings.

Chuck Nolan was interested to learn that the offices of AOGC and several other oil exploration and mining companies in the Top End would soon be visited by ASIO field agents. Most of their questions were about whether or not any explosives had gone missing. Once it became clear that there had not been any explosives thefts, then their questions shifted toward conjecture on how the bombs might have been constructed. This led to several round table meetings.

As an explosives expert, Chuck was called into one of these meetings. The almost unanimous conclusion they reached was that the bombs had been assembled in Indonesia rather than in Australia. As Chuck put it to the ASIO agents, "Modern timer circuitry could have been used to program the devices to detonate several *decades* into the future, and they would have simultaneously done their job. There was no need to assemble or even program the devices here in Australia. In the plastic hard cases they've been describing, the bombs would have been just about idiot-proof. For all we know, they could have been built several years ago. My suspicion is that this is exactly what happened."

The Australian prime minister was absolutely livid when she learned that the Australian Navy had been reduced to one ship, which had a primary fitting of just seafloor sonars.

The news of the simultaneous attacks on so many airplanes and ships was astounding. Australians were glued to their televisions and smartphones, eager for updates. While the authorities did not immediately pin any blame, Peter and Rhiannon were already convinced that it was the Indonesians who were responsible.

The government of New Zealand quickly donated one of their two frigates, the HMNZS *Te Kaha*, to aid in Australia's defense. The media at first mocked the donation of the 118-meter frigate, with one left-wing newspaper headlining that New Zealand's generosity had "doubled the size of the RAN." There was a public campaign to rename the frigate the *Revenge*, but in the end, her original *Te Kaha* stuck, with just her

HMNZS forename changed to HMAS. Both the *Melville* and the *Te Kaha* had senior captains put in command.

In the two years before the Crunch, the Royal Australian Navy had accelerated sales of their older generation warships and transports to meet carbon emission standards that were arbitrarily set by the Canberra government. This reduced the RAN's fleet from fifty-four ships to just forty-two. Most of the surplus ships were sold to Indonesia and Malaysia, some of them complete with armaments and fire control systems. Ironically, these would soon be used to bring Indonesian and Malaysian invasion forces to the Philippines, East Timor, Papua New Guinea, and finally Australia.

Right before the Crunch, Indonesia had also bought up as many surplus landing craft as they could find. They bought three Landing Craft, Vehicle Personnel (LCVPs) from Australia, two Landing Craft Utility (LCUs) from the United States, four *Czilm* class hovercraft from Russia, and seven 1990s-vintage 25-ton Landing Craft Mechanized (LCM) from the U.S., and even three aging WWII-vintage LCMs from Cambodia. Their finest landing craft purchases, however, were two Landing Craft Air Cushions (LCAC) through the U.S. Foreign Military Sales (FMS) office and another nearly identical one that came from the Japanese Defense Force.

In his visit to Indonesia in 2010, President Obama announced the gift of twenty-four former USAF F-16s—multirole fighter aircraft—as a sign of friendship to the Muslim world. The gift was building on his first inaugural address, in which he said of other hostile nations, "We will extend a hand if you will just unclench your fist." Two years later, the Australian government sold four C-130H transport planes to the Indonesian Air Force. And in 2013, Indonesia received six Sukhoi Su-30 Mk 2 multirole fighter planes purchased from Russia in a $470 million deal. This increased their fleet of Su-30s to twenty-nine planes.

Indonesia's many acquisitions fit into their strategic goal of territorial expansion and jihad. Without all this new transport, their large armed forces wouldn't have been able to be used offensively. Their capability to project force over long distances was unprecedented. Because they had acquired equipment from so many far-flung sources, the aggregation of the new transport was ignored by all but a few Western intelligence analysts. Even then, they did not raise the alarm about the full strategic implications. Indonesia and Malaysia had built a war machine, and the world was too distracted to notice.

31

MONITORS

"Someday, we'll go to war over rice."

—*The Dogs of War,* screenplay by Gary DeVore and George Malko,
based on the novel by Frederick Forsyth

Australia—February, the Third Year

Piecing together the details of the coordinated attacks, ASIO and the Australian news media slowly gathered more information about the naval time bombs. The bombing plot was so devious, so dastardly, that it seemed almost unimaginable. The simultaneous death of so many Australian sailors was hard for most Australians to accept. For Ava, who had a cousin in the RAN who was on the Missing List, the emotional impact was much greater than losing her grandfather, who had insulin-dependent Type I diabetes.

The time bombs were shaped charges in 252 magnetically attached gray plastic boxes 9 inches square and 2.5 inches thick. Each bomb contained three pounds of pure crystalline RDX explosive in a shallow cone-shaped charge, with a coating of paraffin phlegmatizer around their edges. This made the charges less fragile in rough handling. The charges each had two electric blasting caps for redundancy.

The labels on the plastic cases were marked ENVIRONMENT PROTECTION AUTHORITY (EPA) AIR QUALITY MONITOR and had detailed instruction labels. They looked very convincing. Their labels described them as carcinogen air sampling monitors. If their Quick Check codes were scanned with a cell phone or PDA scanner laser, the correct URL for the Australian EPA, "Australia's Air Quality Monitoring Program" website would be brought up. This legitimate website even had a mission statement: "Implementing the requirements of the Ambient Air Quality National Environment Protection Measure (Air NEPM), and building data for State of the Environment (SoE) reporting."

The monitors' labels also included a phone number that during business hours connected callers directly to a smooth-talking Indonesian-born agent in Canberra with a perfect Australian accent. He had a variety of carefully worded scripts close at hand, to assuage any doubts or concerns about the monitors. These scripts quoted actual NEPM rules and URLs for real Australian EPA web pages. He also had detailed lists of the monitor serial numbers, so that if asked, he could say, for example, "Our records indicate that the monitor in question is on board HMAS *Bathurst*, is that correct?"

What looked like angled air vents in the face of the cases were actually dummy slots. The plastic outer cases were actually hermetically sealed. Both the devices themselves and the website had stern "anti-tampering" warnings, threatening a $10,000 fine for any individual who might "remove, destroy, or tamper" with a monitor. A single green LED status light showed that each mine was operational.

The Collection Date markings for retrieval of the monitors were all three to eleven months after they were timed to explode.

The clamshell plastic bomb boxes were epoxied shut, making them truly tamperproof. They had been assembled at a factory in Malang, on Java, using crystalline RDX explosives. The RDX had been made by PT Dahana in the city of Bogor, twelve miles south of Jakarta. The powerful alnico-type magnets were unwittingly supplied by an industrial magnet maker in New Taipei City, Taiwan. The five-year-life lithium manganese dioxide batteries for the bombs were sourced from mainland China.

In Malang, the employees who installed the RDX explosives were told that bombs were being built under contract for the Russian FSB for use against "radical Christian separatists." Strict "need to know" compartmentalization kept almost everyone involved in the dark about the real destination of the mines. The exterior adhesive labels were printed by a separate company in Banjarmasin, in Kalimantan on the island of Borneo. These labels were not attached to the faces of the boxes until *after* the bombs had arrived in Australia. An all-Indonesian cell within the Australian EPA handled all of the paperwork and distribution to Australia's east and west naval bases.

Always sticklers for working "by the book," Royal Navy maintenance duty rosters were updated to include checking the status lights on the monitors, once every thirty days.

The monitor boxes were attached by powerful alnico permanent magnets, built in to the bottoms of the boxes around the perimeter. These magnets were so strong that the stacks of monitors had to be separated with sheets of Teflon so each box could be slid off of a stack. Even with the Teflon, it took considerable effort to slide the boxes apart.

The instructions printed on the labels dictated "... because many airborne contaminants are heavier than air, this monitor should be mounted directly on the inside of the ship hull, as low as possible but above the bilge line. Monitors should be spaced approximately twenty meters apart on both sides of each vessel."

The beauty of the plan was that modern electronics allowed the detonator timers to be set months or even years in advance. Every mine and thermite device was timed to be activated at precisely the same time: 1:15 A.M. Western Indonesia Time (Waktu Indonesia Barat or WIB) on February 5th. This day was the Birth of the Prophet, a national holiday in Indonesia. It was also known as *Rabi' al-awwal* 12 in the Islamic calendar. WIB was one hour behind Western Australia time and three hours behind eastern Australia time. The planners also had to take into account the three-hour difference between eastern and western Australian time zones.

It was a RAN maintenance officer who immediately thought of the EPA monitors when he saw the pattern of explosions in press photographs following the ship bombings. His theory was later proved to be true.

The explosions took place at 2:15 A.M. in Western Australia, and 5:15 A.M. in eastern Australia just as dawn was breaking.

32

THE RAIDS

"No battle plan ever survives contact with the enemy."

—Field Marshall Helmuth Karl Bernhard Graf von Moltke

Robertson Barracks, Palmerston,
Australia—February, the Third Year

Robertson Barracks already seemed fairly empty. The U.S. Marine Corps contingent had left just as the Crunch began, having been "retrograde deployed" to Hawaii. When rumors of the invasion began, all of the other tenant units at Robertson Barracks were moved to Queensland and New South Wales. Politically, it was deemed important to put an emphasis on defending Australia's major population centers. Less well publicized was the fact that, strategically, it was seen as best to briefly "give ground" at the Top End to allow time to make a decisive counterstrike, to hit the invaders on Australia's terms.

Australia's newly drafted war plans included plenty of mistakes. For example, there was a misallocation of troops sent to defend Pine Gap, the joint Australian/U.S. intelligence-gathering satellite ground station center twelve miles southwest of the town of Alice Springs. The base was near the geographic central point of Australia. Pine Gap had dozens of satellite ground station dishes. Many of its antennas were enclosed in more than a dozen white domes that ranged in size from three to thirty meters. The long-term strategic importance of Pine Gap gave it unequal weight when choosing deployments. In the end, the majority of the troops sent there were shifted to fight the invaders, but initially their deployment seemed idiotic. In an e-mail to Chuck, Caleb Burroughs called the Alice Springs deployments "an enormous thumb-twiddling and navel-gazing exercise."

The invasion of Papua New Guinea began on the morning of February 5th. With no air cover and only three oil slicks to show where Royal Australian Navy ships had been sunk at their moorings while anchored at Port Moresby, resistance by the Papua New Guinea Defence Force (PNGDF) was pitiful. Their two light infantry battalions (one at Port Moresby and one at Wewak) were quickly overwhelmed by the much larger invading force. With no weapons heavier than 81 mm mortars, they were no match for Indonesia's assault troops.

Landing first at Milne Bay, the Indonesians quickly set up a base and with several subsequent landings soon controlled all of the cities and major roads in Papua New Guinea. The three HMPNGS patrol boats were quickly sunk and their two Landing Craft Heavys (LCHs) were captured. The only two operational PNG aircraft—a CASA CN-235 transport and a UH-1H Huey helicopter were both intentionally destroyed by friendly fire to avoid having them captured by the advancing Indonesian troops.

Papua New Guinea's Firearms Act of 1978 had mandated that all pistols and "high-powered firearms" (which included nearly all rifles and shotguns, except for air rifles) be registered. Seizing the registration records was at the top of the Indo-Malaysian Army's priority list. Within a week, they had disarmed the populace almost completely. A handful of registered gun owners had disappeared, along with their guns. They became the focus of a manhunt that offered nearly twenty ounces of gold (payable in ten Tola bars) for information leading to the death or capture of each of the fugitives.

The Indonesian press hailed the early morning hours of February

5th as Heroes Night while the Aussie media compared it to the December 7, 1941, Pearl Harbor attack, calling it the Night of Infamy.

The surprising effectiveness of the attacks defanged both the Navy and Air Force and turned the Indonesian invasion into a conventional ground war with very little air power involved.

When news of the EPA monitor bombs became public, it caused a near hysterical panic. The hundreds of *genuine* air monitors were removed by bomb squads with much scrutiny and covered by television news crews in great detail. It was learned that most of the Indonesian agents who had infiltrated the EPA left the country before the coordinated attack. Just one of them was captured, put on trial, and given a life sentence. The outcome of his trial triggered many vocal public protests, calling for reimposition of the death penalty for mass murder.

The months following the attacks brought more bad news for Australia. In March, HMAS *Melville* was sunk in the Coral Sea, and in May the frigate HMAS *Te Kaha* was sunk at the mouth of the Bay of Carpentaria. Both ships were defeated with repeated strikes by Chinese-made C-705 missiles launched from the Indonesian Navy's fast missile boats KRI *Clurit* and KRI *Kujang*. In both engagements, the missiles were launched from a distance of more than thirty-five miles. In the three weeks before she went down, HMAS *Te Kaha* had sunk six Indonesian ships, mostly cargo vessels.

The losses of Australia's two remaining warships were crushing blows to morale in Australia. Aside from a few civilian cargo and pleasure vessels that were hastily fitted with missile launchers and torpedo tubes, Australia had no significant naval power. While large numbers of civilian aircraft had been purchased or donated to the RAAF, most of them weren't useful other than as spotter planes or light transports.

One defeatist Tasmanian journalist compared the sinking of HMAS *Te Kaha* to the fictional sinking of the British ironclad torpedo ram

Thunder Child, in H. G. Wells's 1898 alien invasion novel, *The War of the Worlds*. He asked, "What was the difference between the Martian's heat ray and the Indo's missile technology? Only that *one of them* was fictional. Nothing now stands between us and the invaders."

Watching the parade of bad news on television, Alvis Edwards became increasingly angry, both at the Indonesians and at the lack of preparedness shown by his own government. The most telling details came in confessions from captured Indonesian saboteurs. They revealed that the target list for the 786 Heroes included not just RAAF aircraft at Amberley, Edinburgh, Richmond, Tindall, and Williamtown, but also telephone networks, bridges, power generation stations, and refineries. They had even prepared to poison civic water supplies.

The telephone networks were both soft and hard. The soft attacks were made via hacks on telephone software. The largest number of hard attacks involved thermite incendiary collars on cell phone towers with timer igniters smuggled via diplomatic pouch. The bulk aluminum and iron oxide powder to make the thermite were purchased locally and aroused little suspicion. There were also thermite and explosive attacks on most long-haul military communications (multichannel) shelters. Alvis later heard that some older Australian Army Reserve RATT rigs were overlooked and later proved to be crucial in providing military communications across the vast expanses of the Australian continent.

Alvis and Vivian had a long talk about the recent events, and they decided that their frustration would be relieved only if they did something to get involved with the war effort. "There has to be something we can do, to pitch in. I think I should ask about volunteering with a weapons contractor," Vivian said.

Alvis nodded. "Yes, please do. We may be too old to be fighters on the front lines, but we can still do *something* to do our bit."

Following the demoralizing sinkings of Australia's last two RAN ships, the Indonesian Navy began some daring nighttime raids, landing

Pembebasan Kerombakan Komando (PKK or "Liberation Demolition Commando") teams and shelling Australian coastal locations, often without any substantive opposition.

Their naval gunfire targets were coastal airports, refineries, radar installations, bridges, port facilities, and a few selected factories. The shells were mainly fired from the 4.5-inch guns on their seven *Van Speijk* class Dutch-built frigates. These seven frigates were 113 meters in length and had 120-man crews. They all had their original Harpoon anti-ship missile launchers replaced by C-802 missiles from China, and the original Sea Cat anti-aircraft missile launchers replaced by Simbad (Mistral) launchers from France.

Most of their nighttime approaches were feints, designed to un-nerve the Australian defenders. These feints usually ended three to twenty miles from shore with the Indo ships veering off. A few pressed on close to shore, and the shelling commenced. In one instance what looked like a feint was actually an attack: After an Indonesian *Klewang* class trimaran had veered off, it fired two C-705 missiles—one each at a pair of tankers anchored at the Bulwar Island Refinery, sinking both of them in spectacular blazes. These composite-hulled trimarans were particularly feared because the 63-meter ships each carried eight C-705 missiles and were purposely built for stealth. The trimarans were also fast, with a top speed of thirty-five knots.

One much-publicized night, the Indos risked staying until dawn, repeatedly shelling the BP Kwinana Refinery on the shore of Cockburn Sound near Freemantle in Western Australia. This was Australia's largest oil refinery, with a capacity of 138,000 barrels per day. Ava Palmer heard about this event firsthand in a telephone conversation with her grandmother, who lived just one block off the beach at Freemantle. Her grandmother described it as a night of intense fear. Sirens wailed all night. The concussion of the secondary explosions at the refineries could be felt and rattled windows up to fifteen miles away. The glow of the fires at the refineries could be seen from twenty-five miles away. Ava later learned that the lengthy shelling took the refinery off line for nearly a year.

The main goal of the Indo raids was to bluff the Australian military into moving their field artillery and few remaining air assets to defend cities on the east and west coasts rather than on the north coast, where invasion was most likely. Ironically, the 8th/12th Regiment of the Royal Australian Artillery, normally headquartered at Robertson Barracks near Darwin, had all of its 155 mm guns defending Brisbane when the Indonesians invaded.

Australian military planners still had doubts about Indonesian intentions, and they had gaps in their knowledge of the enemy's order of battle and transport capability. There was also still plenty of turmoil at home as economic adjustments were made to adapt to the post-Crunch world. This would be a "come as you are" war, and Australia was far from fully ready.

33

DISPATCHED

"All men dream, but not equally. Those who dream by night in the dusty recesses of their minds wake in the day to find that it was vanity: but the dreamers of the day are dangerous men, for they may act their dreams with open eyes, to make it possible."

—T. E. Lawrence, *Seven Pillars of Wisdom,* 1926

7th Combat Service Support Battalion (CSSB) Headquarters, Gallipoli Barracks, Enoggera, Queensland—February, the Third Year

Caleb Burroughs was summoned to the colonel's office with vague word that he needed information about a forward logistics base. As he donned his hat, Caleb muttered to himself, "An FLB? *What* FLB?" He arrived at the brigade headquarters office to find Colonel Jack Reynolds poring over several maps that he'd spread over his desk. Reynolds, a balding man with a bristly mustache, was known for his informality. He waved Caleb in without giving him time for a salute. "Burroughs, I know you were reared around Darwin, so I'd like your advice for some FLBs for Task Force Dingo. We've been tasked with replacing the lost assets of the 1st CSSB at Robertson Barracks, just south of Darwin." He gestured to the topmost Geoscience Australia 250K Series topographic map.

Slightly puzzled, Caleb approached the desk hesitantly and

Reynolds said, "No need to be nervous. We haven't had any direct dealings, but you've come very well recommended by the staff. I've been told that you know the bush and you've got common sense. You also seem to be a good judge of character. For example, I heard that you carefully kept your distance from Captain Eggers back when he was one of the most popular men in the officer's mess. That is, before his muck-up and fall from grace. That alone tells me a lot about you."

Reynolds looked back down at the maps and said, "We have plenty of time, so just begin at the beginning. It may sound odd, but honestly I've never been up the Top End. So brief me as if I'm tabula rasa on the Northern Territory. I suppose you should start with the climate first."

Caleb cleared his throat and said, "Sir, the dry season of course comes in winter, usually between May and October. The wet season up at the Top End is in the summer, from November to March. In a really wet year, we can get up to one-point-two *meters* of rain. People really can't appreciate that figure until they've seen it firsthand. Back in 2011, we had eighty-nine full-on rain days, which was a record breaker. Not much gets accomplished out in the bush during the worst of it. The roads simply become impassable—that is, any of the unsealed earth roads that haven't been paved or graveled. Therefore, in the summer much of the Northern Territory becomes classic 'slow go' or even 'no go' terrain, as the Plans and Operations folks call it. We call the humid period between the dry and wet seasons the buildup. People tend to get tense during the buildup, waiting for the first rains to come. When the rains do come, it is a relief since it cools off a bit."

Reynolds nodded, and Caleb continued. "The real wild cards are the tropical cyclones, which can't be predicted other than arriving in a general season, which runs from November to April. I was there for Cyclone Monica, back in April of '06. That was a bad one, still a Category 2 cyclone when it went through Darwin. Then there was Helen in January of 2008, and it tracked around just south of Darwin for five days. Helen wasn't quite so intense, but it was still quite a mess. More rain than you can imagine."

After a pause he continued. "The climate is tropical, so the humidity plays hell with any stores. The humidity is always fairly high, but it gets insanely high for part of each year. Corrosion of metal and mildewing of canvas is a constant struggle. Silica gel and grease are our friends. The Army will have to busy itself like the Navy, just to keep pace. Lots of wire brushing and spot painting—that sort of thing. Cardboard boxes get soft and rot. Tinned foods get rusty. So I'll have to coach the troops on the local tricks like lacquer-painting tins and how to dip boxes and cans in melted paraffin."

Reynolds nodded. "What else will we be facing?"

"Well, then there are the spiders and snakes. There are half a dozen varieties of snakes up there that are deadly. Some of our soldiers that grew up in the big cities will need some coaching. They don't even understand the importance of shaking out their boots in the morning. We'll have to remedy that, straight away."

Caleb gestured to the map and continued. "The terrain is varied and the vegetation runs the gamut from saltwater swamps to dense jungle—that's also called closed forest canopy—to open forest, to some scrublands. Some of the steep jungle country is practically impenetrable. But a lot of the better land has been cleared and put to use for cattle stations."

"What about the people and the economy?"

"Well, the economy is relatively weak. The standing joke is, 'The Top End is just another Third World country, only with better roads.' I can honestly say that the Northern Territory was an *interesting* place to grow up. It is hard to describe, but personalities seem more amplified up there. There are some world-class eccentrics. But by and large, the people are hardworking, neighborly, and self-sufficient, especially the farther you get out of town. The old Australia is still alive and well up there."

Putting on a slight lecturing tone, Reynolds said, "What we have before us is an unprecedented situation, Caleb. The distances are vast, and our numbers are going to be mismatched against the Indos.

Because of the great distances involved, there will be considerable delay in moving our forces to react to any Indonesian landings. Our problem is that *they* can pick anywhere they'd like along two thousand miles of coast to make their move. For small garrisons there, it might turn out to be a classic 'hold until relieved' scenario. But that naturally is suboptimal. What are your thoughts?"

"Well, sir, rather than having this turn out to be another Rorke's Drift or, God forbid, Gallipoli, I think the best thing for us is to keep the Indos guessing. We can use the heavy vegetation to our advantage to conceal our locations. I'd much rather try to keep them in a muddle, guerilla style, than face them in a set-piece fight."

The colonel nodded and said, "That's it, precisely. I've heard that you're keen on military history. Tell me, have you read much about T. E. Lawrence in the First World War, or David Stirling in the Second?"

"Yes, I've read *Seven Pillars of Wisdom* and as much as I could find about the early days of the SAS. And I'd say that I'm fairly well read about North Africa in World War Two. Fascinating stuff, sir."

The corners of Reynolds's mouth turned up as he responded, "The 1st CSSB, as you know, had been at Robertson Barracks in Darwin since the late 1990s. Soon after, they got warned out in support of the 3rd Brigade's deployment to East Timor. After that, they got comfortably settled back into Robertson Barracks, but then just before the Crunch, they got deployed again even more heavily to Papua New Guinea. Communications have been spotty, but as near as we can tell, they were obliterated there by the Indos."

The colonel paused to let that sink in. "So we've been tasked to take over their loggy role in that region, covering about two hundred fifty miles of the northern coast."

Burroughs nodded. "I see."

The colonel went on. "But we don't want to make the mistake of just taking up their old digs and carrying on in a quasi-peacetime mode. That would be a huge blunder. We'd be sitting ducks in range of naval gunfire. Instead, we'll use Robertson Barracks only temporarily for staging. Everything should be hidden, out in the bush. I want you to go up there and select three widely separated FLBs. Each of them will be like a brigade maintenance area, and they'll have the same functions as a standard BMA, but the military staffing will be light. The same number of soldiers that would normally staff one BMA will be spread out over three sites. We'll be hiring civilians to make up the difference in requisite manpower. With the redundancy of three sites, we won't have all our eggs in one basket.

"There'll of course be more FLBs at other points up and down the northern coast, but those will be handled by other brigades. Just concern yourself with the three sites we'll need near Darwin. Your three sites should all be in no more than a two-hundred-mile radius."

He gestured to the map again. "So think *Lawrence of Arabia*. The Top Enders are going to be our Bedouins, Caleb. Instead of riding camels and horses, they'll be driving Toyota utilities, but the principle is the same. Our job is to provide the logistics. There'll be regular maneuver units to follow up, but odds are that for the first week—or perhaps even the first *month*—you and the local Stay Behinds will be left to your own devices. In the logistics world, all our bag and baggage denies us the advantage of great maneuverability. So you'll have to be very clever in choosing the locations for your FLBs. You'll need to pull a magic trick to make the FLBs disappear. Strike a balance between good camouflage and accessibility all within a short time frame. Obviously, you can't bury it all, or it will be no good to us. Nor can you leave it where the Moslem hordes can find it."

The colonel paused, and then added, "I need you get up there, go through the PEACHs site selection process, and get the stores left behind at Robertson as well as those we shuttle up there in position quite quickly. And—how do I put this?—Be bold, but don't be *hasty*. A lot will be riding on your decisions. Consider that, if you miscalculate, you could be providing logistics stockpiles for the Indos rather than our own forces."

Caleb gave a grim nod. "That's a heavy responsibility, sir." Caleb looked down at his clasped hands for a few moments and then asked, "Sir, to have recourse to a Plan B, I'd like your permission to bring along enough demolitions and thermite to deny everything we have to the invaders in case they *do* fix any of our hardstand positions and roll up on us."

"That would be wise, Caleb. I'll see to it that you can requisition whatever demo gear you need, and I'll have someone from the Engineers give you the über short course in making things go boom. If need be, I'll have a sapper detailed to go with you to provide refresher training to your logisticians. Most of us haven't discussed demo-ing our own supplies since we took our branch courses—and for me that was *many* years ago."

He brushed his hand over his bald head, for emphasis.

"The position I'm giving you is something I'd normally give to a major. And in fact if it were in my power, I'd promote you before sending you out. But as you know, the promotion process has become very bureaucratic in recent years, and the promotion boards hold inordinate power. In some ways, we're still stuck with the peacetime army mentality even though we're on the brink of war. So I'm making the recommendation that you be given a standard commission *and* that you move up in rank. While we wait for the gears of bureaucracy to turn, I'm sending you with a letter that gives you a lot of leeway—more or less a roving commission, with a checkbook to match. I trust that you won't disappoint me."

"I'll do my best, sir."

"Very well, then. Ready a small advance party to be on the road within thirty-six hours. You'll have to do a lot of thinking on your feet. The PM said 'improvise,' so make that happen. You'll be counting a lot upon the cooperation of the local civilians. Anything they might lack in volunteer spirit, you can make up for with the Crown's good checks."

"Understood, sir."

Reynolds sat down in his desk chair to indicate that their meeting was drawing to a close. Waggling his index finger to punctuate his words, Reynolds said, "Again, be bold, but don't be hasty."

"Will do, sir."

34

CRESCENDO

"If it were possible for members of different nationalities, with different language and customs, and an intellectual life of a different kind, to live side by side in one and the same state, without succumbing to the temptation of each trying to force his own nationality on the other, things would look a good deal more peaceful. But it is a law of life and development in history that where two national civilizations meet they fight for ascendancy. In the struggle between nationalities, one nation is the hammer and the other the anvil: one is the victor and the other the vanquished."

—Bernhard Heinrich Karl Martin von Bülow,
German Secretary of State for Foreign Affairs and
later Chancellor of the German Empire

Gallipoli Barracks, Enoggera, Queensland, Australia—February, the Third Year

The evening after his briefing by the brigade commander, Caleb sent Chuck Nolan an e-mail. He wrote a one-line message that simply said, "Check Your Inbox (NTXT)."

By prior arrangement, Chuck knew this meant he was to use their "not secure but semiprivate" method of avoiding e-mails, which could be intercepted. With this method, rather than sending e-mail back and forth, they would log in to Caleb's DarwiNet account using Caleb's password and check the "Drafts" e-mail folder. There, he found an e-mail that originated from his office computer, which was unusual. It read:

(UNCLASSIFIED)

FROM: WO1 CALEB BURROUGHS

HQ, LOG GRP 2, 7 CSSB, GALLIPOLI BARRACKS, ENOGGERA, QLND

PRIORITY: HIGH

TITLE: Most Urgent: Need Your Southern (Not Yankee) Ingenuity

Chuck:

I will be arriving in Darwin in three or four days. I must ask you to clear your calendar so that we can meet to discuss some pressing issues related to my branch of service. I've been put in charge of a project of great importance that will see me posted there for an extended period. I will be arriving with a few subordinates. I can't go into any details via phone or Internet. Can you be ready to quit your civvy job to be a contractor for my endeavor? Treat this with the utmost discretion. *Consilio et animis.*—Caleb

(UNCLASSIFIED)

Reading between the lines, Chuck recognized that "issues related to my branch of service" could only mean a military logistics operation of some sort. He quickly replied, also in the form of an unsent draft, in the same folder:

Caleb:

You can be assured of my full cooperation. Given the current exigencies, my boss would probably be agreeable to a leave of absence, or if need be, even releasing and rehiring me. I'll put myself at your disposal for your project. I'm sure that Ava will understand, given the circumstances. You have my mobile number to coordinate a meeting.

Amat Victoria Curam—Chuck

Caleb arrived in Darwin four days later in an Australian Army Bushmaster Protected Mobility Vehicle (PMV) that had been requisitioned from the Army Logistic Training Centre. These Irish-designed and Australian-built vehicles could carry up to nine passengers. This one carried just Burroughs, the truck's driver (a female lance corporal with a plain face), a supply sergeant, and a load of mixed cargo in the back. All three of them were wearing MultiCam Australian Defense Force (ADF) uniforms with the latest-issue bush hats of the same camouflage pattern.

They seemed particularly proud of their vehicle because it was equipped with a Common Remotely Operated Weapon Station (CROWS)—a piece of weapons technology that came to the ADF by way of the U.S. Army.

All around them, there was a steady stream of civilian evacuees heading south. The Indonesians had warned that they "could not be responsible" for the safety of anyone who remained north of the 24th parallel. The Australian government grudgingly echoed this, urging evacuation. They did mention that there would be "an undetermined number" of stay-behind resistance forces operating in the north. They asked all civilian refugees to leave their houses unlocked to accommodate these Stay Behinds.

Caleb met Chuck at the main gate of Robertson Barracks, which had recently been evacuated. There were no longer soldiers manning the gate. Caleb had a standard issue AUG rifle slung across his chest. Chuck could see the glint of brass cartridge cases through the rifle's translucent magazine. Seeing this *loaded* rifle was a reminder that Australia was now on a war footing and that their conversation would be serious business.

Leaving their vehicles parked in what had been the security inspection lane, they sat down to talk at the desk of the guardhouse. After in-
quiring about each other's health and pouring a couple of lukewarm
cups of Daintree tea that Caleb had brought in his thermos, he gave
Chuck a ten-minute briefing about his mission. He concluded by re-
questing, "So . . . I'd like you to be our explosives expert, bouncing between all three sites, training both those in uniform and the civilian
contractors. You might even be training some of the civilian Stay Behind militia members. You'd also oversee the safe storage and handling
of all explosives, rockets, and mortar bombs at the FLBs."

"I know something about civilian explosives, but I don't know much
about military explosives or artillery shells," Chuck protested.

Caleb wagged his finger dismissively. "You haven't had military
courses, but you still have all those military manuals that we put on our
memory sticks, right? Well, just consider this the on-the-job training to
'go with.' And for whatever it's worth, there will be no artillery shells.
The biggest thing that goes bang we'll be handing out will be some
81-millimeter mortar rounds and some satchel charges, but those are
just like civilian explosives. There will be some rockets, but this isn't
rocket *science*. I just need you to teach everyone the common sense
stuff, like not transporting detonators and the explosives in close proximity, and warning them about static electricity around blasting caps,
that sort of thing."

Chuck nodded. "Okay, I'll do it."

35

TO YOUR GUNS

"Had the Japanese [army's territorial conquest in Asia] got as far as India, Gandhi's theories of 'passive resistance' would have floated down the Ganges River with his bayoneted, beheaded carcass."

—Mike Vanderboegh, in *Sipsey Street Irregulars* blog

Darwin, Northern Territory, Australia— February, the Third Year

With war imminent, AOGC had minimized all of their oil and gas exploration in the north to concentrate on production and distribution in the southern half of the country. So Chuck's boss was willing to release him on an unpaid leave of absence. Chuck Nolan cleaned out his desk, and his ADF contract started the same day. He was asked to "find some trustworthy fellas who can think outside the box, to come on board, to help man the FLBs." He immediately thought of Peter Jeffords and Joseph Navarro and called both of them.

Joseph agreed to work as a contractor without any hesitation. Peter asked for a night to think about it. He called back the next morning. "Rhiannon and I talked and prayed a lot about it. We decided that she ought to take Sarah down south where it's safe. But we agreed that it would be a good idea for me to stay here and help out for two reasons: First, I'm *done* with running. We were run out of the Philippines because we had no choice. *Here*, I have the opportunity to help stop the

Indos, at least in some small way. Second, I got to thinking about what it will be like living at those logistics base camps that you have planned. It'll be a lot of foul-mouthed soldiers from the Big City together with an assortment of rough-around-the edges Top Enders. A bunch of bogans, mostly. In other words, it'll provide a great opportunity for Christian witness! Sign me up."

Chuck began work the next morning. He enthusiastically plunged into his job, and soaked up the military logistics jargon. His years of field work in harsh conditions in the oil fields and in oil field wildcatting prepared him well for life at an austere logistics base in the jungle.

Chuck soon learned that a CSSB normally included a headquarters element, a transport squadron, a health company (with medical and dental assets), a field supply company, and a field workshop. Normally a CSSB is responsible for maintaining three to fourteen days of supply depending on the commodity. But for the Northern Territory FLBs, the guidance was for twenty-one to twenty-eight days until any re-supply.

Caleb was specifically tasked with scouting locations for three forward logistics bases (FLBs). He was tentatively given direction to locate them on Crown land, but private property could be also used with compensation, at his discretion. The stated goal was to set up the bases on well-drained level ground in forested areas. By cutting just a minimum number of trees and through skillful use of camouflage netting, it was hoped that these bases would be difficult to spot from the air. Each of the FLBs would be provisioned with stocks of fuel in 2,500-gallon flexible rubber "pillow tank" blivets, ammunition field rations, batteries, and water trailers. To conserve precious military manpower, the FLBs would be staffed with eighty percent civilian contractors and just a few army officers and enlisted personnel.

The first site Caleb selected was a forested tract near the town of Batchelor that was owned by a private plantation company. They were gradually cutting mixed stands of native timber and replanting to create African mahogany plantations. He eventually picked a particularly dense tract of mixed mature second-growth timber that had originally been logged in the 1950s. The tract, in a broad north-south valley, was thirty-four miles out of Darwin. The trees were tall and dense, and inside the grove he could barely see the sky. Old logging roads that could easily be upgraded to accommodate large trucks crisscrossed the grove.

Hiking the property, he found that it was so deeply shaded, it felt almost claustrophobic. But he could see that all that would be needed was limbing some trees for truck clearance and felling a few trees to make room for storage tents and hardstand parking places. The access was perfect: a number of lanes that turned out directly onto Litchfield Park Road—a paved secondary road. He was surprised to see that the lanes had been kept free of deadfall. He later learned that it was feral pig hunters who had kept the lanes cleared. The hunters liked to retain the ability to haul out the heavy pig carcasses (up to 115 kilos for boars) in their utilities.

The FLB site would be almost undetectable, even to someone driving by on the paved road. To the casual observer, the lanes would be indistinguishable from dozens of other existing logging roads. With some gravel, these lanes would be drivable even in the wet season. This FLB site was dubbed Site G and informally nicknamed the Grove by everyone involved.

When Caleb approached the plantation company about leasing two hundred hectares, the plantation manager told him, "My price is firm at one dollar for the duration of the hostilities. Just do your best not to burn it down."

Once the lease was signed, a flurry of activity began at Site G. More than forty camouflage nets arrived on contract commercial contract trucks, driven by "red right arm" civilian truckers who seemed confused why they had been directed to GPS coordinates rather than to a street address.

Next came a pair of 2.5-ton capacity rough terrain forklifts—made by YTO in China—painted bright yellow, but that was soon remedied with two coats of flat olive drab spray paint. Caleb had thought ahead

and had directed his NCOs to bring forty-eight cans of military specification black and olive drab spray paint.

Chuck Nolan helped set up the site. It was laid out in what the Australian NCOs called a defensive donut. The only access road ended in a
lollipop-shaped road loop with hardstand position under the thickest
clumps of trees. The donut was about three hundred yards across, so
Chuck soon found that it was easiest to use his mountain bike to make
his rounds.

Nolan's work clothes were usually a pair of Aussie Army MultiCam
trousers, one of his forest green AOGC button-down long-sleeve shirts
(still with an AOGC logo above the left pocket, embroidered in dark
blue), a pair of Bates American-made lightweight hiking boots, and the
MultiCam boonie hat that his sister had given him just before he moved
to Australia. That hat originally had its left brim tacked up with a few
stitches of thread to make it look like an Australian bush hat. Thinking
it looked too trite, Chuck cut out those threads before his flight to Australia. Another gift from his going-away party became something he
carried every day. It was a Leatherman Wave multi-pliers tool with a
special blasting cap crimper built into the pliers' jaws. This Leatherman
had been given to him by his parents and was one of his favorite and
most useful possessions.

The FLBs were thrown together in a hurry. They were short on men,
short on supplies, and they were desperately short of knowledge about
what would happen next. But they were diggers, and diggers always
found a way to muddle through.

36

EXIGENCIES

"A person can be a partisan or a survivalist, but not both. The survivalist defends himself, his people and his redoubt against all comers. It's not just his right, it's his duty. He may have standing patrols or mount a rescue operation, or do a preemptive strike against bad guys advancing on his community, or even take control of a strategic hilltop. He may make arrangements with other survivalists for mutual aid, much like volunteer fire departments do. All this is defensive. What he will not do is join with others in wholesale annihilation merely to expand turf. Legitimate defense does not involve gang war. The survivalist wins this game by not playing, which is to say he wins by staying away from crowds. Same as always."

—Ol' Remus, *Yer Ol' Woodpile Report* blog

Darwin, Northern Territory, Australia—
February, the Third Year

Peter Jeffords and Tatang Navarro came to work at the Site G base while it was still under construction. Tatang brought his M1 Garand and Jeffords had his Pindad SS2 .223. Because it was standard issue with both the Indonesian Army and Marines, Caleb asked Peter to give training classes on it at all three FLBs. "I want every man—whether army or civilian—to be able to pick up a Pindad and know how to load it, shoot it, and clear stoppages. And if you have the time, even teach them how to field-strip it."

After introducing himself, Peter always started his lectures and demonstrations by holding up the SS2 rifle and saying, "I inherited this Pindad rifle from an Indonesian soldier who passed away rather *suddenly.*"

After the minimum age restriction for army contractors was dropped to age eighteen, Joseph Navarro also came to work at Site G. He was quickly and informally issued a greasy L1A1—a UK Commonwealth inch pattern FN FAL—that the Australians preferred to call SLR or Slur—Self-Loading Rifle. This obsolete 7.62 mm rifle, manufactured in the 1960s at the Australian Lithgow Arsenal, had been pulled from deep war reserves. It had a wooden stock and handguards which distinguished it from the other FAL variants he had seen when he was in the Philippines. Long after even the Australian Army Reserve had transitioned to the F88 Austeyr (the ADF's version of the Steyr AUG), there were still thousands of L1A1 rifles held in reserve. This was one of them. Joseph immediately recognized the rifle's design since it was the granddaddy of Peter's Pindad.

Peter was issued a set of military web gear and a pair of 7x32 binoculars. He selected his particular binoculars from among the packing crate because of the small reference number painted in red enamel: 316. This number resonated with him because of John 3:16, the most-cited verse in the New Testament.

While the Indonesians lacked side-looking airborne radar (SLAR) to provide moving- and fixed-target indicators, they did have aerial reconnaissance drones with traditional cameras. This left the Australian ground forces at risk of detection. Even vehicles and encampments hidden in dense forests or beneath camouflage nets were still at risk of other habitation indicators through pattern analysis. Muddy tire tracks emerging onto paved roads was only one example.

On one of his scouting trips, Caleb heard about the McKenzie horse farm, four miles up the Adelaide River. It had several large hay barns and an enormous covered riding arena. The elderly owners of the farm had scaled down to just a few horses and were anxious to move to southeastern Australia. Caleb was able to negotiate a lease for the Army on the entire 1,800-hectare farm and unlimited use of the water bores for just two thousand dollars per month. The buildings provided excellent concealment for the FLB, so long as all of the vehicles were kept indoors. The farmhouse was used for officer billeting and administrative offices as well as relatively cool storage for field rations.

The McKenzie farm was dubbed Site M. The riding arena provided a concealed location for supplies that was large enough for trucks to drive in and drop off cargo. Only the fuel blivets were stored outdoors, well away from the other supplies, under redundant cover of both camouflage nets and eucalyptus trees. There were large ventilation fans mounted at both ends of the arena. Since the Mains grid power had been shut down, the fans no longer worked and the temperature quickly rose. But power from a trailer-mounted 12 KW multifuel generator set soon remedied the problem. The same genset also provided power for lights inside truck-mounted shelters. Given the blackout in the region, the shelter doors had to be kept closed to maintain light discipline. The last thing they wanted was to be a target.

The interior of the farmhouse became cramped after cases of CR1M, PR1M, and CR5M rations were stacked from floor to ceiling in every available space, making the hallways quite narrow.

The Combat Ration, 1 Man (CR1M, spoken "Crim") was the army's ubiquitous field ration. It was the equivalent of the American military Meal, Ready to Eat (MRE). Like the MRE, the CR1M was the butt of many jokes, both exaggerated and fabricated. For example, Army legend had it that CR1M rations had been invented by "a ninety-five-year-old German nutritionist named Herr Doktor Crimspeil who's first job was planning menus at Dachau."

One step up from the CR1M was the PR1M: Patrol Ration, One Man, or "Prim." These were similar to a CR1M, but with some more palatable freeze-dried components. The PR1Ms were sought after by Aussie soldiers whenever they had the chance.

All three of Caleb's FLB sites were designed to strike a balance between camouflage and ease of access. Roads were laid out in sweeping curves rather than straight lines. Road gravel was used sparingly and was carefully selected to about the same color of the soil at each site. It was hoped that the graveled areas would blend in, at least from aerial or satellite observation. They made the decision to minimize the amount of gravel spread and to immediately add some grass seed from the local native grasses both to the roads and to the adjoining soil to make the roads at the FLBs blend in. They wanted aerial observers to see only irregular green blotches—no sharp contrasts or straight lines.

The Crunch removed most of Australia's access to satellite reconnaissance. Long accustomed to being granted access to this compartmented access intelligence, Australia's spy agencies were suddenly left in the dark. The American National Reconnaissance Office (NRO) constellation of Keyhole series spy satellites were no longer being properly controlled from their ground-based satellite control facilities, so they reverted to default "dumb" orbits and their cameras went "off gimbal"—meaning that they ended up pointing almost randomly. Only one satellite was still producing any useful imagery, but its highly elliptical orbit brought it over successive swathes of Australia and Papua New Guinea only once every sixteen days.

Under the exigencies of the expected hostilities, Task Force Dingo tossed many regulations and procedures out the window. For example, there was extensive use of civilian housing for billeting. Civilian trucks, SUVs, and aircraft were rushed into military service, often without a new paint job—or with just a perfunctory slap of flat tan or olive drab paint with a hand brush. Some off-road vehicles like Volkswagen Amaroks were also used "off the shelf" in large numbers.

Another striking change was the rejection of the long-standing admonition that soldiers, sailors, and airmen should never take their issued weapons off post. Soldiers soon were seen carrying their AUG rifles at all times on and off post, even when they went home on leave. Likewise, civilian contractors were no longer restricted from having firearms, but in fact were encouraged to do so, especially in forward areas like northern Australia.

The government in Canberra also rescinded most of the civilian firearms restrictions and declared a general amnesty on the possession of any previously banned weapons or explosives. These moves offended many staunch anti-gunners. Newspaper editorials bewailed seeing Australia "turned into an armed camp" and warned of a "resurgence of the gun culture" that they had spent the past four decades systematically destroying.

Back in Wyndham, Alvis Edwards scoffed at these gun control proponents. He told his wife, "That band of fools would rather see us invaded and subjugated than let the general populace have guns. They won't see the error of their ways until they're behind Indonesian barbed wire."

Having the general populace armed at all times was reminiscent of the darkest days of early World War II, when a Japanese invasion—or at least air raids—had seemed likely.

After the Indonesians made their evacuation decree, a large number of men opted to serve as Stay Behind resistance fighters. Most of these individuals formed into loosely organized groups of two to four men.

The Stay Behinds ranged from ages seventeen to seventy and came from all social strata. Among them were a sixty-seven-year-old retired male park ranger who carried a Mini-14 rifle he had kept tucked away in his attic during the ban; a twenty-three-year-old female grocery store employee who had a penchant for kung fu movies; and a nineteen-year-old male skateboarding champion who was armed with just a .22 bolt-action rifle. His hope was to use the rifle to get something better.

Another Stay Behind was an Aborigine named Sam Burnu. A thirty-five-year old ex-convict bachelor, Sam worked as a groundskeeper in Marrakai Heights. Like most aboriginals, he had two names: an

English name and a "skin name," representing the section of his kinship group. But because of his criminal record, he used a third, fictitious name when he signed the Stay Behind roster. From the items offered, he took only CR1M rations, a MultiCam bush hat, and a set of web gear with a canteen. He already owned an old Essex 12 bore single-shot shotgun, and he knew its shooting characteristics intimately. He did accept the offer of four boxes of Hexolit shotgun slug ammunition from a friend who was about to take his family to Brisbane. These slugs were specially segmented to splay out into bladelike structures that looked almost like a hunting arrow broadpoint when they hit their target. He subsequently used these slugs to great effect. He killed seven Indonesian soldiers over the course of three weeks, most of them sentries. Each time he took a life, he would go back to his solo camp and sing a death song. Then, before going to sleep, he would prepare his mind to direct his dreams. His father had always said, "Those who lose dreaming are lost."

37

LUAU

"The only things of value which we have at present are our arms and our courage. So long as we keep our arms we fancy that we can make good use of our courage; but if we surrender our arms we shall lose our lives as well."

—Xenophon, The Persian Expedition

Near Darwin, Northern Territory, Australia— February, the Third Year

Even after nearly one hundred truckloads of supplies had been stockpiled at the FLBs, the tents had been erected, and the camouflage nets strung in position, Caleb Burroughs still didn't feel quite "ready." Each night became progressively more tension-filled along the coast in the Top End, with wild rumors circulating of Indonesian and Malaysian Army landings. The only sleep they got came from the utter exhaustion of working sixteen hours a day.

The same night that there was the first confirmed report of a landing at the Bay of Carpenteria, there was a false alarm on the perimeter of Site G, caused by two feral pigs. A nervous guard felt convinced that Indonesian Kopassus troops were probing their lines. He "dialed Triple Zero" to let loose two full 30-round magazines from his Austeyr, pulling the trigger all the way back to the full auto position in long bursts. The next morning, following a reprimand of the guard, the debate centered on how to roast the 70- and 100-kilo pigs without generating smoke that could be seen from the air. They ended up eating boiled pork, cooked over gas burners, which didn't provide quite the same festive atmosphere of the boar roast that most had expected.

Before the Indonesians arrived and forced the FLBs to hunker down in stealth mode, Caleb's unit was able to distribute gear to some of the local Stay Behinds. The gear included camouflage nets, hand grenades, satchel demolition charges, Claymore command-detonated mines, and dozens of cases of CR1Ms. There were also a few L1A1 rifles available for veterans who lacked combat-capable rifles of their own.

More than ninety-five percent of the population had already fled from the Darwin area. Evacuation was recommended, but not required. Those who remained were mostly scrappy bogans and a few assorted eccentrics. Some of them claimed they were too set in their ways to leave their homes. There were also some naïve internationalist idealists who hoped they could carry on their lives under Indonesian rule. Caleb was worried that some of the latter might talk too much to the Indos. Therefore, everyone involved with the FLBs was warned to keep the FLB locations on a strict "need to know" basis. Similarly, the Stay Behind fighters were warned to avoid all contact with the starry-eyed idealists.

Randall Burroughs and Bruce Drake both accepted job offers with the same commercial explosives company near Brisbane that had recently turned to making military demolitions. With Chuck's urging, Ava Palmer and her parents evacuated to Adelaide and lived with relatives. Rhiannon Jeffords and her daughter, Sarah, accompanied them, with Rhiannon driving the rusty Datsun ute. The truck made it to Adelaide despite a leaking radiator that had to be refilled seven times en route.

Thomas Drake packed up his guns and relocated to his hunting property, which bordered Garig Gunak Barlu National Park. He fully expected to die fighting the first time an Indonesian patrol entered his property, but that never happened.

Wyndham was occupied six days after Darwin. The town had been

completely abandoned. Driving the Tanami Road in their Range Rover
towing a trailer loaded with gas cans, Alvis and Vivian Edwards relocated from the Kimberley region to Geraldton, but soon after moved
on to Perth, where they both worked at a small factory that made camouflage nets for the war effort.

Other than the troops at the FLBs, the only regular Australian Army
troops still in or near Darwin were seven widely scattered two-man
Stinger missile teams. These teams were directed to lie low, hiding in
abandoned houses or bivouacking in small camouflaged tents, waiting
for opportunities to shoot down Indonesian aircraft. The teams each
had eight Stinger RMP missiles with passive infrared seekers. These
missiles were man portable—about the size of a bazooka. After firing, a
new missile tube could quickly be mounted to the gripstock, allowing
another missile to be launched in less than a minute. The shoulder-fired
Stinger was added to the Australian Army inventory shortly before the
Crunch to supplement the heavier and more bulky Swedish RBS-70,
which was launched from a pedestal mount. This procurement was
dubbed Project LAND 19—Interim MANPADS. Because of their
compact size, the more portable Stingers were particularly suitable for
guerilla warfare. Meanwhile, the larger RBS-70s were all used in the
defense of the large cities on the southeastern coast.

The main goal of the Indo-Malaysian invasion was to seize intact all
of the oil and natural gas fields in the northern half of Australia, along
with their associated ocean shipping terminals at Darwin, Weipa,
Townsville, Broome, and Dampier. The largest population center in the
Top End was Darwin. It needed to be secured first before the petroleum facilities.

The Stay Behinds were a thorn in the Indonesians' side from the beginning. Snipers like Quentin Whittle would fire just one or two shots
from long range and then disappear into the jungle. Indonesian infantry platoons dispatched to find them were nearly always frustrated.
Through the use of foxholes with well-camouflaged covers, the pursu-
ing soldiers would walk right past the snipers and spend an entire day

fruitlessly searching the jungle, returning exhausted. The next day there would be another shot, another dead Indo soldier—usually an officer or NCO—and the process would be repeated. On the few occasions when a fleeing sniper would engage his pursuers, the Indos often found themselves out-ranged. At distances between four hundred and seven hundred yards, their 5.56 rifles lacked the requisite accuracy when they were up against a man armed with a .243 or .308 bolt action with a 9-power scope.

Meanwhile, the Stinger teams took a deadly toll on any low-flying aircraft. The rate of attrition grew so high that the Indonesians' few remaining aircraft were effectively grounded. The few planes that found shelter from the sappers in the six-pointed star revetments on the south side of the Darwin airfield were eventually picked off by the Stinger teams whenever they would take off or approach for landings. Only ship-based helicopters were safe, and then only if they stayed well offshore. The combined efforts of the Stay Behinds and the Stinger teams turned the campaign in northern Australia into a ground war for both sides.

38

IBOMB

"Besides black art, there is only automation and mechanization."

—Federico García Lorca

Near Darwin, Northern Territory, Australia—
February, the Third Year

Colonel Reynolds arrived at Site G just as stocking the three FLBs was nearly finished. He arrived in his personally owned Audi Q5 luxury sedan that had been turned into an ersatz staff car using some flat tan paint with a few irregular wisps of flat olive drab.

Over the course of two days, Reynolds inspected each of the three sites. He thought their site selection and layouts were quite clever and made very few suggestions for improvements. He did recommend erecting a few additional camouflage nets and constructing overhead cover for some of the recently dug perimeter foxholes.

He also wanted to address as many of the Stay Behinds as possible. He repeated essentially the same briefing three times for groups of between six and forty men. He was quite upbeat. He wanted to encourage active resistance and to reassure the Stay Behinds that they'd be given the logistics support they'd need.

One key portion of his briefing was a rundown of instructions from the top command. "We can be as aggressive as we'd like. The PM has said that 'the gloves are off.' The rules of engagement are *loose*. You can fire on any invading soldier at any time. You can destroy any materiel that they might find particularly useful, but please use discretion in destroying telephone or pipeline infrastructure. You may use flame weapons. You may use dynamite, plastique, and even fuel-air explosives. Your only limitations are: No use of chemical weapons—other than irritants—no use of biological weapons, no radioactive dirty bombs, no poisons, and no use of *contact-initiated* mines or any explosives with a time delay greater than thirty minutes. This is all designed to minimize any collateral damage and to assure the safety of the citizenry when everyone returns. You can do whatever you'd like in the way of command-detonated explosives, but you *cannot* use traditional booby traps that could go off days or weeks later. So get cracking and make the Indos pay *dearly* for trying to take Australian territory."

Palmerston City, Northern Territory, Australia—February, the Third Year

Samantha Kyle had become the top-grossing independent systems installer in the Northern Territory, and she excelled in both sales and installation. Samantha was an attractive and slim redhead of average height who walked with a cane. She never had to play the sympathy card to book orders, but she often suspected that customers opted for a lot of add-ons to their systems after noticing her prosthetic legs.

Her disability was self-evident and most new customers, upon seeing her uneven gait, would ask about it. They each got the same thirty-second summary: "I was a RAAF communications specialist with the 114 MCRU—that's a Mobile Control and Reporting Unit, stationed at Kandahar Airfield in southern Afghanistan. On one of my few convoy trips outside the wire, the five-ton lorry I was riding in got blown up by an IED—a command-detonated mine. I lost both of my legs, below the knee. It doesn't affect my ability to do installations. I just have to be extra careful when I'm up a ladder. No worries."

Samantha was an independent sales rep for OzCyberHomeAnd-Office, a systems integration company that sold hard wire and wireless automation systems from major makers like INTEON, UPB, X10, Z-Wave, and ZigBee. These systems allowed home owners to control everything from lights and burglar alarms to lawn sprinklers remotely—either from a laptop or from a smartphone. Home automation was gaining popularity in Australia. As system prices fell, Samantha's customer base widened. It was no longer just rich doctors and lawyers who had their homes wired.

Samantha was one of just a handful of women who attended the Stay Behind briefings. She met with Caleb Burroughs after the briefing in Palmerston City, just south of Darwin. She was nervous at first and addressed Caleb formally as "sir" and "Warrant Officer Burroughs," but Caleb's informality and his genuine Top Ender manner quickly put her more at ease. Samantha told Burroughs that she was familiar with Robertson Barracks. She explained that as a disabled veteran with a Gold Repatriation Health Card, she visited there regularly. She made Caleb blink when she said, "Look, I know Robertson quite well. We need to be ready to blow part of it up if the enemy gets too possessive, with appropriate size devices, as needed. This isn't a job for time fuses. We need to be able to do it by command detonation. I have the technology to make that work."

She presented her "shopping list" to Caleb. He was taken aback but, to his credit, recovered quickly after she told him her thoughts and outlined her plan.

After describing her qualifications and the particulars of the systems she had been installing, Samantha talked her way into being issued forty complete M18A1 Claymore antipersonnel mines—the largest number issued to any Stay Behind. Along with them came forty-four electric blasting caps. The green plastic 3½ pound mines used C-4 plastique to propel hundreds of steel ball bearings in a sixty-degree arc. The front of each mine had FRONT TOWARD ENEMY molded into the plastic.

"I know wireless home automation systems forward and backward, but my knowledge of explosives is limited," Samantha explained. "Can I get the help of someone who really knows explosives, for a day or two?"

"I know just the man for the job," Caleb replied. He loaned her Chuck Nolan.

The 1st Brigade Headquarters was the most impressive building in the Robertson Barracks complex. Built in 2006, the two-story structure had a large open two-level reception terrace that extended toward a reviewing stand and parade ground on the far side of Malaya Street. Samantha felt confident that the Indos would try to occupy the building. General officers of any nation, she surmised, would have a weakness for teak paneling.

Atop a stepladder, her first look above the ceilings showed that they were insulated in conformance with the recent rulings for public buildings that had been promulgated by Standards Australia. Normally, she dreaded the sight of itchy fiberglass insulation in an attic crawl space, but she was thrilled to see so much of it in the brigade headquarters building since it would conceal her upcoming handiwork.

Chuck handled arming all of the mines, inserting a blasting cap into one of the pair of provided cap wells of each mine. They used all forty of the Claymores, facing them downward beneath the batts of insulation. There were two for the brigade commander's office—one each for the inner and outer offices—sixteen for the various staff offices, eleven for the small conference rooms, ten for the main assembly hall, and one for the men's washroom that was closest to the brigade commander's office. Samantha did not want to risk missing her primary target.

Emplacing and wiring the controller and the Claymores took her two long, exhausting, and sweaty days, even with Chuck's help. Rather than using the reels of brown two-conductor wire that were provided with the mines, she opted to use Romex type insulated wire that had been liberated from a post facilities workshop. This wire, she judged, would attract less suspicion if the Indonesians searched the attic spaces. By tapping into power junction boxes in the attic and putting all of the mines as well as the controller underneath the insulation, she hoped they would be missed unless there was a detailed inspection.

The controller that she had available supplied only 230 volts, AC, but she reckoned that voltage would work just fine to set off forty blasting caps wired in parallel. The Ensign-Bickford blasting caps were designed for 30 to 60 volts, DC, as the triggering voltage. Just to make sure they'd work with the available voltage, she and Chuck did a test outside the office of an adjoining building on Lighthorse Drive using a spare blasting cap. The cap lead wires were inserted in the receptacle at the end of a yellow AC extension cord. The other end of the cord was plugged into one of her web-based controllers. After the shunt for the cap was clipped, she touched it off using a command from her iPhone. The noise made by just that one blasting cap was louder than she expected. It shattered a window and made her ears ring. When she saw the broken window, she said, "Uh-oh. There I've done it. Destroying government property. Tisk-tisk." As she pocketed her iPhone and began to coil up the extension cord, she joked, "Steve Jobs is probably doing turns in his grave about now."

Chuck mimicked a television narrator's voice and said, "The new, improved iBomb—yep, there's an app for that. Making the world a better place."

Laughing at Chuck's impression, Samantha said, "If you log in with the password and bring up the Palmerston Beach House web page and then click 'Air Conditioning On,' the Indos will be the recipients of quite a fireworks show. We'll wait, of course, until the maximum number of Indonesian field-grade officers are present."

Chuck nodded. "Yes, it would be wise to wait."

39

RULE .303

"The more you know, the less you need."

—Australian Old Saying

Site G, Near Darwin, Northern Territory, Australia— February, the Third Year

L ike all of the other civilian employees, Chuck Nolan was asked to not leave Site G once the Indos began their landings. He mainly assisted with the sporadic nighttime visits by the FLB's supported units. These vehicles would arrive using only blackout lights, with the drivers wearing the standard issue ITL N/SEAS night vision monocular, very similar to the American PVS-14 system. They would load up quickly—mostly rations and ammo—and then be gone in less than an hour. These "pull" missions were straightforward, and became almost routine. There were of course nagging fears that the Indos might observe the routes they took, but that level of risk couldn't be avoided. They hoped that within a couple of weeks, there would be a major Australian Army advance and that they'd soon be inside friendly lines.

There were also three daring nighttime "push" logistics runs to re-supply isolated units. These were just individual trucks from the FLBs, driven by soldiers wearing NVGs. Also in the cab was a navigator, who usually spent most of each run with a poncho draped over his head so the light from the GPS screens wouldn't blind the driver. They intentionally left the infrared blackout light on the vehicles turned off, realizing that they could be spotted from a great distance by any night vision equipment. In Afghanistan, their IR lights had even proved vulnerable to detection by inexpensive consumer video cameras used by the Taliban. This combat lesson was still fresh in their minds.

The first Indonesian landings were conducted at night, but once they had large numbers of troops ashore, they began to feel confident and ran their landings twenty-four hours a day. For Caleb Burroughs and the men at his FLBs, an anxious waiting game began.

Nine days after the landings began, Site G had their first enemy contact. Word came from a concealed ridgeline observation post (OP) that was three kilometers to the southwest. The observer reported a possible dismounted Indonesian patrol advancing toward the FLB. A minute later, he radioed a follow-up: Based on their uniforms and weapons, they were definitely Indonesians—either army or marines. The FLB was quietly put on full alert. Their usually shunned Tiered Body Armour System bullet-resistant vests and helmets were enthusiastically donned, and the perimeter foxholes were all manned. Caleb Burroughs ran from foxhole to foxhole, imparting some strict rules of engagement. He hoped the FLB would go undetected and that the Indo patrol would pass them by.

As a civilian, Chuck Nolan felt redundant in this buzz of activity. He donned his Camelbak and boonie hat, picked up his rifle and approached Caleb. He said hurriedly, "I'm not really needed here. Everyone's been trained and equipped to demo the whole site without my help. You know I'm a good runner, fast on a bike, and a good shot, so what do you say I go east of here and draw them off?"

Burroughs hesitated for just a moment before firmly ordering, "Go!"

Chuck didn't waste any time. He cross-slung his rifle and jumped on his mountain bike. Pedaling furiously, he was out to Litchfield Park Road in less than a minute. Four more minutes of riding brought him to the base of a brushy hill that gave him a commanding view of the valley. He left the bike fifty yards into the jungle on the east slope of the hill and started to climb. In another few minutes he was atop the hill, lying prone and observing the eleven-man Indo infantry patrol through the scope on his Enfield. They were arrayed in a shallow V in fairly open ground. They were now just three hundred yards from the FLB's southern perimeter. Chuck was nearly perpendicular to the patrol's avenue of advance.

By their casual movements, Chuck could tell that they weren't expecting contact. Even without military experience, he knew that if they were anticipating trouble, they would be using bounding maneuvers. This looked more like a nature hike—just a typical security patrol with only the precaution of the wide wedge formation. But he could also see that if they continued in their direction of advance, they would eventually impinge the west side of the FLB's defensive donut.

Chuck sighed. He pulled back the bolt hammer that he had *slowly* released earlier on a live round. It served as a nice additional safety on a chambered round, on the SMLE. There was no wind, but this would be a very long shot—he roughly estimated it at seven hundred yards—and he was shooting slightly downhill. His rifle was zeroed for two hundred yards. Referring to the drop table taped to the rifle's forend, he saw that he had to hold over by six feet four inches. But he came back down eight inches to compensate for shooting downhill, which would otherwise make the bullet impact too high. Chuck also had to lead slightly, compensating for their steady walking speed. He aimed for the second man back from the point man. Realizing that he had little chance of a hit when shooting so hastily from such a long distance, he squeezed the trigger anyway. His job, he reasoned, was just to *make noise* and draw them away—not to win any awards for marksmanship. The rifle bucked against his shoulder.

By the time he got his scope lined up again, all of the men in the Indo patrol had dropped to the ground. He slowly cycled the rifle's bolt. With the patrol in high grass and brush, Chuck could see only two of the Indo soldiers. He took a steady aim and fired again. This time, he could see a puff of dust kicked up by the bullet's impact—slightly high and to the right. The Indonesians started to return fire. Despite the range, the Indonesians peppered the hilltop. Chuck could hear some rounds going over his head, a queer sound that he had never experienced before.

Instinctively, Chuck began crawling backward. The bullet impacts were getting closer. Dirt kicked up on both sides of him, but after just thirty seconds of crawling, Chuck was safely below the crest of the hill. Holding his rifle at high port position, he took a couple of jumps and then started running down the reverse side of the hill. As he ran, he glanced up and picked out another small hill near the winding road, about a mile up the valley. He was quickly on his bike again and pumping the pedals. His mouth had gone completely dry, so he took a few pulls from the bite valve on his hydration pack. He had a lot of ground to cover in a hurry. Once he was a half mile down the road, he heard more firing coming from the hilltop he had just recently occupied. At first sporadic, their rifle fire became intense, coming in long volleys. A few rounds twanged on the pavement ahead of him and beside him.

Finding an untapped reserve of energy, Chuck rode even faster. A few hundred yards farther down the road, a curve took him behind a hillock, blocking the Indos' line of sight. The shooting stopped, and Chuck started laughing. "I can play this game all day!"

He continued cycling rapidly. As he worked his way up the valley, he changed his mind about the hill he had picked out, deciding that it would be too obvious. He opted instead for another hill on the left side of the road, slightly closer. This one wasn't in line of sight to the hill from which he'd fired before.

He intentionally rode beyond this hill as well, to be able to approach its reverse side. Walking carefully with the bike's frame over his left shoulder, he did his best to avoid leaving a trail in the grass. This made for uncomfortable walking, especially with the rifle slung over his other shoulder. He left the bicycle in the jungle—farther in this time, and broke a few tree branches off to camouflage it.

Chuck started up the hill at a slower pace, stopping to take several pulls from his Camelbak. Even if they ran, the Indos wouldn't be close for another half hour.

He reached the crest of the hill in twelve minutes. This hill, slightly higher than the first, was more heavily covered with trees. It made observing the valley more difficult, but it gave him better camouflage. This time, he carefully selected his position with his eventual retreat in mind. He picked a hollow near the summit, one that was particularly brushy. Just a ten-second scoot backward would take him safely behind cover. He decided that to avoid being predictable, this time he wouldn't go back to his bike. Instead, he would plunge into the dense jungle to the north. "Try to find me out there," he whispered to himself.

After he got his breathing under control, he took stock of his situation. He reloaded his rifle with two fresh rounds from a stripper clip of the same Greek ball ammo that he'd been shooting. With the rifle topped off, he examined the scope and wiped the dust off its objective lens with the tail of his T-shirt. Alternating between scans of the valley with his scope, he inventoried his pockets and his Camelbak pack. He found his wallet, his Leatherman Wave tool, six granola bars, an Aquamira Frontier siphon straw water filter, ten stripper clips of .303 ball (one of them now short two rounds), one full Enfield box magazine of .303 soft-nose, two melted Cherry Ripe chocolate bars still in intact plastic wrappers but feeling squishy, a similarly squishy Aero Chocolate bar, six toilet paper packets (from CR1Ms), a small bottle of Italian Gun Grease brand gun oil, a Bic lighter, four Band-Aids, a mini Maglite, a handkerchief, a C-A-T tourniquet, and two Australian Army battle dressings.

He scanned the valley again, and took a few more sips of water from the tube over his shoulder. As a new believer in Christ—a "baby Christian" in Baptist parlance—Chuck had not yet memorized much scripture. He had, however, committed to memory the first four verses of Psalms 91, which he said aloud, nervously.

"He that dwelleth in the secret place of the most High shall abide under the shadow of the Almighty. I will say of the Lord, He is my refuge and my fortress: my God; in him will I trust. Surely he shall deliver thee from the snare of the fowler, and from the noisome pestilence. He shall cover thee with his feathers, and under his wings shalt thou trust: his truth shall be thy shield and buckler."

After pausing for a moment, he added a phrase that had caught in his memory from a movie he had seen about the American Revolution: "Lord, make me fast and accurate. Amen."

Realizing that he might need a quick reload with the same type of cartridges he'd been using, Chuck methodically unloaded the spare 10-round magazine of soft-nose and refilled it with ten of the Greek ball cartridges. He needed to be sure the rifle would have the same point of impact with every shot. As he was reloading the soft-nose cartridges into the emptied stripper clips, the Indonesians came into view. He took a long look through the scope. There were still eleven of them. He could see that they were now in staggered file on both shoulders of the road and moving at a trot. He estimated their range at twelve hundred yards. He toyed with the idea of engaging them at this extreme range, but then decided against it. He again donned his Camelbak and waited.

He suddenly wished that he had better camouflage. Lacking a typical three-color camouflage face paint compact, he picked up a handful of mud from a low spot that was just within reach. He rubbed the mud over his face and neck, the exposed V of skin at the top of his green shirt, and the exposed backs of his hands. Noticing the shiny finish on his scope, he also smeared mud on the scope tube. He used some more of the mud on the back of his neck.

Taking another look through his scope, he saw that they were now about eight hundred yards away. Even at this distance, he could see that most of the soldiers were nearing exhaustion. The soldier in the lead turned and shouted to the others. Chuck surmised that this was an NCO.

Thankfully, there was no breeze as he readied his rifle. Since they were only slightly quartered to him, there was no need to lead to compensate for their rapid pace. He had just confirmed the holdover required for seven hundred yards, so he decided to engage them at the same distance. They would also be in an open stretch of ground with no brush.

His first shot missed, going just over the soldier's shoulder. The second shot, fired right as the soldier crouched down after stopping, hit him in the solar plexus. He went down hard, flat on his back.

The Indos, now prone, began answering with bursts of fully automatic fire, vaguely in Chuck's direction. Chuck took deliberate aim. With his subsequent eighteen shots, he hit three more soldiers—two of them were decisively hit and left sprawling belly-up, like the first one.

At least one of the Indonesians must have caught a glimpse of Chuck or seen a muzzle flash, because the incoming rounds were coming in uncomfortably close. The Indos moved off the road and maneuvered toward the base of the hill, running in pairs. Chuck slid backward, crawling behind cover. A 5.56 bullet caught the top of his boonie hat, spinning it around and nearly plucking it from his head. As he reached full cover, Chuck felt a warm trickle running down the side of his head, parted by his ear. He reached under his hat and felt a three-inch-long grazing wound to his scalp. Only after he'd touched it did it start to sting.

Chuck started down the ridge, picking up speed. He reloaded his rifle from stripper clips as he ran.

40

DEBRIEF

"Whoever looks upon them as an irregular mob will find himself much mistaken. They have men amongst them who know very well what they are about, having been employed as rangers against the Indians and Canadians; and this country being much covered with wood, and hilly, is very advantageous for their method of fighting."

—Hugh Percy, 2nd Duke of Northumberland, from a letter written April 20, 1775

Site G, Near Darwin, Northern Territory, Australia— February, the Third Year

Three days after he had first engaged the Indos, Chuck Nolan stumbled back into Site G. In a close call, he was nearly shot by anxious perimeter sentries for his failure to know the day's password.

Chuck reported to Caleb's truck-mounted shelter, which served as both his office and sleeping quarters. Caleb took one look at his haggard face and his filthy, bloodstained shirt before declaring, "Good Lord, Nolan! You look like a box of blowflies, and you smell like a big two-day-old Bondi. What happened out there?"

Caleb chewed an Anzac chocolate bar from a CR1M ration as he answered. "I was running and gunning with them for a day and a half. I kept moving and fired anywhere from two to six rounds every hour or so, leading them on a merry chase. Most of those shots were just to make noise. I was about twenty miles northeast of here when I fired the last few shots. Then I went and found myself the most gosh-awful dense patch of jungle to crawl into and slept for about ten hours. After that, I very quietly made my way back here, using a circuitous route."

Caleb watched Chuck practically inhale the ration and immediately open a second one. "What did you eat for the past three days?" Caleb asked.

"Other than a few candy bars I had in my hydration backpack, just a few bush bananas and a couple of snakes. One of them was a big mulga and the other was some variety I didn't recognize. But I assumed it was poisonous, too. I pinned their heads down with the muzzle of my Enfield and then cut their heads off with my Leatherman. I ate them raw."

"Crikey."

"Well, like they say, 'protein is protein.' Anyway, I was moving too fast to do any serious foraging, so here I am with one heckuva appetite."

After taking a sip from his Camelbak, Chuck asked, "Did you have any enemy contact here?"

"No, it's been quiet. The Indos seem pretty clueless. No systematic patrolling despite our proximity to where you first started shooting. That was fantastic of you, playing offsider for us. It was like seeing a Spur-winged Plover faking a broken wing. You fooled the Indos, so you're going to be the camp celebrity for sure, mate."

"I just want to clean my rifle, get a shower, get some more to eat, and some rack time. I also need to scrounge for some .303 ammo since I shot up almost sixty rounds."

"No worries, Chuck. Your low ammo supply justifies me issuing you an SLR and a pile of ammo and magazines."

"An L1A1? Really? That would be great."

Caleb shook his head. "Don't mention it. That's just fair dinkum."

As Nolan pulled off his boonie hat to show Caleb the scabbed-over wound, he said, "Oh, one more thing. I'd like the medic to look at this little bullet graze."

Caleb chortled. "Ooh, that was close. An inch lower and that round would have emptied your skull out like shooting a melon."

Chuck let out a grim laugh. "Yeah. I've thought about that. *A lot.*"

"Oh, but Ava is going to love it, after it heals. It'll make quite the dashing *Mensur* or *Studentische Fechten* scar for her to admire," Caleb said. He ran the tip of his forefinger across his own cheek in a slashing motion to emphasize his point.

"Yeah, right. Some fencing scar. *Schön und hässlich, gleichzeitig.* She'll probably tease me about it, endlessly."

The wound had already filled with pus, which the medic said was typical in the Northern Territory, even with well-treated wounds. After his initial assessment, the medic painfully cleaned out the wound, re-bandaged it, and counted out a bottle of flucloxacillin. He also issued a stern warning to use up *all* of the pills in his prescription even if any signs of infection had disappeared.

All in all, Chuck considered himself lucky to have made it back to the FLB in one piece.

Headquarters, ADF Special Operation Command, Near Bungendore, Australia—February, the Third Year

Just hours after emplacing the Claymore mines in the headquarters building at Robertson Barracks, Samantha Kyle had packed her SUV and joined the stream of refugees heading south. She got to Canberra as quickly as she could and then drove twenty miles east to Bungendore. After spending just eight hours in a motel, she drove seven miles south to Headquarters Joint Operations Command (HQ JOC), the ADF's top operational headquarters. Arriving at seven thirty A.M., she found that her ADF Disabled ID card and a warm smile got her past the main gate of the General John Baker Complex to the HQ JOC building. The one-story glass-fronted building looked more like a modern college classroom building than it did a military headquarters. She was directed to the desk of a secretary in the office of the deputy commander. After explaining why she was there, Samantha was immediately referred to the Special Operations Command (SO-COMD), which was also headquartered in the same base complex. "They're the ones who handle all of the Stay Behind issues," she was told. Samantha looked displeased until the secretary said, "No worries. I'll give you directions and I'll phone ahead."

Once at the SOCOMD headquarters, an armed SAS trooper escorted Samantha to the commander's office. There, she was met by the commanding general's aide-de-camp. A first lieutenant with deep-red hair, he sat at a surprisingly Spartan steel desk. His beige SAS beret was tucked into the left epaulet of his MultiCam shirt. The doorway behind him had a doorplate stenciled SOCAUST, which she knew stood for Special Operations Commander, Australia. Samantha explained that she had been involved with the Darwin Stay Behinds and that she needed to brief the commanding officer. The lieutenant explained, "The general will be in late today. On Wednesday mornings he does his longest run of the week. He should be here at 0815." He gestured to a nearby chair for her to wait.

The lieutenant did his best to pry some more information out of her, but Samantha clammed up, saying, "I'm not certain you have a need to know." The lieutenant seemed nonplussed and quickly transitioned to chatting up Samantha. Most of their conversation was about crocodiles and beaches.

The commander arrived at 0814 wearing MultiCams and a beret. He immediately went into his office, with his aide following close behind. Three minutes later the lieutenant emerged from the inner office and gave Samantha a thumbs-up, holding the door open for her.

The aide shut the door from the outside to give them privacy. Samantha was nervous. This was the first time she'd ever spoken to a general officer. Major General Rex Raymond was near sixty years old but still lean and fit. He had a pencil-thin mustache, short-cropped gray hair, and a deep tan. The walls of his office were lined with photos and memorabilia.

After brief introductions, Samantha haltingly described the preparations being made with the Darwin area Stay Behinds. Then she explained her civilian work in home remote-control systems and how she had just wired the headquarters at Robertson Barracks.

General Raymond laughed. "That's simply brilliant. I'll give you full marks for that."

Emboldened by the general's response, Samantha pressed on. "So now I want to wire some more Claymores in the control tower at the Amberly Air Force Base."

The general laughed again, and said, "You don't bandy about, do you?"

Without giving Samantha a chance to respond, he said, "I don't think the Indos will ever advance down the east coast far enough to threaten Amberly. Our ASIO liaison and all the top planners and analysts agree with that. The Indos have delusions of *adequacy*. Granted, they've got superior numbers, but they don't have the nakas for a big stand-up fight, and that is what they'll get if they try to advance south of Townsville."

He hesitated for a moment and then said, "I do like your idea, but it is far more likely to be put to good use if you emplace Claymores in the control tower at Townsville. I can send you up there with a couple of my troopers and a few Claymores, but you'll have to convince the civil air authorities that stray RF from their radios or radars isn't going to set off your blasting caps prematurely. That would be most unpleasant."

41

DENIAL

"The more I learn about people and society the more I love guns and explosives. Guns and explosives are more understandable, more predictable, and less hazardous."

—Joe Huffman, in his blog *The View from North Central Idaho*

Darwin, Northern Australia— March, the Third Year

Four days after Chuck Nolan returned to Site G, an Indonesian patrol discovered Site M, the McKenzie farm.

The patrol consisted of six Indonesian Army (TNI-AD) troopers on green-painted Kawasaki 275-cc off-road motorcycles. They had been tasked with following every road and track in their operational area to search for any signs of resistance, and for any materiel that could be exploited. That day they had already used their bolt cutters to cut the locks on more than twenty gates on the Adelaide River Road.

Although the McKenzie farm was hidden by hills, a pair of the cycle troops found it simply by following the road. The cycle scouts rode up to the farm house with nonchalance. The farm looked abandoned and no vehicles were visible. Their eyes were drawn to the big riding arena building, so it was where they started their search. It was also where it ended.

The younger of the two troopers slid back the big door of the arena and his eyes grew wide as saucers. Inside were enormous piles of supplies on pallets and more than a dozen Australian Army vehicles and civilian trucks parked in a herringbone pattern, nose out. There were eight rifles pointed at him. An Australian sergeant who had combat experience in East Timor shouted, "*Opgeven!*" the Dutch word for surrender. Rather than surrendering, the soldier grabbed the MP5 submachine gun that was slung across his back and spun it around to fire.

He went down in a fusillade of bullets. The Indonesian managed to fire only one short burst into the ground before a hit to his upper spine caused him to lose control of his grip. A few moments later, a second burst of fire killed the other TNI-AD trooper.

One of Site M's outlying sentries reported that other Indo troops had heard the shooting and could be seen radioing in a report. Realizing that Indonesian aircraft might respond in just a few minutes, or ground troops might arrive in less than an hour, the lieutenant commanding Site M wisely ordered an immediate evacuation and destruction of all of the FLB's stored supplies.

In just five minutes all of the fuse igniters had been pulled. The site's entire complement of vehicles headed out individually to a predesignated rally point that was fifty-five miles to the south. From there, they would convoy to Alice Springs.

Within a few minutes of their evacuation, the farmhouse was fully engulfed in flames—accelerated by ten gallons of gasoline. The explosions of the fuel blivets and stacks of mortar ammunition began another eight minutes later. The explosions and resulting smoke could be seen and heard for miles.

The vehicles headed south quickly, each following a preplotted GPS route. This circuitous route used all secondary roads until they were south of Katherine, in the hopes of avoiding contact with Indo-Malaysian forces. For the first fourteen hours, the convoy stopped only to refuel, using their Mack MC3 diesel tanker truck. They jokingly called this camouflage-painted turbocharged diesel nine-ton truck their *Mad Max 2* Tanker.

At near midnight they reached the Ti Tree Airport, which was just inside of friendly lines. Ti Tree was an old cattle station town. A RAAF and RAAAF contingent at the airport were there to greet them and to direct them to a vehicle dispersal area. The airport had already been bombed once and was under sporadic observation by Indonesian drones, so it was not considered safe to leave the vehicles near the airstrip or to park in a regular pattern.

After six hours of sleep, they resumed their convoy to Alice Springs. In all, the drive was eight hundred miles, and they covered most of that in the first day. Once they reached Alice Springs the following day, the officer in charge made inquiries with his brigade commander via the RAAF's satellite phone. Ironically, he was ordered to set up a new FLB in the bush at a water bore three miles east of Ti Tree Airport. This was less than one and a half miles beyond where his unit had bivouacked the night before. They spent the afternoon shifting supplies, refueling all of their vehicles, and refilling the tanker.

By the next evening they were establishing the new Ti Tree FLB on Anmatyerre aboriginal land. His men were exhausted by the time they had the camouflage nets suspended above all of the vehicles. The lieutenant had thought it was important to do so before dawn. Some of the men grumbled about this, but they stopped complaining when they heard the sound of RAAF machine gunners shooting at a Wulung drone as it passed overhead.

The dusty Ti Tree FLB was not nearly as comfortable as Site M, but it would be their home for the next three weeks.

42

A TIME TO EVERY PURPOSE

"When it comes time to die, be not like those whose hearts
are filled with the fear of death, so when their time comes
they weep and pray for a little more time to live their lives
over again in a different way. Sing your death song, and die
like a hero going home."

—Chief Aupumut, Mohican, 1725

Near Darwin, Northern Territory, Australia—
March, the Third Year

Soon after their invasion of Australia began, the Indonesians
started to shuttle fighter aircraft and fighter-bombers to airfields
in northern Australia. Because they lacked aircraft carriers, this
necessitated flying with minimal armaments and carrying drop tanks.
Ordnance for the planes all had to come to Australia, so the planes had
only limited operational capability with a low operational tempo, allowing just two sorties per day.

When war with Indonesia began to look likely, a Civilian Auxiliary
Australian Air Force (CAAAF) was created almost spontaneously.
Most of the volunteers were retirees who owned their own light planes.
The CAAAF—also jokingly known as the Old Farts' Australian Air
Force (OFAAF)—had two distinct cadres of members: those who had
family obligations, and those without. The latter formed the nucleus of
the organization. Many of them were self-designated as "too old or too

sick to care" and volunteered for the riskiest missions. These were mostly "teaser" flights aimed at getting the Indonesian Air Force to scramble their fighter planes. The goal was to flush the Indonesian fighters out of their hardened revetments so they could then be shot down by any of the dozens of Stinger Stay Behind teams that were deployed along the northern Australian coast. Since the Indonesians had more operational aircraft than the RAAF, it was essential that they be destroyed either on the ground or as they were taking off or landing. Everyone realized that if their air superiority were allowed to continue, the Indo planes would make it very costly for Australian Army forces to maneuver. Only with freedom of maneuver would they be able to counter the Indo-Malaysian advances.

One much-publicized septuagenarian couple in the CAAAF was Edward and Paula Hadley from Alice Springs. Edward Hadley was a retired banker. Before they left on their final flight, Mr. Hadley told a reporter from *The Australian*, "When you're seventy-three and have been diagnosed with Stage Three pancreatic cancer, you can be a lot more fearless than a healthy twenty-something who has a wife and kids."

They day before they left, they visited their son, who agreed to take charge of their mixed-breed Bitzer dog, Max. When they left Max and his leash and food bowl, their son realized they weren't coming back.

Mr. Hadley was flying his Turbo Mooney 231, which he had owned and meticulously maintained for twenty-five years. His wife was flying a donated twenty-three-year-old Cessna 172. The Hadleys spent their last night before the fateful mission at an abandoned cattle station near Stapleton. Like many other stations with its own airstrip and AVGAS fuel tanks, the owners had willingly donated their use to the CAAAF.

At just after eight A.M. the next morning, the Hadleys came into Darwin at treetop level. Two Indonesian F-16 fighters were scrambled in response, taking off side by side. The Indo pilots foolishly left their flare dispensers turned off. Before the jet fighters could turn toward the two light planes, they were downed in rapid succession by Stinger

POST missiles while still less than eight hundred feet off the ground. Five minutes later, after the Hadleys had circled the Darwin Airport several times, they lined up their planes' noses toward the military ramp at the south side of the airfield. Another Indonesian fighter—an F-5—taxied out of its revetment. The Hadleys' two planes dropped their flaps and angled toward it, making a well-calculated approach at ninety miles per hour just off the deck. In rapid succession, they slammed the Mooney and the Cessna into the F-5, spraying wreckage across the taxiway and setting all three planes ablaze.

In the preceding year and a half, most of the Australian Army had been tied down with quelling civil disturbances in major cities on the south-eastern coast. A limited call-up of the Australian Army Standby Reserve had only been partially successful, given the chronic fuel shortages and general chaos in the cities.

Before the Crunch, Indonesia had about 235,000 men under arms, including one armored cavalry brigade and fourteen infantry brigades. These brigades included ninety infantry battalions, one parachute battalion, nine artillery battalions, eleven antiaircraft battalion, nine engineer battalions, one independent tank battalion, seven independent armored cavalry battalions, and four independent para-commando battalions.

After some reshuffling three of Malaysia's four army divisions were put under the operational control of Indonesia, bringing with them the majority of the Malaysian army's one thousand armored vehicles.

After the Crunch, the Indonesians also hastily assembled another eleven reserve infantry brigades. These units were led primarily by retired officers and NCOs who had been recalled to active service. The second-line units were equipped with older-generation equipment, some of which dated back to World War II. These brigades were intended for protection of the home islands, thus freeing up the regular army for the planned invasions.

There were also twenty-seven new Pembebasan Kerombakan Komando (PKK) battalions formed. These 140-member units were a separate organization from the 786 Heroes. The PKKs trained to infiltrate enemy territory to mine roads and to blow up bridges, trestles, communications facilities, port facilities, and other key infrastructure *south* of the 24th parallel. Given the strategic goal of the invasion, oil fields, fuel pipelines, and terminals in the northern half of the country were intentionally ruled out as potential targets. But fuel refineries and related infrastructure south of the 24th parallel were on the target list.

The Indonesian general staff set the following targeting priority for the PKKs:

1. All surviving RAAF aircraft
2. Civilian communications infrastructure
3. Military communications infrastructure
4. Civilian and military air defense and ATC radars
5. Power generation and distribution infrastructure
6. Intelligence gathering and analysis centers

Facing the 350,000 Indonesian and Malaysian invaders, the Australian Army had just 25,000 Regulars in the country, and between 55,000 and 170,000 Reserves—depending on whether or not the Standby Reserves were counted. Many of these men had not had any military duty for twenty-five years. As the Crunch set in, the Australian soldiers deployed for Operation Slipper became stranded in Afghanistan. And since the deployment had gone "up-tempo," its numbers had surged from 1,500 to 5,000 men just before the Crunch.

The original Indonesian invasion plan had included seizing the huge Kwinana refinery near Perth. But that part of the plan was later discarded after the manpower required to depopulate and control the Perth region was studied in detail. The final plan—Plan Capricorn—sought to control all of the territory and oil assets *north* of the 24th parallel, and carry out a "depopulation and denial" terror campaign south of the 24th parallel. The long-term goal of the invasion was to terrorize Australia into permanently ceding all of the land north of the 24th parallel to Indonesia. They reasoned that since the vast majority of the Australian population already lived south of the 24th parallel, the Australians could be bullied into submission.

For more than a decade, Indonesia had been developing its own drone aircraft. The main UAV program was development of the Wulung, a 264-pound drone with a twenty-foot wingspan and a T-tail. It had a four-hour flight endurance and a cruising speed of sixty-nine miles per hour. The data link limited it to operating only within forty-five miles of its ground controller. Crude by the standards of developed nations, the Wulung had a very noisy engine and simple avionics, but it still provided fairly useful tactical imagery. The Wulung had gone into mass production in 2014, but most of them were destined to service in foreign militaries.

The Wulung UAVs were difficult to spot and shoot down. Only one was downed by ground fire, but two of them were downed by CAAAF pilots, who discovered that the unarmed UAVs could be approached from behind by a light plane that slowed to near stall speed. Closing on the UAVs slowly, their fragile tails could be quickly chewed off by just a touch of an airplane propeller. Tailless, the UAVs were sent spinning out of control.

The Australian Army had its own UAVs, the larger and slower but more sophisticated RQ-7B Shadow 200 drones. Since the Wulung had a single tail boom and a T-tail, and the Shadow had a twin tail boom and an inverted V-tail, there was little risk of misidentification. The Aerial Threat Briefings given to all ADF units and even the ABC television news shows about the invasion emphasized this key difference in their designs.

The American-made Shadow UAVs weighed 458 pounds and had a sixteen-foot wingspan. They had up to nine-hour flight endurance. The Australian Army, however, had only seventeen of them at the onset of the Crunch, and nine of those were deployed in Afghanistan, and hence left out of the equation. Then, on the night of the synchronized Indonesian attacks, four of their Shadow UAVs were destroyed on the ground by thermite charges. The four remaining Shadows were used quite effectively and none of them were lost to ground fire or Indonesian fighter planes. The problem was that there were simply *too few* Shadows available. The expansive distances of the Northern Territory also limited their effectiveness. The Shadows worked well in Papua New Guinea and in Afghanistan, but in Australia's Top End, the flying distances were so great that the UAVs were either completely out of range or so close to their maximum range that they had hardly any loiter time before they had to return to their airfields.

The drone war was just one small piece of the parrying that took place between the Indos and the Australians. Both sides, like chess players, were waiting for their enemy to make a decisive move.

43

THE SPIRIT

"Of course most people underestimate the warrior characteristics of the Anglo-Saxon and Norman peoples anyway.
It takes a heap of piety to keep a Viking from wanting to go
sack a city."

—Jerry Pournelle, in a reply to reader e-mail, in *Chaos Manor*
Mail 141, February 19-25, 2001

Jabiru, Northern Territory, Australia— February, the Third Year

Quentin Whittle was typical of the solo Stay Behinds in the Northern Territory. He had military experience and few family con-
nections. A self-proclaimed "spitting chips mad bogan," Whittle
was a former bush logger and commercial hunter. He was forty-three
years old and divorced, with no children.

When he was in his early twenties, Quentin had served just two
years in the Australian Army as an infantryman before a trailer hitch
accident crippled his left hand—leaving him with only one finger and
very limited strength in his thumb. Although the army would have allowed him to continue with active service if he transferred to a support
branch, he opted to take a disability "early out." He eventually settled
into a job as a truck driver and log loader operator with Kasun Logging
headquartered in Rapid Creek, a suburb north of Darwin.

After the Crunch curtailed most logging, Quentin took up commercial hunting. His hunting territory ranged mostly east into the Garig

Gunak Barlu National Park where he mainly went after feral pigs, feral banteng cattle, feral sambar deer, and magpie geese. He sold or bartered all of the meat that wasn't necessary for him to survive and drove a battered old Toyota HJ75 trayback ute that was equipped with a pivoting hoist and electric winch for lifting the heavier animal carcasses.

Quentin was one-eighth aboriginal by the blood of his great-grandmother Polly, but his fair skin and light brown hair didn't show it. His status as an "octoroon" gave him aboriginal hunting and fishing privileges under the Territory Parks and Wildlife Conservation Act 1976 and the Cobourg Peninsula Aboriginal Land and Sanctuary Act of 1981. He was occasionally confronted by the Parks and Wildlife Commission of the Northern Territory Rangers. When showing the Aboriginal Land Council hunting permit and the Aboriginal Status Declaration documentation that he always carried in his wallet, he would often play it up, putting on a heavy aboriginal accent. "Why you blokes always harassing us hard-yakka black fellas, uh?" This infuriated the park officials since his status made him immune from enforcement of most of the game laws, and even from the requirement to purchase any hunting permits under the most recent legislation.

Whittle's small and nondescript rented house outside of Jabiru, about 150 miles east of Darwin, was notable only for having three chest freezers filled with frozen meat, and rawhides dominating the living room. His next-door neighbor was a full-blooded aboriginal named Sam who made his living catching and drying freshwater barramundi. When the Indonesian invasion started to look imminent, Quentin gave Sam two of his three freezers. With Sam's help, they loaded the third freezer into Quentin's ute bed. Towing a trailer containing only the most valuable and useful items from his other household goods, Quentin drove to Rapid Creek. Among his other gear was a duffel bag of military field gear that he had stolen several years before from a fellow army private in retribution for a barracks prank that went too far.

In Rapid Creek, Quentin took up residence in the disused gardener's house on the grounds of an estate owned by Kasun Logging. The owner was about to "head for the Big Smoke" (a big city) with his family and was happy to have a caretaker.

Quentin Whittle owned just two guns: a 1920s-vintage Belgian-made Liege 12 bore double-barrel shotgun with almost all of its original bluing worn to a gray patina, and a Remington Model 7 .308 Winchester bolt action. The latter was equipped with an inexpensive Simmons variable 3-9-power scope. The rifle's buttstock was badly battered from constant use in the field.

As a designated Stay Behind, Quentin was issued four pale olive green 200-round cans of ammunition marked 7.62 MM BALL F4 on their sides and 7.62 BALL BDR-CHGR on their lids. Each can held four green canvas bandoleers of ammunition in stripper clips. The ammo was compatible with his .308 Winchester rifle. His prior army qualifications also made him eligible to be issued fragmentation hand grenades and Claymore mines. After a half-hour refresher course, he was given ten frags and six Claymores with one proviso from Caleb Burroughs: "Be sure to put them to good use. Do not bury your talents."

By training, an infantryman's first instinct is to dig. During the week before the Indos landed, Quentin selected, developed, and stocked sites for three hidden firing/hide positions on the periphery of Darwin and one bivouac site. He spent the next two nights shuttling clothing, rations, ammo, and gear from the guest house to the four sites. At the three chosen firing positions, he dug foxholes with wooden lids, commonly called spider holes.

According to his laser range finder, each of the holes was between 350 and 550 yards from positions that would likely be occupied by the Indonesians. The first spider hole was on the military crest of a knoll near the edge of Holmes Jungle Nature Park. This hole was 407 yards from the junction of Vanderlin Road and McMillan Road. He called this his Jungle Park hole.

The second spider hole was in Charles Darwin Nature Park and had a view across Sadgrove Creek to a long stretch of Tiger Brennan Drive. Even before he finished digging it, the bottom of this hole began to fill with seeping swamp water. This "swamp hole" was in a wetland location that would be difficult for the Indonesians to pinpoint and even harder to access.

The third spider hole was on a triangle of scrubland at the junction of Howard Springs Road and the Stuart Highway southeast of Palmerston City. He called this his Road Watch hole. This one was just sixty yards from Taylor Road, but he didn't plan to shoot in that direction. Anticipating that the Indonesians would quarter some of their troops at the abandoned Robertson Barracks and that they would frequently use the Stuart Highway, he hoped this would be a prime sniping location.

His main bivouac—a "sleeping hide"—was one and a quarter miles northeast and just a mile east of Robertson Barracks, just beyond a group of small lakes. He found one of the thickest patches of brush in the area, crawled in, and leveled off a shelf on a gentle slope that was not much wider than his bivy bag. The brush was so thick that he could hardly see the sky. This bivouac site was just a few yards uphill from a small creek where he could refill his filter canteen. From his position, he could hear the Indo ships unloading vehicles at the East Arm docks. Darwin Harbor was full of Indonesian and Malaysian ships of all descriptions. A few of these were civilian roll-on, roll-off (RORO) ferryboats that had simply been painted gray and pressed into navy service.

Quentin plotted the coordinates for the three spider holes and his sleeping hide with his GPS, offsetting each sixty yards to the east, in case his GPS receiver was ever taken.

The spider holes were armpit deep. He used thirty-inch square scraps of Australply laminated plywood for their lids. With a jigsaw, he cut the lids into curving oblong shapes to reduce their chance of detection.

Quentin then camouflaged them further with a generous coat of Clag Kid's PVA white glue and sprinkled them heavily with soil and dried leaves. A few small downed tree limbs were then attached with finishing nails. He was careful to use soil, leaves, and limbs gathered in the immediate vicinity of each spider hole so they would look natural.

44

CONTACT

"A fine marksman with a second rate rifle is far more effective than the reverse."

—Colonel Jeff Cooper, writing in Mel Tappan's newsletter
Personal Survival (P.S.) Letter

Darwin, Northern Territory, Australia— February, the Third Year

Just as he was finishing up camouflaging the lid of his third spider hole, Quentin caught his first glimpse of the Indonesians: a Korps Marinir scout vehicle roaring through an intersection a quarter mile away. It was a French-built AMX-10P, but Quentin initially mistook it for an American-made M113—a model he'd once ridden in. It was not until he had a chance to look at the vehicle through his rifle's scope that he could see the distinctive 25 mm gun turret atop the APC.

Quentin spent the next three nights further stocking his three spider holes. On a packboard, he carried three four-liter water jugs and one case of CR1M rations to each hole. He also spent a few hours at the Road Watch spider hole observing the Indos' vehicle movements on the Stuart Highway through his binoculars or rifle scope. A huge variety of vehicles passed by, most of which looked unfamiliar. Nearly half of the trucks appeared to have been of civilian manufacture and simply painted in tan and reddish-brown blotches to prepare them for use in the Australian invasion.

The vehicle movements initially looked chaotic, but then he noticed a pattern: at five P.M. each day, an Alvis Stormer tracked APC stopped on the shoulder of the Stuart Highway just south of Howard Springs Road. There, a soldier set up a small satellite dish on top of the vehicle and connected it to a backpack SATCOM radio. Once it was set up, another soldier—presumably an officer or NCO—climbed atop the APC to read a message into the SATCOM radio's handset, referring to pages on his clipboard. Each message seemed to take about five minutes to transmit. Then the subordinate soldier would disassemble the radio, collapse the folding dish, and stow the gear. Each time, they'd make a 180-degree turn and drive back in the direction of Palmerston.

Whittle surmised that they chose the spot near the road junction because of its excellent line of sight to the north. He decided that if the opportunity arose again, he might have the chance to take out an officer or a senior NCO.

The next day, Quentin spent the late afternoon watching the highway through his rifle scope instead of his binoculars. The Stormer APC arrived on time as usual. As the radio man set up the SATCOM dish, Quentin used his rangefinder and confirmed that the APC was 570 yards away. He tested the wind with a spittle-moistened finger. There was a very slight breeze from the south. The soldier with the clipboard climbed atop the APC and began sending his message. He was facing almost directly toward Whittle, but the other soldier was looking southward.

Quentin started feeling anxious. He knew his rifle was zeroed for three hundred yards, so at this distance he would have to hold high. With the rifle steadied on a Harris bipod, the scope crosshairs tracked smoothly. In a way, this almost felt like harvesting a roo, but he had never shot a man before, and this seemed particularly cold-blooded. The man with the clipboard droned on. Quentin decided to aim at the top of the man's left ear to allow for both the bullet drop and the slight wind. He clicked the rifle's safety forward and took deliberate aim. He could see a slight oscillation in the crosshairs caused by the pounding of his heart. He fought to control his breathing. A seven-vehicle convoy approached, so Quentin decided to wait.

Once the convoy was out of sight, Quentin again took up his normal cheek weld on the Remington's stock. He settled the crosshairs above the soldier's ear. He let half a breath out, and gently squeezed the trigger with the first pad of his trigger finger. The bullet struck the Indonesian just to the right of the center of his chest. As the rifle came down from the recoil jump, Quentin caught a glimpse of the soldier going down. But he didn't wait to observe any longer. He slipped into his spider hole and slowly slid the lid in place. He was breathing rapidly, feeling overwhelmed. In the almost pitch-blackness of the spider hole, he methodically cycled the rifle's bolt and flipped the safety back to the safe position.

Just then, the 25-millimeter atop the Stormer came to life. Firing in long bursts, the gunner expended 120 rounds. Of all those rounds fired, Quentin heard just two rounds zip over the top of his spider hole, so he knew that the Indos had only a vague idea of the direction from which his shot had been fired. There was a pause in the cannon fire as the gunner switched to a fresh ammo can. During this lull, Quentin could hear sporadic lighter-caliber fire. He surmised this was from the 5.56 mm rifles he had seen the Indos carrying. The gunner cycled the first round from the belt into the cannon and resumed firing. This time the bursts were shorter—just three to six rounds per burst. Again, the gunner burned up an entire belt, but unlike the previous belt, Quentin heard no near misses. He snorted to himself and mouthed silently, "Those wankers have no clue where I am."

The firing ceased. Quentin could hear other vehicles stopping near the APC. There were many shouted orders. After five minutes, Quentin heard a whistle blowing. It sounded just like his rugby coach's whistle from twenty years ago. Expecting a dismounted infantry advance in his direction, Quentin's attitude quickly changed from curiosity to fear. He wished he had a miniature periscope or something like a webcam so he could see what was going on around his position. He didn't dare lift the lid of the spider hole. There were a few rifle reports as the skirmish line of nervous Indonesian soldiers shot at any suspected targets.

After a couple of minutes, Quentin could hear the voices of individual Indo soldiers. It wasn't long before the voices became quite distinct. He heard the crunch of approaching footsteps. Quentin's breathing grew more rapid, and he could hear the blood pounding in his ears. His hands began to shake, but the Indonesians passed by his undetected spider hole. The voices faded into the distance. There were still a few occasional rifle shots, but none came close to his hiding position. Sitting in the darkness, Quentin grinned in relief. He whispered to himself, "What galahs."

Other than cracking the lid roughly once an hour for fresh air, Quentin stayed hunkered down in the spider hole. He took sips of water and nibbled on a packet of prawn crackers, but he didn't feel very hungry. He waited until his wristwatch showed three thirty to fully open the lid and investigate his surroundings. The Indo vehicles had long since departed. A sliver of moon was setting in the west. He waited, watching and listening intently for ten minutes. After the moon had set, he hopped up out of his hole and carefully replaced its lid. He moved very slowly and quietly in case the Indos had left an ambush patrol.

Quentin sprinkled a bit of earth around the edges of the spider hole's inset lid. If it weren't for the distinctive Y formed by the limbs atop the lid, it would be very hard for him to locate, even in full daylight. Forty minutes later he was resting in his daytime hide. He had trouble getting to sleep. Just before falling asleep at sunrise, he thought to himself, *One down, three hundred thousand to go.*

The next morning the sky became overcast early and it began to rain. Quentin spent some time deepening the draining trench at the uphill side of his sleeping platform. He crawled back into his bivy bag, zipped the mosquito netting closed and shifted the thin tropical-weight sleeping bag beneath him for extra padding. He fell asleep. After a half hour the rain transitioned to a torrent. He zipped the bivy bag's end flap shut. He chuckled and said to himself, "Try using your tracking dogs now."

45

HEAD SHOT

"All warfare is based on deception. Hence, when able to attack, we must seem unable, when using our forces we must seem inactive, when we are near, we must make the enemy believe that we are away; when far away, we must make him believe we are near. Hold out baits to entice the enemy. Feign disorder, and crush him.

"If he is secure at all points, be prepared for him. If he is superior in strength, evade him. If your opponent is of choleric temper, seek to irritate him. Pretend to be weak, that he may grow arrogant.

"If he is inactive, give him no rest. If his forces are united, separate them. Attack him where he is unprepared, appear where you are not expected. These military devices, leading to victory, must not be divulged beforehand."

—Sun Tzu, *The Art of War,* Translation by Lionel Giles, 1910

Near Robertson Barracks, Northern Territory, Australia—February, the Third Year

After two nights in his bivouac hide, the rains lessened. Quentin Whittle repacked his rucksack and hiked a mile north to the quarry lakes east of Robertson Barracks. Passing by the lakes, he approached the recently active sand quarry on Thorngate Road. Slowing to an almost creeping pace, he skirted the south edge of the quarry. When he was 110 yards from the road, he transitioned to a high crawl. He moved forward slowly through the brush and took up a hide position 70 yards west of the gate on Robertson Road. Avoiding any sudden movements, he spread out an oblong camouflage net with the green side up. (It could be reversed to tan for use on sandy ground.) This eight-foot-long and six-foot-wide plastic net took up half the volume of his pack. Draping the net over himself, Quentin looked like just another bush.

His vantage point was fair, though he wished there was higher ground available with a more commanding field of view. Aside from the obstruction of the guardhouse, he still had a very good view down Robertson Road, across the parade field, and beyond the reviewing stand to the 1st Brigade Headquarters terrace and its covered parking circle.

He could hear the whine of large generators running somewhere at the post but outside of his line of sight. He cranked his scope up to 9-power and flipped down the rifle's bipod legs, moving them very slowly to avoid having the leg springs make the annoying twang that they made if this was done in haste. The floodlights at the entry gate were dazzlingly bright. He could just make out the outline of the headquarters building in the distance. He decided to stay in this temporary hide for at least eighteen hours to observe the daily rhythm of activities. Four guards lolled at the gate. At 190 yards, they would be an easy shot. The terrace at the headquarters building was 500 yards away, which would be a much more difficult shot. His mission, however, was to observe, not to snipe.

As dawn broke, his view of the headquarters building improved when the floodlights were extinguished. He could see Indonesian officers smoking on the upper terrace deck. One of them had his hand on the rail. He was facing directly toward Whittle, who could see the man take repeated puffs on his cigarette. As the soldier dropped his cigarette butt, stamped it out, and turned to go back indoors, Quentin mouthed, *You don't know how lucky you are, mate.*

After it was full daylight, Quentin pulled out the iPhone he'd been given by Samantha Kyle. Removing it from the Ziploc bag, he powered it up. It showed 94 percent of battery capacity. There was no telephone

service, but the Wi-Fi indicator popped up, showing three signals—
two of them weak, and one fairly strong. The latter was labeled
HOLSWORTHY-02. Quentin tapped the screen twice and a password
entry box popped up. He pulled out his notebook and opened it to the
page of passwords that Samantha had provided him. The first four passwords were rejected, but the fifth one worked.

"Ace!" Quentin whispered.

Next, Quentin brought up a browser window. Buried among more
than 500 web page bookmarks was the Palmerston Beach House page.
Opening it and then selecting the pull-down menu for HOUSE CON-
TROLS, he clicked on AIRCON. At the top of the next screen was a pair of
toggle buttons marked A/C ON and A/C OFF. Below them was a temperature control slider with Celsius numbers in a blue-to-red gradation.
He hovered the pointer over the A/C ON button and grinned. He whispered, "You found your true calling, Miss Samantha." He gazed up at
the brigade headquarters. Then looking back down at the iPhone, he
closed the browser, checked the battery once more—now down to
ninety-two percent—and powered down the phone. After rebagging
the phone and notebook, he took a sip of water from his Camelbak. It
was going to be a long day of watching.

That evening, Quentin decided to visit his other spider hole sites over
the next several nights. He started by visiting his swamp hole, in
Charles Darwin Nature Park. Walking stealthily, he covered the distance to the park in six hours. Most of the city was blacked out. There
were just a few islands of light, mainly near the docks where the Indonesians and Malaysians had generators running. They were still landing, troops, vehicles, and innumerable pallet loads of artillery shells.
Their incessant activity reminded Quentin of ants.

Quentin skirted around several buildings that were occupied by Indonesians. He was amazed to see that they took few, if any, light and
noise discipline measures and their sentries did not look particularly

alert. Using his GPS, he took note of the date and unit locations in his notepad.

Arriving at Charles Darwin Nature Park, he was disgusted to find that the spider hole was nearly full of water. He grumbled, "So I've dug myself a well. I'm such a boofhead. Scratch that."

He retrieved the ammo can from under the water. He was surprised to find that despite some newly formed exterior rust, the can's contents were dry. The can's rubber gasket had done its job. He stowed the can in his pack and trudged back to his bivouac site, arriving just before dawn.

The next night he "tabbed" to the Holmes Jungle Nature Park, which was a shorter walk. He was surprised to find a noisy Malaysian Army unit set up there. Their sprawling encampment actually straddled the hillside where he had constructed his spider hole. Seeing this, Quentin muttered to himself, "Well, forget that one."

Resting prone a hundred yards away, Quentin studied the encampment through his binoculars. The Malaysians were talking, joking, and even occasionally shouting. They seemed to be quite unconcerned. In three hours of watching, Quentin saw only one roving sentry. The Malaysians had two large AC generators running and their light discipline was pitiful, with no attempt to conceal their generator-powered light strings. His observations that night were bemusing. Based on the configuration of their truck-mounted shelters and the many antennas, he determined that it was a communications unit of some sort.

He decided that this was too good a target to pass up. It would be the perfect place to use his Claymores.

Quentin could see that one of the open-sided Malaysian tents had a map board. There were lots of folding chairs in the tents, so he presumed the space was used for briefings during daylight hours. The area appeared to be the Malaysian equivalent of a Tactical Operations Center (TOC). There was just one officer there. He was drinking coffee and holding a nightlong vigil next to a radio and a field telephone that were set up on a table.

Quentin noticed that the four tents nearest to the TOC tent were different from all of the other bivouac tents, which were smaller two-man pup tents. These were more spacious, looking like they could each hold three or perhaps four cots. He could occasionally see the flare of cigarettes being lit in these darkened tents, so they were obviously occupied.

As he watched the activity in the camp, Quentin repeated to himself, "Too good to pass up."

46

CLAYMORES

"... When you're a pessimist, the worst that ever happens is that things go exactly the way you were prepared for them to go, and half the time you're pleasantly surprised."

—Massad Ayoob, *Backwoods Home Magazine*, January 1, 2009

Near Robertson Barracks, Northern Territory, Australia—February, the Third Year

Quentin returned to the Holmes Jungle Nature Park the next evening, but first he walked quietly through a blacked-out suburban neighborhood to the west, checking door locks. About half of the houses were unlocked. After five houses, he found what he was looking for—a moldy-smelling house on Spathe Court that was so messy he could barely walk from room to room. This house had belonged to a hoarder. The rooms were so heaped up with boxes and piles of newspapers that it would be almost impossible to search them effectively.

He unpacked everything from his rucksack except the six Claymore mines and left them in a box in one of the bedrooms. There, he spent an hour organizing as he developed a sort of nest behind the headboard of a king-size bed. In the nest area, he prepositioned a small foam mattress, a child's Spider-Man sleeping bag, three cases of bottled water, a variety of tinned foods, a couple of empty milk jugs with caps, and the box of miscellany from his rucksack. Making note of the address, he shouldered his pack and tabbed his way back to the nature park.

Just after nine P.M. the following evening, Quentin settled into the observation point he had used two days previously and watched and waited for two hours to ensure the guard schedule was the same. Setting up the five Claymore mines took a nerve-racking forty minutes. He used just one electric blasting cap. The other four mines were tied together in a daisy chain of PETN blasting cord that went from cap well to cap well.

He aimed each mine by laying a pencil across the inadequate plastic sights that were molded into the top of each mine. The pencil provided a longer sighting plane, making this part of the job easier, even in the dim light. He combined four sets of the brown firing wires to give himself more standoff distance.

His goal was to be as far away as possible when the mines went off, giving him a head start on anyone who might pursue him. He hoped the miniature "clacker" detonator would have enough of an impulse through the extra-long firing wire. He wasn't disappointed. The five targeted tents were shredded by the blasts. The camp was chaotically roused to attention. Malaysians fired erratically all around their perimeter with no particular targets. Tracers arced out randomly in all directions. Whittle laughed quietly at their confusion and thought to himself, *What a beautiful sight!*

Quentin was already over the park's north fence by the time the first patrol was initiated in reaction to the blast. He spent the next three days in the Spathe Court house in his dusty nest. He eventually found a package of AA batteries, so he was able to read a few paperback books that he'd picked out from among the hundreds that were stacked in the house. It proved to be a quiet way to spend the next three days as he waited for the local patrols to die down. They never searched the Spathe Court house, but he did hear squealing tires several times, and searchlights washed the front end of the house two nights in a row.

Five days later, Quentin was back at his temporary hide site opposite the Robertson Barracks gate. He lingered there until after dark. There was a steady stream of vehicles to and from the headquarters building, but no sign of any big meetings. He wondered when the right opportunity to strike would present itself.

Continuing his vigil on Tuesday, he was excited to see an unusually large number of vehicles arriving in front of the headquarters and dropping off passengers. It was obvious that there was a high-level meeting about to start. After 12:50 P.M., there were no more arriving vehicles. At 1:04 P.M., Quentin hit the A/C ON button. Although they didn't look dramatic from his vantage point, the results were devastating.

The simultaneous explosions roared and a cloud of dust rose from the roof of the headquarters building. He saw the windows shatter and paper floated down like confetti. But the sprinklers worked as designed, and immediately prevented any fires from spreading and burning down the building. Quentin stayed and watched the whole show. By the number of stretchers carried out to military ambulances, he presumed that there were at least sixty casualties. It wasn't until two months later that he learned there were eighty-two WIAs and sixty-two KIAs, including six field-grade officers. The commanding general was missed only because he was late arriving at the staff meeting. Quentin Whittle's decapitation of the Indonesian invasion command structure resulted in confusion, hesitation, and what turned into indefinite delays in their forces advancing south to the 24th parallel. The decisive hit, however, was not enough to completely stop the invasion from advancing.

The Big Push began. The Indo-Malaysian army had already been stopped twelve miles north of Port Hedland in the west, forty-five miles north of Alice Springs in the center of the country, and eighteen miles north of Townsville in the east.

Holding fast to their front lines on the coasts, the Australian Army shifted and advanced into the Northern Territory on three main axes of advance: west from the town of Mount Isa, north from Alice Springs, and east from Port Hedland.

Assuming that the Aussie Army would avoid the major highways and attempt to cross the Tanami Desert via the Tanami Road, the Indos had positioned a large portion of their ground forces south of Halls Creek, expecting an epic ground battle. Instead, they were outmaneuvered before they could even react.

In the end, the combined Indonesian and Malaysian armies proved to be too poorly trained to stand up to the Australians, despite their larger numbers. It was the Australian Army's artillery that proved to be the decisive blow. Light spotter planes, flown by both RAAF pilots and CAAAF Reserve pilots radioed in the locations of Indonesian and Malaysian vehicles and troop concentrations. If artillery wasn't already within range for an immediate barrage, it often could be relocated within a few hours to inflict devastating strikes. Then, per their modern doctrine, the artillery units would quickly displace, leaving the Indonesians wondering from whence the fire had originated. The Indonesians lacked counterbattery radars.

Indonesian aircraft dispatched to spot the Aussie forces quickly fell prey to the Australian's ground-based air defenses. Left blind, the Indos maneuvered ineffectively, and most units were cut off and were then handled piecemeal. Their large force at the edge of the Tanami Desert was isolated and attrited by both artillery fire and by CAAAF pilots flying private planes packed with explosives in suicide attacks.

The only major battle of the war took place at the edge of the Barkly Tableland, between the towns of Katherine and Tennant Creek. This three-day conflict resulted in a horrific loss of life. The final tally was 22,800 Indonesian KIAs, 1,850 Malaysian KIAs, and 15,812 Australian KIAs. And 307 of the invaders' vehicles were also destroyed. Most of the Australian casualties were Australian Army Reserve unit members. More than 20,000 Indonesian and Malaysians were taken prisoner and 151 vehicles were captured intact. The Battle of Tennant Creek (as it was later known) broke the will of the Indonesians in the ground war. The Australian press described this as "the only real knock-down, drag-out fight" between the two armies. The Indos started their peace overtures the following week via HF radio.

In the end, Caleb's two remaining FLBs became just a minor footnote in the history of the conflict. They did, however, provide some badly needed fuel and replenishment of ammunition as the army advanced. With the FLBs in place, a portion of the army was able to press on to attack the Indonesians without having to wait for their logistics "tail" to catch up with them as they normally would.

The cease-fire and withdrawal of the invasion forces was facilitated by the holding of 536 Australian civilians hostage in Papua New Guinea and forty-six in East Timor. Some of these hostages were from the Australian mainland and forced to board ships as the Indos started their withdrawal. The Indonesians made a show of calling them "guests of the peace-loving Indonesian government," but they made it clear that they would not be released until every Indonesian and Malaysian POW was released and repatriated. Video footage of the Australian hostages was shown endlessly on ABC television. In the end, the Indos got their way. But the Australian prime minister made it clear that because hostages were used, normalization of relations between the two nations would be delayed for a decade or more, even *if* the agreed reparations were paid in full, in gold bullion.

Refugees began to return to their homes in the Northern Territory even before the bilateral cease-fire was formally announced. As news of the Indonesian withdrawal from each city became public, long convoys of refugees' vehicles returned. They found that some towns had hardly been touched while others had suffered widespread destruction at the hands of the retreating Indo troops.

Following the return of the refugees to the Top End, there was a huge quantity of captured Indonesian and Malaysian materiel. Mountains of Indonesian military Composite Rations (similar to CR1M rations) mysteriously hit the civilian market. The Northern Territory newspapers had many stories about civilians attempting to register captured vehicles with the Department of Transport's Motor Vehicle Registry (MVR). This caused a huge row in the editorial pages. The large number of captured firearms created an even larger uproar as people debated the legality of civilians possessing these weapons. Some called for reinstating the ban on civilian-owned semiautomatics, while the majority—and an overwhelming majority in the Northern Territory and Western Australia—thought a renewed ban would be ridiculous. In the end, a general consensus developed that Australia needed a well-armed citizenry to help defend against invading armies. One newspaper editorial summed up the decision with the pointed headline: WHAT IF CHINA COMES NEXT TIME?

47

STAR OF COURAGE

"All you need for happiness is a good gun, a good horse, and a good wife."

—Daniel Boone

7th Combat Service Support Battalion (CSSB) Forward Headquarters, Robertson Barracks, Palmerston, Northern Territory, Australia—April, the Third Year

Chuck tapped on the brigade commander's door. After Colonel Reynolds shouted, "Enter!" Chuck stepped into the office and found the colonel tapping away at his laptop keyboard. Looking up, he smiled and said, "Good to see you, Nolan. Do shut the door."

After Chuck had closed the door behind him, Reynolds flipped the laptop screen closed and said, "How are things getting along with your Inventory, Destruction, and Safe Storage project? We've been hearing the explosions from quite a distance."

"It's all gone quite well. It was my pleasure to stay on for an extra couple of weeks to see it all wrapped up. The dugout space for the captured artillery rounds and other explosives was limited, so we had to be selective about what we destroyed, what we sold, and what we put into storage. Much of it had no commonality with our logistics and no civilian use, so that material was burned in place, or for any *contained* explosives—like artillery rounds and mortar bombs—blown in place."

The colonel nodded, and Chuck continued, "There was a large quantity of the Indo's bulk explosive in twenty-kilogram bags, essentially a clone of commercial AMEX explosive. Along with that was about twenty thousand feet of detonating cord. That stuff is identical to commercial Cordtex or Primacord except for its outer casing color. Those explosives and det cord would have been a shame to burn up, so it was disposed of at auction via a six-way phone conference call. The high bidder was a big mining supply company in Malaga. They bought it with the understanding that they had just four days to haul it away. It was all gone by Wednesday. At this point, I'm just down to having someone proofread the report that you requested, and scheduling my last day."

"I think Saturday should be your last paid day, assuming that you get your report in tomorrow. No need to come into the office on Saturday, mind you. Does that sound good?"

Chuck smiled. "Yes, sir. So what is the procedure for ending my contract?"

"Well, Chuck, it's pretty simple when we're talking about an open-ended 'at will' contract. In essence: you stop showing up for work, and we stop paying you."

Both men laughed.

Chuck asked, "Okay, now what about my SLR—how do I go about turning that rifle back in?"

The colonel cocked his head and smiled. "You know, in all the confusion and tumult of combat, there was a tremendous amount of materiel that was captured by the Indos, destroyed, or otherwise went missing. Why, even my own AUG went missing and had to be replaced with one that came from a wounded trooper who was sent off to hospital. In your case, your SLR will be logged as an 'unavoidable combat loss, captured by the enemy with no possibility of recovery' or some such."

Chuck grinned in response and said, "That has a nice ring to it: 'unavoidable combat loss.' Thank you, sir."

Within three weeks of the cease-fire, most Darwinites had returned to their homes. Many parts of Darwin and its suburbs were just as the refugees had left them. But even in the untouched houses, the lengthy power outages had left refrigerators and freezers a stinking mess. Nearly all of these had to be discarded and replaced. Livestock that was left out to pasture generally fared well, although the Indos had helped themselves to some steak on the hoof. On two farms, dozens of cattle and sheep had been indiscriminately machine-gunned and left to rot.

One family in the Darwin suburb of Berrimah came home to find a sink full of dirty dishes and a garage stacked full of cases of Indonesian Composite Rations and more than a hundred cans of 5.56, 7.62 and .50 caliber ammunition. Their garden shed was stacked full of diesel fuel cans. They assumed that their house had been used as a TNI-AD supply cache of some sort.

Another family in the posh Darwin suburb of Cullen Bay returned to find that an Indonesian officer with a penchant for larceny had occupied their house. In just a few weeks he had accumulated thousands of pieces of loot, including dozens of oil paintings from several different galleries, sacks of gold and silver coins, dozens of pocket watches and wristwatches, several stamp collection albums, nearly a thousand audio CDs and Blu-ray DVDs, seventy-five laptop computers, 127 iPads, twenty-three Kindle readers, seventy-eight smartphones, and more than a dozen high-grade shotguns. It took months to track down the owners of these items.

Peter Jeffords reunited with Rhiannon and Sarah, and the three found that their rental house was just as they had left it, except for the musty smell that permeated all the rooms. It took three days to air out the house to Rhiannon's satisfaction.

Ava Palmer and her parents returned home to find that their house was also fine, except for a rank-smelling fish aquarium and a lawn that had grown so tall that their gas-powered lawn mower's grass catcher had to be emptied five times to complete the job. Their three vegetable gardens survived quite well despite the depredations of birds during their absence.

Chuck proposed to Ava Palmer two days after his army contract ended. She immediately accepted. Given the calamitous times they had just survived, neither wanted a long engagement. They decided to get married two weeks later at Casuarina Baptist Church. Ava's parents were delighted.

On the first weekend between his proposal and their wedding, there was an awards ceremony at Robertson Barracks. Caleb Burroughs was one of the organizers of the event. He arrived wearing his olive green Ceremonial Dress Uniform with Sam Browne belt and saber.

Chuck Nolan and Quentin Whittle were both to be awarded the Star of Courage. This silver star with a red and orange ribbon was awarded to civilians for "acts of conspicuous courage in circumstances of great peril." They were among just fifteen civilians awarded the medal for their service in the recent conflict with Indonesia. Nine of those commendations were made posthumously, mostly to CAAAF volunteers.

Before the ceremony began, Samantha Kyle caught Caleb's eye, and he approached her. Smiling, he said, "Well, it's good to see you again. Miss Claymore, was it?"

She laughed and replied, "It's Samantha Kyle. I promise I'm not here to beg you for any more Claymore mines. They're going to give me a Commendation for Brave Conduct, for emplacing a few remote-control goodies. But honestly, I don't think the trifling things that I did deserve any recognition."

Caleb shook his head. "Oh, quite the contrary! I'm told that it was the loss of their key leadership that made the Indos blink, and that it may have changed how everything got sorted out. You *do* deserve a commendation."

After a pause he added, "Can I be so bold as to ask you to dinner, this evening?'

"Wouldn't that be considered fraternizing, since you're an officer?"

"Well, since you had *prior* service in Other Ranks and are now a civilian, technically no, it would *not* be considered fraternization. And I'd consider it an honor if you would accompany me."

Samantha smiled and said, "Then yes. I'd be delighted."

The church was well known locally as the Food for Life charity church because they operated a food bank. It was also a source of controversy after the church opened its doors to foreign asylum seekers who were held in detention. Most of them had been arrested immediately after arriving on Australian soil. Each Sunday, buses from three of the four detention centers around Darwin arrived and SERCO contract guards wearing their insipid pale blue uniforms escorted the detainee "clients" into the church building. The Christian detainees included Afghanis, Iranians, Nepalese, Sri Lankans, Turks, and Vietnamese.

The pastor, who had been a fireman earlier in his life, conducted the wedding ceremony. Caleb stood up as Chuck's best man. The church was quite crowded with the regular congregation, plus Ava's many local friends and several of Chuck's coworkers from AOGC, as well as several friends he had recently made while working at Site G. The Jeffords family was there, along with Paul Navarro, his grandson, Joseph, and Joseph's girlfriend.

Ava wore a white wedding dress that she had been preparing for six months. (She had seen the proposal coming.) Chuck wore his black "weddings and funerals" suit with a crimson red tie. It was a wool suit but made with lightweight fabric, in deference to the Texas climate, so it served him well in Australia. Ava insisted that Chuck wear his Star of Courage on his suit pocket.

Since the wedding was to be held immediately after the church service, the asylum seeker "clients" asked to stay late to attend. Many of the wedding pictures included both asylum-seeking detainees as well as their detention center guards in uniform. The pastor asked Chuck whether the extra guests bothered him, but he didn't mind. "The more the merrier," Chuck said. "It was already an international wedding, so this just adds some more international color."

One of the guests at the wedding was Samantha Kyle. Caleb had been courting her in earnest since they saw each other at the awards ceremony. Even though she had worked with Chuck only for one day—wiring the explosives at Robertson Barracks—she came to the wedding as Caleb's guest. Caleb was clearly smitten with Samantha. He took Chuck aside and confessed that he was already thinking about asking Samantha to marry him. Not wanting to discourage his friend, Chuck still considered it his duty to advise Caleb to be just a little more patient.

The ceremony was brief, but it included a gospel message for those attending in the Baptist tradition. They sang just one hymn, which dated back to eighth-century Ireland, "Be Thou My Vision":

> Be Thou my Vision, O Lord of my heart; Naught be all else to me, save that
> Thou art. Thou my best Thought, by day or by night, Waking or sleeping,
> Thy presence my light.
> Be Thou my Wisdom, and Thou my true Word; I ever with Thee and Thou
> with me, Lord; Thou my great Father, I Thy true son; Thou in me
> dwelling, and I with Thee one.
> Be Thou my battle Shield, Sword for the fight; Be Thou my Dignity, Thou my
> Delight; Thou my soul's Shelter, Thou my high Tower: Raise Thou me
> heavenward, O Power of my power.
> Riches I heed not, nor man's empty praise, Thou mine Inheritance, now and
> always: Thou and Thou only, first in my heart, High King of Heaven, my
> Treasure Thou art.
> High King of Heaven, my victory won, May I reach Heaven's joys, O bright
> Heaven's Sun! Heart of my own heart, whatever befall, Still be my Vision,
> O Ruler of all.

Ava had long been considered the most eligible and attractive young lady in the congregation. After the ceremony, as Chuck and Ava shook hands with everyone in a receiving line, one of the detention guards summed up how many of the young men in the church felt when he commented, "You don't know how many hearts you've broken today, Ava, but we all wish you half your luck." This confused Chuck, who had never heard the expression. He just smiled and gave Ava a quizzical glance. Later, Ava explained to him that "half your luck" had been derived by shortening the phrase "I'd be happy if I had half your luck."

48

A NEW FLAG

"'Tis mine to seek for life in death,
Health in disease seek I,
I seek in prison freedom's breath,
In traitors loyalty.
So Fate that ever scorns to grant
Or grace or boon to me,
Since what can never be I want,
Denies me what might be."

—Miguel de Cervantes Saavedra, *Don Quixote*

170 Miles Northeast of Darwin, Northern Territory, Australia—May, the Third Year

Still stinging from their defeat and hasty withdrawal from northern Australia, the Indonesian high command issued orders for a series of punishing raids. Not expecting to do any substantive damage, these raids were designed to boost morale and to demonstrate that Indonesia was still in the fight. If nothing else, they distracted the media's attention away from the unending parade of photos and interviews with bedraggled Republic of Indonesia (RI) soldiers and sailors who had made it out of Australia in the "miracle evacuation." The Indonesian press was playing it up as a latter-day Dunkirk.

At the same time, Indonesia and Malaysia were dragging their feet on making their war reparations, which under the terms of the cease-fire agreement were primarily to be paid in the form of natural rubber.

Once all of their soldiers, sailors, and aviators had been released and allowed to return home, their conciliatory tone changed to something
more brash, Islam-centric, and nationalistic.

Captain Soekirnan Assegaf watched most of the invasion of Australia
on television. Other than ferrying some communications security
equipment to an invasion ship that had already left port, Assegaf and
his patrol boat did not play a major part in the invasion effort. They
were, however, involved in the aftermath. In mid-May, the *Sadarin* was
tasked with ferrying a fourteen-man PKK commando team to infiltrate
northern Australia for a sabotage mission. The orders were hand-
carried by the commando team leader and included the seals of both
the TNI-AL and BIN headquarters. To assure deniability, they included the proviso that the orders themselves were to be burned once
Sadarin was within 125 miles of Australian waters.

To fit so many soldiers and all of their gear on board, Assegaf opted
to crew his boat with just himself and three sailors. All three of them
were in Assegaf's cell. Like Assegaf, they were Muslim in name only
and therefore deemed expendable by their superiors. Suspecting they
might be used as scapegoats, the sailors confided to him that they
wanted to defect to Australia.

In the first leg of their mission the seas were rough, and some of the
commandos were seasick. Assegaf watched the commandos do their
daily prayers with quiet amusement. There was much debate each time
about the direction of Mecca so they would be sure to bow down in
the correct direction.

Instead of dropping them off on the coast north of Tiwi as he
had been ordered, Assegaf deposited them on uninhabited North Vernon Island. In the dark of night, the commandos didn't know the difference. Watching his depth finder carefully, he crept up to the shore.
Then he heard the familiar grind of beach sand at the ship's bow. The
men jumped off in just two feet of water in very light surf. The beach

ahead could just barely be seen in the moonlight. As soon as the last man had slipped over the bow, Assegaf gave a wave and reversed his engines.

A few minutes later, after sprinting off the beach and into some rolling dunes, the commandos unpacked one of their GPS receivers from one of their Chinese-made waterproof bags. It was then that they learned they had been deceived.

Wishing to look inoffensive when they surrendered, Assegaf and his crew dismounted the Browning .50s from the ship. Working in pairs, they carried them below to stow in their canvas cases. They hoisted a white flag that was fashioned from a bedsheet.

As they pulled *Sadarin* up to the newly installed floating dock at Fannie Bay, they were greeted by the muzzles of more than twenty guns held by Australian civilians. Captain Assegaf shouted to the gathered crowd, "We are here to surrender this ship and to seek asylum. I also need to tell you about fourteen Special Forces soldiers I stranded last night on North Vernon Island. They are heavily armed and I'm sure that by now they're as mad as Tasmanian Devils."

49

RESTORATION

"Guerilla war is a kind of war waged by the few but dependent on the support of many."

—B. H. Liddell Hart

Fort Knox, Kentucky—
January, the Fourth Year

As the resistance continued to gain ground, the ProvGov tried to sound upbeat in their propaganda broadcasts. The UN's Continental Region 6, which included the territory that had been the United States, Mexico, and Canada, was in a losing war with the guerrillas. The growing resistance throughout the region ranged from passive protest to sabotage and overt military action. The UN was steadily losing control of the former United States.

It was becoming clear that resistance was the strongest, the best organized, and the most successful in rural areas. Unable to wipe out the elusive guerrillas, the UN administration and their quislings began to concentrate on eliminating the guerrilla food supplies.

The ProvGov's army was bolstered by large numbers of soldiers from the United Nations Protection Force (UNPROFOR). In areas where resistance was rampant, "temporary detainment facilities" were constructed to house anyone thought to be politically unreliable. Special emphasis was placed on rounding up suspect farmers or ranchers, or anyone remotely connected with food distribution businesses. When farmers were put into custody, their crops were confiscated, plowed under, or burned. Bulk food stocks were carefully monitored by the authorities.

Despite the ProvGov's efforts, the guerrillas rapidly gained in numbers. As the war continued, resistance gradually increased beyond the UN's ability to match it. Every new detainment camp spawned the formation of new resistance cells. Every reprisal or atrocity by the UN or federal forces pushed more of the populace and even federal unit commanders into active support for the guerrillas. Increasing numbers of commanders decided to "do the right thing" and abide by the Constitution. The decision to support *the document* rather than the Provisional Government's power elite at Fort Knox was becoming widespread. Units as large as brigade size were parlaying with the guerrillas and turning over their equipment. In many instances the majority of their troops joined the resistance.

County after county, and eventually state after state, came under the control of the resistance. The remaining loyal federal and UN units gradually retreated into Kentucky, Tennessee, and Southern Illinois. Most held out there until the early summer of the war's fourth year. Militias and their allied "realigned" federal units relentlessly closed in on the remaining federal territory from all directions.

Fort Knox, Kentucky—Early July, the Fourth Year

The ProvGov collapsed following a fait accompli roundup that was led by rogue officers at Fort Knox. The UN flag was lowered and the Stars and Stripes were raised in a ceremony at a Fort Knox parade field on July Fourth.

The UNPROFOR's prison gates were opened, releasing tens of thousands of suspected resistance fighters and those who had been deemed "politically unreliable." Only common criminals remained incarcerated, and each of their cases was carefully reviewed.

The defeated armies were soon disarmed and demobilized. Apart from a few soldiers who were put on trial for war crimes, the rest of the U.S.-born soldiers were allowed to return to their homes by the end of August. The new interim Restoration of the Constitution Government (RCG) made it clear that if the "bounty" reparation payments stopped, the demob flights would stop.

Maynard Hutchings committed suicide before his extradition process was completed. Most of his staff and a few divisional and brigade commanders were eventually extradited from Europe, given trials, and shot. Hundreds of lower-ranking military officers and local quislings were arrested and similarly put on trial. Sentences included head shavings and brandings. In a few rare cases, death sentences were given. Only a few UN troops who professed fear of retribution if they were returned to their home countries were granted asylum. Each of these individuals was given separate hearings by the RCG. Most of them eventually gained citizenship.

The first elections since before the Crunch were held throughout the United States in the November following the federal surrender at Fort Knox. The Constitution Party and Libertarian Party candidates won in a landslide. A former Wyoming governor—a Libertarian—was elected president. Based on rough population estimates, the new House of Representatives had just ninety seats.

To the Altmillers, the RCG represented a great hope for restoration of all that had been lost, even before the Crunch. Their prayer was that the RCG would usher in an era of minimalist government, negligible taxes, and maximum individual liberty. They also prayed that commerce would flourish, that honest money would prevail, and that the nepotistic relationship among the bankers, Wall Street, and Capitol Hill would not be repeated.

50

O CANADA

"Once a nation parts with the control of its currency and credit, it matters not who makes the nation's laws. Usury, once in control, will wreck any nation. Until the control of the issue of currency and credit is restored to government and recognized as its most conspicuous and sacred responsibility, all talk of the sovereignty of Parliament and of democracy is idle and futile."

—William Lyon Mackenzie King (1874-1950), prime minister of Canada, 1935 speech

Tavares, Florida— March, Eleven Years After the Crunch

The Super Osprey II eight-passenger amphibian plane touched down on Lake Dora and taxied to the City of Tavares Seaplane Base. The breezy day made the water choppy. The Altmillers were waiting excitedly for them at the dock.

It had been nine years since the families had seen each other face-to-face. Lance Altmiller was now nineteen years old. He had found part-time work in the local thrift store, moving and sorting boxes of donated household goods. He still lived at home with his parents. Sarah Jeffords was fifteen and had recently begun arguing with her mother about whether or not she could wear eye makeup. Peter and Rhiannon Jeffords were happy to be back in America, but Sarah felt as if she had left her home—and all of her friends—in Australia.

The first thing Rhiannon said when she saw her sister was "Uggggh. You got old."

"You've got wrinkles, too, sis," Janelle replied.

"Well, we can count our blessings. At least you never got fat, and I got skinny and I stayed that way. And we all have our health."

Janelle nodded. "Yes, God is good."

Unloading their luggage was tricky, even with the amphibian plane pulled up on the gently sloped ramp. The Jeffords had brought seven suitcases, two Pelican pistol cases, and four Kolpin long gun cases. The six people and luggage were a tight squeeze in the two vehicles that the Altmillers had driven to the seaplane base.

The conversations on the short drive to the Altmillers' home focused on the Jeffords' lengthy trip. They had taken flights on an Airbus A380 and a Boeing 747-8 to Miami, and then the charter in the smaller amphibian to Tavares. The men were in one vehicle, and the women in the other.

When they reached the house, the day guard ushered them in. Their housekeeper, Elena, already had lunch prepared for them. The habana sandwiches and mojito salad were served with coffee and iced tea. Over lunch, the conversation quickly turned to their family in Bella Coola, British Columbia. Janelle and Rhiannon's parents, Alan and Claire McGregor, were in their mid-seventies and still living at the ranch there.

"There's talk of outright resistance in Canada. Almost everyone has wanted the UN troops out for *years*," Jake said emphatically.

"I've already been praying about this. I suppose we'll have to do something about Canada," Peter said.

"Do you suggest that we support the resistance or *join* it?" Jake asked.

Peter sighed. "If not now, then when? And if not us, then who?"

GLOSSARY

000: The Australian emergency service phone number, called Triple
  Zero. The equivalent of 911 in the United States.

10/22: A semiautomatic .22 rimfire rifle made by Ruger.

1911: *See* M1911.

2-D: Two-Dimensional.

3-D: Three-Dimensional.

.303 British: The British Commonwealth's standard rimmed .30
  caliber rifle cartridge from the 1890s to the 1950s. Also known as
  7.7x56mmR. Used primarily in SMLE rifles and Bren light
  machine guns. It was replaced by 7.62 NATO with the adoption of
  the L1A1 rifle.

5.56 NATO: The current standard rifle cartridge for NATO countries.
  Dimensionally, it is nearly identical to the .223 Remington but not
  completely interchangeable.

7.62 NATO: The former standard rifle cartridge for NATO countries.
  Still used in many NATO machine guns. Dimensionally, it is nearly
  identical to the .308 Winchester but not completely interchangeable.

9/11: The terrorist attacks of 9/11/2001, which took three thousand
  American lives.

A572: A common structural steel.

AAA: American Automobile Association.

ABC: Depending on context: Australian Broadcasting Corporation or American Broadcasting Corporation.

Abu Sayyaf: One of several militant Islamist separatist groups in the Philippines. Also known as al-Harakat al-Islamiyya. *See also* ASG and ILF.

AC: Alternating Current.

A/C: Air-Conditioning.

ACP: Automatic Colt Pistol.

ACU: Army Combat Uniform. The U.S. Army's "digital" pattern camouflage uniform that replaced the BDU.

ADF: Australian Defence Force.

AFB: Air Force Base.

AHRC: U.S. Army Human Resources Command. The current personnel management command for the entire U.S. Army, both Regular Army and U.S. Army Reserve. Formerly PERSCOM (U.S. Total Army Personnel Command) and AR-PERSCOM (U.S. Army Reserve Personnel Command). Decades of incompetence and mismanagement at U.S. Army Reserve HRC at St. Louis, MO, were finally addressed during the early years of the Iraq and Afghanistan occupations, thereby creating a consolidated management system, based at Ft. Knox, KY.

AIDS: Acquired Immune Deficiency Syndrome.

Aircon: Slang for air-conditioning.

AK: Avtomat Kalashnikova. The gas-operated weapons family invented by Mikhail Timofeyevitch Kalashnikov, a Red Army sergeant. AKs are known for their robustness and were made in huge numbers, so they are ubiquitous in much of Asia and the Third World. The best of the Kalashnikov variants are the Valmets that were made in Finland, the Galils that were made in Israel, and the R4s that are made in South Africa.

AK-47: The early generation AK carbine with a milled receiver that shoots the intermediate 7.62 x 39 mm cartridge. *See also* AKM.

AK-74: The later generation AK-family carbine that shoots the 5.45 x 39 mm cartridge.

AKM: The later generation 7.62 x 39 mm AK with a stamped receiver (Avtomat Kalashnikova Modernizirovanniy).

AKO: Army Knowledge Online.

ALICE: All-Purpose Lightweight Individual Carrying Equipment.

Alpenflage: A defunct Swiss military camouflage pattern with a significant percentage of red.

AM: Amplitude Modulation.

AMEX: A brand of commercial explosives, primarily used in the mining industry.

AMX: Atelier de Construction d'Issy-les-Moulineaux. A French armored vehicle manufacturer.

Angkatan Laut: Indonesian Navy. *See also* TNI-AL.

AO: Area of Operations.

AOGC: Australian Oil & Gas Corporation.

AP: Armor Piercing.

APC: Armored Personnel Carrier.

APEC: Asia-Pacific Economic Cooperation.

AR: Automatic Rifle. This is the generic term for semiauto variants of the Armalite family of rifles designed by Eugene Stoner (AR-10, AR-15, AR-180, et cetera).

AR-7: The .22 LR semiautomatic survival rifle designed by Eugene Stoner. It weighs just two pounds when disassembled.

AR-10: The 7.62 mm NATO predecessor of the M16 rifle, designed by Eugene Stoner. Early AR-10s (mainly Portuguese, Sudanese, and Cuban contract, from the late 1950s and early 1960s) are not to be confused with the present-day semiauto-only AR-10 rifles that are more closely interchangeable with parts from the smaller-caliber AR-15. *See also* AR, AR-15, and LAR-8.

AR-15: The semiauto civilian variants of the U.S. Army M16 rifle.

ARM: Australian Republican Movement.

ARRL: American Radio Relay League. National association for amateur radio.

ASAP: As Soon As Possible.

ASEAN: Association of Southeast Asian Nations.

ASG: Abu Sayyaf Group (Grupong Abu Sayyaf). *See also* Abu Sayyaf and ILF.

ASIO: Australian Security Intelligence Organisation. The Australian equivalent of the U.S. CIA. *See also* CIA.

ASP: Ammunition Supply Point.

ATC: Air Traffic Control.

ATF: Bureau of Alcohol, Tobacco, Firearms and Explosives (a U.S. federal government taxing agency).

AUD: Australian Dollars.

AUG: *See* Steyr AUG.

Aussie: Slang for Australian.

Austeyr: *See* Steyr AUG.

AVGAS: Aviation Gasoline. The most commonly used aviation gasoline is 100 octane, low lead (100LL).

Ball: Ammunition made with a nonexpanding full metal jacket.

BATFE: *See* ATF.

BBC: British Broadcasting Corporation.

BDR: Short for Bandolier.

BDU: Battle Dress Uniform. Also called camouflage utilities by the USMC. Most BDUs were made in the Woodland camouflage pattern.

BIN: Badan Intelijen Negara. The Indonesian State Intelligence Agency.

Bitzer: Australian slang for a mixed breed dog. ("Bits of this and bits of that.")

Black Rifle/Black Gun: Generic terms for a modern battle rifle— typically equipped with a black plastic stock and forend, giving these guns an all-black appearance. Functionally, however, they are little different from earlier semiauto designs.

BLM: Bureau of Land Management (a U.S. federal government agency that administers public lands).

BMA: Brigade Maintenance Area.

BMG: Browning Machine Gun. Usually refers to the .50 BMG, the U.S. military's standard heavy machine-gun cartridge since the early twentieth century. This cartridge is also now often used for long-range precision countersniper rifles. *See also* M2 Browning.

Bogan: Australian slang, usually pejorative, for an individual who is from an unsophisticated background. *See also* CUBs.

BP: Depending on context, British Petroleum or Blood Pressure.

BPS: Australian Customs and Border Protection Service.

Bravo Sierra: Military slang for lies or lying.

BSA: Birmingham Small Arms Company Limited, a British company that originally made guns but later became best known for making bicycles, motorcycles, and taxicabs bodies.

B.U.L.L.: Basic Utility Locking Liner. A folding pocketknife made by CRKT that was designed by Aaron Frederick. *See also* CRKT.

C-4: Composition 4, a stable plastic explosive. It is ninety-one percent RDX.

CAAAF: Civilian Auxiliary Australian Air Force.

Camo: Slang for camouflage.

CAR-15: *See* M4.

CAS: Close Air Support.

CASA: Depending on context, either Construcciones Aeronáuticas SA (a Spanish aircraft manufacturer) or Civil Aviation Safety Authority (Australian government agency).

C-A-T: Combat Application Tourniquet.

CB: Citizens' Band radio, a VHF broadcasting band. No license is required for operation in the United States. Some desirable CB transceivers are capable of SSB operation. Originally twenty-three channels, the Citizens' Band was later expanded to forty channels during the golden age of CB, in the 1970s.

CD-ROM: Compact Disc Read-Only Memory.

CETME: Centro de Estudios Técnicos de Materiales Especiales. Best known as the maker of the Spanish army's predecessor of the HK G3 series rifles. Thousands of CETME rifle parts sets were imported into the United States in the late 1990s and rebuilt into semiauto-only sporter rifles.

CHGR: Short for Charger.

CIA: Central Intelligence Agency.

Claymore mine: The M18A1 is a command-detonated antipersonnel mine in the military inventories of many NATO and ASEAN countries.

CN: Phenacyl chloride. A military tear gas. Can cause vomiting in high concentrations. *See also* CS.

CO: Commanding Officer.

CO2: Carbon dioxide.

COD: Collect on Delivery.

COMINT: Communications Intelligence.

COMSEC: Communications Security.

CONUS: Continental United States.

Cordtex: *See* Det Cord.

CP: Command Post.

CPY: Ham radio shorthand for Copy.

CR1M: Combat Ration One Man (spoken "Crim"). The Australian equivalent of the U.S. MRE field ration. *See also* MRE and PR1M.

CR5M: Combat Ration Five Man.

CRKT: Columbia River Knife & Tool.

CROWS: Common Remotely Operated Weapon Station.

CS: 2-chlorobenzalmalononitrile (also called o-chlorobenzylidene malononitrile). A military and civilian tear gas.

CSSB: Combat Service Support Battalion.

CUBs: Cashed-Up Bogans. *See also* Bogan.

CUCV: Commercial Utility Cargo Vehicle. The 1980s-vintage U.S. Army versions of diesel Chevy Blazers and pickups, sold off as surplus in the early 2000s.

DC: Direct Current.

Demob: Short for demobilization.

Det Cord: Slang for detonating/detonation cord.

Detonating/Detonation Cord: A small-diameter plastic tubing filled with PETN explosive and a plasticizer, often used to tie together separate explosive charges to cause them to detonate almost simultaneously. Sold under trade names like Primacord and Cordtex.

DF: Direction Finding.

DMV: Department of Motor Vehicles.

DPM: Disruptive Pattern Material. A British military camouflage pattern, with colors similar to the U.S. Army's defunct Woodland BDU pattern.

DPMS: Defense Procurement Manufacturing Services. An American maker of AR-10 and AR-15 family rifles.

DVD: Digital Video Disc.

E&E: Escape and Evasion.

ELINT: Electronic Intelligence.

Enfield: *See* SMLE.

EPA: Environment Protection Authority (Australia) or Environmental Protection Agency (USA).

E-tool: Entrenching tool. A small folding shovel.

F88 Austeyr: *See* Steyr AUG.

FAA: Federal Aviation Administration (U.S.).

Fair Dinkum: Australian slang for the spirit of fair play in personal or business dealings.

FAL: *Fusil Automatique Léger* (Light Automatic Rifle). *See* FN FAL.

FEMA: Federal Emergency Management Agency (a U.S. federal government agency). The acronym is also jokingly defined as "Foolishly Expecting Meaningful Aid."

FFL: Federal Firearms License.

FLB: Forward Logistics Base.

FM: Field Manual.

FMA: Filipino Martial Arts. *See also* Pekiti-Tirsia Kali.

FMS: Foreign Military Sales. Program of U.S. Defense Department.

FN: Fabrique Nationale, a Belgian gun maker.

FNC: A 5.56 mm NATO battle rifle originally made by the Belgian company Fabrique Nationale (FN). *See also* Pindad SS2.

FN FAL: A 7.62 mm NATO battle rifle originally made by the Belgian company Fabrique Nationale (FN), issued to more than fifty countries in the 1960s and 1970s. Now made as semiauto-only "clones" by a variety of makers. *See also* L1A1.

FOB: Forward Operating Base.

FORSCOM: U.S. Army Forces Command.

FPI: Front Pembela Islam (Islamic Defenders Front). *See also* PKS.

Frag: Slang for fragmentation.

FSB: Federalnaya Sluzhba Bezopasnosti. Russia's main successor to the Soviet KGB.

FTV: Fast Troop Vessel(s).

FUBAR: Fouled Up Beyond All Recognition.

FV: Fishing Vessel.

G3: A 7.62 mm NATO assault rifle designed by Heckler & Koch, developed in the 1950s, based on the CETME rifle design.

G36: A 5.56 mm NATO assault rifle designed by Heckler & Koch. It replaced the G3 in the late 1990s.

Galah: A Rose-breasted Cockatoo, native to Australia. The term *Galah* is derogatory Australian slang meaning "fool" or "idiot."

Galil: The Israeli battle rifle, based on Kalashnikov action. Most were made in 5.56 mm NATO, but a variant was also made in 7.62 mm NATO, in smaller numbers.

Garand: *See* M1 Garand.

GB: Gigabyte.

GCA: The Gun Control Act of 1968. The law that first created FFLs and banned interstate transfers of post-1898 firearms, except "to or through" FFL holders.

GDP: Gross Domestic Product.

Geoprime dBX: A pentolite high-explosive tailored for seismic surveys, made by Dyno Nobel, a subsidiary of the conglomerate Incitec Pivot Limited.

GIS: Geographic Information System.

Glock: The popular polymer-framed pistol design by Gaston Glock of Austria.

GMT: Greenwich Mean Time.

GoldenRod: A brand of compact electric dehumidifier designed to protect the contents of tool cabinets and gun vaults from rust.

G.O.O.D.: Get Out of Dodge.

GPS: Global Positioning System.

Ham: Slang for amateur radio operator.

HDPE: High Density Polyethylene.

H-E or HE: High Explosive.

HF: High Frequency. A radio band used by amateur radio operators.

HK or H & K: Heckler & Koch, the German gunmaker.

HK91: Heckler & Koch Model 91. The civilian (semiautomatic-only) variant of the 7.62 mm NATO G3 rifle.

HMAS: His/Her Majesty's Australian Ship.

HMNZS: His/Her Majesty's New Zealand Ship.

HMPNGS: His/Her Majesty's Papua New Guinea Ship.

HQ: Headquarters.

HQ JOC: Headquarters Joint Operations Command (of Australian Defence Force).

Humvee: High Mobility Multipurpose Wheeled Vehicle (spoken "Humvee").

IBA: Interceptor Body Armor.

ID: Identification.

IED: Improvised Explosive Device.

IFV: Infantry Fighting Vehicle.

ILF: Islamic Liberation Front. One of several militant Islamist separatist groups in the Philippines. Also known as the MILF, or Moro Islamic Liberation Front. In Arabic, Jabhat Tahrir Mooroo al-Islamiyyah. *See also* ASG.

Indo: Slang for Indonesian.

ISAFP: Intelligence Service of the Armed Forces of the Philippines.

Ithaca: Ithaca Gun Company. An American gun maker, best known for its shotguns.

JI: Jamaah Islamiyah (Islamic Congegration), Southeast Asian Islamic terrorist group.

Kapten: Indonesian for Captain.

KD: *Kapal Diraja* (Ship of His Highness, Royal Malaysian Navy).

Kel-Tec: Kel-Tec CNC, Inc. A firearms maker headquartered in Cocoa, Florida, that specializes in making polymer frame firearms.

Kevlar: The material used in most body armor and ballistic helmets. Kevlar is also the nickname for the standard U.S. Army helmet.

KIA: Killed in Action.

KJV: King James Version of the Bible.

Klick: Slang for kilometer.

Kopassus: Special Forces Command in Indonesian Army.

Korps Marinir: Indonesian Marine Corps.

KRI: Kapal Perang Republik Indonesia (Navy Vessel of the Republic of Indonesia).

L1A1: The British Army version of the FN FAL, made to inch measurements. *See also* SLR.

LAPAN: Lembaga Penerbangan dan Antariksa Nasional (Indonesia's National Institute of Aeronautics and Space).

LAR-8: A variant of the AR-10, made by Rock River Arms (RRA), that accepts FN FAL or L1A1 magazines.

LAW: Light Anti-Tank Weapon.

LC-1: Load Carrying, Type 1. U.S. Army Load Bearing Equipment, circa 1970s to 1990s.

LCAC: Landing Craft Air Cushion.

LCH: Landing Craft, Heavy.

LCM: Landing Craft, Mechanized.

LCVP: Landing Craft, Vehicle, Personnel.

LCU: Landing Craft Utility.

LDS: The Latter-Day Saints, commonly called the Mormons. (Flawed doctrine, but great preparedness.)

LED: Light Emitting Diode.

Lee-Enfield: *See* SMLE.

Lenten Sate: Indonesian for first lieutenant.

LOB: Line of Bearing.

Loggy: Slang for logistician or the logistics role in military planning.

LP: Liquid Propane.

LP/OP: Listening Post/Observation Post.

LRRP: Long Range Reconnaissance Patrol.

M1A: The civilian (semiauto-only) version of the U.S. Army M14 7.62 mm NATO rifle.

M1 carbine: The U.S. Army semiauto carbine issued during WWII. Mainly issued to officers and second-echelon troops such as artillerymen, for self-defense. Uses .30 U.S carbine, an intermediate (pistol class) .30-caliber cartridge. More than six million were manufactured. *See also* M2 carbine.

M1 Garand: The U.S. Army's primary battle rifle of WWII and the Korean conflict. It is semiautomatic, chambered in .30-06, and uses a top-loading, 8-round en bloc clip that ejects after the last round is fired. This rifle is commonly called the Garand (after the surname of its inventor). Not to be confused with the U.S. M1 carbine, another semiauto of the same era, which shoots a far less powerful pistol-class cartridge.

M1911: The Model 1911 Colt semiauto pistol (and clones thereof), usually chambered in .45 ACP.

M2 Browning: The .50 Browning belt-fed heavy machine gun, in service with ninety-five nations.

M2 carbine: The selective fire (fully automatic) version of the U.S. Army semiauto carbine issued during WWII and the Korean conflict.

M4 carbine: The U.S. Army-issue 5.56 mm NATO selective fire carbine. (A shorter version of the M16, with a 14.5-inch barrel and collapsing stock.) Earlier issue M16 carbine variants had designations such as XM177E2 and CAR-15. Civilian semiauto-only variants often have these same designations, or are called M4geries.

M4gery: A civilian semiauto-only version of an M4 carbine, with a 16-inch barrel instead of a 14.5-inch barrel.

M9: The U.S. Army issue version of the Beretta 92 semiauto 9 mm pistol.

M14: The U.S. Army issue 7.62 mm NATO selective-fire battle rifle. These rifles are still issued in small numbers, primarily to designated marksmen. The civilian semiauto-only equivalent of the M14 is called the M1A.

M16: The U.S. Army issue 5.56 mm NATO selective-fire battle rifle. The current standard variant is the M16A2 that has improved sight and three-shot burst control. *See also* M4.

M18A1: *See* Claymore mine.

M60: The semiobsolete U.S. Army issue 7.62 mm NATO belt-fed light machine gun that utilized some design elements of the German MG-42.

M113: A tracked armored personnel carrier made by FMC Corporation, in the United States.

Maglite: A popular American brand of sturdy flashlights with an aluminum casing.

MANPADS: Man-Portable Air Defense Systems.

MARPAT: Marine Pattern. A highly effective digital camouflage pattern adopted by the United States Marine Corps that is predominantly green and brown.

MCRP: Marine Corps Reference Publication.

MCRU: Mobile Control and Reporting Unit.

MCWP: Marine Corps Warfighting Publication.

MD: Medical Doctor.

MHz: Megahertz.

MILF: *See* ILF.

Mini-14: A 5.56 mm NATO semiauto carbine made by Ruger.

MOLLE: Modular Lightweight Load-carrying Equipment.

Molotov Cocktail: A hand-thrown firebomb made from a glass container filled with gasoline or thickened gasoline (napalm.)

MRAP: Mine-Resistant Ambush Protected vehicle.

MRE: Meal, Ready to Eat. *See also* CR1M.

MSDS: Material Safety Data Sheet.

MSS: Modular Sleep System.

MTU: Motoren- und Turbinen-Union, a German conglomerate.

MultiCam: *See* OCP.

MVR: Motor Vehicle Registry (Australia).

Nakas: Australian slang for testicles.

Napalm: Thickened gasoline, used in some flame weapons.

NATO: North Atlantic Treaty Organization.

NAVFORCEN: Naval Forces Central of the Philippine Navy.

NBC: Nuclear, Biological, and Chemical weapons.

NCO: Non-Commissioned Officer.

NEPM: National Environment Protection Measure. *See also* EPA.

NiCd: Nickel Cadmium (rechargeable battery).

NiMH: Nickel Metal Hydride (rechargeable battery). Improvement of NiCd.

NRETAS: Australia's Northern Territory Department of Natural Resources, Environment, the Arts, and Sport.

NRO: National Reconnaissance Office (U.S.).

N/SEAS: Monocular night vision device (NVD). Standard issue for the Australian Defence Force. It is very similar to the U.S. military's AN/PVS-14 monocular NVD.

NTXT: No Text.

NVG: Night Vision Goggles.

NWO: New World Order.

OBTW: Oh, by the way.

OC: Oleoresin capsicum. The main ingredient in pepper spray.

OCONUS: Outside the Continental United States.

OCP: Operation Enduring Freedom Camouflage Pattern. Commonly called by its civilian trade name, MultiCam.

OEF: Operation Enduring Freedom.

OP: Observation Post. *See also* LP/OP.

Op Order: Operations Order.

OPSEC: Operational Security.

Oz: Slang for Australia.

PCS: Permanent Change of Station.

PDA: Personal Digital Assistant.

PEACHS: Protection, Existing tracks, Camouflage and concealment, Hardstanding and Space. A field logistic site selection process.

Pekiti-Tirsia Kali: One category of the Filipino Martial Arts (FMAs.)

PETN: Pentaerythritol tetranitrate. Also known as PENTA. The explosive filler used in detonating "det" cord. *See also* Det Cord.

PFC: Private First Class.

PHP: Philippine Peso.

P.I.: Slang contraction for Philippine Islands.

Pindad: An Indonesian arsenal that produces military firearms and ammunition.

Pindad SS2: The Pindad Senapan Serbu 2 is an Indonesian variant of the FN FNC 5.56 mm battle rifle. Made in four variants. *See also* FNC.

PKK: Pembebasan Perombakan Komando (Liberation Demolition Commando), Indonesia.

PKS: Partai Keadilan Sejahtera (Justice Welfare Party), Indonesia. *See also* FPI.

PM: Prime Minister.

PMV: Protected Mobility Vehicle.

PN: Philippine Navy (Hukbong Dagat ng Pilipinas).

PNG: Papua New Guinea.

PNGDF: Papua New Guinea Defence Force.

Pogue: A term of derision for military men assigned to support positions rather than front-line units.

POL: Petroleum, Oil, and Lubricants. A category of products used by U.S. military.

POST: Passive Optical Seeker Technique. *See also* Stinger and RMP.

POW: Prisoner of War.

PR1M: Patrol Ration One Man (spoken "Prim"). Similar to a CR1M, but with some more palatable freeze-dried components.

Pre-1899: Guns made before 1899—not classified as firearms under U.S. law.

Pre-1965: U.S. silver coins with 1964 or earlier mint dates, usually with little or no numismatic value. They are sold for the bullion content. These coins have 90 percent silver content. Well-worn pre-1965 coins are sometimes derisively called junk silver by rare-coin dealers.

Primacord: *See* Detonating/Detonation Cord.

ProvGov: Provisional Government.

PSYOP: Psychological Operations.

PT: Physical Training.

Purple Patch: Australian slang for good luck.

PV: Photovoltaic (solar power conversion array). Used to convert solar power to DC electricity, typically for battery charging.

Qantas: Originally acronym for Queensland and Northern Territory Aerial Services Limited, 1920–1947.

QRP: Ham radio shorthand for low-power (less than 5-watt) transmitters.

QRT: Quick Reaction Team.

RAAF: Royal Australian Air Force.

RAN: Royal Australian Navy.

RTTY: Radio Teletype.

RBS 70: A Swedish-made pedestal-mounted surface-to-air missile.

RCG: Restoration of the Constitution Government.

RCS: Radar Cross Section. The unit of measurement that defines how detectable an object is with radar.

RDX: Research Department Explosive. A nitroamine-based high explosive (cyclonite or cyclotrimethylene trinitramine) that is more powerful than TNT. It is the main component in C-4 plastic explosive.

Reg: Short for Regulation.

Remington: An American gun maker.

RI: Republic of Indonesia.

RMN: Royal Malaysian Navy.

RMP: Reprogrammable Microprocessor. *See also* Stinger and POST.

ROF(F): Royal Ordnance Factory, Fazakerly, England.

RORO: Roll-on Roll-off. A type of ship specifically designed for transporting vehicles.

RPG: Rocket-Propelled Grenade.

RQ-7B Shadow 200: An Australian UAV with a sixteen-foot wingspan. They weigh 458 pounds. *See also* UAV and Wulung.

RRA: Rock River Arms. A firearms maker headquartered in Colona, Illinois, that specializes in AR-15 and AR-10 variants.

RTA: Radio Traffic Analyst. *See also* TA.

RTB: Return to Base.

Ruger: An American gun maker.

SALW: Small Arms and Light Weapons.

SAS: Special Air Service, British Army.

SATCOM: Satellite Communications.

SBI: Special Background Investigation.

SCI: Sensitive Compartmented Information.

SCUBA: Self-Contained Underwater Breathing Apparatus.

SERCO: Service Corporation.

SH: Student Handbook.

SIG: Schweizerische Industrie Gesellschaft, the Swiss gun maker.

SIGINT: Signals Intelligence.

Skype: A commercial Voice Over OP (VOIP) video-telephone service.

SLR: Self-Loading Rifle. The generic term used by Australia for the L1A1 rifle.

SMLE: Short Magazine Lee-Enfield rifle.

SOCAUST: Special Operations Commander, Australia.

SOCOMD: Special Operations Command.

SOP: Standard Operating Procedure(s).

SPF: Sun Protection Factor.

SS2: *See* Pindad SS2.

SSB: Single Sideband. An operating mode for CB and amateur radio gear.

Steyr AUG: The Austrian army's 5.56 mm "bullpup" infantry carbine. Also issued by the Australian Army as the model F88, as their replacement for the L1A1. This AUG variant is often called the Austeyr.

Stinger: An American-made shoulder-fired surface-to-air missile. *See also* POST and RMP.

Strac or Strack: A complimentary term for a military member who is well disciplined. Also sometimes applied to a field gear locker box—a "Strack Box." The origin of this word is debated. Some say that it is an acronym for "Strictly Regular Army Commission" (STRAC), while others attribute it to the family name of Army Air Corps (later USAF) Brigadier General Harold Arthur Strack.

S&W: Smith & Wesson.

SWAT: Special Weapons and Tactics. SWAT originally stood for Special Weapons Assault Team until that was deemed politically incorrect.

TA: Traffic Analyst. *See also* RTA.

TAB: Tactical Advance to Battle. Tactical movement is often called tabbing in Commonwealth countries.

Tavor TAR-21: A bullpup configuration .223 rifle designed in Israel.

TBAS: Tiered Body Armour System (Australian Army issue).

TBD: To Be Determined.

TC: Training Circular.

TCCC: Tactical Combat Casualty Care.

TDY: Temporary Duty.

Thermite: A mixture of aluminum powder and iron rust powder that, when ignited, causes a vigorous exothermic reaction. Used primarily for welding. Also used by military units as an incendiary for destroying equipment.

TM: Technical Manual.

TNI-AD: Tentara Nasional Indonesia Angkatan Darat. The Indonesian Army.

TNI-AL: Tentara Nasional Indonesia Angkatan Laut. The Indonesian Navy.

TNI-AU: Tentara Nasional Indonesia Angkatan Udara. The Indonesian Air Force.

TO&E: Table of Organization and Equipment.

Top End: Australian slang for the Northern Territory.

TOW: Tube-launched, Optically tracked, Wire-guided missile.

Triple 0: *See* 000.

TSA: Transportation Security Administration (also jokingly defined as: Thousands Standing Around).

UAV: Unmanned Aerial Vehicle. *See also* Wulung and RQ-7B Shadow 200.

UH-1: The venerable Huey helicopter. In service from the Vietnam War to the present.

UN: United Nations.

UNPROFOR: United Nations Protection Force.

UPS: Uninterruptible Power Source.

USAF: United States Air Force.

USB: Universal Serial Bus.

USD: United States Dollars.

USMC: United States Marine Corps.

Ute: Australian slang for utility vehicle.

VAC: Volts, Alternating Current.

Valmet: The Finnish conglomerate that formerly made several types of firearms.

VDC: Volts, Direct Current.

VOI: Voice of Indonesia.

VW: Volkswagen.

WD-1: U.S. military issue two-conductor insulated field telephone wire.

WIA: Wounded in Action.

WIB: Waktu Indonesia Barat (Western Indonesia Time).

Wi-Fi: Wireless Fidelity.

Winchester: An American gun maker.

WO1: Warrant Officer 1.

Wulung: An Indonesian-built 264-pound propeller-driven UAV with a twenty-foot wingspan, a four-hour flight endurance, and a cruising speed of sixty-nine miles per hour. *See also* UAV and RQ-7B Shadow 200.

XD: Extreme Duty. A line of pistols with parts made in Croatia, produced by Springfield Armory in the United States.

Yakka: Australian slang for work or working.

ACKNOWLEDGMENTS

My sincere thanks to my editor, Jessica Horvath. I'd also like to express my thanks to the many other folks who have encouraged me, who contributed technical details, who were used for character sketches, and who helped me substantively in the editing process: Edwin B., Bob G., Danielle, D.L., Dr. Craig in New Zealand, Gil R., Stephen H., Steve G., Josh S., Maid Elizabeth, S.L.M., M.B., M.E.W., Nate, Jerry J., J.I.R., Reggie K., Robert L. in Florida, Alan S. in Australia, S.O. in Australia, Kody, Kory and Owen, the family of the late John Kofler ("John the Bowhunter," who was mentioned in the credits of my previous novels), and the family of the late Pat Jones (also known as SLR-5000 on FALFiles.com.) Pat was born in Australia but worked and died in America, his adopted home. He personified the greatness of the Australian spirit while at the same time he was a true American patriot.

Lastly, I wish to honor the memory of Major Damon Gause (1915–1944). His daring escape from the Philippines in a small boat during the World War II occupation by the Japanese was the inspiration for one passage in this novel. (I highly recommend his published journal, *The War Journal of Major Damon "Rocky" Gause*, edited by Damon L. Gause, with a foreword by Stephen E. Ambrose, published by Hyperion Books, 1999.)

ABOUT THE AUTHOR

Former U.S. Army Intelligence officer and survivalist James Wesley, Rawles, is a well-known survival lecturer and author. Rawles is the editor of SurvivalBlog.com—the nation's most popular blog on family preparedness. He lives in an undisclosed location west of the Rockies and is the author of the bestselling *Founders: A Novel of the Coming Collapse*; *Survivors: A Novel of the Coming Collapse*; *Patriots: A Novel of Survival in the Coming Collapse*; and a nonfiction survival guide, *How to Survive the End of the World as We Know It.*